MW01068946

ROYAL
HEIRS
ACADEMY

ROYAL HEIRS ACADEMY

Lindsey Duga

Christy Ottaviano Books

LITTLE, BROWN AND COMPANY

New York Boston

Christy Ottaviano Books
Hachette Book Group
1290 Avenue of the Americas, New York, NY 10104
Visit us at LBYR.com

First Edition: January 2025

Christy Ottaviano Books is an imprint of Little, Brown and Company. The Christy Ottaviano Books name and logo are registered trademarks of Hachette Book Group, Inc.

The publisher is not responsible for websites (or their content) that are not owned by the publisher.

Little, Brown and Company books may be purchased in bulk for business, educational, or promotional use. For information, please contact your local bookseller or the Hachette Book Group Special Markets Department at special.markets@hbgusa.com.

Library of Congress Cataloging-in-Publication Data
Names: Duga, Lindsey, author.
Title: Royal heirs academy / Lindsey Duga.
Description: First edition. | New York : Little, Brown and Company, 2025. | Audience: Ages 14–18. | Summary: Told in alternating voices, three royal grandchildren and one fortuitous commoner compete to inherit the kingdom of Ashland while attending Almus Terra Academy.
Identifiers: LCCN 2024009110 | ISBN 9780316578660 (paperback) | ISBN 9780316578691 (hardcover) | ISBN 9780316578714 (ebook)
Subjects: CYAC: Boarding schools—Fiction. | Schools—Fiction. | Inheritance and succession—Fiction. | Love-hate relationships—Fiction. | Interpersonal relations—Fiction. | LCGFT: Novels.
Classification: LCC PZ7.1.D83424 Ro 2025 | DDC [Fic]—dc23
LC record available at https://lccn.loc.gov/2024009110

ISBNs: 978-0-316-57866-0 (trade paperback), 978-0-316-57869-1 (hardcover), 978-0-316-57871-4 (ebook)

Printed in Indiana, USA

LSC-C

Printing 1, 2024

To Meaghan:
my soulmate I found in the YA section

PROLOGUE

LEANDER

PEACE IS AN ILLUSION.

Leander scraped his thumbnail across the charcoal words inked into his skin, embedded beneath an angry rash that was spreading like flames over his arm.

Allergic reaction be damned. The mantra would be permanent, the pain temporary. And that's what he was looking for: permanence.

His advisors had scoffed at the idea of a tattoo on a man approaching sixty—more so, on a man in his position. Even so, Leander knew gold-plated words would never suffice to commemorate this day, or the steps he'd taken. It wasn't penance, but it was as close as he dared.

A knock sounded at the door and Leander tugged his shirt sleeve down to his wrist, adjusting the cuff without a sound, though the cotton against his inflamed skin made his back molars grind in annoyance. The captain of his royal guard stepped inside his office, bending at the waist in deference. "Your Majesty. Apologies for the interruption."

Leander merely nodded at the formality. He had long ago established he could be called upon at any moment, for any reason. A king had no privacy, and no time off.

"Headmistress Aquila has arrived."

Thanks to an internal clock he'd maintained since his days as a soldier, he didn't bother glancing at the old grandfather one in his study. He knew she was early.

"Bring her in," Leander said. Hardly a need to keep her waiting merely to show he could.

"Yes, Your Majesty." His captain disappeared and the next moment, the door opened fully to allow a tall, striking woman to step through. The ivory pantsuit was a lovely contrast to her brown skin, while a pearlescent duster hung off her shoulders like a royal mantle. The headmistress took the seat before his desk, shrugging off her coat, and fixed Leander with her dark gaze as if he were a student she was about to lecture.

"Tell me you're joking."

Leander regarded the woman seated in one of his wingback chairs with grudging respect. He might be two decades her senior, but he'd rather chew glass than pull rank with her. The blood of Nelson Mandela ran through Zuri Aquila's veins, and as powerful as King Leander of Ashland might be, Zuri had been charged with the world's future leaders. On a global scale, she eclipsed him.

"You've had a long day of travel. Can I get you a drink, Headmistress?" Leander reached for the bottle of one-hundred-year-old brandy in the cabinet under his desk.

"No, thank you. I'd like to get straight to why you summoned me here. Unless..." Zuri tilted her head, her braids draping down one shoulder. "The rumors aren't true?"

He'd known Zuri would have questions—just as the press had. Though he hardly needed to defend his actions to someone so young with no descendants, who'd never been charged with governing a country, he valued her opinion. Her expertise in economic and sociological theory, as well as moral philosophy, made her one of the most erudite scholars in recent generations.

Unconsciously, Leander rubbed his left inner wrist, and he felt something warm and wet bloom under his thumb. Blood. The tattoo was bleeding. Ah well. He had plenty of good shirts.

"They are true," Leander said slowly.

It was the closest he'd ever come to seeing the headmistress in shock. For a long moment she said nothing, relaxing further into her chair.

"Do you think it wise? Separating children from their parents?" Zuri finally asked.

"Normal children? Certainly not," Leader replied. "My grand-children? Unequivocally, yes."

Zuri scoffed under her breath. "Your grandchildren are no different from their peers."

"You're wrong, Headmistress." Leander's tone was neither angry nor dismissive. It was emotionless. Dry, like he was plainly quoting a statistic. Opening his top drawer, he withdrew a black leather box about the size of a glasses case and set it on the desk.

With a raised brow, Zuri took the hint, picked up the box, and flipped it open. Her eyes widened, but her response was otherwise restrained. Then again, people saw fingers all the time...though rarely severed.

"And whose is this?" she asked, snapping the case closed and passing it back.

"Emmeline's nanny. She was caught trying to poison the child's bottle."

"Poison?"

"Traces of lead and mercury. Seemingly low doses that would lead to defects, not death...most likely." Leander flicked his wrist dismissively. "Already, political interest groups are aligning with my children, making moves in the shadows. I have not spent thirty years working toward stability only to let it all go to hell."

"You should've appointed your heir a long time ago and avoided all this," Zuri countered. "Your son—"

"My sons are worthless. They're all greed with no ambition. And my daughter is too frail." With a heavy sigh, Leander stood from his desk and turned to face the window. "If I were to perish tomorrow, the line of succession would be determined by my advisory council. I pity their prospects."

The Cliffs of Durah dropped to the frigid Atlantic down below. Waves frothed and foamed, clashing against the rocks, warning of the incoming downpour. It stormed often enough in eastern Ashland to warrant an old superstition: If the Cliffs of Durah were ever dry for longer than a day, they would crack off into the sea and take the Heres Castle with them. Locals liked to say a castle drenched with blood would appease the old sea gods. Iron into salt.

Leander could count on one hand the number of times he'd admitted mistakes—not for excessive pride; simply because the occasions were few. But there would be no appeasing Zuri without divulging his biggest regret.

He turned back to her calm gaze. It was the same expression she wore at the Peace Summit last year when she was appointed Headmistress of Almus Terra Academy.

"My children know nothing of how to shepherd a country *and* grow an economy, Zuri. I was a negligent father, too busy repairing my kingdom wrecked from centuries of civil wars to pay them mind. You know I speak the truth. I see who they are. What they have become. I never groomed them, and therefore I cannot entrust the fate of Ashland to them. But my grandchildren...they have a chance. A real chance at greatness."

Zuri closed her eyes and sighed. When she looked back up at Leander, there was something in the angle of her chin and the simple elegance of her posture that was telling. Though morally it still felt wrong, she was intrigued by the concept of innate potential, of "nature" without the inevitable flaws of "nurture."

"I suppose this is why I'm here? I don't fly halfway across the world during my summer holiday for just anyone, Your Majesty."

With the barest traces of a smile, Leander opened his desk drawer for a second time. The envelope he produced was slim, but the paper was a substantial weight, top quality, and sealed with a deep scarlet wax.

Unceremoniously, Zuri ripped open the wax seal. The check inside boasted nearly three million euros from the treasury of Ashland, made out to her school.

"I'd rather not wire such a hefty sum. I hope you understand," Leander said.

Zuri frowned at him. "This amount is incorrect."

"I assure you it isn't."

The headmistress stuffed the check back into the envelope, annoyed. "I know our deposit fees, and this covers four students, not three."

"Correct."

Her maroon lips pinched. "You've publicly stated no more heirs would be born."

"No more heirs *by blood*," Leander stated, his thumb massaging his inner wrist where the tattoo oozed and burned. Pain and prickling numbness swirled under his skin, but it felt good. Oddly centering.

Zuri gazed at him, waiting for an explanation.

"I'll need a name for the fourth student, Leander. To secure their spot."

"And you'll have it. But not yet. List the deposit under the Eldana name."

"Leander—"

"On my honor, Headmistress, four Ashland heirs will matriculate at Almus Terra."

"Fine." Zuri stood, tucking the envelope into her coat. "But they'll be held to our scholarly requirements for acceptance, like all students."

Leander dipped his head. "Naturally."

Zuri started for the exit of her own volition, unfazed by the precious customs of royalty. Then she stopped, her fingers curled around the door handle, her broad shoulders tense.

Her eyes moved back to the king, landing on him with bold admonishment. "Let me be clear: My students will not become pawns in the battle for your succession. I won't allow it."

The heavy door shut behind her with a deep echo just as the rain started pelting the windows, louder than the ancient Norse drums on the battleships that landed in Ashland millennia ago.

"My dear Headmistress," Leander murmured, pushing back his cuff to press hard into his raw, aching skin. "That is entirely up to them."

1

ALARIC

Sixteen Years Later

THERE WAS A SLIGHT CHANCE HIS JAW WAS BROKEN.

Alaric tested it by slowly rolling it back and forth, left to right. Another explosion of pain reverberated through his skull, this one magnitudes worse than the hit that likely fractured his jaw in the first place.

It was concerning, but not because of splintered bones. He was pretty sure he'd shattered his jaw back when he was thirteen. And *that* hadn't resulted in any lasting damage—that he knew of. He worried, instead, because head pain affected the whole body, and he couldn't afford to pass out. Not right now.

"Kneel, yeh arsehole." McKennah's voice came with a ringing sound in his head. "Kneel and I'll go easy on yeh."

Lie. The second he cowered they would kick and kick and kick.

"C'mon, Durham. On the ground. Or yeh want me to mess up more of yer pretty face?"

"Yea," snorted Walsh, "*Game of Thrones* that shite. Bend the knee."

A cacophony of laughter echoed in the tiny alley behind the convenience store off Old Ballymun Road and it made Alaric's skull throb in pain again. If only he'd eaten lunch before his shift, then he would've made it home in peace. But there was bound to be retaliation for Brody. If one of his own guys had been beaten to a pulp, he'd do the same.

My chicken is getting cold. The flimsy plastic bag sat at his feet, right next to an old sock and empty slushy cup. Even the smell of fried batter couldn't cover the stench of fluids from the previous night's pub patrons a block away.

Careful with his jaw, he spat a wad of blood onto McKennah's shoes.

The gang leader jerked away. "Son of a—"

Alaric rocketed forward with a right hook to McKennah's nose. Delicate bones crunched under his knuckles as a slasher-movie scream tore from McKennah's throat. McKennah stumbled backward, falling to his knees. One down, three to go. On his left, Alaric slammed an elbow into the side of Walsh's head, sending the scrawny boy into the brick wall with a groan.

Two more of McKennah's goons were next. Alaric had forgotten their names, and he didn't care to keep track—McKennah liked to switch his guys out.

They rivaled Alaric's size, but in the narrow alley, it was easy to move over the bodies of McKennah and Walsh and throw an uppercut into the first one's face, then grab the back of his Members Only jacket to knee him in the solar plexus—once, twice. The second swung wildly once his buddy was on the ground. Alaric ducked and, without mercy, slammed his fist right into the guy's groin. He went down hard with a scream that rivaled McKennah's.

Breathing heavily, Alaric turned, finding McKennah's collar amidst the groaning bodies. He hauled the gang leader up and felt McKennah's blood and spit speckle his face and shirt.

"Yeh put Brody in the hospital. Yei dead, Durham."

Alaric would've laughed if not for his jaw.

"Yeh already gave it a lash. Better luck next time." Alaric pressed the pad of his thumb into McKennah's already busted nose, applying pressure, and the boy whimpered.

"Brody got what he deserved, McKennah." Alaric's voice dropped dangerously low, fury rippling through his veins at the scum around him. "If any more of yeh harass Kyle's little sister I'll skip the hospital and send yeh straight to the morgue. Walsh, phone."

Walsh slapped his phone into Alaric's open hand, which Alaric then dropped to the ground and smashed under his foot. The glass and little metal bits inside crunched into near dust.

"Jaysus, Durham," Walsh groaned, still holding the side of his head that Alaric rammed.

"Next time don't take pictures of thirteen-year-olds." Alaric turned to grab his chicken, then thought better of it. Already the putrid stench of the alley had infiltrated his boxed dinner. Alaric couldn't well afford to abandon food, but then he tested his jaw and another wave of pain rushed him—he wouldn't have been able to eat anyway.

Hands in his pockets, Alaric legged it home. He was tired from work, hungry, aching all over, and now in a rotten mood. *Damn.* He'd been really looking forward to that fried chicken.

Dublin traffic was light on Saturday afternoons, especially on the fringes of Glasnevin and Ballymun. He barely had to check for cars as he jogged across the street, his phone buzzing in his back pocket. Ignoring it, he climbed the stairs to his flat. Likely a group text, with his crew laughing and cutting up about McKennah's defeat. Word got around fast among the gangs in north Dublin. Well, *they* called themselves gangs.

Alaric was sensible enough to know they were just children playing at being men. What happened between them didn't matter. None of it.

The reality was that Alaric would be back in that alley, stopping by the same Tesco, cutting classes to play on Kyle's Switch, or moving boxes at the shipping company day after day. Week after week.

But this was his lot in life. He'd long since accepted it. At least he wasn't in foster care. He had his own place, however run-down it was, and he had trashy blokes like Brody to take everything out on. Which reminded him...

As he unlocked his studio flat, he slipped out his phone and texted Kyle. **Pics of Kaylee gone.**

Kyle responded immediately. **I owe you, lad.**

"Alaric," barked an old, raspy voice to his left.

Alaric turned to find Mrs. Tuttle standing there in her stained muumuu, her wispy gray curls unkempt. Watery eyes squinted at him in displeasure and Alaric mentally prepared himself for whatever nonsense his old neighbor had to spout today.

"Aye, Mrs. Tuttle. Howsagoin?"

"Two blokes came looking for yeh today. Same ones as yesterday."

Alaric stopped short of knocking his head against the door. For one, his head still hurt. For another, it would irritate Mrs. Tuttle. Though she was a cranky old lady, he sometimes got paid for random odd jobs she couldn't do herself—sometimes in quid, other times in stew. And her cooking was unreal.

"Sorry they disturbed yeh, ma'am," Alaric said, throwing his weight against the old, warped wood of the door; it shuddered open. He stepped inside, hoping to end this conversation fast. Painkillers were his top priority.

"I told them to come back this evening," Mrs. Tuttle continued, clearly not caring what these men wanted, or if they meant trouble. As long as it didn't bother her.

"Right, then. Cheers, ma'am." Alaric shut the door and tossed his keys on the counter. He stripped off his jacket, threw it on the back of the one kitchen chair he owned, and crossed to the freezer for ice. There was none—he forgot to refill the tray—so he settled for a bag of frozen peas.

With a sports drink and two ibuprofen, he sat at the rickety table and pressed the bag of peas to his face while his empty stomach churned.

Part of him knew he should be concerned about the two strange men, but he couldn't bring himself to care. When Mrs. Tuttle told him about the visitors yesterday, he'd spent almost an hour on his phone messaging anyone he knew to figure out who the men could be. Nothing panned out.

According to Mrs. Tuttle, they didn't look like cops—at least not beat cops—and were too posh for detectives. Instead, they wore suits and drove a fancy car. Alaric figured they were maybe lawyers. Maybe even Brody's . . . though he couldn't imagine the coward getting some personal injury solicitor involved.

Ah, well. Whatever.

Cradling the frozen peas to his face, he ignored his stomach. He'd wait for the pills to settle in and then find a protein shake or soup for dinner—nothing he had to chew.

He was half out of it when a pounding sounded through his little flat. The nearly defrosted bag of peas slipped from his grasp and dropped to the floor while he strained his tired eyes open.

"Alaric!" screeched Mrs. Tuttle through the thin wall they shared, "open the feckin door!"

A bolt of fear suddenly went through him. He didn't know who was looking for him or why, and the not knowing made him feel unprepared. Out of control. Then the trepidation was quickly replaced with irritation.

This whole evening was a bust. After his chicken, he'd planned to watch the latest episode of *Jujutsu Kaisen*. The current season of the anime was shaping up to be deadly, and now he'd be behind when all his friends met up tomorrow to debrief. With a groan, Alaric pushed himself from his chair, slid off the lock, and pulled the door open.

Two men stood before him. One was big enough to play rugby, maybe professionally, while the other was tall, but leaner. Both wore stern expressions and pristine navy-blue suits, polished all the way down to their dress shirts and ties.

Okay, so they didn't look like solicitors either. Hell, Alaric didn't know *what* they looked like.

"Alaric Durham?" the rugby-man asked.

Alaric tried to place the strange accent. It definitely wasn't from the UK. It sounded vaguely American, but he'd briefly dated a girl from the States who'd taught him different American accents, and none of those seemed to fit. Perhaps Canadian? That could be it, though he'd only met someone from Montreal once.

"Alaric Durham?" the man repeated, now annoyed.

Alaric's gaze dropped to a phone in the man's hand. The screen was still illuminated with a somewhat blurry picture of Alaric at school. His pulse skipped. *Who are these guys?*

The fight-or-flight instinct was kicking in, but Alaric urged himself to relax. These men weren't law enforcement and if they really were here to bust his face in, they'd already be swinging. With a picture, they didn't need him to confirm their target.

"Yeh know I am. Who's askin'?"

"May we come in?"

Polite too. This was, hands down, the weirdest ambush of his life. But what was he supposed to do? The men already proved they would keep coming back.

Alaric stepped aside and they entered his tiny flat. Their gazes roamed around his bedroom slash living room, the tiny kitchenette, the pile of graphic novels from the library, the comic books he'd bought at cheap secondhand stores, the mound of dirty clothes, and the door that led to the water closet.

It was clear these men came from money, but their looks didn't seem judgmental, more...appraising. Taking stock.

"All right, lads. What's the craic?"

"'Craic?'" the second guy muttered.

"Irish slang. What's the situation," the rugby-man said to his partner. Alaric rolled his eyes. "Christ. What do yeh want?"

"Have you been receiving your mail?"

Pointedly, Alaric looked at the pile of junk mail and bills sitting on the slim counter not a foot away from them. It was right next to his schoolbooks left untouched since the end of the term a month ago. Clearly these men loved rhetorical questions.

"Yeh lads from the electric company?" Alaric said following their silence. "I pay on time."

The rugby-man slipped his hand into his suit pocket and Alaric tensed, but all he withdrew was an envelope.

An envelope Alaric had seen more than once. It was an expensive off-white paper with a wax seal and some fancy crest on the front. The missive was addressed to him, Alaric Durham, with his flat number and everything, in loopy calligraphy.

Four times now Alaric had found that same letter in his PO box. He'd read the first one, then thrown the rest out, because there was no way the content was meant for him. Or it was some kind of weird scam.

"And have you been receiving this letter?" the man asked.

Alaric collapsed into his kitchen chair. "Yeh sure yeh have the right Alaric Durham?"

The two men exchanged glances.

"I mean, there's got to be another one out there better fit to go to yer fancy wee school. That's for sure." Alaric gestured at the envelope in the man's hand, then took another swig of his Gatorade. The ibuprofen and electrolytes were slowly making their way through his system, but not nearly fast enough for this conversation.

The rugby-man cleared his throat. "We're quite certain of your invitation to Almus Terra Academy, Mr. Durham. We're here to make sure you matriculate."

The school's name made the hairs on the back of Alaric's neck stand up. When he'd received this letter the first time, he'd been curious and done some googling. But there wasn't much about the school online. All he could really tell was that it was an insanely rich boarding school. There were no news articles, no admissions website with photos and curriculum listed—just brief mentions in certain famous people's education histories. Like, important public figures. The president of France. The CEO of a global billion-dollar green energy corporation.

"We're also here to ensure you get your uniform, schoolbooks, and travel accommodations prepared before the start of the term," the man continued.

Alaric stared at him while the absurdity of those words sunk in. After a moment, he let out a snort of laughter. "Is this some Harry Potter hoax? Are yeh about to tell me I'm a wizard?"

The men shared a loaded look, and Alaric's annoyance shot up ten more notches. He was used to adults diminishing him, but never in his own home.

Alaric nodded toward the door. "Not interested, lads. See yerselves out. Cheers."

The men didn't move, and Alaric's head gave a painful throb. The ache in his jaw was nearly to the point of needing a strong shot of whiskey. He didn't usually drink, because it guaranteed more trouble, but he found it to be an effective painkiller.

"I'm afraid that's not an acceptable answer, Mr. Durham. We have very specific instructions to secure your arrival at the Academy by September first," the leaner man replied.

Alaric raised his head, pain momentarily forgotten. The man's words didn't make sense. They *barely* registered in Alaric's foggy mind, but enough for him to grasp something important.

Alaric squinted at them. "Whose instructions?"

"Your family's."

Alaric exploded in laughter, his aching jaw almost bringing tears to his eyes. But the statement was so absurd—so inherently *wrong*—it was all he could do.

When his chuckles subsided, Alaric slouched fully in his chair, the suspense melting away. The men *were* here by mistake. Alaric had no family. He never had.

"I told yeh, I'm not yer guy," Alaric said, leaning his head back and closing his eyes. His independence and isolation had become a rigid second skin over the years, protecting him from any false hopes. There was no emotion in his voice when he continued. "Do yeh see a Mr. and Mrs. Durham anywhere? Yeh've got it wrong."

There was a moment of silence where even though Alaric couldn't see them, he was sure they were exchanging another weighty look.

"Seventeen years ago you were born. May sixteenth. Nine pounds, fifteen ounces, blood type AB positive."

Alaric froze, making his muscles lock and pain ripple through his body enough to nauseate him. That was his birthday. And his blood type.

"If you're concerned about the tuition, your family has taken care of it."

Truthfully, the tuition had never crossed Alaric's mind, positive as he was that it had all been a mistake. But now that they brought it up, a school that educated prime ministers and CEOs—it certainly wasn't cheap. And if his family was loaded enough for boarding school, where the hell had they been for the last seventeen years?

Back when Alaric was quite small, he remembered someone watching over him. This guardian changed every few months. At some point, one person left, but no one came to take their place. He was moved into government care. Eventually he'd gotten old enough to get a job, and he'd been looking out for himself ever since. Just last year he'd earned enough to pay for his own flat. His life had been one long lesson in survival. An endless stream of disappointments.

Was there really some rich family out there that had simply ignored him all these years?

His right hand slowly curled into a fist. The skin across his knuckles, broken and bleeding, stretched painfully across bruised bone. For years, he'd hated his parents for abandoning him before they even gave him a chance to be a person worth sticking around for.

But what tormented Alaric the most was how little his life mattered. All he knew was boring school with teachers who thought he was a lost cause, inane classes that never challenged him, tedious part-time jobs, hanging with his friends, watching videos on his phone, reading comics, and occasionally ending fights. It was tolerable for now, but his future was scary. He'd seen the men stumbling out of pubs every night after soulless work drove them to pints.

Sure, university might be an option, but could he ever get a respectable job? Would people take a chance on him? No one had yet. Not even his own family... until now.

But why *now*? If they were going to abandon their kid, may as well commit for life. If this letter was real... he could trace his past and remake his future all at once. There really wasn't much of a choice to make.

"This school...," Alaric muttered, staring at the grimy floor of his flat, feeling his stomach churn with nerves and his blood burn with resentment, an emotion he thought he'd long since overcome. "Yeh sure it's free?"

2

EMMELINE

A FRESH WAVE OF TURBULENCE ROCKED THROUGH THE PASSENGER jet, making Emmeline white-knuckle her armrest. Not for the first time, she was glad she had declined any tea or coffee. It would be all over her Dolce dress and cropped blazer by now.

Imagine: her first appearance at Almus Terra Academy, covered in faded beige stains. At that point, she wouldn't leave the airstrip. She'd rather return to Manhattan as the city's most beautiful—albeit lonely—society girl than appear sloppy on her first day at the most prestigious school on the planet.

Butterflies fluttered in her stomach at the thought of the academy. Flying across the Atlantic over the last six hours, she'd been trying *not* to hyper-fixate. Because she wanted her head clear when they landed, she'd avoided Dramamine or any other anti-nausea pills. Her poise, her attitude, her wit—all hinged on a sharp mind. She had to be at the top of her game.

"Another sparkling water, miss?" a flight attendant asked above her.

Emmeline had barely even touched her first glass, which was now well past flat.

"I'm fine, thank you," Emmeline replied. She didn't need to factor in potential burping from the carbonation.

"You should eat something," Heather said once the flight attendant had moved on, not even glancing up from a novel she was reading—likely a Brontë sister. Heather never read anything from this century, and the Victorian classics were her comfort reads. Which was telling since Heather, like Emmeline, had been a wreck of nerves for days.

Hardly surprising, as this happened to be the biggest moment of both their lives.

"Not hungry." Emmeline glanced out the window hoping to see their destination in the distance. No southern coast of France, not yet.

If she checked the plane's trajectory, she would see they were still a couple hours out. No different from when she checked it eleven minutes ago. *Get a grip, Emmeline.*

"It's not about hunger. It's about having energy for the day. Would you rather be sluggish when you meet your peers?" Heather asked, tapping the digital reader screen to turn the page.

Emmeline hated when Heather did that. Question her with something so obvious it bordered on moronic. But that had been Heather's method for raising Emmeline since she was nine. *Do you want to watch shows that will rot your brain? Do you want to inevitably grow out bangs? Do you really want nails that garish?*

Over time, Emmeline understood the psychological game in each of those questions, and she slowly began to overcome them. But it took her many years, given how deeply the expectation of perfection was ingrained in her subconscious. From Emmeline's rough calculations, her victory rate against Heather's manipulative barbs was about 45 percent.

"I'll have a protein bar later," Emmeline acquiesced. *Forty-four-point six percent.*

As usual, Heather showed no signs of approval. Emmeline was used to it. In fact, it would be somewhat disturbing if Heather suddenly became a loving, doting parent. She would never be what Emmeline wanted, because Heather was her…guardian? Governess seemed more applicable, if also extremely dated.

But just as Heather had manipulated Emmeline over the years, Emmeline had learned to do the same.

"This is a private charter, am I right?"

Heather still didn't look up. "Correct."

Another bout of turbulence rocked the plane and Emmeline wished she were flying on a massive transatlantic flight. She'd heard that larger planes were a much smoother ride. At this point she'd even consider—*shudder*—premium economy.

"Who do the flight attendants work for?"

Finally, Heather relinquished her attention. Seated across from Emmeline in a massive armchair likely made from the coats of a baby llama or something else horridly expensive, she looked comfortable. As she should. As Emmeline's governess of eight years, Heather had lived in the same Manhattan high-rise and dressed and dined in the same luxury.

She straightened in the high-back chair and lowered her e-reader. "Why?"

Emmeline shrugged. "Just wondering if they work for my family or not."

She could feel Heather getting agitated. Her governess hated when Emmeline refused to get to her point fast enough, drawing it out so Heather had to keep pushing, pulling, prodding.

"Your family hired the charter. They do not own it."

"Right. Interesting." Emmeline pursed her lips, drumming her nails on the llama leather.

"What's interesting, Emmeline?" Heather hissed, her patience running out.

"Well…I don't want to get anyone into trouble." Emmeline's

words were smooth and practiced, not sweet but earnest. "I thought I saw the flight attendant out with her phone. And given where we're going and my family's discretion—"

Heather made a growling noise in the back of her throat, clicked off her e-reader, and stood. Her heels padded on the carpeted floor of the jet toward the back of the plane, where the flight attendant was probably just playing *Candy Crush* on her phone.

Finally. Moving quickly, Emmeline pulled out the two pieces of paper that she'd slipped into the crevice of her seat. The first was her acceptance letter to Almus Terra—a document she'd coveted since she was eleven.

Before Heather, she'd had a fairly pleasant childhood. While she didn't have normal loving parents, her nanny had been kind and cheerful. However, Tilde had still treated Emmeline as a job, no more than a handsome paycheck, choosing not to get too close. Exactly *who* was paying for Tilde, for Emmeline's designer clothes, private schools, and high-rise apartment, Emmeline was never told. And when Tilde was replaced with Heather, whose job was to mold Emmeline into a brilliant scholar and socialite, the lonely girl became even more aware of the fact that her life was not normal.

Who exactly was this familial benefactor willing to invest millions to ensure Emmeline grew into someone important, when she was a stranger to them? It didn't add up.

For years, she and Heather worked tirelessly to ensure she got into Almus Terra Academy. But soon after the enrollment documents came, the biggest mystery of her life began to unfold. Another monumental letter arrived, addressed to Emmeline from her parents.

By now, the paper was crinkled and worn from the many times Emmeline had folded and unfolded it, smoothed it, and read it.

Though she'd memorized almost every word, her eyes raked over the letter, hungrily eating up the pretty loops and swirls of her mother's cursive.

Dear Emmeline,

At last, we welcome our beautiful daughter back into our lives. For reasons we cannot yet divulge, we have had to endure the past sixteen years apart. But our separation, and these wretched secrets, will end once you embark on the next chapter of your life. Your entelechy awaits at Almus Terra. Though you will be tested, your father and I both believe that you will rise far beyond our expectations. Remember always: passion in the pursuit of perfection.

With Highest Regards,
Your Mother

Emmeline had to look up the word *entelechy*, but more importantly—*they had reasons*. She had clung to that line—read it over and over until she was breathless with hope, desperate to be anything other than some unwanted dependent.

Either her mother had never wanted her and had been knocked up by some rich guy who'd agreed to pay a billionaire's version of child support...or her mother was so rich and successful that the burden of taking care of a child was something worth her money but not her time. Both possibilities were devastating but theories she'd lived with, and at various points accepted. Until this letter.

Whatever the reasons were, it almost didn't matter. Even if they were misguided, paltry excuses, it was better than being unwanted. And in her heart, she knew she would accept them.

At the sound of Heather's footsteps returning, Emmeline shoved the letters back into the gap between her cushion and her arm rest.

Heather took her seat, glaring furiously at her ward, but said nothing, as usual. Whenever Emmeline was able to manipulate, Heather never scolded her. Because that would mean admitting defeat to a seventeen-year-old. And in truth, elegant manipulation was probably the most important lesson for Heather to impart.

They lapsed into silence. Emmeline checked the flight path. One hour and forty-two minutes to landing.

For all of Emmeline's family wealth, she'd never traveled. At least, not outside the US. She'd flown to Chicago and LA for academic decathlons and school field trips that Heather had approved. But her mysterious family had been content to keep her without a passport.

So it was hard to maintain indifference as their private Audi drove them along the coast of southern France. The climate was hot and sunny, but dry. The sea was the brightest blue Emmeline had ever seen, rivaling the shade of the sky. Vineyards stretched out to the left in rows of peridot. Emmeline wondered if they were grenache grapes or the cabernet sauvignon variety. She had been given one glass of wine twice a month since her sixteenth birthday—not as a treat, but as a lesson. Heather expected Emmeline to know enough to smartly converse with a sommelier, though Emmeline had never really understood why.

Having landed in Marseille, they were now headed toward a small port town called Toulon. Not that anyone had told her this. Emmeline was following the car's route on her phone. The town was beautiful and exotic, so very different from New York, with clay shingle roofs and a backdrop of limestone mountains. But as they came and went through Toulon, Emmeline's anxiety grew.

The driver exited off the main highway onto a smaller road, and Emmeline shifted in her seat, her stomach doing aerial flips.

"Stop squirming," Heather commanded sharply.

The subtext screamed in Emmeline's head. *Nervous looks weak.*

Emmeline didn't move again until the car pulled into a small, well-kept port. Paved stone the color of rust, bronze, and gold bordered the rocky coast, and a single sturdy dock made of gleaming wood stretched out into the calm waters. At the end of the dock was a yacht...ferry? Emmeline didn't know ships very well, but this one had the sleekness of a luxury yacht with the broad, flat decks of a ferry. At its helm was a crest that she recognized well. A silver shield with the earth's four main landmasses—Africa, the Americas, Europe, and Asia—surrounded by olive branches and backed by crossed sabers.

ALMUS TERRA ACADEMY

For so long those three words had been a lucky charm for Emmeline. Something to whisper to herself when she felt helpless and alone. She'd wished for a place so powerful that it would catapult her confined life into something more.

Here, she'd find not just the right path, but true allies. A real ride-or-die squad. Her "friends" back home had been convenient at best. Enjoying Emmeline's wealth but loving the mystique of her lonely existence even more. Who *was* Emmeline Rhodes? Who were her parents? Where did her money come from? The constant well of gossip was a way to keep her separate and different from the kids at school. Not that Emmeline wanted to be like anyone else.

But she *had* wanted people she could belong to. Thanks to Heather and a revolving door of large security men instructed not to socialize, Emmeline was never allowed to get truly close, to be vulnerable, with anyone.

Almus Terra offered freedom and, according to the worn letter in her bag, *family.*

Heather stepped out of the car and without a word headed for the small rust-colored building where several other adults were already congregated, talking to the faculty, who were wearing pressed academy uniforms of gray, ivory, violet, and emerald.

Emmeline stayed by the car while the driver silently unloaded her several bags. To distract herself from the gathering of students at the dock, Emmeline checked her nails, trying to exude nonchalance. She was meant to be here. This was nothing.

Yet her whole life had led up to this moment. And she was just… standing by the car?

Emmeline glanced over at Heather, who was speaking with one of the school's representatives, doing her job. Nothing more than that. In so many years of companionship, Heather had never been cruel to Emmeline, but she'd never shown attachment to her either. There was no deep love between them. If anything, there was relief that they would finally part ways, from this day forward.

So, without a single goodbye, Emmeline flipped her long honey hair over her shoulder and strode toward the Almus Terra students on the dock, looking every bit like she belonged.

And deep in her bones, she knew she did. Since birth.

3

SADIE

Covered parapets, an outer curtain wall, ramparts connecting towers that flanked the outer walls—and that was all Sadie could see just downhill. There was likely more—the main keep, a chapel tower, turrets, and hidden posterns, but until the next bend in the road, the rest of Almus Terra would be left to Sadie's overactive imagination.

Fig and cypress trees bordered the one-way country lane that wound up the elevation of the small isle in southern France. Behind her, the laughter and chatter of her new classmates played as a background score to the title credits of Sadie's previously simple life. Hans Zimmer, Howard Shore—hell, even John Williams would be impressed with the composition of her new life's soundtrack. *Holy Medieval Battlements, Batman. Here I am.*

Sadie nudged Remy next to her. "What do you think the bailey looks like?"

The only other student from Ashland looked annoyed, but just slightly. Which Sadie considered a win. Remy had looked *very* annoyed the whole journey: From the Ashland flight to Paris, from the Paris train to Toulon, and finally the Toulon bus to the ferry, she'd been sour.

Still, they'd stuck together. They were hardly best friends, Remy being the daughter of Ashland's most successful CEO and Sadie being…well, no one, but the two Ashlandic girls found it easier to pair up than to introduce themselves to strangers so soon.

"What the hell is a bailey?" Remy asked.

"It's a leveled courtyard within castles, surrounded by walls for—"

"I don't care," Remy muttered.

"I bet they have some statues from the Holy Roman Empire, like Frederick II or Ramon Berenguer IV of the Catalan Dynasty…." Sadie tilted her chin to get a better look as the trees gave away to a broader angle of the thirteenth-century castle. "It has a barbican! That's a—"

"Sadie. Don't. Care," Remy snarled next to her.

Outer gatehouse for fortification, Sadie finished in her head as the piece of medieval architecture came into full magnificent view.

Behind her, the score changed tempo. From enthusiastic conversation to gasps of awe, excited whoops, and a few relieved sighs. The journey to the castle had been on foot, half a mile uphill. Now that they were so close, Sadie relished this moment to admire the school of her dreams. The ancient gray stone, the towers with the bronze corbels nearly touching low-lying clouds, the hanging purple banners fluttering from the ramparts…it was all really real.

It had been the beginning of eighth grade when she'd first heard of Almus Terra Academy. As one of the top students in her district, Sadie had been among the chosen few to enter Ashland's National Merit Scholarship Program.

It was a four-year program designed to motivate Ashland's young scholars and send one lucky child to the world's most prestigious preparatory school. Almus Terra was dedicated to educating the brightest students so they may lead their home countries on a mission for global economic prosperity and world peace, and the National Treasury of Ashland would foot the admissions bill for one lower-income contestant every few years. When King Leander had announced the program, he'd gained a lot of admiration from the media—people loved the idea that the king was taking a personal interest in the hopes and dreams of his young subjects.

It was a lofty ambition for a twelve-year-old from a working-class family, but Sadie had been inspired. She had studied so hard, achieved perfect grades for four years, and then...last year her pristine record was destroyed.

The scholarship application deadline came and went. Her spotless attendance, her roster of extracurricular activities, her flawless GPA—all of it tarnished. In just one night, her future was washed away.

Sadie shook her head quickly, her ponytail nearly whipping Remy in the face. She would not think about that night. She couldn't afford to.

"Aren't you getting in line?" Remy snapped.

Mentally Sadie kicked herself; she hurriedly stepped behind Remy. She wasn't going to ruin her dream in the present by dwelling on the past. Reaching this moment should've been impossible since she'd missed the scholarship deadline and her grades had taken a nosedive. Yet the acceptance letter had still arrived. She was still *here*.

Her neck craned backward as she marveled at the old moldings on the barbican restored to their former ancient glory.

A hard poke jolted Sadie, and she dropped her head to notice the older, brown-skinned woman in the bright-colored head wrap and gray power suit waiting for her with a tablet. Remy was already walking across the bridge through the gates, toward the main castle entrance.

"Welcome to Almus Terra. Name?" the woman asked.

Sadie squeezed her fists at her sides, keeping herself from vibrating with excitement. "Sadie Aurelia."

The woman's fingers, poised to tap across her tablet, remained frozen as she raised her eyes to meet Sadie's for the first time.

"Sadie Aurelia?" she repeated.

Sadie blinked, the temperature of her skin suddenly heating and cooling in a flash. A symptom of anxiety she'd never quite been able to control, especially not since...

Don't.

"Y-yes," Sadie breathed. Her pulse started to spike, and oxygen suddenly felt out of reach. But she managed to grab control—like the therapist had taught her. "That's me." Good. Her voice was steadier now.

"Stand here, please," the woman instructed, pointing to the space right next to her.

The blood drained from Sadie's face. The rest of the students were all told to head in. She hadn't been out of breath walking uphill, but she could collapse if all this crumbled before her. If her miracle had been a mistake.

"Is something wrong?"

"Here, please," the woman repeated, her features growing stern.

Sadie complied and tried not to ask more questions. Almus Terra surely did not tolerate any form of disobedience, and she wasn't about to get in trouble before she'd even stepped foot inside—though it seemed like maybe she already had.

The line of students slowly trickled down, nearly every one of them giving Sadie a curious look. Why was she just standing there on display? What made her so special?

Almost twenty minutes later, when the last of the students had been checked in, the teacher turned to Sadie. "Follow me, Ms. Aurelia."

The teacher headed under the barbican and over the cobbled walkway through Almus Terra's inner gates. Her heels clicked across stone, and she moved with such poise that Sadie couldn't help but stare before registering her instructions. *Follow.*

The entrance hall was as impressive as the exterior of the castle. With a thirty-foot ceiling, the hall opened to a grand atrium where sunlight filtered down through a stained glass window. The window art displayed the school's crest and had probably been installed when the castle was restored. Potentially post–World War II. According to Almus Terra history, that's when the school grew significantly in popularity and prestige, its mission even more critical. Almus Terra had always been a renowned institution—famously boasting connections to scholars like Galileo, Isaac Newton, Immanuel Kant, and Voltaire—but the devastation wrought during World War II gave the school a new sense of purpose: world peace.

"Ms. Aurelia," the teacher called.

Sadie hurried after her—she was already going up a narrow stone staircase on the right. The teacher opened a door to a long corridor covered in tapestries on one side and tall windows bordered by thick, rich purple curtains held by gold cords on the other.

The afternoon sun shone brightly on the tapestries, illuminating rutilant threads and making the weaving around them shine. Each tableau depicted moments of great significance in world history—the burning of Rome, the Xinhai Revolution, the Declaration of Independence, D-day, the Fifth Pan-African Congress, the founding of the UN. Sadie would've stared at them for hours, taking in every detail and committing each one to memory, but she couldn't fall behind again. Hopefully there would be time later to take a closer look.

Please, please, please, let this not be a mistake.

After going through another door and up a second staircase, this one a spiral, the teacher stopped at a door larger and grander than the rest. The wood was a deep cherry red, and the knocker was metal worked to emulate the shape of a dove.

For peace, Sadie noted.

The teacher rapped on the door and pushed it open. "Ma'am, I brought the last one."

The last one?

"Thank you, Professor Haji," a smooth, slightly accented voice said through the door.

Professor Haji dipped her head and then promptly left, heading back down the stairs without another word.

"Come in, Ms. Aurelia."

Relax, Sadie. If they sent you an acceptance letter by mistake, it's their fault, not yours.

But still, her gut clenched at the idea that she could be going back home. No. There was no home to go back to. Almus Terra was her only path forward.

Taking a deep breath, Sadie stepped through the door and had trouble deciding where to look first.

The room was an office, and it was huge. It could've easily been the bedroom of a lord or a member of the holy church a thousand years ago. Now it had giant volumes of text on shelves, world maps encased in glass on the stone walls, and statues of historical figures.

There were four people in the office—three teenagers about Sadie's age, and then clearly the most important person in the room, perhaps the school. The woman standing behind the massive desk was stunning, with light brown skin and black braids threaded with silver and purple strands. Her back was to the windows, and her fingertips rested lightly on the wood surface. She was dressed in lavender slacks and a matching light purple vest, showing off muscular arms with an impressive amount of ink. When she spoke, Sadie's spine straightened on instinct.

"Welcome to Almus Terra, Ms. Aurelia. I'm your headmistress, Zuri Aquila. Please, join us." The headmistress beckoned Sadie to the empty spot between two of the three teens.

Slowly, Sadie shuffled forward, unable to stop herself from openly staring at the other... well, they obviously had to be students too. But that's where the similarities ended.

All three looked like they'd stepped out of a TV show. Some ridiculous American drama where every person is obnoxiously attractive. But it wasn't just their looks—they seemed to exude confidence and an aura of…superiority? It was hard to discern self-assurance from snobbery, but they seemed to possess some kind of divine right.

The office was quiet as the three larger-than-life teenagers regarded Sadie, just as she sized them up herself. The guy to the far left was the most intimidating since he radiated hostility as well as power. He was also probably one of the tallest and broadest boys Sadie had ever seen—plus he had a nasty multicolored bruise traveling from the side of his pale face down to his jaw. Unlike the other two, he was dressed more like Sadie, in simple, worn clothes. His hands were tucked into a hoodie once black but now a dark gray. A green Henley that he'd seemingly outgrown strained across a muscular chest. He wore jeans that had seen many washes and had many stains (one that looked suspiciously like blood). His hair was a dark brown cropped close on the sides and unruly on top, and his eyes reminded Sadie of storm clouds over the coast of the Durah cliffs back home.

The girl next to him was his opposite in both attire and bone structure. Her features were delicate and perfectly symmetrical. She was rather tall, built like a model, really. She wore a peach dress, clearly some designer label, and a blazer that stopped above her waist like a business crop top. Her light brown hair resembled liquid honey and fell down her slender back in silky waves. Her eyes, too, were gray, though they shined more like silver. She was, quite possibly, the prettiest girl Sadie had ever seen in real life.

The second young man, whom Sadie now stood next to, resembled a real-life Greek god Apollo. He was tall, but where the dark-haired boy was bulky with muscle, Apollo was leaner, more like a swimmer than a hockey player. With perfect posture, his arms rested easily, and somehow respectfully, at his sides. He wore slacks, a button-down, and a sports coat, and like the girl's outfit, everything seemed cut from money and stitched with style. Blond hair, bordering on gold, a straight nose and accented cheekbones—he could've been Chris Hemsworth himself. Except for his eyes. Not a Hemsworth blue. Gray, again, like iron.

"Late," Headmistress Aquila said, sighing and glancing at the clock on the wall.

"O-oh, I'm sorry," Sadie said on reflex, not that it was *her* fault she was late for . . . whatever this was.

"Not you, Ms. Aurelia," the headmistress said kindly, then nodded toward the door. "Him."

When Sadie and the others turned, she almost choked on air—somewhere between a gasp and a squeak. Standing before her in the doorway was the king of Ashland.

King Leander was easily over six feet tall. With broad shoulders, he was well-built for a man in his mid-seventies. Though he was getting on in years, he exuded authority and elegance. His gray hair was cut short like a soldier's, and his suit was so crisp and simple, it could have been a military uniform. There were no dazzling embellishments like sashes, badges, or epaulets to signal his royalty, but Sadie knew him all the same.

He'd ruled Ashland for over fifty years now. The longest reign in their country's existence. His face was everywhere—television, stamps, statues, history books.

Two men in navy suits flanked him, both rather large, imposing, and capable—Sadie was sure—of killing anyone at a moment's notice. They made the enormous office feel a little tighter.

The blood rushed back to Sadie's face as she dropped to one knee, her heart pounding. *Why was the king here?*

"Rise, Ms. Aurelia." Amusement colored the king's tone. "No need for formalities."

Face even hotter, Sadie unsteadily got to her feet, realizing no one else had moved to kneel. In fact, the other students were looking at her like she was a creature from outer space.

"Oh, for heaven's sake. This is a school, not the Kremlin. Please tell your guards to wait outside," Headmistress Aquila said, clicking her tongue.

With a surprisingly chill shrug, the king muttered a few choice words to his men. The guards responded with the Ashlandic military salute, then headed back down the stairs.

Once the door was closed, King Leander turned to regard each person in the room, his gaze lingering longest on the three pairs of dazzling gray eyes. A smile tugged at the corners of his mouth, though the man's face was so harsh it seemed more like a grimace to Sadie.

"I've waited years for this day," he said, his low voice rich in depth and class.

Sadie twisted her fingers against her stomach, unsure if she was more nervous or confused.

"Aye? And what day is that, lad?" the dark-haired boy drawled in a thick Irish brogue.

Sadie's fingers tightened, locking together so hard her knuckles turned white. The king of Ashland wasn't anybody's *lad*.

King Leander's smile grew, his own gray eyes seeming to spark with intrigue. "Headmistress, I appreciate you gathering them for me."

The headmistress flicked her wrist toward the clock. "Time is of the essence, Leander. I have a speech to give and these four must attend the welcome banquet with their classmates."

"Straight to business, then. Please, let us sit." The king gestured to an area with five chairs and a coffee table before them. A Japanese tea set rested on the table, though Sadie highly doubted they'd be offered any.

The dark-haired boy dumped himself onto the chair nearest to where he stood, and the pretty girl took the seat next to him. The blond demigod and Sadie took the other chairs across the coffee table, and King Leander sat in the last seat.

"First, let me congratulate you all on your acceptance into Almus Terra," King Leander began, his heavy gaze scouring each of them. "Though I paid your tuitions, *you* had to meet the academic requirements on your own in order to be admitted."

Sadie bit her tongue—literally—to prevent herself from interrupting a king. Though she was practically bursting at the seams. Wasn't the National Merit Scholarship funded by the Treasury? Was the king claiming to have *personally* paid? Were these other students *also* Ashland scholarship winners?

Lacing his fingers together, the king continued. "A long time ago, I decided that my succession would be determined not by lineage or politics, but by strength. Skill. Knowledge. You've all been gifted a spot at Almus Terra because of your birthright. But only one of you will inherit my throne, and that"—his index fingers dipped downward, hands still clasped—"must be earned. Won."

The room was completely silent. Not a single outside bird, clearing of throat, or sound of footfalls could be heard. Nothing. It was as if God—or whoever might be out there watching with popcorn—wanted to press pause. Sadie blinked. Hard. She pinched her thigh. It *hurt*.

"Excuse me, sir," the other girl said, her voice as lovely as her face. Soft, melodic, perfectly pitched, and clear.

King Leander turned to her. "Yes, Emmeline?"

"What do you mean by birthright?"

"Ah, yes. That." The king reached into his jacket pocket, withdrew folded sheets of paper, and then unceremoniously dropped them onto the coffee table. "The three of you—Alaric, Titus, and Emmeline, are my grandchildren. With the blood of House Eldana running through your veins, you are viable successors to my reign. You're welcome to verify your birth certificates and medical records if you wish. The documents are all right here."

No one moved to reach for the papers.

Sadie's gaze shot to the three heirs sitting around her. It wasn't every day you got to watch someone find out they were royalty.

The girl, Emmeline, was staring at King Leander with a mix of realization, surprise, and...triumph? Her silver eyes seemed to blaze, and her hands curled into fists on her lap.

The dark-haired boy, either Alaric or Titus, looked as if he'd just eaten something poisonous, like weeks-old sushi. An expression something close to horror and utter revulsion.

But the blond one, amazingly, wasn't even looking at his surprise grandfather—he was staring at Sadie. His eyes were as sharp as steel, and his perfect mouth was set in a firm line.

"And Ms. Aurelia?" he asked, his voice coated with a thick high-society British accent. "You said the three of us. If *she* is not of your blood, who is she?"

An excellent question, my dear Watson. This was quickly escalating to K-drama status and Sadie tended to react to discomfort with humor.

Sweat broke out between her shoulder blades and she felt like laughing or throwing up, it could really go either way.

Thankfully, the king answered—as he should, since the question certainly hadn't been directed at her. "Sadie Aurelia is one of my subjects. Born and raised in Ashland's capital and an exemplary student with a brilliance that her teachers have long praised. She won a national scholarship to attend Almus Terra. Little did anyone know, this year's scholarship comes with the chance at my crown. I am honor-bound to challenge unbridled nepotism. The best and the brightest deserve a path to Ashland's monarchy."

This can't be happening.

At everyone's stunned silence, the king chuckled. "I am not so arrogant as to believe my own blood are the only ones fit to rule. Any citizen has a right to prove themselves worthy of leadership. I believe Ms. Aurelia could have what it takes, and I want someone born and raised on Ashlandic soil to stand as an equal contender alongside the three of you."

"We would have been born and raised in *our* country had you not sent us away."

"Titus." Warning cut through the king's tone as his eyes flashed over to the blond boy next to Sadie. "Believe what you like, but I sent you three away to save your lives *and* our country. As I had not yet chosen an heir, predators were plotting left and right to eliminate you as possible successors. And I did not want to see my grandchildren murdered any more than I'd want to see my homeland ravaged by another civil war. Our kingdom was healing, our people finally working and thriving. I did what I did for the good of Ashland. But now we have nothing to hide. A press release will be issued within the week and once that happens, you will officially be known as the royal heirs of Ashland. Learn everything you can at Almus Terra, and then bring that bounty of training and knowledge back to your homeland."

Powerful words for powerful people. But Sadie wasn't one of them. She was a nobody. Chosen *why*, exactly?

According to Ashlandic law, the ruling monarch could choose their own successor regardless of birth order or blood relation. In the event a monarch dies prior to naming an heir, the Royal Advisory Council would choose. It wasn't a foolproof system by any means, which was partly why it had been so easy to wage wars during transitions of power. Nevertheless, it was tradition. So while choosing a non-related heir was exceedingly rare, it wasn't against custom.

Though *how* King Leander could take on a random girl as an heir without—wait, did her social worker even know about this?

Then again, did it matter? He *was* the king, and she supposed he could enact whatever law he liked, appoint whomever he wanted as his heir. He could make her a princess under his royal decree. *Whoa. No way.*

Suddenly, the dark-haired boy shot to his feet and started for the door.

"Alaric?" Headmistress Aquila asked from her desk. Sadie had forgotten she was still there "Where are you going?"

"Back to Dublin," he snarled, tossing the words over his shoulder. "This was an absolute gas. But yer all off yer head if yeh think I'm some eejit prince."

"And what's in Dublin?"

Alaric froze, fist on the door handle, his big shoulders stiff at the king's words.

"Don't you want to know why, Alaric?" King Leander continued lightly, as if he were talking about the weather.

Why what?

Alaric slowly turned back around, the good side of his jaw moving and grinding. But he didn't leave... and he didn't say anything more.

Satisfied, King Leander reclined in his low cushioned chair.

"Today is just the beginning. Settle into your classes, make your new friends, and we shall reconvene before long. In the meantime, you will be judged. Not just on your grades, but by your character and your actions here at Almus Terra." King Leander crossed his legs, his chin tilting up in a tenebrous look that made Sadie shiver.

"This school breeds world leaders and revolutionary thinkers. That's why you're here. I have no doubt each of you will do well. But doing well is not enough. You must be exceptional. You must be the best to inherit my legacy."

No one said a word. No one even breathed. Sadie's nerves were shot, a numbness starting to spread through her limbs as she realized something very important: The king of Ashland would never make the mistake of getting the wrong girl. If he chose Sadie as part of his game of succession, he meant it. Still—*why me?*

"Now, there's a banquet to attend... is there not, Headmistress?"

Headmistress Aquila swiveled in her chair, her fingers drumming on the arm rests and her mouth turned down in aggravation. Her glare was fixed on the king.

"Indeed. Students, wait for me down at the base of the tower. I'll escort you to the Banquet Hall. Right after I have a quick word with your king."

Formally dismissed, Titus, Emmeline, and Sadie stood from the sofa, while Alaric, closest to the door, was already stomping down the stairs.

Though it wasn't Sadie's place to judge, she did find it extremely strange that there was no tearful reunion. The king had just met his grandchildren for the first time in what, sixteen years? And there wasn't a single embrace or even a pat on the back. It was just so cold. King Leander hadn't rejoiced at seeing them because he missed them. He'd brought them here to compete for his crown, and then dismissed them like mere employees. Sadie was glad he wasn't *her* grandfather.

As Emmeline and Titus followed Alaric out, their footsteps echoing in the hollow archway, Sadie paused at the door, casting one look back at her king.

His iron gaze found hers and the corner of his mouth hitched up. "Yes, Ms. Aurelia?"

Sadie licked her lips, her throat suddenly so dry. There must have been thousands of other Ashlandic children to choose from. For example, she knew one boy who'd moved to the States to join a team of kids training to go to Mars one day. Sure, she was intelligent, maybe more than the average student, but she was nothing so special as to belong here. And, more importantly, none of the other scholarship contenders had botched their applications.

"Your Majesty, I...I missed the deadline. My schoolwork fell apart. Why was I still considered?" she asked, her pulse rocketing.

"Sadie," King Leander said, his hands slipping into his pockets, "do you believe in second chances?"

Her heart clenched painfully, and it was a struggle to keep her voice level. "Yes."

He smiled kindly. "So do I."

4

TITUS

"YOU KNEW."

Titus raised his head. He wasn't entirely surprised to find the American girl—Emmeline—standing in front of him with her hands on her hips, looking quite cross.

Well, he supposed she was partly American, just as he was partly British. They would never be fully, or *only*, Ashlandic.

Titus looked away from his cousin, his gaze pointing toward the guards awaiting their king at the end of the hall. He hoped to God they were out of earshot.

He'd been trying to ignore her and Alaric while the other girl and the headmistress made their way downstairs. It took everything in him not to sprint up the steps and grab Sadie Aurelia. Why wasn't she down here yet? What were they still talking about?

Emmeline gave a sharp tap of her heel on the stone floor, her throat clearing in an obnoxious demand for attention.

With great practice, Titus kept his face blank. "I'm sure I don't know what you mean."

For years, Titus had been anticipating the moment where his royal heritage would be revealed to him. He needed a surprised look, but nothing too shocked. It should be genuine, if also within the typical range of his highbrow composure.

But he blew it when he found out there would be a *fourth*. Not just a fourth...an outsider. Neither an Eldana nor someone from a distinguished social rank. She was, for lack of a more modern label, a commoner. This must be a bloody joke.

"Bullshit," Emmeline hissed. "I saw your face."

"That language is a little uncouth for a princess," Titus murmured, and his cousin's eyes flashed with rage.

Footsteps came from above and Emmeline pursed her lips, stepping away from Titus. Alaric hadn't budged from leaning against the wall with his arms crossed. His gaze didn't even flicker toward the staircase as Sadie came down, her dirty Converse echoing on the stone steps.

Titus didn't like how still Alaric was. It reminded him of an animal predator about to strike. That said, he didn't seem to be much of a threat. Until a few minutes ago, Alaric was ready to walk out on this whole thing. Besides, judging from his bruised face and scuffed-up knuckles, he was hardly king material.

"O-oh, excuse me," Sadie said.

Titus had strategically positioned himself at the bottom of the steps so when Sadie came through, he had to stand back and make room, giving himself an excuse to take a closer look.

She was shorter than average, and her jeans and oxford shirt seemed to hang loosely on her petite frame in a way that wasn't fashionable. Which told him two things: She had either lost a significant amount of weight recently, or she'd lost weight over time and didn't have enough money to purchase new clothes. Her light red hair was oily at the roots and dry in the ends, bound up in a ponytail with ginger and strawberry tones. Long bangs brushed the square frames of glasses shielding hazel-colored eyes.

Though her features were not unpleasant by any stretch of the imagination, nothing about her was notable. Nothing about her was royal. Yet that didn't seem to matter, thanks to his grandfather's ridiculous scholarship program.

His back molars grinded in frustration. This girl would never beat him, of course, but the added hurdle was irritating. After years of training, this was only the beginning. Besting two heirs to the throne was stressful enough, but now some New Age peasant was in the race as well?

Titus forced a smile down at her. "Forgive me, I was in *your* way."

Sadie's brows furrowed; she wasn't buying it. She would be wary of him. As she should be.

"Students," Headmistress Aquila's voice rang from above as she rounded the bend in the stairs, "let's not delay a moment longer. We're already holding up the food."

Sadie and Titus practically jumped aside as the headmistress of Almus Terra reached the bottom and breezed past them all. The woman moved with the kind of authority that Titus couldn't help but admire. Her strides were fast but not rushed, and her gaze was focused like an arrow intended to meet its target.

Emmeline fell into step behind her, nearly matching the headmistress in confidence and poise. Then Titus and Sadie followed, while Alaric pushed off the wall with a growl. At least they were moving again. He'd hated standing in one place for too long while waiting in the headmistress's office.

Already the stiffness in his feet and ankles was beginning to recede as they headed down the tapestry corridor and the steps into the entrance hall of the castle. Crossing diagonally under the stained glass reflection of the school's crest, they went through a side door that led them into a long, smaller antechamber with more statues, books, and sitting chairs, along with a few desks. The next door took them into the bailey, the courtyard that Titus assumed served as the school's quad. Benches, covered parapets, and elegant landscaping went by too fast for Titus to drink it all in.

Before long they were out of the gardens and up steps into a stone building that Titus had to bet was once the castle's main keep. This antechamber had even higher ceilings, more stained glass windows, and yes, more doors. As soon as they entered, a male teacher in a gray suit and a purple-and-green-striped tie hurried to greet them.

"Headmistress, everything is ready."

"Shimizu-sensei, can you please escort these students through the western postern?"

"Mochiron desu," the professor said with a small dip at the waist.

"Arigatō gozaimasu." The headmistress mirrored his bow, then continued her brisk pace across the antechamber.

Shimizu-sensei lifted his arm toward the opposite end. "This way, students. Hurry, please."

Like before, Emmeline was the first to follow, then Sadie and Titus, with Alaric bringing up the rear. The next door led into a back corridor clearly meant for staff because it was full of excess stacked chairs and giant carts with food ready to serve. The hall smelled delicious, like a blend of hundreds of spices from dozens of cuisines. The Japanese professor ushered them through one final door, and upon entering, even Titus had to stop and stare.

They'd emerged into a giant ballroom easily the size of Westminster Abbey's Lady Chapel, the length of it at least. With ceilings almost as high as the room was long, the floor was swirls of peach, ivory, and pearl—the finest marble that Titus had ever seen, and he'd seen a lot. Between fifty and seventy round tables adorned with elegant place settings were in the back half of the ballroom; the students congregated before a stage with a lectern and a row of chairs, and the faculty was already seated.

Without a word—just a sharp, angry glance at Titus—Emmeline strode toward the sea of students with a hair flip and her heels clicking on marble.

"Umm…"

Titus could hear Sadie fretting beside him but said nothing to assuage her. *Let her sweat.* She didn't belong here. The sooner she drowned, the better.

Eager to ditch his rivals, Titus followed Emmeline into the crowds of his classmates, though he noted the direction she took and went the opposite.

He was relieved that his peers also remained in their travel clothes. As one of the first to arrive, he'd been in the headmistress's office for too long and would've been annoyed if he'd missed the chance to check into his dorm, meet his roommates, and settle in.

Hands in his pockets, Titus prowled the edges of the groups, observing. One thing he had missed, it seemed, was the opportunity to network—*er*, socialize. Clusters had already begun to form, and it was such a pain to infiltrate when you were far too late.

He was used to events like these—if you acted like you belonged, then you did. The problem was choosing a group that would accept him immediately.

In about a hundred different ways, Almus Terra Academy was not a normal prep school. Somewhere between a high school and university, it took students whenever they managed to meet the requirements. Which meant ages tended to vary. Thirteen-year-old savants could be third-years, while seventeen-year-old rich kids could be first-years. Much like in the outside world, their standing mattered. If Titus accidentally picked a group full of seniors, they'd bully him for being two years behind in academia.

Inevitably, Titus was forced to take a chance. Otherwise he ran the risk of being an awkward loner, and *that* he could not afford. Choosing a well-dressed circle that appeared equal in both age and social standing, he sidled in, and no one even spared him a real glance.

"Trust me, the strike is going to happen. There's no way Ford,

GM, or Stellantis are meeting the union's demands. They're calling for a forty percent wage increase and a thirty-two-hour work week *without* pay cuts," a pale girl with short black hair said.

The South Asian boy in an Armani suit next to her scoffed. "Simple economics says the manufacturers will cave. Across all three companies, it would cost five billion and reduce an already low inventory. Do you know what kind of impact that would bring? Besides, they can afford it. I mean, just look at the profits they've raked in the last few years."

Titus was ready to add his own two cents about the auto workers' strike, because he agreed with the raven-haired girl—the union president had all but trashed the contract on Instagram Live—when he felt an arm sling around his shoulders.

"Titus! Mate! What're you doing here?"

The voice was all too familiar, as was the suffocating Kilian Black Phantom cologne.

"Sebastian Bane," Titus said, his stomach sinking. *And the hits just keep coming.*

The small group pivoted their attention over to Titus and his old schoolmate. With their debate interrupted, Armani suit guy quirked an eyebrow while raven-haired girl shifted from one heeled boot to the other, her look expectant.

"Bane?" Armani said, raking his eyes over Sebastian. "As in Warburton Bane, the prime minister of England?"

"Dear old dad, the one and only." Seb flashed a toothy smile at the rest of them, then gripped Titus by the shoulders. He didn't bother asking the names of anyone else. So long as they knew who *he* was, that's all that mattered. "Why didn't you say anything, mate?"

Titus should've anticipated this. Out of all the highbrow Eton grads, Sebastian Bane was the most obsessed with himself. With his pore-less ivory skin, inky black waves, and precisely symmetrical features, he was popular enough to be parliament's Prince Harry. It made sense that he'd be aiming for ATA. Titus just thought Seb hadn't possessed the IQ to get in.

"For the same reason you didn't, I suppose," Titus said with a nonchalant shrug.

Seb's smile stretched and Titus had the primitive urge to knock it off his arrogant face. The reason—which neither of them could say out loud—was the fear of rejection. You could be the crown prince of England, the Chinese president's daughter, Einstein's great-grandchild, and still not get in. Not if the admissions board deemed you unworthy. Every single student was hand-selected by a committee using a hundred qualifications and differentiating factors. ATA favored diversity and inclusion, not social stratification. Though based on the student cliques he could already discern, the diversity efforts weren't entirely successful.

"Nah, just didn't want you to feel bad knowing I was leaving you all alone at Eton next year," Seb said, digging his knuckles into Titus's rib cage rather hard.

"Like I said." Titus forced a grin. "Same."

Seb's smiled tightened, almost imperceptibly, but Titus knew him all too well. They'd been—and he loathed this term—frenemies since their first day at Eton four years ago. And he could tell there was a retort on the tip of Seb's forked tongue, but mercifully he was spared. A sweeping hush fell across the ballroom as Headmistress Aquila stepped up to the lectern.

"Scholars," she began, her distinguished baritone carrying through hidden speakers, "it is my privilege to welcome you to Almus Terra Academy, where the future of our world is decided every day. Looking out at each of you, I wonder who will set the course of history. Who will get us to Mars, who will abolish world hunger, who will reduce fossil fuels and bring clean, sustainable energy to every home in every country...*who*, indeed."

The headmistress paused and let her eyes drift slowly across the crowd. "I have no doubt those minds are in this room. You are here because you have shown great potential. It is our responsibility as your teachers to harness it with the belief that *you* are our planet's greatest hope. *Pax in terra.* May this be your creed. Learn all that you can and become more than you imagine. Your time here is pivotal. Not just for your personal growth, but for the legacy you stand to leave this world. And if you've come here to serve your ego or ambitions, you will be known."

Students glanced warily at each other.

This time, Titus noticed her piercing eyes land on him. It might just be paranoia, but it felt like she drilled right through his soul. And for whatever reason, he was keenly aware of the rest of Ashland's heirs standing in the crowd. Emmeline to the far right with a group of other gorgeous, well-dressed girls. Sadie straddling two cohorts, trying to bond with both but ultimately claimed by neither. And Alaric, in the back, brooding alone.

"Now, I won't delay your meal a moment longer. I'm far too late as it is." Again, her punishing gaze seemed to flicker in his direction.

Not my fault, Headmistress, Titus wanted to say. *I never asked for any of this.*

If Titus thought the Sadie Aurelia plot twist was bad, it was nothing compared to his roommate situation. Surely this was by design. Some kind of cruel joke or one of those inane "tests" his grandfather had mentioned.

Without a word, Alaric chucked his ratty duffel bag onto one of the two bottom bunks. Then he turned and glared at the rest of the guys, daring them to challenge his claim.

Titus, Sebastian, and Oliver—a Black American guy with a vaguely Midwestern accent wearing thick glasses and a beanie—didn't move until Alaric had flung himself across the mattress and turned to face the wall.

But then, remembering himself, Titus surged forward to claim the other bottom bunk. Not for the same reasons as Alaric, but he knew in his bones he'd pay for it later if he didn't.

After Sebastian made a disgruntled noise about getting third pick, he tossed his jacket on the bunk above Titus.

Ignoring him, Titus glanced around the dorm room. It was a decent size. Large enough for four grown boys to move around relatively easily, and honestly, wide enough for the beds to be lined up on the floor without stacking. But then there'd be no room for the desks. And at a place like ATA, desks were nonnegotiable.

The only one who'd yet to move was Oliver. But the uncertain look on his face at the prospect of sharing a bunk with Alaric was brief. The next second, he stalked over to the top bunk and threw his laptop bag onto the pillow—as if he could purposefully claim something that was left for him as a last resort. Titus gave him points for pride.

Sebastian's phone rang and he answered immediately, his entire demeanor adjusting like a dimmer on a light switch. "Hey, Cami, I was just thinking about you," he purred as he slipped into the shared bathroom to check his reflection. Once he was satisfied with what he saw, he headed for the door. "Yeah? Where do I meet you?"

Moments later he was gone, leaving behind a trail of his exorbitantly expensive cologne thick enough to choke on.

Unbelievable. He was hooking up with a girl already. Meanwhile, Oliver had climbed into his bunk, taken out his laptop and headphones, and started typing.

Alaric shoved a pillow over his head.

Brilliant. So much for friends on the first day.

Titus decided to unpack. There seemed to be plenty of room in the walk-in closet, as well as a standing wardrobe and dresser. Since the other guys hadn't claimed any of that space, he'd get first dibs there. He was unlatching a suitcase when his phone went off.

Dread slithered through him like a python as he envisioned the inevitable lashing about how royally he'd screwed up. *Pun intended.*

Casting a glance at his two antisocial roommates, he checked his phone. The number was BLOCKED. Unknown. But the message was painfully predictable.

> UNKNOWN:
>
> How many times have we prepared for this? I hope your ruinous slip-up doesn't affect your standing with your grandfather. Surely WE will suffer for it.

> UNKNOWN:
>
> After all that we've done...

> UNKNOWN:
>
> I shouldn't be so surprised, I suppose. I hope you're proud of yourself.

Titus guessed it was his mother texting. His father was more blind rage over shame, while his mother had finesse. His thumbs hovered above the letters, preparing to type out an apology. An excuse.

He'd been caught off guard by Sadie's appearance. How could he have known his grandfather would invite a *commoner* into the competition for Ashland's crown? But his reaction easily revealed he'd known about his true heritage for years. And that broke the rules.

Time and again, his parents reminded him they'd been instructed to stay out of his life, that they were taking a risk by even speaking to him. Because according to King Leander's conditions, Titus should've grown up like Emmeline and Alaric, oblivious to his royal blood. Instead, his parents had made him complicit in their play for the throne, communicating with him through blocked numbers and discreetly hiring tutors to ensure their son was prepared.

Prepared for the crown that was *his*.

Titus had earned this far more than the other three. He'd studied much harder, suffered for much longer—he deserved the gold at the end of the rainbow.

His phone dinged again, and Titus closed his eyes, breathing through the need to punch something. In the back of his mind, Titus wondered when he had stopped celebrating the fact that his parents had broken the rules and instead started regretting it.

5

SADIE

SADIE COULDN'T BELIEVE HER LUCK. FIRST, SHE GOT INTO THE school of her dreams for free. Second, she got the bunk bed next to the window overlooking the Mediterranean Sea. Perhaps she was a banana slug in her previous life, and this was karma making up for it.

Of course, there was the whole competing for her country's throne with her royal classmates—she had no idea what to think about *that*. The thought of ruling a country was just as absurd as the idea of becoming royalty. It was so far away from Sadie's reality that it might as well be a world where people had hot dogs for fingers; Sadie had seen that in the movie *Everything Everywhere All at Once*, and it had been *weird*.

But that's what this whole thing was. Indisputably and ludicrously weird.

Still, she was terrified to tell the king that she wanted out of the running for his succession. Setting aside the fact that he was extremely intimidating, ultimately she feared he would rescind her Almus Terra tuition. He sponsored her for the sole purpose of having her compete against his grandchildren. If she refused, then what was all his trouble for?

Sadie couldn't go back to Ashland. She had nothing to return to. Speaking of—she tapped her phone screen, waiting for a reply from

Mrs. Higgins, her legal guardian. The last notice was the tiny "Read" receipt under Sadie's last message.

> MRS. HIGGINS:
>
> Someone contacted me from the Office of the King this morning. I hung up because I thought it was a joke.
>
> SADIE:
>
> It's DEF not a joke!!
>
> MRS. HIGGINS:
>
> I know that NOW. I just had a Royal Secretary in my living room.
>
> SADIE:
>
> So what do I DO?

Ever since the worst night of her life nine months ago, Sadie had been in a strange limbo. At almost seventeen, she couldn't yet be declared a legal adult in Ashland, but she was also rather old to enter foster care. Her middle-aged workaholic neighbor, Mrs. Higgins, had taken pity on Sadie's situation and offered to act as her guardian. The woman was a civil servant in Ashland's government with no kids of her own. It had been easy enough for Mrs. Higgins to step into the role knowing that Sadie would be off to ATA at the start of the school term.

Accepting a fancy scholarship was one thing. But being catapulted into Ashland's court made the prospect a lot less appealing. How could this be a real thing that the king was allowed to do? Snatch her up and declare her an heir? Using the scholarship program to find his fourth contender seemed reckless. Not that she dared to dissent—turning down the offer didn't seem to be an option. How could she? She'd be refusing her king.

Her phone dinged.

MRS. HIGGINS:

As I'm sure you've already guessed, if you turn
down this offer, you will be asked to return
home. I'm sorry, Sadie, but there's not much
more I can do. I hope you understand...

Sadie quickly typed out a message thanking her and emphatically saying she *did* understand. If not for Mrs. Higgins, Sadie might have had to move into a foster home rather than stay in her familiar—albeit lonely—house. Mrs. Higgins had only guaranteed Sadie stability until she went off to school. Nothing past September 1, though.

That's it, then. This succession competition was her only way forward. After all, she should be grateful. If she hadn't been chosen for the scholarship program, she'd still be . . . lost.

All at once Sadie's throat tightened, cutting off the memories threatening to rise. She swallowed and refocused on the absurdity of her future, rather than the pain of her past.

Luckily, nothing particularly royal had been asked of them yet. Sadie had time to figure this out. Maybe she could concentrate on her school life and simply come in "last place" in whatever strange tests the king had devised.

"Are you going to unpack or just stare out the window?"

Sadie dropped her phone and looked down from the vantage point of her top bunk. Emmeline was back from the bathroom looking fresh, her complexion glowing with some magical (in other words, expensive) serum. As soon as they'd received their dorm assignments she'd learned that her newly minted "rival" was also her roommate. *Oh joy.*

Emmeline hadn't said a single word to her until now. She'd just strutted into the bathroom with her toiletry bag and slammed the door. Which had left Sadie to attempt to engage their third roommate in friendly small talk. But Trang Nguyen, an extremely shy (or just antisocial) Vietnamese girl, didn't give up a single word. Instead, she pulled out her headphones and started watching something on her tablet, tucked into the corner of the bunk beneath Sadie's. In fact, Sadie only knew the girl's name because of the complete list of roommates posted on their door.

"Er, I already did." Sadie pointed to the dresser. "I took the bottom three drawers, and my uniform is hanging up in the closet. Hope that's okay."

Emmeline stared at her like she'd just sprouted two additional heads. "That's it?"

With great effort, Sadie pursed her lips to prevent herself from saying, *We're not all loaded, Your Highness*, and merely shrugged in reply.

As the silence between them stretched, the door suddenly burst open. A girl with brown skin, a nose piercing, and black spiral curls, wearing a sports bra with overalls and platform shoes, barged in. Oakley Strider, their fourth and final roommate, dropped her bag and, with the enthusiasm that Sadie shared but all the confidence she lacked, threw jazz hands into the air.

"ROOMIES!"

Sadie gave a tiny, nervous wave. Emmeline just stared at Oakley like she, too, had the three heads of Cerberus. Trang didn't even flinch.

Before Emmeline could dodge, Oakley ran up and squeezed her around the shoulders. "Welcome to ATA, nerds! We are going to have soooo much fun being roommates." The words came out in a rush, with such a heavy Australian accent that Sadie could hardly pick them apart.

Emmeline was frozen in place, crystal-gray eyes wide, as if shocked that someone would dare touch her.

But Sadie, hungry for that same warm, enthusiastic greeting, quickly climbed down from the bunk bed and accepted the friendly embrace. Oakley smelled fantastic—like cinnamon.

Except in the next instant, she nearly regretted it. A slight burn pricked her eyes and Sadie again had to force herself to stave off the well of emotion that sometimes came out of nowhere. How long had it been since she'd had a hug?

"So, I'm a second-year," Oakley continued. "Last year, all my other roommates were third-years, which means now they've abandoned me to, you know, go change the world." Oakley flitted her hands, imitating a butterfly, and her many rings and bracelets flashed in the late-day sunlight. "Ask me anything you want about ATA and the castle. We can talk bathroom and dorm rules later, but my old roomies and I had a great little whiteboard we used to map out our schedules. It was really e-and-e. Oh, and you can also ask me anything outside ATA, of course. I'm an open book. For example, I'm a Gemini vegetarian, blood type O negative. I have two horses back home—Pinkie Pie and Fluttershy. And I'm in a committed relationship with Danica, my girl-friend of exactly ten months, almost to the day. Want to see a picture? She's a total smoke show."

Oakley whipped out her phone and showed them the lock screen photo of an attractive girl with light brown skin, purple-and-pink hair, and loads of freckles making two peace signs and beaming at the camera.

"Freaking adorable, right?"

"Adorable," Sadie agreed. "Um, what's e-and-e?"

"Oh, efficient and effective," Oakley said, tucking her phone back into her overalls. "So...let me guess. Sadie"—she pointed at Sadie, then to the princess—"and Emmie?"

Emmeline scowled. "Emmeline."

"Right. Do you two want a tour?"

Sadie was liking Oakley more by the second. Everything about her screamed fun and friendly, and so far, this was Sadie's first indication any of that existed within Almus Terra.

"Desperately," Sadie gushed.

54

"How about you, Trang?" Oakley called, cupping her hand around her mouth to project her voice into Trang's bunk. Their roommate didn't respond, and Oakley nodded as if this was expected. "Okay, you do you. Shall we?"

"Pass," Emmeline said, turning toward her mountain of suitcases.

But Oakley seized Emmeline by the elbow and hauled her back to her side without much resistance. "C'mon, Emmie, it'll be a fun bonding experience! Besides, you don't want to be late for your classes tomorrow, right? I can show you where most of them are."

"Fine," Emmeline relented, and to Sadie's surprise, didn't try to pull away, though she did grab her purse on the way to the door. "But if it's longer than an hour, I'm heading back here. I need to press my uniform for tomorrow."

Oakley cast a look at Sadie over her shoulder as she steered Emmeline into the hallway. "Don't we all."

Sadie stifled a giggle and followed them out.

Oakley's tour of Almus Terra Academy was nothing short of a five-star rating on Google—the legit kind. Most dorms were located toward the western back wing of the castle, but some were in flanking towers on the east wing. Oakley told them proudly that the ATA staff had worked hard to ensure that the living quarters were comfortable and inclusive. There was a tower dedicated to LGBTQ students that they could opt into ("Danica lives in one of them with her trans roommate, Ross"), and the school bathrooms were unisex. The central part of the castle held the entrance hall, the admin offices, and three classrooms.

"The one with the window facing the sea is where you'll have any poli sci classes. Professor Hendrick says the waves soothe him through the garbage fire that is politics."

Oakley took them through the bailey and into one of the curtain walls of the western wing. More classrooms, but smaller, for more intensive, narrower subjects; several clubrooms; a computer lab with an apex to the observatory tower complete with a donated NASA telescope. In the eastern part of the castle, there was a massive gym, dance studio, band and choir room, chem lab, and self-study classrooms.

It was all so impressive. State-of-the-art technology in all the labs, and brand-new equipment and furniture. But nothing—*nothing*—compared to the library. Sadie immediately recalled the library from *Beauty and the Beast*, complete with sliding ladders.

"Neat, right? But don't push people on them. Mrs. Harakka gets suuuper mad."

Oakley took the girls through the unofficial student places too. For instance, the western rampart was a hooking-up spot where students would meet before curfew to make out. Sadie could see why. She wouldn't mind kissing someone with the sun setting over the sea like that.

Then there were things like how the second-floor bathroom next to the drama classroom turned into a nail salon on Saturdays and a student named Fern offered appointments. *Fortnight* tournaments and anime watch parties took place in the third-floor eastern lounge. Book clubs, fantasy premier leagues, D&D, and table-top gaming sessions—there were too many things to count. Sadie wondered how anyone had time for their classes.

"Where are we going now?" Emmeline nearly shouted over the sound of the waves crashing below. The wind tossed her hair about, and the last rays of the sun painted the strands of her honey locks in gold.

They were on the north ramparts, the back side of the castle, where the light was quickly fading. Sadie could feel the temperature begin to drop, and the crashing waves were so close she could taste the salt. It reminded her a bit of home.

"Last thing, I promise," Oakley said with a smile, and waved them over. She pointed to a section of the stone rampart that had graffiti all over it. *"This is Almus Terra."*

Sadie's brow furrowed as she tried to pick out the words in the shadows on the rock wall, trying to understand what Oakley meant. That was when she saw one name that made a bolt of excitement arc through her veins. *Augusta Ada King.* Otherwise known as Ada Lovelace, a countess in the early 1800s who was a brilliant mathematician and is known as the founder of computer programming.

Sadie held her breath as her gaze hungrily raked over the wall, looking for another of her heroes' names. And there were many more. Some modern. Some extremely old and faded, like Ada's. *Teddy Roosevelt, Nikola Tesla, Lonnie Johnson, Philippe Leopold, Indira Gandhi, Hassanal Bolkiah, Wangari Maathai, Lise Meitner...*

A US president, two brilliant inventors, the Belgian king, the first woman Indian prime minister, a sultan, an environmental activist, and a physicist. Historical leaders in their countries or their fields. World changers.

Sadie understood now. *This* was the Academy. Its students and its history.

"There's a legend about this wall," Oakley said as Sadie and Emmeline continued to ogle the renowned names scribbled on it. "That if you put your name up here, you'll go down in history. But there's a risk. Because it might be good, or it might be bad."

As Sadie caught sight of more names—*Nicholas II Alexandrovich Romanov, Franz Ferdinand, John F. Kennedy, Diana Frances Spencer, Marie Curie*—she realized what Oakley meant. Famous, but terribly tragic.

Before Sadie could ask another question, Emmeline stepped up to the wall, withdrawing from her purse a bottle of crimson nail polish. Using careful, deliberate strokes, she wrote her name with the nail polish. Her *real* name. It shined like blood on the stone.

Emmeline Eldana.

Right next to Leander Eldana, her grandfather.

Without a word, Emmeline screwed the cap back on, dropped the bottle back into her purse, and headed down the stairs from the ramparts, her hair flying behind her.

Oakley raised a brow over at Sadie. "Is she always that intense?"

Yes, Sadie thought, *it's hereditary.*

Thanks to Oakley's tour, Sadie found her first class right away. Which was a relief, because she was already running late. They had worked out the bathroom schedules last night. Luckily, Oakley and Sadie liked to take showers before going to bed, because Emmeline *needed* a shower in the morning. Trang had simply nodded at the AM shower slot. But Sadie still needed to brush her teeth and wash her face. When Emmeline *finally* emerged, looking movie-star polished, Sadie knew she'd have to miss breakfast in the dining hall to make it to class on time.

Rather than getting angry at her inconsiderate roommate, Sadie adjusted her phone alarm so she'd be sure to wake up earlier the following morning. Nothing was going to ruin her first day of classes at Almus Terra Academy.

International Econ 101 was held in the basement of the corner tower of the castle's southwest wing in a round classroom with elevated seating modeled very loosely after a Greek amphitheater. A lot of students were seated already, their laptops brightly lit, ready to take copious notes.

Sadie hovered at the door, tightly clutching her bag straps and trying to decide on the best place to sit. Down below, closest to the professor, to show her interest? Or maybe the back row to slip out first so she could catch a snack before her next class?

"Yeh gonna just stick to the doorway?" a deep voice rumbled from behind.

Alaric Eldana towered over her looking as broody as the day

before. Except this morning he wore ATA's uniform, the gray slacks and sports coat, the ivory collared shirt, and a first-year emerald tie. Unlike Emmeline's, Alaric's uniform was *not* pressed. His shirt looked rumpled, and the tie was so loose the knot hung down to the second button, which was nearly undone—showing more of his muscular chest than was appropriate for the world's best prep school.

His eyes narrowed as if he could tell she was judging his appearance. Sadie quickly looked away as she made space for him to enter the classroom.

"S-sorry," she muttered, looking everywhere *but* him.

Surprisingly lithe for someone so big, Alaric brushed past and slid into the first available spot.

Now Sadie felt rather silly for taking so long to decide. Cheeks warm, she skipped down several rows and moved through the circular aisle to take a desk opposite from where the prince of Ashland sat. It was far from him *and* the best logical position—perfect visibility for the lectern. She was just opening her laptop when an email notification popped up. It was a forwarded email from Mrs. Higgins.

To: saurelia@almusterra.edu
From: henrietta.higgins@ashland.gov
Subject: FWD: Ashland Heirs Press Release

Sadie,

The royal secretary reached out to me about release forms of your guardianship. While there is no formal adoption, the Office of the King is assuming custody until you turn eighteen next year. Before I signed over the papers, I was asked to provide a few details for the press release announcing the heirs.

Rest assured, I stuck to the bare minimum. There are bound to be questions about your past, but because you are a minor, your family records are protected. I have been assured of this fact.

I'm sorry I could not do more for you, but I'm on your side. Others won't be—see below. Beware and stay strong.

Warmest Regards,
Henrietta

To: royalsecretary-office2@ashland.gov
From: titus.rex@gmail.com
CC: henrietta.higgins@ashland.gov, emmeline -pemberley@gmail.com, durhamstriker@gmail.com
Subject: Re: Ashland Heirs Press Release

Ms. Halvorsen,

I am writing with the hope of gaining clarity regarding Sadie Aurelia's status as an heir. I understand this was the result of a scholarship program, but a monarch is not apprised by their intelligence alone.

Other than being good at studying—where all three Eldana blood heirs also excel—what qualifies Sadie as a worthy candidate for the throne? I am struggling to understand why someone with no gentry status or any outstanding qualities has been chosen. I wonder if this is a good use of the country's resources given the precarious political history of our land and the clear need for someone strong and capable as the pillar of our government. Furthermore, any misstep she will undoubtedly make could embarrass the royal family and the government of Ashland.

If this is merely a stunt to gain popular favor among the Ashlandic citizens, don't we as the blood heirs deserve to know? Any insight to this internecine predicament would be greatly appreciated.

Respectfully,
Titus Eldana

Disbelief, shame, and rage hit Sadie like a blue shell in *Mario Kart*. It exploded her psyche, sending all kinds of confidence shrapnel every whichway.

She'd known from the start that Titus was not her friend. The way he'd examined her yesterday—more than once—made it obvious she was little more than gum at the bottom of his shoe. But this? To insult her in front of the others, deciding after one day there couldn't be a single legitimate reason as to why she'd be included among them?

He might have a point there, but *still*.

Oh, but then he'd implied she was weak, incapable, nothing special, and a *waste of resources*, finally declaring that she would inevitably screw up and embarrass them. It was more than mean or rude. It was spiteful.

The instructor approached the lectern and tapped her fingers across the glass surface. A screen instantly lowered from the ceiling, and the slides highlighted the class's name, the professor's name, and their location.

"Welcome, students," Professor Gupta said in a loud, clear voice. "I am Professor Gupta, and this is International Economics 101, located in Churchill Basement."

Sadie snapped her laptop shut, struggling to push aside the waves of fury rolling through her. She'd take notes by hand. She did not need more *royals* ruining this day.

6

ALARIC

All around him, laptops were open with various windows pulled up. The student portal, a note-taking application, digital versions of their textbooks—not a single tab open to social media or online zines. Alaric knew those sites weren't banned from the ATA network—he'd already tried them.

Christ, I'm surrounded by nerds, he thought. Then again, it was the first class of the first day—even the most indolent student would probably try to act like they were paying attention at this point. Alaric, on the other hand, didn't bother pretending. He folded his arms and sank low into his chair, his long legs sprawling underneath the vacant desk in front of him.

"The syllabus is online within your student portal," the professor said, then clicked through to her next slide. "I suggest you read through it at your convenience. Now, who can give me a definition of international economics?"

A dozen hands shot into the air. Alaric resisted the urge to roll his eyes.

"Yes, you." Professor Gupta pointed to a boy with a rather pointy face in the front row.

"Raymond Carmichael, professor," the boy said.

No one cares, Alaric thought.

"It is the field of economics concerned with the production of resources and consumer demands in relation to the international institutions that affect them," Carmichael-the-snot said. "International transactions are closely studied to explain patterns and consequences upon economies at a global scale."

"Very good." The instructor used her clicker to change to the next slide: an old image of a man from the 1800s sitting for a portrait. "Who can tell me who this man is?"

More hands. This time, Professor Gupta pointed to a girl a few rows opposite Alaric, whom he recognized immediately.

It was the girl from the doorway. One of his supposed "rivals." She'd been the only one in the headmistress's office who'd looked as confused and shocked as he'd felt. He couldn't recall her name... Katie? Melody? Something sweet-sounding like that.

"David Ricardo. He was an English political economist who developed the theory of comparative advantage. And an alumnus of ATA."

That earned a small smile from Professor Gupta. "Well done. Yes, David Ricardo is international trade's father of classical theory. He sought to explain why countries capable of producing their own goods would look beyond their borders. Ricardo theorized that countries would naturally seek to export the goods they are more efficient at producing and importing the goods that cost more labor. This simple yet revolutionary theory was instrumental—"

Unbidden, a noise of derision rose in Alaric's throat. And it was loud. Loud enough to make everyone in the class turn to stare. Loud enough that Professor Gupta stopped in her tracks and found him immediately with her hawkish gaze.

"You...disagree?"

Alaric's neck grew warm. He wasn't used to having anything to say during class. He let the teachers speak, and if he cared, he listened; if he didn't, he doodled in his books or skipped entirely. Classes like science, literature, maths—he disliked. But history, politics, and economics always pulled him in. He hated to think it, but he wondered if it was in his blood.

With all eyes on him, he felt the weight of his next words like gravity, pulling people into his orbit. So he took his time. He drummed his fingers on the wood of his desk. "I just think yer givin' Ricardo too much credit there, professor. His *revolutionary* theory," he continued, sounding every bit the smart-ass he meant to be, "was the first step away from Mun's balance of trade theories, the beginning of the end of the state's ability to supply for its citizens. And that's why we pay taxes, ain't it? So the state can look after its own?"

Like a game of tennis, all spectator gazes swiveled back to the professor.

"An interesting take," Professor Gupta said with a smile. "And this is where we veer away from objective fact and cross into subjective political reasoning. Ricardo was a powerful influence in international economics, and that is undisputed. That said, does anyone else care to oppose"—Gupta went to her tablet and moved her finger as if scrolling through a list of names—"Alaric Eldana's argument?"

A murmur went through the class and Alaric felt himself sit up straighter. Not out of sudden respect, but annoyance. *That* wasn't his last name, though he supposed his Willy Wonka–wannabe grandfather had enrolled him as Alaric Eldana.

Slowly, a hand went up. Alaric cocked an eyebrow. Doorway girl again.

"Go ahead," Professor Gupta encouraged.

"Mun was a mercantilist," the girl continued, glancing at Alaric. "He cared about his state's political and economic power, not about what increased wealth among the citizenry, of his country or anyone else's."

For the first time, Alaric really looked at her. She was quite small, and undeniably cute. With her round, rosy cheeks, big brown eyes, and gingery hair, she reminded him of a hamster.

A smirk crawled up his features as he forgot the rest of the class entirely. He met her gaze straight on, wanting nothing more than to watch her shrink back into her little hamster house. "Sure, luv, and the state should supply a unicorn to each home too, eh? No, the state's responsibility is to the state."

"The state's responsibility is to its people," she shot back.

"Same thing, basically."

Her cheeks were getting redder. "No, it isn't."

Alaric tapped his index finger on the desk as if to stab the point deeper. "Cop on. A country's economic practices should be about consolidation of wealth for the government, nothin' else. Protective tariffs, trade balances that favor export over import, and strong currency controls."

"Very engaging, students," Professor Gupta interjected, clicking to the next slide, "and the perfect segue. Now. A tariff is a tax put in place to discourage importation of foreign—"

"No modern economist is in favor of tariffs," the girl cut in, her blazing eyes still holding his.

"Ms. Aurelia—" the professor began, looking annoyed.

"And *economists* run governments?" Alaric scoffed, realizing he found a perverse satisfaction in the way 'Ms. Aurelia' leaned over her desk like she was ready to throttle him.

"Can you name a single country that runs on modern mercantilism? High tariffs? More exports than imports?" She didn't give him time to answer. "I can. None of them are particularly wealthy. Most of them have dictators at the helm."

Aye, lookit that, Alaric thought, his smirk stretching, *the hamster has brains.*

"Business leaders or consumers can't be trusted with makin' decisions on an individualized level. And that's a gas to say otherwise," he stated calmly, though a chill bled into his tone. "They'll buy poorly made goods, pay for the cheapest labor, exploit other countries—all in the name of 'free trade.' No doubt, human greed makes the state weak."

She gripped the sides of her desk, looking more infuriated with every word from his mouth. "You're clearly looking for the worst in people."

He smiled. "Because people *are* the worst."

"All right, that's—" the professor tried again.

"There are people perfectly capable of making decisions that are good for their employees *and* their economy. You're just not one of them." Her voice bordered on shouting.

What manic pixie dreamworld was this girl living in? Walking among all these heirs apparent, future presidents and tycoons, she should plainly see that the system was rigged. No matter where in the world, an individual never held as much sway as the multinational corporation, the media conglomerate, or the royal court. Frankly, he despised people like her. They had the luxury of believing people were fundamentally good, when he'd known the truth for a long, long time.

His hands flexed under his desk. "Did yer mam teach yeh that fairy tale at bedtime?"

At that, the girl's face went completely scarlet with rage. "Go to hell, you arrogant—"

"ENOUGH. How *dare* you two make a mockery of my classroom," Professor Gupta roared. "Sunday detention for three months. Both of you. And you're lucky I don't make it the entire school year. Sit *down*, Sadie Aurelia."

Sadie. Alaric committed it to memory.

In the span of seconds, Sadie's face had gone from a red flush to a white pallor. She sank into her chair.

"If I'm interrupted again, I'll dismiss you from more than my class Understood?"

Sadie nodded, her eyes glassy and her cheeks once again beginning to flush, this time with mortification. Alaric simply shrugged and leaned back in his seat, trying to look completely chill. But that couldn't be further from the truth. He was now strangely unsettled.

The rest of the class, he couldn't help but track her movements. Their debate made him realize two things: One, this school was going to be *much* more interesting than he'd originally thought, and two, he'd clearly underestimated Sadie Aurelia.

Though he put no stock in his grandfather's sick game of succession or the possibility of finding a family who cared for him at the end of all this, Alaric was starting to actually look forward to this year. And maybe even detention.

7

EMMELINE

It was lunchtime before Emmeline heard the news of Almus Terra's record-breaking detention assignments. Apparently no student had ever gotten detention within the first class of the first day, let alone two of them. The fact that it was her rivals was so delicious that Emmeline could've survived off that morsel of gossip for the rest of the day.

Nevertheless, she'd gotten her meal and sat next to Oakley and was now delicately cutting into a chicken-and-mushroom fricassee. The food here was, unsurprisingly, divine, with at least seven unique dishes to choose from per meal, including multiple vegetarian and vegan options.

"Poor Sadie. She must've been really upset to talk over the professor like that," Oakley said before taking a large bite of her quinoa-and-gruyère veggie burger.

Emmeline frowned. Whether Sadie had been upset or not didn't matter. Only a child would lose control like that. If this incident didn't convince her grandfather that Alaric and Sadie didn't deserve the crown, then Ashland's standards must be lower than she'd imagined.

Titus, on the other hand, was a force to be reckoned with. Especially since that bastard had already known—maybe everything, it seemed. Unlike *her*. And Emmeline hated being behind at anything.

The moment King Leander had recognized her as one of his grand-children, everything suddenly made sense: Why she'd never known her parents, how she'd grown up in such lavish conditions, the emphasis on her education and class, the mystery in her mother's letter... it all fell into place with such clarity.

The explanation she'd been craving all along was even more perfect than she ever could've dreamed. She was a *princess*.

Naturally, it took her very little time to get over that fact. Now that she was aware of her royal blood, it felt... obvious. Like something she'd known deep down. No wonder there was secrecy; no wonder there was wealth; no wonder she'd always been groomed for greatness.

"I heard the boy goaded her. Like, it was totally his fault," Danica said, stabbing a sweet potato fry into ketchup.

"Nuh-uh, it takes two to tango, sweetie," Oakley said, laughing and lightly bumping her girlfriend's side.

"Agreed. She didn't have to rise to his bait," said another girl, who was Oakley's and Danica's friend. She took a long sip of her Pellegrino, tucked a jet-black curl behind her ear, then calmly inspected her perfect nails. "Students at Almus Terra should be above that."

Oakley rolled her eyes. "Blimey, Kia. Ease off. We're just teenagers. Not Buddhist monks."

Emmeline was beginning to really like Oakley. Or rather, she was starting to respect her. The girl had an effortless way of drawing people in but also shutting them down. She exuded confidence. Whether it was hard-earned, Emmeline hadn't exactly figured out. Regardless, she had a charisma that went beyond just enthusiasm, and it was a testament to Oakley's personality that her table in the dining hall was by far the most popular. It made natural sense for Emmeline to sit here, at least for now. And it had been easy too. Oakley had snagged her while she was in line for her food and ushered her over.

"So how were your first few classes, Emmeline?" Danica asked, then stuffed the fry into her mouth.

In a word: challenging. Which Emmeline was not quite used to. Before, she shined among her Marymount peers. But everyone at Almus Terra was brilliant *and* had something to prove. She was just one raised hand among many.

"Pretty straightforward," she said carefully, intending to sound capable but not overly arrogant.

"What'd you have?"

"Ancient Political Rhetoric and Technology Entrepreneurship."

"Oh, I remember APR," Oakley said cheerfully, wiping her hands on her cloth napkin. "One of my classes as a first-year too. I'm in the sequential class for it. Modern Political Rhetoric. And then there's Advanced Political Rhetoric. But that's on the political track, obvi. I'm not sure what track I want to be in yet, which is why I'm taking a bunch of new stuff this semester. Like Intro to Environmental Food Science."

"Speaking of," Danica said as she wound her arm through Oakley's and placed her chin on her shoulder. "You coming to the greenhouses later, babe?"

"Uh, yeah, duh. I need your help picking out a plot for my capstone project if I've got a fair go at passing. I'm thinking eggplants. At the end of the year, we work with the ATA chefs to help us prepare a dish using our crops that we get to eat."

She suddenly gasped, and everybody at the table flinched—even Danica pulled away.

"Babe, what's wrong?"

"I just realized...if I raise Eggbert the eggplant, how could I possibly eat him?"

Emmeline almost snorted into her sparkling water, but she caught herself and managed to clear her throat instead. "It's not too late to switch classes. If you cut vegetables out of your diet, you'll run out of things to eat."

"Hmm." Oakley tapped her chin. "You've got a point there, mate."

As the conversation shifted into an argument between Kia and a boy with a septum piercing about whose math class was more difficult—Calculus or Statistics—Emmeline noticed her phone buzz. She snatched it out of her bag and tapped on the email notification. She scrolled past the message where Titus had so blatantly undercut Sadie and noticed there was no new reply. But that wasn't surprising. To question the king's reasoning was a bold move that reeked a bit of desperation.

Also, unnecessary. The fact that the royal secretary had reached out to a social worker rather than Sadie's parents, or Sadie herself, told Emmeline all she needed to know. Sadie was an orphan. Why else talk to her guardian about press release information when the secretary had contacted Alaric, Emmeline, and Titus directly? It was because she wasn't yet a legal adult and had no one else to authorize the release of her personal information. Unlike the *real* princes and princess, whose parents had released them (in more ways than one) sixteen years ago.

The new email was from an entirely different thread that Emmeline had started that morning upon receiving the contact information for Ilsa Halvorsen, the royal secretary. Ilsa had replied—hopefully with the information that Emmeline requested. *One step closer.*

She was just about to open it when Oakley's voice stopped her.

"Something good happen?"

Emmeline glanced up to find Oakley, Danica, and Kia looking at her curiously. Annoyance wiped the excited smile off her face, but the irritation was directed at herself. Why was she perusing such a private email in the most public place? She knew better than that.

She threw up her phone screen showing an e-commerce auction site. "Limited-edition Hermès Birkin. I'm the highest bidder."

Oakley cocked an eyebrow while Kia made a groan of envy. "That one's so cuuuute."

"Lucky me," Emmeline said as she stood from the table and grabbed her bag and lunch tray. "I'm going to scope out my next class."

"Later, Emmeline." Danica waved cheerfully.

Without waiting for the rest of their goodbyes, Emmeline briskly walked through the dining hall. She stopped to separate her leftover food (compost) from her dirty dishware, then took the route through the halls that led her to the northeast end of the bailey, where she knew there were gardens for seclusion.

Having grown up in Manhattan, she'd always been good at directions and had an excellent visual memory. It didn't take her long to find an isolated spot behind a tower of viburnums, their blossoms tucked away until next spring.

Once alone, Emmeline took out her phone again and pulled up the email. She first scrolled down to read her initial message. It was a polite request to be connected with her parents. She'd kindly, subtly implied that one of the other Eldana heirs was already in contact with *their* parents. Because how could the king not have inferred the same from Titus's reaction?

But Ilsa's reply was merely an acknowledgment of receipt from the royal secretary's...secretary. She knew important people had assistants to help them manage emails and calendars, but to be rebuffed by an assistant was rather insulting.

After staring at the standard reply with nothing changing, no new notifications, she realized how foolish she was being. If she was going to succeed at Almus Terra and become Ashland's next queen, as her parents obviously intended, this was not the best use of her time.

Stuffing her phone back into her bag, she set off for her next class, Stock Markets 101. Hardly thrilling, but at least this was her comfort zone. She'd been playing with her own stock portfolio since she was twelve.

Another email came at the end of her classes. Her head had been buzzing about the sociology of energy consumption following Principles of

Energy Conservation, but once the notification dinged on her phone, thoughts of all else vanished.

Emmeline went straight to her dorm room and was relieved to find it empty. She dropped her schoolbag on the floor and opened the email on her phone.

> **To:** eeldana@almusterra.edu
> **From:** royalsecretary-office2@ashland.gov
>
> Princess Emmeline,
>
> I apologize for the late reply. I have been attempting to get in contact with your parents, but I'm afraid they are currently unreachable. They are in Rome and have denied our inquiries. However, I have passed along your contact information to their private secretaries so they may contact you at their earliest convenience.
>
> As you know, it is my honor to attend to any of the heirs' needs, so please never hesitate to reach out. I will do my best to see to your requests if they are within my power to do so.
>
> We have waited a long time for our young heirs to return, and in three short years, you will be home for good. Best of luck in all your classes.
>
> Your Loyal Subject,
> Ilsa Halvorsen
> *Royal Private Secretary*
> *Office of the King, Ashland*

The email signature was a bit blurry and shaky. With a gasp, Emmeline swiped at her eyes and dropped her phone, forcing her hand to stop trembling. *This is nothing. This is nothing.*

She would not let this affect her. If anything, she felt naive for getting her hopes up. Her parents were royals. With more responsibilities than she could even imagine. Of course they were busy. Of course they wouldn't be waiting around to FaceTime their long-lost daughter.

Still, the disappointment tasted metallic in her mouth. Followed by a dull throb on the inside of her cheek. *Wait. Did I...*

She rushed to the bathroom and cursed under her breath, Titus's words about her uncouth tongue echoing in her brain. Without even realizing it, she'd bitten the inside of her cheek and now her mouth was bleeding.

She rinsed, ignoring the sting of the fresh wound, then stomped over to the mini fridge and grabbed an ice cube from the freezer. She popped it into her mouth and pressed it against her cheek with her tongue. The pain chased away other emotions at least.

As Emmeline bent down to retrieve her bag, the door flew open, and Oakley and Danica came in. Danica was already out of her school uniform, dressed in baggy jeans, a sleeveless midriff top, and a thin flannel shirt. The door was barely closed before Oakley started to strip. In record time, she tugged on leggings and threw a patchwork denim jacket over a faded tie-dye crop top.

"First day donezo," Oakley said, tying a bandana over her springy curls. "I hate those uniforms. So stuffy."

"So collectivist," Danica agreed, then she turned to Emmeline. "You only have to wear them during class hours, you know. You can wear whatever you want after three thirty."

Emmeline swallowed the last bit of her ice and suppressed a shudder at the cold. "I haven't had time to change yet. I just got back."

"Isn't your last class super close?" Oakley asked.

"Yeah, but I got turned around," Emmeline answered, willing her roommate to drop it.

Oakley hummed in the back of her throat. "Be careful about that. Professors hate when students are late. But anyway, glad we caught you. Do you want to come down to the greenhouses with us?"

Emmeline could certainly use a distraction right now, but she hesitated, looking between the two girls. "I won't be intruding?"

Danica snorted. "Nah, there'll be too many people there right now for it to be romantic. The botany nerds find any spare moment in the greenhouses right after summer to check on their gardens. You'll like them. They're pretty dope."

"Come with us, Emmie," Oakley pleaded.

Emmeline had given up on trying to force Oakley to use her full name. Besides, she'd never had a nickname before, and it was growing on her.

"I'll go for a bit," Emmeline said, then turned to her closet. "Let me change first."

Without shame, she also stripped down and pulled on jeans and one of her more relaxed blouses. With Heather as her default influence, Emmeline's couture wardrobe had always been more "thirty-year-old girl boss" than "stylish seventeen-year-old."

But if Danica or Oakley had thoughts about Emmeline's outfit, they didn't voice them. After Emmeline slipped on her least-expensive pair of platform sneakers, they headed out of the dorm and took the stairs down to the bailey, walked through the courtyard, and headed into the east wing, past the gym and art rooms. The greenhouses were at the bottom of a sloping rock path that led down the hill from the main campus. The glass glinted from the late-afternoon sunlight, nearly blinding her.

In the distance, Emmeline could hear the waves on the eastern shore. She'd forgotten they were on an island and how close the castle sat against both shores. The smell of salt and garigue floated to her on the sea breeze. She'd heard of the signature scent in her study of French wine, as the essence of it is infused into the soil and grapes, but for the first time, she could experience it. Thyme, rosemary, juniper, wild lavender, rock roses—all so fragrant from the region's hot, dry climate.

"You coming?" Oakley called.

Emmeline hadn't realized how long she'd been frozen and found that Oakley and Danica were already far ahead. In an uncharacteristic move, Emmeline hurried down the rock path to catch up, but that quickly proved to be a mistake. With zero traction, her platform sneakers slid on the loose pebbles, and her ankle twisted painfully in an attempt to keep her upright. It worked. She didn't fall, but it *hurt*.

First her cheek bite, and now this. Emmeline had never felt so... *off* in her life. It was starting to freak her out.

Luckily, Oakley and Danica were too far ahead to notice her clumsy slip, so she righted herself and ignored whatever tenderness she felt in her ankle.

The first greenhouse loomed over her in two stories. It was full of contraptions helping the plants grow as organically and sustainably as possible and, as Danica predicted, it was full of students. There were at least ten of them working diligently in various plots, checking soil samples and adjusting panels that accounted for temperature, humidity, and solar energy.

The second greenhouse, a relatively smaller one used for less-advanced students, was where Danica led Oakley to view the open plots. "Eggbert could go right here, babe."

Oakley held up her fingers in a rectangle and squinted through it. "Ace! I can see it. Oliver, what do you think, my dude?"

Emmeline turned away from inspecting a thriving blue trumpet vine to find a boy sitting in the dirt path with a laptop on his thighs. He raised his head and used his index finger to push up glasses that had been sliding down his nose. "The second row, third from the right, has a better statistical chance of surviving under an amateur's care."

The answer was so strangely confident for something that sounded entirely tenuous that Emmeline couldn't help but stare at the boy in awe.

He was still in his uniform and clearly didn't care about it getting dirty on the greenhouse floor. It was impossible to tell his height since he was sitting down, but Emmeline got the impression he was tall. While his accent was American, she couldn't discern from where exactly. His skin was a warm, russet brown, and his black hair was shaved on the sides and done in twists on top. He wore oval tortoise frames that were well-suited to his high cheekbones, narrow chin, and wide forehead. Objectively, Oliver was hot.

Perhaps feeling her gaze, Oliver glanced up, his dark brown eyes meeting hers.

Emmeline crossed her arms and drew an uncomfortable breath, quickly looking away. She couldn't remember staring at *anyone* for that long before.

"Done." With a few taps on Oakley's phone, the tablet at the end of the greenhouse row showing whose plots were whose updated to show Oakley's name.

Danica rested her hand on top of Oliver's head. "Ollie, honey, did you go to class today?"

Oliver didn't even stop typing, let alone look up, or push away Danica's hand. "Yes, I did. My last class happened to be in here."

"Yeah? Good. You like your dormmates?" she asked.

No answer.

"Uh-oh." Danica stepped back and folded her arms. "Ollie, I'm your ambassador. You need to tell me if you're having trouble."

"Ambassador?" Emmeline asked, glancing over at Oakley.

"Scholars are assigned second-year ambassadors on their first day," Oakley explained. "You know, to help them get acquainted with the school and be an advocate for them. Elites and C-Suites don't really need one."

"There's no trouble," Oliver said in a flat tone. His attention was still locked on his computer screen. Except when he'd felt Emmeline's gaze, that is.

"I feel like I'm missing something," Emmeline said. What on earth were they talking about? Weren't they *all* scholars? What were Elites and C-Suites? How did Emmeline not have an ambassador as a first-year? She didn't love the idea of a babysitter, but she hated the idea of falling behind even more.

Oakley smacked her palm against her forehead. "Oh, doih. Of course, you don't know. There's um... okay, well, no school is perfect, right?"

Emmeline shrugged, though silently disagreed. Almus Terra felt pretty close to perfect.

"It's not like... official or anything. Not school sanctioned anyway, but there's three factions at ATA."

Factions were political. A group within a group. How did the student body at Almus Terra have factions? "What do you mean?" Emmeline asked, walking closer to the two girls, careful to avoid Oliver's legs sprawled out across the aisle.

"Like cliques, you know? Normal schools have the drama nerds, the jocks, band geeks, but ATA students are recognized by their background. If you come from royalty or politicians, you're an Elite. If your family owns corporations or major conglomerates, you're known as a C-Suite. But Scholars are here because they got a scholarship. Their family didn't pay for them to be here. Because of that they don't have the same access to school resources that a lot of the Elites and C-Suites do. It's a load of bullshit, really."

"Oakley's a C-Suite," Danica muttered.

Emmeline had guessed that. After learning Oakley's last name yesterday, she'd thought *Strider* sounded familiar, and after a quick Google search discovered why. Her father owned the largest wind farm in New Zealand and supplied half the energy of the island, and parts of Australia.

Oakley moved her hands to her hips and glared at her girlfriend. "I'm an Equalist. Who cares about our backgrounds? IMO, factions are dumb and shouldn't exist."

"Babe, you know there's no way that's going to happen. Social stratification is human nature. Plus, C-Suites and Elites run the student council. They make the rules."

"Almus Terra should be the one place where we're all equal. We're focused on making the world better *together*, and yet we're still divided."

Danica raised her hands. "Hey, you know I'm on your side, but I'm just being realistic."

"Yeah, yeah, I know. Dominance hierarchy, blah blah, blah. Let's go. I'm hungry."

Emmeline was a few paces behind Oakley and Danica when Oliver spoke up again.

"The infirmary is in the eastern wing, second floor."

Strangely, her heart stuttered and she paused, certain she heard wrong. With a glance over her shoulder, she found Oliver looking right at her. His long fingers, previously tapping on his laptop keys, now tapped against the side of his leg.

"Your ankle," he clarified, his voice low and deep.

Unable to hide her surprise, Emmeline's lips parted as she stared back at the very astute boy sitting on the greenhouse floor. Had she been limping? She thought she'd hid it well. With a tight swallow, she said nothing and turned to leave.

For perhaps the first time, she felt seen. For perhaps the first time, someone had surprised her.

8

TITUS

By the end of his first week at Almus Terra, Titus was fairly convinced he was developing a stomach ulcer. He'd had one last year so he knew the signs. Also, he was ready to chuck his phone off the third-floor parapet into the frothing sea.

For four days he'd been on pins and needles waiting to find out if his screwup had knocked him out of the running for the crown. Now that it was clear that Titus had been aware of his royal heritage for the last twelve years of his life, he would likely be disqualified from this unconventional competition. Unfortunately, he had no way of knowing for certain. It wasn't as if there were an official rule book for all this. And even if there were, it's not like *he* had broken any rules. His parents had.

He'd accidentally revealed their breach to the king, which meant whatever happened next was entirely his fault. A point they continued to make in long strands of shaming texts.

Of course, that email hadn't helped either. He regretted it nearly the second he'd pressed send, but he'd just been so *bloody* angry. A press release announcing all the grandchildren of the king plus some complete random chosen as an heir? He didn't care if it was a spectacle for King Leander to gain public support—it basically looked like the king didn't have faith in his own blood, casting Titus and his two cousins as failures before they'd even been given a chance.

The response he'd received had not been encouraging. Ilsa Halvorsen had politely, in more words, replied, "Sadie is in because the king said so." Not a great sign.

But a very secret part of Titus actually hoped he *would* be disqualified. He'd lose a family he'd never met, but at least he'd be free from debilitating stress. Problem was, he didn't know who he'd be without Ashland. His entire self-image involved being the heir to the Ashlandic throne. And building a new identity from scratch was somehow more terrifying than appeasing his unforgiving parents.

Outwardly, though, Titus was a paragon of equanimity. Most classes were a breeze, as his studies had prepared him for the progressive and specialized curriculum of Almus Terra. And thanks to his pseudo friendship with Sebastian, he had enough cachet to be welcomed at any dining hall table. He'd yet to find one core group, but it was easy enough to mesh with most.

The student body of Almus Terra was curated to foster world peace—at least on the surface. Within the first few days, differences between the student factions were widely apparent. Elites and C-Suites got the most convenient study room timeslots; the best tables in the dining hall; private lessons with professors for band, studio art, languages; the choice of which show should be streaming in the student lounges; among other unwritten privileges. The Scholars...well, they seemed to simply exist.

And until the official announcement was made about Titus's background, he was stuck in a strange social limbo. As were the rest of the Ashland heirs. Well, except for Emmeline. She seemed to be doing just fine on her own.

Titus and Emmeline had one class together: Ancient Political Rhetoric. As expected, she was a colossal pain. Her beauty drew the attention of any straight boy who crossed her path, while her friendship with Oakley Strider helped with her popularity among most of the femme, queer, or progressive students. She was annoyingly clever too. With enough sense not to answer every question, she made an impression with replies so compelling as to garner the attention and admiration of professors and peers alike.

Alaric and Sadie were in a couple of his classes too. But pretending the others didn't exist seemed to be an unspoken rule. Which made his dorm situation that much more awkward.

The disparity—in character, circumstance, and appearance—between Alaric and Titus was unbelievable, and yet, they were bound by blood. Honestly, Titus was curious how Alaric had grown up so differently than he and Emmeline did, but he didn't dare ask. It would make him look like an absolute *arsehole* to flaunt his own privilege, and he wanted to keep his bone structure intact, thanks.

His other dormmate, Oliver, seemed to spend as much time out of the room as possible, though Titus had already pinned him as the smartest of them all.

In short, his life at Almus Terra was isolated. With no real connection to anyone other than Sebastian, he flew under the radar for the time being. More than anything, he understood that strong personal relationships were just as influential as money, but until he was publicly known as an Elite, there were no moves to be made.

He didn't have to wait very long, thankfully. His low profile promptly blew up that Friday morning. Titus was enjoying a goat cheese and spinach omelet in the dining hall, having a quiet conversation with Yujiro, a Japanese classmate from his Global Economic Statistics class, when someone grabbed his shoulder.

It wasn't an affable grip. Knuckles dug into his collar bone while a thumb needled hard into his shoulder blade.

"You've been holding out on me, mate." Sebastian's voice was fake friendly, edged like a sword. The same tone he used when he'd found out Titus had tipped off Stephen Foust that Sebastian was on his way to beat him up in the sixth grade.

Titus chewed slowly, his gaze circling the dining hall as he noticed students raising their heads, turning toward his table. Sadie was in the corner of the dining hall receiving the same attention. There was a loud gasp, and a laugh, near Oakley Strider's crew. Emmeline.

What about Alaric? He never made it to the dining hall for breakfast, but Titus would bet all the gold in the Eldana coffers that his cousin would be receiving the very same looks by morning's end.

So. The press release had dropped. *Finally.*

And it appeared Titus was still in the running. He picked up his fork and speared his omelet for another bite, finally answering Sebastian's accusation. "Not by choice, I assure you."

Sebastian squeezed his shoulder painfully, but Titus wouldn't give him the satisfaction of wincing or flinching. "I'm your mate. You could've told me. I would've kept it a secret."

It took everything Titus had not to laugh out loud. It would've been around Eton and all over the internet in a matter of seconds. People complain about women gossiping, but the worst offenders will always be teenage boys with something to prove.

"And defy my king?" Titus said, finally standing and abandoning the rest of his breakfast.

With a disrespectful snort, Seb rolled his eyes and followed Titus toward the exit. "Good lord, Titus. Don't make it sound so bloody archaic."

Out in the hallway, Titus spun on his heel, backing Sebastian suddenly into the wall. For the first time, he allowed himself to pull rank—like a royal.

"Listen, *mate*, in my country, the king is a leader, not some precious antique like the neocolonial British crown. Your father may have authority, but you don't. As a prince, *I* do."

They were so close Titus worried he might gag on Seb's cologne, but he held his ground, and his breath. Sebastian narrowed his black eyes, saying nothing. Then his snake-oil smile slithered across his face. "I like your true colors, Your Highness. You really are one of us."

Titus stepped back, jerking the lapels of his school jacket to straighten his uniform. "Whatever you say. I'm heading to class."

"Just a sec there, prince," Sebastian drawled.

Though he was eager to escape and read the article that had outed him and the rest of the Ashland heirs, he paused and turned back to the son of the British prime minister.

"The other Elites will want to get to know you." Seb's arrogant smile was nauseating. "And see what you can do for us."

Easy. So much easier than he'd thought it'd be to get the attention of the students who really mattered. Then again, his capital extended beyond light political sway, public adoration, or philanthropic hobbies. In fact, Almus Terra might not have seen a consequential royal since Prince Abdul Mateen of Brunei. Now there were four of them. Well, three, really.

"What makes you think I can do anything at all?" Titus raised an eyebrow. "I've been a royal for all of twelve minutes."

"Don't be a git," Seb sneered. Titus hated how on point he was. "This entire week you've been biding your time. I see that now. Let's lay our cards on the table. We don't particularly like each other, but we can use each other. Tomorrow night, eight thirty. Northeast flanking tower, top floor. Don't be late, Your Highness."

Seb pushed past him, his shoulder knocking into Titus's arm, as other students started teeming out of the dining hall toward their first class. Titus headed down the corridor and pulled out his phone. The article was easy to find. Every major media outlet had already picked up the story. Titus chose the news station closest to the source, DAFB, right in the capital of Ashland. He'd followed them ever since he'd learned about his identity.

ASHLAND'S LONG-LOST HEIRS RECLAIMED

By Rosemary Guidry

Published: Sept. 6, 7:30 AM GMT-5

DURAH, Ashland (DAFB)—After 16 years, the grandchildren of King Leander have emerged into the public eye, their identities released to the press this morning at 6 AM.

Alaric Eldana (known as Alaric Durham), son of Crown Princess Rhea and Lord Erickson, has been hiding in Dublin, Ireland.

Titus Eldana (enrolled at Eton College as Titus Cross), son of Prince Magnus and Lady Calliope, has dwelled in London, England.

Emmeline Eldana (formerly masquerading as Emmeline Rhodes), daughter of Prince Frederick and Lady Chloe, has grown up in a luxurious penthouse in New York City.

When the kingdom lost sight of our beloved heirs as infants, every citizen mourned their absence. But now their reemergence is shadowed by the reveal of a fourth and final heir—a 16-year-old nonroyal Ashlandic citizen, Sadie Aurelia. In a press release from the royal secretary, Aurelia is identified as a potential heir to the Ashland Crown under House Eldana.

While she may not be related by blood, she has been hand-selected by King Leander as a worthy candidate to go toe-to-toe with his grandchildren at the prestigious Almus Terra Academy in southern France. It is unclear if or when she will be adopted by the king, but we can all agree that the four heirs will be closely monitored by their instructors and the media.

> The question of *why Aurelia* is itself newsworthy.
> Aurelia was chosen as the recipient for the National Merit
> Scholarship Program. Little did Ashlanders know the
> prize was two-tiered: access to the world's best education
> as well as the chance to one day assume the throne.
>   Growing up in Farach, a suburb of Durah...

A scorching heat seared through Titus's vision, and he pinched the bridge of his nose, his eyes squeezing shut.

For years he'd imagined the day his identity would be revealed to the whole world. And this article—the article announcing him as prince—cited his name in *one* sentence. The rest of it focused entirely on a commoner.

He'd had a hunch this was coming, and it was partly what prompted him to send that desperate email. Naturally, a rags-to-riches story was beloved by all. Discovering that a nobody might have the chance at becoming *somebody* was more exciting than any long-lost blue-blooded heirs. Not to mention, it was obvious that Sadie was an orphan. Though the article made no mention, it was bound to come out and would incite a lot of sympathy for her, as well as adoration for the king. Oh, how noble, gifting a brilliant young orphan an education some would kill for. Then lo and behold, she *also* has a chance at the crown! Ridiculous.

His parents were going to freak. But he shoved that thought aside for now. Anger was easier to manage than the nerves that cramped his stomach when he thought of his mum and dad.

Logically, he knew this attention, or lack thereof, wasn't his fault. At the end of the day, this was politics. Which heir did the court of Ashland favor? Whom would popular opinion side with? A New York socialite, a preppy English schoolboy, an Irish delinquent...or one of their own? Titus hated how obvious the answer was.

Friday's classes were certainly different from the days prior. Professors could barely hold the students' focus. One kid stood in his seat to get a better look at Titus in their Psychology of Marketing class. He caught another girl trying to sneak a photo of him. Murmurs followed him from room to room, while his phone vibrated incessantly against his chest.

Texts from his parents and emails from Ilsa Halvorsen, the royal secretary and emissary to the heirs, kept blowing up his phone. But he didn't check them—none of the messages would be even remotely uplifting.

Meanwhile, Sadie's profile was erupting worldwide. Every form of journalism was obsessed with the ordinary girl being named an heir. And Titus loathed it all.

On his first Saturday at Almus Terra, he mostly hid on the second floor of the library.

As it turned out, Sadie was there too. Since the second floor went around the library like a long continuous balcony, he could see her spot by the lattice window very clearly from his vantage point. Especially with the daylight casting geometric shadows across her laptop and old books.

Titus rubbed his throbbing knuckles with tense, heated fingers and slowly rotated his neck to relieve the strain of staring downward for hours. Really, he should get up and move—that feeling of suffocating stiffness began to overwhelm his body—but he didn't want to alert Sadie of his presence.

She was in his Philanthropy 101 on Tuesdays and Thursdays and the gym period that the first-years had every Monday, Wednesday, and Friday. Ever since she'd gotten detention, it seemed she had folded inward. That was probably for the best. Her buttons were easily pushed—at least from what Titus could tell watching the video a student had sloppily recorded.

She worked quietly, reading and typing, typing and reading. Sipping on a stainless steel water bottle covered in stickers of sea animals. At one point, a third-year stepped up to Sadie and loudly said, "I'm totally rooting for you, girl." Then held out her fist to bump.

Sadie blinked back and, looking bewildered, held out her fist to complete the gesture of good faith. Then the girl and her friends were gone, and Sadie was left staring after them.

Complete strangers offering a nobody support. If Sadie were even a little bit capable, she could make use of all sorts of help from fellow students. After all, at least half the student body had connections of some kind.

Another group then approached Sadie's table and slid into chairs. One of them Titus even recognized: a boy from his Media Studies class who happened to be the son of the man who owned media stations in the US, India, Spain, Japan, Canada, the UK, and Egypt. He leaned forward, speaking to Sadie in a lower register than the previous girl, so Titus couldn't hear. But he could surmise. The press wasn't allowed anywhere near Almus Terra, but that didn't stop a teenage boy from recording an exclusive interview with the new Ashland heir for his dad.

Around the table, other C-Suites gathered. One was a kid whose robotics invention had made its way into the latest NASA project. The daughter of an entertainment executive from Korea leaned in close to take a selfie with Sadie. *Yep*, this girl was going to be a problem.

Titus left his dorm at exactly eight fifteen Saturday night. The northeast flanking tower was a trek across campus and being late was inexcusable.

He chose his clothes more carefully than he'd like to admit: darkwash jeans and a simple heather-blue crew neck tee with a collarless army-green jacket. He had to dress for style, not stature, if he was ever going to have a real chance at this school.

As his feet carried him up the winding stairs to the top floor of the tower, he ran a hand through his blond hair, suddenly nervous. Like many times over the last six months, he ignored the fact that his feet were hurting. After a simple flight of steps, they ached in an all-too-familiar fashion. Luckily, he'd been well-trained in hiding his discomfort. Besides, the queasiness in his gut overpowered all else. With a slow breath, *in* and *out,* Titus yanked the door open.

He struggled to school his features at the sight before him. This was no ordinary classroom—anything but. It looked more like a lounge at Kensington Palace crossbred with a conference room at the United Nations. Nearly floor-to-ceiling windows took up half the western side. The floor was marble with an exquisite rug under a massive mahogany table and a seventy-five-inch television mounted on the wall. The rest of the room held armchairs and couches and a table piled with food.

"Ty, my man," Seb said with a broad grin, walking over to clap Titus on the shoulder. "You made it."

Titus wasn't surprised to find that there were only nine other students apart from him and Sebastian. He couldn't believe the absence of security—like a keypad, a retinal scan, or even a bouncer.

As if reading his thoughts, Seb gave him another patronizing squeeze. "Ah, don't worry. Kids know not to go into the student council room. There are consequences if they do."

"The student council," Titus echoed, glancing at the ATA crest on the wall and at the monitor that had a similar crest, but slightly altered with the Latin words *Princeps Iuventutis.* Leaders Among the Young.

"Makes sense. Appreciate the invite," he said. Though Titus knew Sebastian despised letting him up here. But if it wasn't Sebastian, someone else would've invited him. No doubt, Sebastian was using Titus like a ladder. *Align with the powerful.*

Seb smoothed his hand across Titus's shoulders, practically shoving him forward. "You know I've got your back. Now go meet the leaders of ATA."

An attractive girl who'd been lounging on a wingback armchair as though it were a throne stood and approached Titus. Her skin was porcelain, and her blond ringlets ended in hot pink. Chocolate eyes tracked Titus as he extended a hand toward her, and she to him.

"Bienvenue, Titus," she said, her voice soft and musical, and though her accent belied a French background, it wasn't heavy. With the way she said his name, he was able to place her. The daughter of the French prime minister. She'd attended an Eton formal as Sebastian's date.

"Calixa, nice to see you again."

Her pink lips curled into a smile; she was evidently pleased he'd remembered her. "Who knew I'd been in such regal company back at Eton?"

"Not I," Titus said, returning her smile.

She gave an airy laugh. "My father always said King Leander is a cunning, enigmatic man." Her gaze traveled down his body, then jumped back up to his face. "Can't say I'm shocked, though. You fit the part."

"I'll take that as a compliment."

"You should. Welcome to the ATA student council." Her catlike smile widened. "I'm a third-year and the president."

Just then, another boy about an inch shorter than Titus came up to Calixa Chevalier. His skin was a tan hue, and his hair was full of rich umber tones—black with hints of auburn and chestnut. Titus recognized him at once. He'd seen him in the library talking to Sadie.

"And you're Kavi Sandhu," Titus said, turning to shake his hand.

Kavi flashed a white smile. "A fan?"

"I'll watch any station under Valmiki's flag," Titus affirmed.

Kavi nodded. "Naturally. How do you know Titus, Cal?"

"Seb brought me to an Eton dance once upon a time," Calixa answered, not taking her eyes off Titus, her long, sharpened nails tapping against her arm. "Titus made an impression."

And we snogged in one of the closets. Titus hadn't exactly planned for it, but Sebastian had provoked him with something stupid, as usual, and Calixa had shown interest. He walked off with her when he saw Seb flirting with John Forthright's date, not the least bit guilty.

The way she was looking at him, he knew she was revisiting that memory too. He'd been fourteen, and making out with a beautiful older girl—especially Seb's date—was nothing short of legendary.

Noticing Calixa's seductive eyes, Kavi wound an arm around her waist and tugged her close, nuzzling into her ringlets. "Cal is the best president the council has ever had. And the best girlfriend a guy could hope for."

Something tense flashed across Calixa's face, but she smiled back at her territorial boyfriend nonetheless. "Only the best at Almus Terra. Well, you already know our vice president." She patted Kavi's arm, still around her waist, then pinched his hand to let her go. "Come, let me introduce you to the rest of the council."

Before turning to follow Calixa and Kavi, Titus glanced at the other person sitting in an armchair. Emmeline's eyes were locked on him. And he hated to admit it, but she looked every bit like a princess. The tilt of her head, the way her ankles crossed under fashionably wide slacks, the gloss of her hair, and the serene yet calculating expression.

"Here you go, Emmeline." Seb appeared, handing her a fizzy drink with a lime wedge.

"Thank you, Sebastian," she purred, her voice sickeningly sweet.

Once again, he should've seen this coming. The idea that Sebastian would go after a princess, especially if that princess could take down Titus, was so ridiculously obvious that it felt like a rotten tooth radiating pain up into his skull with poisonous force.

He wanted to tell Seb about that night at Eton with Calixa right now. But he didn't say a word and instead turned toward the council table. Let Emmeline use Sebastian. Let Sebastian use Emmeline. What did he care? They could very well be soulmates.

In quick succession, Titus met the treasurer, secretary, historian, and parliamentarian—all were either Elite or C-Suite with impressive resumes and parents.

The other students gathered were to be chairs, which turned out to be council members in training for when the current position holders graduated. With Calixa, Kavi, and the treasurer graduating this year, three positions would be left open, so three chairs would be promoted.

It wasn't hard to do the math. As the most polished students coming into Almus Terra, Titus, Sebastian, and Emmeline were clearly the right choices. There were two other potential candidates, both obscenely rich: the daughter of a Saudi tycoon and the son of a famous Hollywood actress.

The meeting, Titus observed, was exceedingly well-run. The agenda covered initiatives for that semester, the various clubs and organizations with their annual budget requests, and the end-of-term winter ball, which happened to be a large student-run event. The secretary promised to email the meeting minutes after it concluded.

Seb wandered up to Titus as the rest of the students broke off to chat about their first week back. "Impressed?" he asked, his voice low.

"Very," Titus answered honestly this time. Why be cagey? This place was next-level.

"From what I've heard, the council has always been good, but Calixa really changed the game. And when she and Sandhu teamed up, the school board did stuff like increase budgets and make plans to develop new labs."

Titus believed it. Apart from their tense first impression, Cal and Kavi seemed like a total power couple.

"I'm sure dating helps," Titus muttered, mostly to himself.

"Please." Seb snorted, folding his arms. "That relationship is just like everything else Calixa does. Strategic."

"Pardon?"

"She knew Sandhu was the only real threat to her presidency. I bet you all the stocks in the Bezos portfolio that she seduced him so he'd support her instead."

Titus stilled. His gaze locked on the two young leaders of Almus Terra, mind churning.

"Sebastian?" a sweet voice called from the door. "Walk me to my dorm?"

"You bet, beautiful," Seb called back to Emmeline, then elbowed Titus again in the ribs. "You're welcome again for the invite, ya royal git."

But Titus didn't reply, didn't even look back to watch his fake friend and his rival-slash-cousin walk out the door together. He was too busy staring at Calixa and Kavi, an idea beginning to take root.

9

ALARIC

THE LAST THREE DAYS HAD BEEN THE STRANGEST OF ALARIC'S life. And he'd had some pretty wild times. Like when he and his crew broke into the pub where his friend's dad got drunk every night and ran the taps so all the beer emptied onto the floor. Or when he'd locked out the owner of an auto garage to throw a rave for his friends, and their friends, and friends of those friends. He'd skirted juvie time when the owner received a buttload of business from the publicity.

So yeah, Alaric maybe didn't have the best life, but he'd lived it fully. With what he could, at least.

Now, though, was unprecedented. And unwelcome. Within the span of an hour, he'd become a celebrity. Whispers and stares followed him to Friday classes, to the dining hall Saturday morning, to the gym, and to the track where he ran laps.

By Sunday midmorning, he finally snapped. He was lounging in the courtyard, listening to music, wearing a tee from an Irish electronica group, his hoodie bundled under his head and his long legs hanging off the stone bench, when he heard the shutter sound of a phone camera between songs.

Taking unsolicited photos of him was bad enough, but having the stupidity to keep the sound on really set him off. He sat up, his hoodie falling to the grass, and immediately caught the offender: a girl with ivory skin and long brown hair twisted into some elaborate braid. She stood with her friends and lowered her phone, meeting Alaric's eye.

He swung his legs over, tugged his headphones around his neck, stood, and stalked over to her. "Delete it," he growled.

The girl looked as if she were thrilled to have gotten his attention. "Right away, Your Highness. But you might want to start getting used to it." Her thumb swiped across her screen and Alaric was tall enough to be able to see that it was gone from her photos.

Then it hit him. She hadn't been trying to hide her behavior in the least. She'd *wanted* him to notice. Wanted him to talk to her. Wary, he stepped back, and the girl smiled, batting her eyelashes. "I'm Lotta, by the way. You know...I hate Ricardo too."

A puff of air expelled from Alaric's lips in disbelief. She was hitting on him—in the most manipulative way he'd seen yet. It reminded him of yesterday, when some dude in the boys' locker room offered to help "brand" him. Whatever the hell that meant. But apparently the guy was an athlete influencer with a fitness TikTok worth millions of followers and billions of views.

These students...they were driven. And they seemed to want a piece of whatever Alaric and the rest of the heirs had. To Alaric, that was downright unnerving.

"Stay away from me," he ordered Lotta. He snatched his hoodie off the ground and headed back into the castle. It was almost time for detention anyway, which helped ward off his bad mood.

Sadie. The name rang through his head like a bell. Now there was one person who wasn't going to suck up to him. He was eager to feel her anger. If that was wrong, he didn't care. It was *real*.

Professor Gupta stared at the two of them, her black brows furrowed in irritation. Alaric swore he saw a muscle ticking angrily in her jaw. She leaned back in her office chair, folding her hands and regarding them silently for another long minute.

Alaric could practically feel Sadie sweating next to him. "Professor, I'm so—"

Professor Gupta held up a hand, cutting off Sadie's apology. "Tell me: Was this a ploy?"

"P-ploy, professor?" Sadie asked quietly.

"It wasn't rehearsed, if that's what yeh mean," Alaric grumbled. It was insulting, but given the students at this school, he could see why Professor Gupta thought she'd been played. Alaric and Sadie, two nobodies, making waves on the first day of school, only to then be revealed as royal heirs?

Professor Gupta sighed and shook her head. "I suppose it doesn't matter either way."

She didn't believe him. Naturally.

"Detentions will be whatever I ask of you, every Sunday for the next three months. First, you'll clean up the coastline. A lot of tourist trash from Marseille washes up on our shores." She pointed to bags and two trash grabber sticks leaning against one of her chairs. "You'll be required to sort your findings for recycling. Enjoy."

Dismissed, Alaric and Sadie grabbed their tools and headed out of the office, through the administrative wing and the main gates, past the barbican, and down the winding path toward the harbor.

They didn't talk their entire journey, but once again, Alaric felt Sadie's anxiety and anger pulse around her like waves of deadly radiation. Not great at hiding her emotions, this one. But Alaric liked that. He relished her presence and didn't particularly care to examine why.

Their shoes made loud crunches as they grinded across the pebbly shoreline. Alaric watched as Sadie used her grabber to pinch a can and dump it into her bag. A tendril of ginger hair fell across her cheek and she blew it away, her breath coming out as more of a hiss.

"So...was it?" Alaric finally asked. He wasn't about to let this detention pass in silence.

Sadie stopped, straightened, and looked over her shoulder at him. "Was it what?"

"A ploy." Alaric gave her a sardonic smile. "I know my motives. But I can't speak to yers when yeh talked over a professor."

Sadie visibly winced. "Of course not. I was just arguing my point."

"Aye, rather passionately," he mused.

Her eyes flashed in a challenge. "As if there's any other way to debate."

To that, Alaric had no response, because he agreed. But he hated to relinquish the last word.

"Fair enough. But I'm pretty sure telling yer opponent to go to hell falls outside the conventions of proper debate."

Sadie's face colored, then she turned to fish out a chip bag from between two rocks. *Crap.* He didn't mean to silence her. Just as he was trying to figure out how to resuscitate their banter, she muttered something that he didn't hear over the crash of a wave.

"What's that?"

Her shoulders drooped, then she looked back at him again and met his gaze. "I'm sorry," she said, much louder. "That was uncalled for, and I apologize."

If a wave had dragged him all the way into the Atlantic, he'd be in less shock than he was now at her honest words. No matter how you looked at it, he'd struck a nerve that day. Potentially a bad one. His baiting remark hadn't been kind. But that's all he knew: getting beat down, then hitting back harder. To be honest, he wasn't mad at all. But he didn't want to give her the out. From the moment she'd snapped back at him in class, she had his attention. Perhaps even more than he'd realized.

"Yeah? Well, apology not accepted." He stabbed his grabber at a pebble-crusted bottle and dumped it into his bag. "Thanks to yer temper, I get to do community service."

"Wait—*my* temper?"

"Yeh didn't hear *me* yelling, did yeh?"

The pink of her cheeks climbed up into her hairline. "If it was just my fault, I'd be doing this detention alone."

He smirked back at her. "Maybe she didn't want a wee bird down here all by herself. One wave could wash yeh away."

At that, Sadie's jaw dropped comically. It struck him as hilarious, and Alaric had to turn his head to hide his laughter.

"You're such a jerk," Sadie hissed between her teeth.

"There she is." He jabbed the trash stick in her direction. "Yer far too easy to irk, cailín."

She shot him a glare. "Sadie."

Alaric chuckled. "I know yer name." Cailín was an Irish Gaelic word for girl, common enough in Irish English, but he thought it more fun to keep her in the dark. "Anyway, yeh need to buck up if yer going to rule our country."

Sadie rolled her eyes. "I'm not trying to rule. I'm trying to go to school."

There was that naivete again. "Who says it's any different? Yeh think the king will let yeh stay here if yeh don't try at all?"

She froze, her stick halfway through the water. At least the thought had crossed her mind.

"Sorry, rich people aren't that charitable," he continued. "If yeh don't play at their game, yeh get taken off the board. Might want to adjust yer strategy."

"What about you?" she shot back.

"What *about* me?" he echoed with a smile, knowing perfectly well what she was asking. An odd thrill thrummed through him, and he crouched down on one of the rocks, lowering his tall frame so he could be eye level with her.

More whisps escaped from Sadie's ponytail and batted against her cheeks as the sea breeze tore over the island. She licked her lips and raised her gaze to boldly meet his. "You don't seem like you're willing to play. You were about to walk out right from the beginning. What changed? Why are you still here?"

The waves lapped harshly against the shore. A quarter mile out, one exploded against the outcrop of a rock, throwing salty spray into the air and breaking the silence between them.

Alaric shrugged. "Free learnin'. I'd be an eejit not to take it."

Sadie nodded. "Got it."

"Got what?"

"That you're a liar."

His grin stretched. "Not a liar, just not as honest as *some* people."

Sadie frowned and started walking farther around the coast, dismissing the conversation. She was meticulous as she moved along, scouring through the frothy waves to find some drunk tourist's empty bottle to recycle.

Alaric followed, watching how she climbed on the slippery rocks to reach the harder-to-get ones, putting in unnecessary effort. He doubted very much that Professor Gupta cared how much trash they collected. Honestly, he wondered if the professor had ever even given a detention before. Almus Terra didn't seem like the type of school with disciplinary issues. He also gathered that this might be Sadie's first-ever detention, especially from the way she stood quaking in front of Professor Gupta's office. A thread of discomfort wound through him. He hadn't cared about getting in trouble, but he could tell it had tormented Sadie.

"Yeh really will fall in," he warned as she attempted to stand on a rock taller than her hip.

"How about we make this a silent activity?" Her tone was more biting than the autumn breeze coming off the sea.

Alaric held back a laugh. He suspected that would only make her angrier, and while he very much enjoyed getting under her skin, the angrier she became, the more careless she got.

They'd been picking up trash in silence for over twenty minutes before he noticed her soft humming. Though he could barely hear it over the waves, the melody was familiar somehow. It stirred something in his chest, as though unearthing a memory he'd never known. He dug his fingernails into the base of his neck, feeling a pounding in his skull that he couldn't explain.

About to tell her to quit it, he noticed her climbing over a rock and reaching with a trembling arm to get a piece of trash stuck in a branch hanging over the water.

It was like watching a cut scene in stop-motion. Her foot slipped on the wet stone and her balance teetered. The trash stick clattered against the rocks as Alaric dove forward and grabbed Sadie by the waist. His hand locked onto the branch above to save them both from falling into the ice-cold, rock-filled shoreline.

Sadie gasped and her hands flew to the arm around her waist while the tip of her shoe brushed the surface of the water. It felt like she weighed nothing in his grip, so he held on tighter, as if to assure himself she was still there. His pulse hammered in his neck and ears, but the pounding in his head had been replaced with a sweet scent of sugar cookie and vanilla.

Suddenly desperate to regain his footing, he twisted at the waist, depositing her on the safer part of the shore, away from the rocks and trees. She stumbled, her legs shaky.

"I told yeh ta be careful! How thick are yeh?!"

"I'm sorry!" she shouted back. Her hair had come loose from its ponytail and whipped about in the sea breeze, sending more of that sweet scent his way. He jerked his head to the side, unease and adrenaline swirling in his chest.

It wasn't just that she could've smashed her head against the rocks, it was that she'd been so earnest in picking up the trash. He had an irritating notion that she was always like this—sincere, stubborn, and vulnerable.

For a long moment, the two of them stood there, breathing hard, letting the wind ripple through their clothes and streak through their hair. His hands curled and uncurled at his side.

"Alaric."

The knee-jerk reaction to his name made his neck snap back in her direction, and he eyed her warily.

"You're bleeding."

Now that she mentioned it, he felt the sting on his palm and the wetness gather between his fingers. It was the hand he'd used to grab the tree branch to keep them from falling. He made a move to wipe it on his shirt, but she caught his wrist.

"Don't. Geez. Hold on, okay?"

Sadie kept her hand around his wrist and tugged him toward where they started, where she'd dumped her book bag on a rock while they'd picked up trash. She rifled through it and pulled out a water bottle decorated with cartoon sea lions and otters, and then a bandana. He said nothing as she emptied her water bottle on his palm. It stung like the devil's claws as her thumb gently glided across his open wound through the water, making sure there was no grit or splinters left in his skin. Then she carefully wrapped the bandana around his hand, tying it with a knot.

"Thank you," she muttered.

"Yeh owe me," he grumbled. "Fecking geebag."

A giggle escaped her, and Alaric glanced up in surprise. She was trying not to laugh harder, but for the first time since meeting her, he watched a smile light up her face.

"This a gas?" he asked, waving his wounded hand.

"No, sorry, I mean...you're just so rude."

He scowled. "Yer making this hurt a lot less right now."

But that just made her laugh harder. She tried to smother back more laughter and Alaric could only watch in disbelief.

"I could shove yeh into the water." He'd never make good on his threat, but her curious joy was getting under his skin in the weirdest of ways. Like the humming.

Sadie shook her head. With a sniff, she swiped at her eyes and blinked back at him with flushed cheeks. "Would you believe me if I said it was charming?"

"No," he replied curtly. In what world was being called rude a compliment?

She shrugged and smiled. "It's just . . . this feels like the most genuine conversation I've had in days, you know?"

Alaric felt the blow of her words ricochet through his bones. Because, unsettlingly, that's how he felt too. When Sadie got her laughter under control, she sat back on the wet pebbles, not caring that the rocks were slick and her jeans would soak through. The salt spray caught her cheeks and tangled hair, and though it couldn't have been comfortable, she was still smiling.

"Why."

"Why what?" Sadie asked, glancing over at him.

Alaric sighed, running his good hand across the back of his neck. "I came here because I want to know *why*. Why am I so different from those two?"

Slowly, Sadie tilted her head, but her smile faded. "Got it," she said quietly. "Not a liar."

It was thirty minutes shy of the school's eleven PM curfew by the time Alaric got back to his dorm. At Sadie's insistence, they'd gone to the infirmary after sorting their trash into the castle's recycling bins. His cut had been properly cleaned and bandaged, and now he was looking forward to passing out. Where he wouldn't have to think about being the most vulnerable he's maybe ever been, with a complete stranger or where his grandfather was concerned, a rival.

But there was one more obstacle between him and bed. Seconds from grabbing the door handle and slipping inside, a voice called out to him in the darkened hallway.

"Long detention."

Alaric looked over at his cousin. Emmeline leaned against the wall with her arms folded, wearing fancy loungewear that probably cost more than all the stuff in his flat combined.

"Were yeh waiting for me, stalker?"

"A friend works at the infirmary." Emmeline rolled her eyes and pushed off the wall. "Texted me you were on your way back. I'm here to warn you, as a courtesy."

Alaric raised his brows. "Yer *warning* me? Of what?"

"Stay in line, and stay away from that girl, or you'll be further behind than you already are." Emmeline's silver eyes flashed in the shadows. "Ms. Halvorsen told me you haven't answered any of her emails. Are you even going to try? You'll be gone by spring at this rate."

A fresh wave of resentment rolled through Alaric with such force he had to suck in a breath. It came like a blow to the gut, stealing oxygen from his lungs.

In three short steps, Alaric advanced on his cousin, towering over Emmeline despite her own impressive height. "Get out of my sight, princess. I don't need yer warnings or yer pity."

To her credit, Emmeline didn't step back, but something flickered across her face. "Fine." She turned so sharply her hair whacked him in the face. Five minutes later, Alaric was finally calm enough to head inside and not break anything.

10

SADIE

Sadie no longer recognized her life. She was half a world away from her small duplex in Farach where she'd lived with Mah and Grannah. Now she ate five-star meals, attended university-level courses, slept in a castle, and constantly dodged people asking to take selfies, sit by her at lunch, or walk with her to class.

Not a single person seemed to care what she was actually like. More frustratingly, she was often used as an information source on the other heirs. As a nobody, she was more approachable than Titus, Emmeline, and especially Alaric. Students felt entitled to ask her all kinds of personal questions about the Eldana cousins. What hair products did Emmeline use? What was Alaric's favorite band? What did Titus do in his free time?

Her response was always "I don't know." More than once, she considered telling the whole truth: that Emmeline was cold and bratty. Or that Titus seemed elitist and extremely judgmental. And Alaric was a colossal jerk with more thorns than a prickly pear cactus.

Her reputation as the "commoner Ashland heir with three months' detention" almost guaranteed she'd never make any friends. Oakley and Danica were sweet, but they were constantly busy and seemed to have so many friends, Sadie almost felt bad asking for their time or attention. Besides, Emmeline had already claimed them for herself.

At one point, she thought she was making some headway with Trang when they bonded over a cozy task-management game that Sadie had noticed her playing on her Switch.

Sadie's family had never been able to afford consoles, but there was a mobile app version that she'd been obsessed with last year, so she remembered most of the game's quests.

"You have to play Daria's song at the vending machine, then she's ready to go to the Everdoor," Sadie offered, climbing to her bunk with her laptop, ready to get some studying done.

Trang looked up at her, brows raised, thumbs hovering over the button and joystick. "You've played *Spiritfarer*?"

"Hours and hours of it. It actually helped me get through"—Sadie cleared her throat, sidestepping an emotional landmine—"last year. It's pretty addicting."

Just the thought of *Spiritfarer* had her suddenly wishing they were talking about anything else. The game about helping spirits come to terms with their death had been therapeutic for Sadie at the time, but it brought back a well of grief. Painful memories of days that had felt like eternal dark nights.

A smile pulled at the corner of Trang's lips. And that simple grin was enough to help Sadie breathe—a reminder that time had moved forward.

"Tell me about it," Trang said. "If I fail the Anthropology quiz, I'm blaming this."

A class they had together! This could be Sadie's chance to become a study partner, or better yet, a real friend. Sadie still didn't know if Trang was a C-Suite or Scholar. She quietly hoped for the latter, since most of the C-Suites and Elites she'd met so far were...difficult. But this interaction—about games and classes—seemed easy. Organic. Genuine.

"The quiz shouldn't be—"

The door suddenly opened, and Emmeline and Oakley burst

through with Danica and Kia closely behind. The four girls were so loud, gossiping about Kia's crush on the Venezuelan oil magnate C-Suite, that Sadie was forced to drop her own conversation. Her chance at connecting with Trang slipped through her helpless fingers as all the girls flopped down onto pillows on the floor and started pulling out manicure tools.

"Just don't get too attached," Emmeline said as she filed down one of Oakley's nails.

"I won't," Kia huffed, then shot Emmeline a glare. "Why?"

"The Marquez family is at risk for bankruptcy. Which means Ramon may not be at Almus Terra next year."

"How in the world do you know that?" Kia asked.

"I'm not positive, but according to the IBVC, its continued plummeting stock likely means that reorganization has cancelled the existing equity shares," Emmeline said, moving to Oakley's next nail. "Regardless, the company is unhealthy. Might be a matter of time."

Before anyone could reply, Trang suddenly stood from the bed, throwing her Switch down so hard it bounced on the mattress, stormed to the door, and slammed it behind her. Oakley made a face in the resulting silence. "Maybe we should've gone to Dani's room."

Yeah, maybe you should've, Sadie thought, annoyed.

She didn't know what had made Trang so upset, but whatever it was seemed to linger. When Sadie tried to engage her again about their Anthropology class the next day, Trang just shook her head and muttered something about being busy. A total brush-off.

So Sadie was left to study alone, which sucked because her classes were incredibly difficult. Anthropology required reading a book a week, and its lectures would've been easier (and more enjoyable) with a friend. Professor Gupta piled on mountains of homework and essays, which felt a bit like long-term punishment for the first day of school.

Even her favorite class, Advocacy Studies, involved hours of watching documentaries on civil and humanitarian rights, not to mention reading countless articles and long transcripts of speeches.

But it was Philanthropy 101, her second-favorite class, that threw her a gigantic curveball in the second week. Rather, it was less of a curveball than a hit straight to the batter's head.

Ever since the detention incident, Sadie had tried to keep a low profile. She found a seat in the back corner and pulled out her laptop, piling the books next to her computer in a way that formed a pseudo-protective wall. It seemed to work relatively well. The only time teachers called on her was during random selections from the roll call, though that was rare. The teachers had no shortage of students desperate to prove themselves.

Professor Reyes was one of the wild cards, however, and seemed vindictive enough to call on students who looked confused or unprepared. It was a little ironic considering his whole focus in Philanthropy 101 was charity.

"Philanthropy is a business," Professor Reyes announced in his loud, nasally voice, and he rapped his knuckles hard on his lectern. "Because businesses are meant to make money. It makes no difference, in that sense, that philanthropy makes money for *others*. That is why most successful philanthropic efforts are organized and executed by businesses. They understand strategic planning, operations, budgets, and marketing."

The spry seventy-year-old professor dragged his gaze over the class. Like he was challenging one of them to contradict him. And his gaze lingered on Sadie for one judgmental second too long.

"Which brings me to your semester-long project, worth half your grade," Professor Reyes continued, pulling up his next slide, where a long outline appeared. "Which is to develop a strategic plan for a charity of your choosing. It must be a real charity, as our work here at Almus Terra extends far beyond the classroom. You will donate your skills and time to an organization by creating a three-year strategic plan for them. Using its financial reports, standard operating procedures, long-term goals, and marketing strategies to help you accomplish this. Due to the significant workload, the project will be a partnership."

Hope sparked in Sadie's chest. A joint class project. Another chance at a real friend. Crossing fingers, she stuck her arms under the desk and sent up a quick prayer.

"I've taken the liberty of drawing the pairs already." Professor Reyes tabbed to the next screen with last names in two columns. "Each row of this grid contains a single team. Take note of your partner. We may devote limited class time to working on your projects, but the majority of this will need to be completed outside of class. There will be milestone markers throughout the semester..."

But Sadie struggled to hear the rest. Her head was buzzing, full of angry hornets drilling through her skull. On row six, there was her name, Sadie Aurelia, right next to... Titus Eldana.

First, she's forced to room with Emmeline, then detention with Alaric, and now *this*? Sadie sank in her chair, sliding until her face was hidden by her laptop. No, no, no! *Please* no.

The email Titus had sent burned into her brain. *I am struggling to understand why someone with no gentry status or any outstanding qualities has been chosen.*

The fact that he'd insulted her in an official correspondence rather than to her face felt so much worse. But people were braver behind a screen. Students shifted in their chairs, and she could feel their gazes on her. She refused to look at Titus.

Class continued for the next twenty minutes, Professor Reyes droning on about the project's requirements and timelines until the castle's bell tower chimed. Sadie slammed her laptop shut and stuffed it into her bag along with her books. Once her privacy wall had been dismantled, she slung her bag over her shoulder and made a beeline for the teacher's desk.

"Excuse me, professor?" Her voice was soft but clear. Reyes had given students a hard time about not enunciating well enough during class.

He continued disconnecting his laptop from the classroom's monitor. "Can I help you?"

At that point Sadie felt a tall, imposing presence behind her. *Keep going. Don't let him intimidate you.*

"I was wondering if it was possible to switch partners." *There's no way he wants this either.*

Professor Reyes finally met her gaze, then glanced over her shoulder at you-know-who. "Have you discussed this with your partner, Ms. Aurelia?"

"No." Ashland's golden prince had a deep, commanding voice. A different accent from his cousin's but just as rich. "She hasn't."

Sadie closed her eyes, willing herself to disappear, like Dorothy wishing to go back home to Kansas. She'd also happily melt. Maybe the Wicked Witch didn't have a bad ending after all. Plus, flying monkeys sounded pretty cool.

Pausing to get her breathing under control, Sadie snapped her eyes opened and leaned a little farther across the desk. Her expression was pleading while still maintaining a certain amount of dignity. "Sir, it's just that Titus and I... well, we're under extenuating circumstances that don't allow for much... teamwork."

But those were the wrong words. Professor Reyes's wrinkled lips tipped downward into a deep frown. "Are you saying you cannot work together in the spirit of charity? Is King Leander's competition more important than helping people?"

"N-no sir. Of course not. I just—"

"Ms. Aurelia," Professor Reyes interrupted, tapping his long fingers on the table, "I won't have any of you royal heirs make a joke of my class by throwing your weight around. Did you ever consider I might've put you together on purpose?"

Sadie's stomach fell. "I . . . I understand, sir."

"Good. Now, about-face and tell your partner you look forward to working with him."

A stab of anger made Sadie tremble as she reluctantly turned around. Reyes really was vindictive.

Titus stood just behind Sadie, less than a foot away, so she had to tip up her head to meet his gaze. His uniform was immaculate, his hair in that perfect gold wave. He smelled crisp and fresh, like evergreen boughs. One eyebrow raised, amusement covered his features. He regarded her like she was a puppy who'd just gotten scolded.

Sadie curled her fists at her sides and lied through her teeth. "I look forward to working with you, Titus."

A smile tugged at the corner of his too-perfect mouth. "Likewise, Sadie."

A week later she was still managing to avoid her Philanthropy partner. Titus had yet to prod, except for an email asking when she'd like to meet to start their work. She deleted it immediately, almost marking it as spam. But on the following Friday, he caught her eye during class, giving her a pointed look. As soon as the bell rang, Sadie took advantage of the partners gathering and chairs sliding, and she escaped out the back.

She'd got Friday's dinner to go and ended up eating in a secluded spot within the bailey. When Titus came into the dining hall Saturday morning, she'd nearly choked scarfing down breakfast. She ducked behind a group of girls and slipped out. When his third, very annoyed email pinged her phone, Sadie skipped lunch altogether.

Part of her enjoyed annoying him. *No*, that wasn't quite right. She enjoyed *disobeying* him. He'd probably grown up with the world at his feet. Royal or not, he'd lived the past seventeen years in luxury. Sadie didn't want to be another person he bossed around.

Later that afternoon, he finally cornered her in the library. She'd become engrossed in her Advocacy Studies reading, marveling at Malala Yousafzai's receiving the Nobel Peace Prize at age seventeen, when a hand slammed down on her book.

The clean smell of soap and evergreen needles filled her nose. Gut sinking, she slowly turned to face a chest only inches from her nose. She looked up and finally conceded: "Hi, Titus."

His gray eyes flashed like the sharpened steel of a sword. "Seriously, Sadie?"

As usual, he looked like a demigod in modern times wearing a casual button-down and navy chinos. *He could be cast in the* Percy Jackson *show*, Sadie thought jealously.

She tried to tug her textbook from under his large hand, but he didn't relent. "Having a nice weekend?" she asked lightly.

He cast his gaze up at the high ceiling of the library and released a long-suffering sigh. "Enough. We *have* to work together."

"How about remotely?" Sadie offered. "Entire companies are remote, you know. And software makes collaboration easy—"

"Are you scared of me? Is that it?" Titus cut her off, sliding into the chair next to her instead of across the table.

Sadie bristled, her hands clenching into fists. "I am *not* scared."

"Could've fooled me," he muttered, lifting his bag to pull out his laptop.

"Right, because a girl *must* be scared of you if she doesn't want to be around you," Sadie said dryly.

A muscle ticked in Titus's jaw, which made Sadie smile. She liked cracking the surface of his cool exterior.

"Enlighten me, then. Why don't you want to spend time with me? Even for a school project."

Sadie huffed out a breath. "Please. Why on earth would I want to spend time with someone who hates me?"

Titus had briefly shown a hint of a conceited smile. But now his mouth thinned. "You think I hate you?"

Finally, Sadie was able to jerk her book out from under his hand and close it with a snap. "I *know* you do."

It took him a moment, but then he recovered. "Sadie, that's ridiculous. I do *not* hate you."

Fine. She was tired of dancing around this anyway. With a few clicks of her laptop, she pulled up her emails and turned the screen to him. "Then what is *this*?"

He only had to read the first line for the color to drain from his face. At least he had the decency to look ashamed, but that didn't make Sadie feel any better about it.

Words eventually came to him. "*That* was a mistake," he said with a sigh, squeezing the bridge of his nose.

"Doesn't change the fact that you meant every word."

"No, that's not true. I wrote that out of anger, but not at you."

At that, Sadie laughed without humor. "Could've fooled me. Since you found out I was in the running for your inheritance, you've antagonized me. Admit it."

"No, that wasn't—I was just surprised."

"Not entirely," she fired back, starting to shut her laptop.

He caught the top and pushed the screen back up with his index finger. "All right," he said, drawing out the words long and slow. "I need you to put yourself in my shoes. I was sent away from my home—my *family*—all for the purpose of hopefully turning out the way my grandfather wanted me to. Then I find out he wants to put me up against my cousins to see if I'm good enough, *and he's* brought in an outsider as well. If he was going to look outside our family for his heir all along, then what was the *bloody point*, Sadie?" With his final words,

Titus pounded the table hard with his fist and Sadie jumped, along with her heart.

He sighed, burying a hand in his blond waves. "Sorry, I...look, what I'm trying to say is that email wasn't about you. Clearly I was... lashing out. Like a child. And I apologize. Truly."

His eyes stared deep into hers, willing her to understand. It made Sadie's skin grow hot and her stomach swoop under his raw intensity. There's no way she could empathize, because her family had never sent her away. But she could sympathize. At last, she nodded.

Titus straightened, relief covering his features. "Let's start over, okay? I'm sorry I'm a git, but I don't hate you. In fact, the only way you're really going to make me hate you is if this project tanks. The charity of our choice is due next Friday."

She pulled up a document full of thorough research on each of the charities they could choose from. "I *am* working on it."

Titus glanced at the screen and looked back at her. "Yeah, by yourself. But that's not the assignment."

Sadie chewed on her bottom lip, knowing full well he was right. If she refused to collaborate, Professor Reyes might fail her.

"Fine," Sadie agreed. "Sorry for the wild goose chase, I guess."

Titus let out a little puff of air. "And I guess I don't blame you." Then he looked back at her document. "Hearts First, Minds Follow? So that's your top pick?"

Sadie's ears grew hot. She hadn't meant to show him that list quite yet. It revealed...a little too much of herself. "I'm not done researching."

He skimmed through the notes. "They're not a worldwide charity. Pretty exclusive to Ashland, and parts of Iceland and Scandinavia. Transportation's not easy. Budgets are low. And mental health isn't very valued in—"

"That's exactly why they need help," Sadie said a bit too fiercely.

"Since the end of the civil wars, Ashland has been focused on growing its economy, but its cultural awareness has fallen behind, with a major impact on quality of life. While other countries are implementing mental and emotional health as a valid field in health care, Ashland hasn't. Besides, if it were too straightforward, why bother? The harder the challenge the bigger the impact."

For a long time Titus said nothing. Then— "Okay."

Sadie blinked. "Okay?"

"You convinced me."

"What—I mean...really?"

He gave her a tiny smile. "You seem passionate. And passion is the key in everything that succeeds, right?"

Sadie allowed herself to smile back as her heart beat loudly in her chest. "Right."

The next day was her second detention session with Alaric. After Professor Gupta heard about Alaric's wound from the doctor in residence, she moved them to something arguably more domestic. That's how Sadie and Alaric wound up at the docks of the island, cleaning, sorting, and packaging fish.

Almus Terra's campus comprised most of the island where it resided, but the Academy neighbored a tiny village where fishing was the only real source of income. Freshly caught sea bass, halibut, cod, haddock, and sea bream were sold in Marseille and Toulon, and to Almus Terra.

When Sadie picked up a knife to cut a fish along its lower belly and pull out the insides starting with the spine, as they were taught, Alaric grabbed her wrist.

"Yeh sort them. I'll cut."

Sadie scowled back. "I know how to handle a knife. I'm good at cooking."

"Ain't that grand," he grumbled, nimbly slicing the halibut by the belly. Sadie swallowed, breathing through her mouth to avoid the fish stench. Alaric looked like he could handle a knife just as well, but the last thing she wanted was for him to cut his hand open again.

Sadie tipped her head back on a groan. "Are all you Ashland princes so stubborn?"

With a movement so swift and skilled that Sadie took a surprised step back, Alaric spun the knife and stabbed it into the cutting board. "What's *that* supposed to mean?"

Her eyes widened at the massive shiny blade, edged with blood and fish guts, stuck into the wooden block. "Uh...nothing."

Alaric turned toward her, his massive body caging her in against the old brick wall of the fish house. "Managed to snag more detention with another heir? Boy, yer really stackin' 'em up."

Sadie's cheeks flushed and she hated how often that was happening around Alaric. How easily he managed to goad her. "Not quite. Just a class project."

"Do yerself a favor and don't compare us. We're nothing alike," he said harshly, seizing the knife and reaching for the next fish.

Recalling their previous conversation, Sadie let herself simmer down. This clearly wasn't about her. "Noted."

Alaric said nothing as he gutted and cleaned the sea bream with deft fingers.

His movements were so practiced and easy it was clear he'd be authoritative in the kitchen. "You're good at cooking too."

"That didn't sound like a question," he muttered.

"It was an observation."

"Yeah, well, there was no one to cook for me but me."

Another tidbit of information about Alaric Eldana that Sadie knew only she was privy to. Well, she didn't know that for sure, but she had a strong hunch. Five fish later, it occurred to Sadie that this was much like the time before.

"Yeh really will fall in."

"Yeh sort them. I'll cut."

A slow smile crawled across her lips, and she turned her face to hide it. Alaric really was a prickly pear cactus. Spiky outside, quite sweet inside.

11

EMMELINE

"YOU'RE REALLY GOING OUT WITH HIM?"

Oakley stood in the doorway of their bathroom, interrogating Emmeline as she released a curl from the iron, steam rising into the light.

"He asked me, and I haven't been down to the village yet."

Though if it smelled as bad as Sadie had coming back from her fishmonger detention, Emmeline wasn't sure she wanted to experience it.

"But he's the biggest tool out of all the first-years," Oakley said with an exaggerated eye roll. "He's been through eight girls already and it's the first month of school."

Emmeline clicked her flat iron at her roommate. "He's also the son of the prime minister of England, a shoo-in for student council, and Mr. Darcy hot." *Most importantly, the roommate of Titus and Alaric.*

"As in, he'll insult you before he asks you out? Then sure," Oakley replied.

Emmeline giggled and ran the tool through the last section of her hair, flipping it expertly off her shoulder. Oakley might have a point, but unlike the Ashland heirs, she wasn't competing for her future—she was the only child and successor to her father's green energy empire.

There was a knock on the door. "Your tall, dark, and boorish awaits," Oakley grumbled.

"Be nice," Emmeline sang as she spritzed on some perfume.

Oakley yanked the door open. "Well, if it isn't the scourge upon women."

"Funny. I haven't gotten any complaints," Sebastian's cool voice came as Emmeline grabbed a jacket from her bed. "You ready?" he asked, poking his head over Oakley's shoulder.

"Maybe not to your face," Oakley muttered.

"Ready!" Emmeline elbowed Oakley in the ribs as she passed. "What happened to nice?"

"That *was* nice," Oakley hissed back.

Shaking her head, Emmeline shut the door on Oakley's grimace and took Sebastian's arm.

It wasn't that Emmeline entirely disagreed with Oakley. Rumors of Sebastian's conquests blazed around like a tornado, but that didn't stop girls from lining up. Because everything Emmeline said was also true: He had power and status, and he was fine as hell. Not that his looks factored into this date whatsoever. Nor, really, did his status.

She was eager to get to know the person closest to Titus, Emmeline's only legitimate rival. And like any good politician, she needed information from the other side.

Though she hated to be counted in a long line of girls, it was necessary in the long run. Three weeks into the semester, Emmeline still had no clue how the heirs would be "tested." After emailing Ilsa Halvorsen her statements for the press, Emmeline hadn't received any more communication from the king's office. And nothing from her parents.

"I'm surprised we're allowed to wander the village," Emmeline said as they passed the barbican and started down the winding cobbled road.

"Well, the Norms aren't," Seb chuckled, pulling her a little closer as a sea breeze wound through the tunnel of trees.

"Why not?" she asked, pretending to be curious, letting him teach her something. It wasn't the first time she'd heard the term "Norms" used in reference to Scholars.

"That's how it is. It makes practical sense more than anything. If something were to happen to them down in the village, the school would be held liable. But Elites and C-Suites, we pay additional tuition for our own insurance and security."

She supposed it made sense, except it was blatantly unfair. But also, what real harm would come to the students in a tiny old fisherman village? It felt like an excuse to widen the gap between the haves and the have-nots on campus.

But Emmeline kept her mouth shut. She couldn't be outspoken like Oakley. It was a risk if King Leander didn't agree with her taking a political stand. What if he didn't like her criticizing his beloved academy? Or what if she offended powerful students who could help her gain connections? No, best to be focused on her end goal: becoming queen of Ashland.

Sebastian led her through the main street of the little village, bypassing tiny shops and French cafes that catered to wealthy students. An elderly Frenchman in a bowtie and vest welcomed them into a swanky-looking bistro. "Monsieur Bane, your table is right this way."

Emmeline raised an eyebrow, impressed. Seb smirked back. From what she knew, other girls got little more than quick hookups in his dorm or a deserted classroom. At least he was making more of an effort with her. *And he should,* Emmeline thought righteously, *I'm a freaking princess.*

"So have you given any more thought to being a chair on the student council? You're the only one who's yet to reply."

Emmeline waited until the waiter finished filling their crystal glasses with chilled water before replying, "Oh, I've given it thought. Just not entirely sure it's for me."

"Because of Oakley?" Seb scoffed. "That girl needs a reality check."

A flare of irritation ignited across Emmeline's skin, and she locked her jaw in order not to reply with, *Oh, is having values unrealistic?*

"I'm not weak, Seb. Don't mistake me for a follower," she said with a tight smile.

"Weak is the last word I'd use to describe you, Emmeline."

Their wineglasses were filled with a dark red blend. Emmeline didn't know what the drinking age was in France or the UK—maybe younger than in the States—though she doubted that mattered anyway. She lifted the glass to her nose and took a deep whiff. There it was again. Garigue. Divine.

They talked about classes and professors through appetizers, an easy conversation to engage in. He even asked about archery and when she first started taking lessons—apparently he'd done his homework on her as well. But it wasn't until their entrees arrived that Emmeline broached the topic on her mind.

"So, what was my cousin like at Eton?" Her tone was casual, but the smile on her lips suggested she knew he was too clever not to see through the inquiry.

Seb chuckled. "He was a bloody stuck-up bastard, which now makes all the sense in the world."

Emmeline laughed. *Not helpful.*

"Oh, come on, Sebastian." Emmeline leaned forward, her elbow on the table, as she batted her pretty lashes. "Besides the king, he and Alaric are the only family I've ever met. Can't you tell me a bit more?"

Sebastian stabbed at his saumon en croute and smirked. "Hmm, not sure I'm ready to betray my best mate just yet."

"Please. Who said anything about betrayal? I just want to get to know my cousin."

"Then ask him yourself. Unless... there's a reason to betray him?"

Emmeline wanted to pour her barely touched wine down his lap, but she settled for tightening her fingers around the stem of her glass instead. She forced a smile. "Not in the least."

The rest of dinner had been painful, but she'd played her part well. She'd deftly pivoted to asking about his father. Sebastian was all too happy to talk about the prime minister's success, to the point where he wouldn't shut up. He droned on about foreign policy until they got to her dorm room. At the sound of his voice in the hall, Oakley opened their suite door and stared menacingly at them. Emmeline gave her a grateful smile as Sebastian's next move was restricted to a good night kiss on the cheek.

"Well?" Oakley asked, "how was it?"

Emmeline spotted Sadie up in her top bunk with a book on her stomach. She wasn't about to run her mouth with *her* present, so she brushed it off and said, "Lovely. I'm going to grab a sparkling water from the dining hall. I'll be back before curfew."

After changing into loungewear, she took a detour through the bailey for some alone time. The moonlight was bright, bathing flowers and stone statues in silver. Emmeline could distantly trace the garigue, but now it felt cloying, as if tainted by her obnoxious date.

For the thousandth time, she checked her email. No change. The back of her throat felt itchy, and with a groan, she dragged her nails through her scalp, tossing back her long waves.

It was then that she heard something else. Low voices but harsh, coming from the other side of the towering honeysuckle bushes.

"Just this one test, Ollie my man."

"Carlton's exams are impossible. One hack, that's all we're asking— a cinch for you."

"Then you should start studying *now*."

Emmeline froze. She knew that third voice. She shouldn't recognize it as surely as she did, not after one little greenhouse conversation, but...

The bushes next to her shuddered. That did not seem good. Ignoring the inner voice that usually kept her in check, Emmeline rounded the flowering wall.

"Listen, you—"

She could hardly believe her eyes—bullying still happened at a school like this? Two second-years stood with their hands on Oliver's hoodie, and their heads snapped toward Emmeline. Caught. They didn't let go, though, as if assuming Emmeline wouldn't care. Or that she'd be on *their* side.

Fury spiked through her. "Problem, gentlemen?"

No one said a word, but the two bullies exchanged glances. Oliver kept his gaze trained on Emmeline, looking at her like he didn't quite believe she was real.

"Move along, princess," one of the boys gritted.

Try again, asshole. Emmeline stepped forward and dipped her chin, leveling them with a piercing glare. "Professor Carlton teaches Data Analysis, correct? Should I inform him that two students are looking to cheat on his upcoming exam? Or maybe Headmistress Aquila would like to be notified?"

The taller guy uttered a foul curse under his breath, then patted Oliver hard on the shoulder. "Not at all, *Your Highness.* Just a little negotiation about Ollie here tutoring us."

"Huh," Emmeline said with a fake, vulpine smile. "What kind of morons need tutoring at a school like this?"

All three boys stared at her in disbelief. Without another word, Emmeline reached over and grabbed Oliver's arm, pulling him against her side. Strangely, his arm felt vastly different from Sebastian's. In a good way.

They started across the courtyard at a brisk pace.

"Emmeline?" Oliver finally said in a low voice, a few feet away from the dining hall.

Emmeline braced herself, fully expecting something macho like, *You didn't have to do that* or *I could've handled it.*

"Yes?" she asked, letting go of his arm.

He waited until she was looking up at him, then smiled gently. "Thanks for that."

She was stunned into silence.

"How's the ankle?" he asked when she remained quiet for a full embarrassing minute.

Emmeline glanced down. "Oh, uh...fine. It wasn't even a sprain."

Oliver nodded thoughtfully, as if he really *did* care. "Good. Well..." He glanced down the corridor. "I'm that way. Tell Danica her friends are doing a good job watching out for me."

Wait...what? For the first time in perhaps, well, ever, Emmeline's cheeks flushed because of a boy. "I didn't do that for Danica."

It was the way she said it—angrily, fiercely—that made Oliver look at her with wide eyes behind his lenses.

Before she had a chance to make a bigger fool of herself, Emmeline turned on her heel and headed back the way she came. She could still feel him staring in confusion, his gaze leaving frissons of heat across her skin.

12

TITUS

WHEN TITUS WRENCHED HIS EYES OPEN, IT WAS STILL DARK. VERY dark. With a curse, he turned to the windowsill and checked his phone. Two AM. *Not again.*

He was tired, that's for sure, but he knew from experience that attempting to go back to sleep would prove futile. Just like trying to figure out the *why.* The first time he'd complained of restless sleep his guardian at the time had told his parents, who then assessed that Titus should be working harder. If he was waking up in the middle of the night, it was clearly because he wasn't studying enough during the day. Their remedy: an extra ten hours of cram school a week.

He'd kept his mouth shut about the occasional insomnia after that.

In fact, he'd kept his mouth shut about... many things. The stiffness in his arms and legs when he was too stagnant, for example, or the frequent dull aches in his hands and feet. Stress had been Titus's constant companion since he was twelve, but the physical effects on his body seemed to have gotten worse in the last year. At first, he'd chalked it off to the anxiety of getting into Almus Terra, but the pain and fatigue were becoming more consistent, as if his body was finally rejecting years of pressure. Not that he could confide that to anyone.

Sharing, Titus found, always invited more problems in. The first time he mentioned the random pain, his parents had him seen by three different specialists. When nothing was definitively diagnosed, and more tests were requested, his parents simply called it a "cry for attention." He would never forget the scathing letter he received after those doctors' visits—the final confirmation that not all parents can love their child.

He'd hoped that being away from his guardian, who was really his parents' spy, would help ease his afflictions. But things were getting worse, not better.

I've got to do something about these stress levels. That was his main thought as he scrolled through his emails. Before he could talk himself out of it, he went ahead and contacted the ATA infirmary, setting up an appointment with the in-house physician. At the very least, maybe they could prescribe him something to help with sleep.

After the email was sent, he continued through his inbox. Then he paused at a calendar invitation for next weekend from Ilsa. The fourth weekend in September, all the heirs were expected for... something. The invite "September Check-In" was annoyingly cryptic, by design.

He scrolled past four more emails from his parents, all complaining his latest grades (As) weren't good enough. Then he landed on another message he'd opened the night before.

His chest rose and fell with a deep breath as he stared at Sadie's name and her reply. **Saturday morning at 10 works for me. See you then** ☺

Since their confrontation in the library, Sadie had started warming up to him. All he'd had to do was let her lead most of their meetups and agree with her in a way that was respectful but not pandering (which wasn't hard, because most of her ideas had merit). Occasionally he slipped in small talk, like, "Professor Reyes was in a foul mood today, huh? You've got a lot of stickers of otters, that your favorite animal?" Pleasant but not overly personal.

He started light, considering her Cold War response after that bloody email. How could he not have assumed the chain would get back to her? By the king's nose hairs, he'd managed to appease her. Sadie didn't need to know he stood by 60 percent of what he'd written. Maybe more. But he did need her to accept his apology, believe his words, and eventually fall for him.

The approach was simple yet ingenious. Rather than have Sadie as a rival, he could neutralize her as a romantic partner. She'd never oppose him if she were in love with him. If Calixa could fake her way through a strategic relationship, so could he. With that initial idea, he thanked whatever karmic god made her his project partner. It was the *perfect* pretense for seduction.

Sadie sat at their usual table with her laptop out and books littered around her like she was studying for the bar exam. If there was one thing he'd learned about Sadie so far, it's that she was a multitasker. She moved from subject to subject when she got bored or unfocused, and it seemed to serve her well.

He slid into the chair next to her, and she flinched, her gaze flickering to the spot across the table. It almost made him laugh at how obvious she was in her expressiveness. *What are you doing? Sit over there.*

"Good morning."

"Morning. Did you finish reading the executive summary?" she asked.

Titus nodded, pulling out his laptop, and the screen lit up in white documents, showing that the last thing he had in fact been reading were the mission, vision, core values, and objectives for the Hearts First, Minds Follow organization.

"Looks good, but I tweaked the fourth objective. Makes it SMART." A SMART goal was a common business term for specific, measurable, achievable, relevant, time-bound. Surely Professor Reyes would appreciate it.

Sadie leaned over, tapping the mouse pad to highlight the changes with editing mode. With her so close, Titus couldn't help but catch a hint of her scent. Her hair was unbound and falling down her shoulders in frizzy waves, smelling like vanilla and bergamot. Though he knew it was strange, he swore she smelled like the earl gray tea he drank every morning back in London. . . .

"Did you swim this morning?"

Titus jerked backward, all too aware that he'd nearly leaned in farther to get another inhale of her shampoo. "What?"

"Either that or you bathed in a tub of chlorine," Sadie said with a grin.

Maybe it wasn't weird if she was able to smell him too—though chlorine had a much stronger scent.

"Yeah. Got up early." He shrugged. "Couldn't sleep."

"I'm sorry." And it sounded like she genuinely meant it. "Insomnia is the worst." She clicked to approve the edit in the document. "I like your change. Thanks for fixing it."

That was another thing he noticed. She said thank you to everything. Even for just working on their project, *his* project, making suggestions, agreeing with hers.

"Why do you thank me for something that's going to improve my grade—our grade?"

Sadie glanced at him, blinking in confusion. "I . . . I don't know. I guess because I'm learning something from you and I appreciate it?"

Titus rubbed an aching hand along his jaw, feeling that same grinding frustration of which he couldn't explain the origin. All he could think was, *I've lived my whole life for my parents. Have I ever been thanked? Have I ever thanked them?*

"Whoa, what's got you all V brow?"

"What?"

Sadie made a V motion with fingers between her eyebrows. "You know, when you get mad enough your eyebrows make a V. V brow."

"That's the strangest thing I've ever heard."

"Then you have lived an extremely sheltered life."

Titus sank into his chair, feeling oddly more relaxed. Calmer. "Look who's talking."

"Excuse you, I'm not sheltered. I've seen *Game of Thrones*. There are naked people in that show."

A snort-laugh exploded out of Titus, shocking him as much as Sadie. He ducked his mouth into his elbow as a few more chuckles escaped. He hadn't laughed like that in...geez, he couldn't remember how long.

"You're ridiculous," he said. With a genuine smile, he leaned forward, itching to tease her. "No naked people in real life, though?"

A lovely red blush spread across Sadie's cheeks, covering her light freckles and making her hazel eyes appear a vibrant sea blue.

Okay, she was pretty. Titus could admit it. She wasn't model pretty, but rather adorable. A slim nose that wrinkled easily, round cheeks with freckles that made interesting patterns down her neck, and a heart-shaped face.

"That's absolutely none of your business," she replied, but it wasn't very snappish, as she was well aware she was being teased.

He grinned. "You're right. My bad."

"That's okay." Sadie turned back to her laptop, muttering, "At least the V brow's gone."

Titus's chest tightened with a strange, indescribable feeling. Had she done that to cheer him up? Before he could stop his body or understand *why*, he was shifting in his chair, his thigh nudging against hers, and his hand reaching for her cheek. He stopped short of touching her, knowing she might not welcome it.

Though he couldn't stop his gaze from dropping to her mouth. A perfect cupid's bow, heavy lower lip and the shade of light coral, like the inside of a seashell.

He watched those lips suck in a breath, then her gaze, too, dropped to his mouth. Her hazel eyes shot back up, as if startled by her own interest. But she didn't move away, and so he allowed himself to trace his knuckles along her cheekbone and down her jaw.

He enjoyed watching her expressions. So real and earnest.

Footsteps, voices, laughter echoed through the library, but still Titus didn't move. Not as fast as Sadie. Her hand curled around Titus's wrist and shoved his arm under the table, and she simultaneously jerked her head back toward the computer screen.

Shit.

Titus cleared his throat. "There was an eyelash. On your cheek. I got it."

"*Oh,*" Sadie whispered, releasing his wrist. "Thanks. So um..." She tucked a piece of hair behind her ear, fingers shaky. "The strategic analysis is next. We need to evaluate the organization. Which part do you want to take?"

Even the tips of her ears were red.

Titus couldn't take his eyes off her. "Weaknesses."

13

ALARIC

"Whoa, dude, is that a VNV Nation tattoo?"

Alaric froze in pulling his shirt over his head. He'd just had a long run and was in the middle of changing after a hot shower. The tattoo was on his left shoulder blade. He'd gotten it when he was fifteen—an older brother of a friend had given him VNV's records, introducing him to the band and telling him that they would help with all his juvenile rage. Strangely, it had.

Alaric glanced over his shoulder to find a kid, kinda scrawny, wearing old workout clothes and thick glasses. He must be one of those Scholars. The *really* smart ones who got here on pure academic merit and came into ATA much younger than most students.

"Uh, yeah, it is," Alaric muttered, pulling down the hem of his shirt. He was honestly surprised someone had even recognized the logo.

"Dude, that's so cool. Ronan is legit," the younger boy said excitedly. "You're Irish, huh? You saw him in concert?"

Again, Alaric was surprised and...amused. A smile tugged at his mouth. "Yeah. Me and my crew have seen him a couple times."

"I wanted to see his *Electric Sun* tour, but he didn't come anywhere near my hometown in the States. I'm Jacob, by the way."

"Alaric."

Jacob nodded as if he'd already known this, then deflated. "Oh, sorry. Didn't mean to bother you. I just think your tattoo is cool."

This was the first time another student seemed genuinely interested in something Alaric liked. Nothing to do with royalty. Just an electronic artist they both liked.

"That's okay," he said after a beat. "Find me later. I'll show you some clips from his concert on my phone."

Jacob's face brightened, his eyes lighting up. "That would be *awesome*." With a nod, Alaric grabbed his gym bag and headed out, his phone suddenly buzzing in his jeans.

It was a summons from the school's receptionist. There was still time before his detention with Sadie, and the admin wing was technically on the way. Plus, it would be more trouble to deal with the aftermath if he skipped it, rather than just going. So he changed course and headed through the bailey into the corridor full of offices.

The receptionist, a sweet hijabi woman with weathered tan skin, grinned at Alaric. "That was fast, Alaric."

"I was on the way. What's the craic?"

The old lady gave him a tender, pitying look that immediately set Alaric on edge. "Down the hall, last door on the left. But perhaps it's best you wait a moment."

That didn't sound good. Unfortunately—he checked his watch—he'd be late for detention if he didn't get going now. "I'll risk it. Cheers, Mrs. Khalid." Ignoring her worried look, he followed directions and slipped into the room.

He knew he'd made a terrible mistake at once. Standing at the window was a tall man wearing a crisp navy suit with a watch and shoes likely worth thousands. His hair was brown with a few streaks of silver, and a trimmed beard lined his sharp jaw.

Something deep down in Alaric's bones screamed in rage and pain. And that something told Alaric everything he needed to know.

This man was his father.

The man's coal-black eyes narrowed. And suddenly Alaric recognized the emotion on his father's face. Hatred.

It wasn't exactly surprising. If there had been any love at all, why had Alaric grown up the way he had? Especially seeing Emmeline and Titus. *They'd* been provided for. They'd had homes and money and food and someone to care for them. Not Alaric.

So yeah, his father's hatred was par for the course but a blow nonetheless. He wouldn't show it, though. He'd sooner die.

"Oy, Da', how's the form?"

The man's lip curled in disgust. Whether it was from the casual tone or the obvious Irish slang, or maybe just the sound of his voice, Alaric didn't know, and he tried not to care.

But he did. Especially now that he knew about his parents. Unable to stop himself, he'd looked them up after reading one of the many articles about the Ashland heirs. The Crown Princess Rhea, his mother, had apparently died shortly after he'd turned two. He'd searched for sadness in that, but...he hadn't known her. How could he feel grief for a total stranger? Then this man—Lord Erickson—was some kind of economics genius who worked closely with the king on his advisory council.

"So." Lord Erickson turned from the window. "Here you are."

Disdain. Hatred. Regret. It was all there. It cut into Alaric's skin like a fisherman's knife. But he didn't flinch.

"Aye, here ah am," Alaric drawled, emphasizing his accent, which seemed to piss off his father even more.

The man pressed his fist down against a nearby desk, pale knuckles turning white. "Listen here, you little punk. You're going to keep your mouth shut. About the orphanage, the foster care, all of it. Not a word to the press."

Alaric stared at him, ice replacing the warm blood in his veins. "What?" he said.

This was what he'd come to say? After years of abandonment...a *fecking threat?*

"You heard me, boy. It's best you stay quiet."

Fury rippled through Alaric—it was hard to even *speak* through the rage. "Why?" Alaric hissed, "so the world won't know yeh abandoned me"—he was yelling now, yelling, and he didn't want to, but he couldn't control it—"to foster systems and poverty?"

The poverty hadn't even been that bad. He could've survived being poor, but it was the exposure to people's hatred of their own miserable lives that really did him in.

Hurried footsteps echoed down the hall.

"Don't you *dare* complain like an ungrateful brat," the man roared back.

At that point, the door behind Alaric ripped open.

"Lord Erickson!" Headmistress Aquila gasped. Alaric could feel other bodies fill the room, but they could livestream this moment for all he cared.

"Your meeting here isn't sanctioned by—" the headmistress continued, but Alaric didn't hear anything over the outrage roaring in his ears.

"I'm not a snitch." Alaric slammed his fist against the wall, and this time his rage made his thick brogue all but disappear. "Maybe *you* would go to the press, but I'm nothing like you. For instance, I'd never abandon my own son."

"You're NOT my son!"

Heavy silence fell like a guillotine. The ice in Alaric's veins cracked.

"You're a bastard," Lord Erickson snarled. "Your grandfather would never admit his daughter was a whore who—"

Alaric grabbed the closest chair—it was heavy and wooden and ornately carved, and it would do damage.

"Alaric! Don't—" Headmistress Aquila and Mrs. Khalid both

screamed, but he was already in motion. Rage gunning him forward like nothing ever had.

But then a small, warm body slammed into him from behind. Fragile, slim arms gripped him by the waist, attempting to heave him back. Alaric stumbled, dropping the chair. A leg cracked under its own weight.

Puffs of breath into his spine, an erratic heartbeat pounding against his back, shaky fingers digging into his stomach. A soft sweet vanilla scent. *Sadie.*

Alaric closed his eyes and breathed. Breathed in deeply while his chest rose and fell with exertion. He'd never wanted to hurt something so badly. To administer the same level of pain ricocheting through him. Never. Not in all his fights.

With as much gentleness as he could muster, Alaric gripped her slim shoulder and pushed her back, but not hard. As her arms fell away, he turned on his heel. Careful not to look at her, careful not to look at anyone, he stormed off through the castle.

As soon as he felt wind on his face, as soon as the barbican disappeared behind him, he started running. He was going to run and run and run until his legs fell off. Or his heart stopped. Whichever came first.

14

SADIE

"Sadie. Sadieeee."

Oakley lightly poked a makeup brush in Sadie's right eye, which finally got her attention.

"W-what?" Sadie jerked her head back, blinking rapidly. It didn't hurt, but it startled her.

"I said open your eyes." Oakley tapped the brush against the eyeshadow palette.

Sadie licked her lips, glad there wasn't gloss on them yet. "Right. Sorry."

It had been a *week*. First the strange moment in the library with Titus on Saturday, then the awful scene with Alaric and his father from hell. Detention that day was obviously canceled, with Headmistress Aquila promising to inform Professor Gupta about the incident. *"Just forget about today, Sadie."*

Forget—ha. Six days had gone by, full of classes and reading and homework, and she'd thought of little else. Alaric's huge body trembling with rage and pain in her arms was something that haunted her. Her only other concern was the royal summons on her calendar for today, which had also consumed her mind far too much.

Because she was so nervous, and to hopefully not make a complete fool of herself, she'd asked Oakley to do her makeup and Danica to do her hair. Thanks to them, her untamable waves were all glossy and smooth and her face didn't look like a child's. There was nothing to be done about her minimal wardrobe, so she simply wore her best dress—a skater skirt design, navy blue with little white flowers—and the only heels she had—tan with a strap around her ankles.

Of course Emmeline looked ready for the runway, with her long legs and stylish pantsuit. To help with her nerves, Sadie left their dorm early to grab a drink at the dining hall, something with ginger and lemon to help settle her stomach.

She didn't know why she was such a mess. It's not like she believed she was seriously in the running for the crown anyway.

Not with Titus's charm, Emmeline's brains, or Alaric's strength pitted up against . . . her. Although she had been angry at Titus's email, he hadn't said anything that wasn't a *little* true.

A taunting whistle pierced Sadie's thoughts and she looked up. Without her even clocking their approach, four girls were now next to Sadie's table regarding her with vindictive looks.

"Someone's all dolled up," one of them said. Sadie immediately noticed Remy—the other Ashland citizen who'd made it to ATA—in their midst. They hadn't talked since their arrival. It was uncomfortably apparent that Remy oozed jealousy.

The whistler grinned, placing one hand on her hip and the other on the table. Her name was Lotta *something* from Anthropology.

"Off to cozy up to Prince Titus, Your *Highness?*"

Sadie's gut clenched. Telling the truth would not be a good idea. Especially if these girls were *fans*. Obsessed with Titus and Alaric, the Ashland princes. All over social media and school forums, students had separated into rival hashtags: #TeamTitus vs #TeamAlaric. Absurd but predictable.

Lotta lunged forward, knocking over Sadie's drink and spilling it down her dress—her only nice dress. The ginger and lemon and sugar now sticky across her thighs and arms.

"Oops. Let me help you." The mean girl leaned in to whisper in Sadie's ear, "That whole scene in the library was pathetic." Then she moved back far enough to gauge Sadie's reaction.

Try as Sadie might, it was hard to keep her face neutral. That moment in the library had been so unexpected and strange. But not unpleasant. Sadie was still wary of Titus, but the last week or two had been nice. *He'd* been nice.

Plus, Titus Eldana *was* gorgeous. When he'd looked at her like that, she'd felt herself helplessly drawn in.

Something must've shown on Sadie's face, because Lotta's sneer grew, and she drawled, "Awww. Falling for Prince Titus? Get real. Give up." She squeezed Sadie's arm painfully, then straightened and glided away, the rest of her posse giggling in tow.

But Sadie sat frozen, unseeing, unhearing. . . .

"I can't do this anymore, honey. I just want to give up."

Words from months ago locked her in place. They echoed, spreading darkness through her mind like spilled ink. Her chest constricted and her ears buzzed. *Give up.*

Suddenly, someone gripped her shoulder tightly and Sadie gasped like she was coming up for air. Like she'd been drowning. Her vision swam into focus again and a face sharpened into view. Pretty, pale, and familiar. A curtain of silky black hair and a beanie with headphones around her neck.

"Trang?" Sadie asked, confused. She hadn't even seen her approach.

Her dormmate pointed to the clock on the dining hall wall. "Don't you have somewhere to be?"

"What?" Sadie asked, confused, then gasped and jolted from her sticky seat. She had three minutes until the mystery meeting in the State Room.

Being late was bad; being late for a king was unacceptable. How long had she been just sitting there, lost in the past? She didn't want to think about it. Didn't want to be sucked back into that dark abyss in her mind where she couldn't breathe...

No. Right now she couldn't breathe because she was sprinting—through the bailey, up the staircase to the southeastern tower, past the historical tapestries that billowed behind her and flapped against the stone wall. She wrenched the door open at exactly two PM.

Everyone in the room turned and stared, and Sadie stifled a groan of frustration. Her dress was wet, her thighs and arms still glistening in tea. Her face was sweaty and her once-nice hair was jostled from running. So much for the extra effort.

Wheezing, Sadie inched into the room, her panicked gaze jumping from person to person. Emmeline was pristine but looked appalled at Sadie's appearance. Titus stared at her all handsome and confused. Alaric didn't acknowledge her. He faced away, arms crossed.

But Sadie knew it ran deeper than that. She hadn't talked to him since that wretched day, and every time she'd gathered the courage to check in, he disappeared.

Then there were the adults. Two thick, tall men in suits were off to the side, while a woman with pale skin, blond curls, and smile lines stood with a tablet in the middle of the room. The headmistress was also there, along with a photographer and a young woman with a makeup kit and garment bag slung over her shoulder. And of course, the king of Ashland.

His Majesty sat on an armchair looking perfectly poised and not at all surprised to see Sadie flying in at the last minute like a bat out of hell.

"My dear, right on time," King Leander said with a smile that didn't reach his eyes.

"This way, Sadie." Ilsa Halvorsen, darted forward, steering Sadie out the door by the shoulders. "Margaret."

The woman with the makeup kit and garment bag followed them into a vacant room next door, smaller and less ornate, without all the fancy plush furniture.

"Heavens, girl," Ilsa said, "what is all over you? Margaret, we need wet wipes."

"Ginseng lemon tea," Sadie said numbly.

"Well, at least your hair looks decent. Needs a brush, though."

The next eight minutes were a whirlwind. Sadie was stripped down to her underwear by complete strangers, wiped down, then swapped into a form-fitting peach satin dress with a pencil skirt and capped sleeves. She was given new five-inch heels that pinched her toes, and heavier foundation on her face that covered her freckles and gave her color "for the camera." Lips painted, hair teased, she returned to the room, where everyone else was already posed. *It's like a royal Addams family portrait,* Sadie thought with horror. And she was expected to be in it.

King Leander stood between two armchairs; Emmeline already sat in one. Alaric leaned against Emmeline's armchair and Titus's spot was next to the vacant one, left for Sadie.

Positioned with her hands gracefully in her lap and ankles crossed, Sadie barely had time to blink before she smiled and flashes went off. Thirty minutes, five new poses, and one hundred photos later, they were done, and Sadie couldn't feel her cheekbones or her toes.

"Well done, children," King Leander said, consulting his watch. "I'm told your studies are coming along, aside from a few"—his gaze roamed between Alaric and Sadie—"hiccups. My visit today is three-fold. The official photos, of course, debriefing with your headmistress, and letting you know what the rest of the semester looks like for all of you.

"Fall break is a few weeks away, in mid-October, just after mid-terms. At that time, you will fly home to Ashland to have a family dinner at the palace as well as attend a few public events we have planned."

Silence filled the room, but there were subtle changes that even Sadie picked up on. Alaric had turned to stone. Emmeline's spine straightened, while Titus shifted from one foot to the other.

"Don't look so excited," King Leander said with a chuckle.

Sadie had to turn away so the king wouldn't scan the anger on her face.

As if Alaric would cheer after meeting his butthead of a dad. Seeing him again for some formal dinner sounded like hell.

Titus and Emmeline had never even met their parents. They must feel sick with nerves.

As for Sadie... the idea of returning to Ashland was painful. And that overshadowed any giddiness about staying in the legendary Heres Castle.

"Is that all, Your Majesty?" Emmeline asked, interrupting the awkward silence.

"Pardon?"

"The rest of the semester. That's only until October, sir. What happens after fall break?"

"Ah, yes." King Leander relaxed deeper into his chair. Sadie wondered whether he considered every chair an extension of his throne. "At the end of the semester, during Hibernia, Almus Terra's winter ball, I plan to announce one of you as heir apparent."

15

TITUS

"I believe it's only fair at this point," Titus's grandfather continued, completely unaffected by the bomb he'd just dropped in the room.

Fair to whom? Titus thought viciously.

"The country has gone long enough with no clear successor in sight. Announcing the four of you as my heirs was a step in the right direction, but let's face it," he said with a wry smile. "I'm not getting any younger, am I?"

"Isn't it too . . ." Emmeline stopped herself, realizing she was about to question the king in front of everyone. She'd probably remembered the last time that happened—when Titus had spoken out of turn.

But King Leander merely smiled. "Go ahead, Emmeline. Too what?"

"It just feels rather soon, Your Majesty. To evaluate us, I mean. For such an important decision."

He dipped his head graciously. "Ah, yes, a valid question. You're likely unfamiliar with Ashlandic laws, so let me assure you: I can revoke the title of heir apparent so long as I live and rule. That being said, my advisors have urged me to plan ahead so more formalized training may begin for my chosen heir, as a precaution."

He paused, a quick look of irritation flashing across his face, which made Titus suspect his grandfather did not care for this reminder of his mortality. "Rest assured, I will not relinquish my throne until I believe the heir apparent is ready. Perhaps not for another five years. Until then, we will establish a clear succession line as I continue to evaluate each of you. Understood?"

No one said anything, but Titus sensed they didn't have to. Most questions from authority figures were rhetorical anyway.

Damn, he was tired of standing. His feet and big toe (especially) were aching, and he wanted to get away from Alaric's hostile mood and Emmeline's thick floral perfume.

At last, they prepared to leave, but then his grandfather paused at the door. "Oh, yes, and make sure you two know how to dance." His gaze flicked to Alaric and Sadie, not the least concerned about emphasizing the gaps in their upbringing. "Titus and Emmeline, perhaps you can teach them the basics of ballroom." With that, they were gone.

"I'd be happy to teach you, Sadie," Titus said as the door shut, turning to admire her once more. She'd come through those doors panting like a dog escaped from a bath, and then reemerged like... hell, like a princess.

In a few short minutes, she'd been transformed. The dress accentuated her curves, and those devilish heels shaped her calves in a way that was borderline witchcraft.

Sadie stared up at him with huge eyes framed by thick black lashes and makeup that highlighted all the blue in her hazel irises. Her expression clearly read, *What just happened?*

He took her hand, helping her to stand in those shoes, which seemed to jar her a bit.

"Oh, um. Thanks. That would be helpful. I guess..." She looked to Alaric, who was already striding for the door, his shoulders hunched and tense. His arm shot forward and ripped the door open, and he disappeared behind it. Emmeline made an annoyed sound, then tossed a look at them over her shoulder before she, too, left.

"My pleasure," Titus said, ignoring his cousins. "Can I accompany you to your dorm? You...um..." He glanced down at her feet. "You look like Bambi learning how to walk."

Sadie let out a little puff of laughter. "Sure, that'd be great, actually."

Titus offered his arm and together they started a slow trek through the castle.

"Oh shoot," Sadie muttered, which made Titus grin. "Do you think I'll get my dress and shoes back?"

"Ask Ilsa. Though I think they'll keep putting you in whatever clothes they want. Alaric too. They got him into that suit just before you walked in."

Sadie frowned but nodded, accepting it. Then nearly rolled her ankle out of nowhere. Titus had to grab her waist and haul her back up. "Okay, first step in ballroom dancing is teaching you how to walk in heels."

"These are medieval torture devices. I can't feel my toes."

"You have my sympathies. So...what happened?" he prodded.

"Nope, not going there," Sadie said. Her light tone made it seem like no big deal, but Titus sensed the weight underneath. He had a feeling it wasn't carelessness that had made her late.

"Keeping a man in suspense. Excellent strategy," Titus whispered, leaning down toward her ear. He sensed her shiver right before she tensed up again. *Slow down*, Titus told himself, *or you'll scare her off*.

"I read your half of the SWOT analysis. With my weaknesses and opportunities section, we should be pretty convincing," he said, casually switching to schoolwork.

The rest of the walk to her dorm room was all about their project, but parting was awkward, because Sadie kept glancing back and forth down the corridor. When Titus finally finished outlining his plan for their next session, Sadie vanished with a rushed goodbye that bordered on rude.

Outside his own dorm room, Titus had no issue being rude

himself. He let out a large and audible groan at seeing Emmeline, still done up in her power suit and slingbacks, leaning against his door.

"I'm tired, Emmeline. If you're looking for Sebastian, he's probably out with another girl."

An angry flush started across her cheeks. "I was waiting for *you*, asshole."

"There's that mouth again," he muttered. But when Emmeline seized his arm and dragged him down the hall in a death grip, he didn't fight it.

"I see what you're doing," she snapped as soon as they were in the north covered parapet walkway.

"Oh? And what's that?" he said in a flat, bored tone.

"You're seducing Sadie." Lips curving into a smile, she continued, "People saw you two all close in the library. And now teaching her to dance? Escorting her back to the dorm? Please."

Emmeline was too bloody clever. He'd always known she was going to be a difficult rival. Even so, she was quickly exceeding his expectations.

"Wow," Titus said, laughing. "Just because that's what you're doing with Seb doesn't mean the rest of us are so conniving."

"Go ahead and deny it. It serves me as much as it serves you anyway."

Annoyed at this truth, Titus leveled her a glare, giving her the attention she demanded. "What's your point, Emmeline? Why draw me out here?"

She took a step closer, her pretty face all sharp angles in the shadows of the fading light off the west coast. "An alliance. We both know that we're the only real contenders for the crown, but Alaric and Sadie are distractions. If you can make sure Sadie stays out of the running, I'll deal with Alaric. He's halfway gone already. He doesn't even want to be here."

Titus regarded her for a long, heavy moment. She wasn't wrong. And once those two were out, Titus and Emmeline would be free to compete on equal footing.

But he didn't trust Emmeline. She was too strategic. Like a brilliant chess player, seeing all the pieces on the board and all the possible moves. She'd always be one critical step ahead.

"C'mon, Emmeline," he said, staring out at the sunset. He remembered seeing her name in bloodred paint across the stone wall with the rest of the historic monikers. She was willing to risk everything to succeed—to inscribe herself into history, no matter what—like he was.

At that moment, his phone started buzzing in his jacket pocket. He pulled it out and glanced at the screen, a terrible, tightening sensation forming in his gut.

He cleared his throat. "There's no way the two of us could work together because I don't trust you, and you wouldn't trust me. Now, I have to take this.... Excuse me."

Without awaiting her response, he turned and headed down the staircase, lifting the phone to his ear. "Hello, Mother."

"Titus, darling, how'd it go today?" His mother's highborn Ashlandic accent was already grating on him, and he'd only spoken with her on the phone three times. Their first call had hardly been a loving conversation between mother and son.

"Seeing as how I don't know what the headmistress told Grandfather, I can't say for sure. But I've been succeeding in every class, I'm up for a student council chair, and—"

"Yes, yes," she cut him off, tired of his talking already. "Did he tell you about Hibernia?"

Grinding his teeth, Titus headed down the stone path that led outside the inner wall toward the rocky coast. He didn't want anyone overhearing this conversation. "About choosing the heir apparent? A heads-up would've been nice."

"And have you mangle things again?" His mother's voice was low and dangerous.

Titus winced, gripping his phone so tight his knuckles ached.

"Listen, Titus, the heir apparent is critical. They will shadow the king. You'd have more privileges at school and new responsibilities in court. There's no more room for missteps. Be prepared for your return to Ashland."

There was a click, and then a tone. She hung up. No goodbye, much less an *I love you* or even *I'm looking forward to seeing you after sixteen years.*

With a sigh, Titus was about to tuck his phone back into his pocket when another call came through. He frowned, recognizing the number as the in-house physician at ATA. Last week, he'd visited the doctor to check on his insomnia, the stiffness in his limbs, and aches in his hands and feet... he thought it was just stress, especially when Dr. Sharrad hadn't been able to tell him much more than those other specialists. So why was he calling now?

"Hello? Dr. Sharrad?," he answered.

"Titus, hello. Do you have a moment to come by the office?"

Titus felt his entire being tense as if he were on a precipice about to fall. Something was wrong. Something *felt* wrong.

"No," Titus said, his voice strained. He was already behind on his study time thanks to walking Sadie back to her dorm, Emmeline's proposition, his mother's warning. He didn't have time for whatever *this* was.

There was a pause on the other end. "I see. Then please stop by the infirmary tomorrow."

"Just tell me now." Titus didn't mean for his words to come out so sharp. He sounded vicious, demanding—like his mother. "I'm sorry, I just... please, doctor."

He was careful to make sure his voice did not break.

A deep sigh. "Well, as an ATA student, you're under my care, so I was given full access to your previous medical records. Apparently, you've been to quite a few doctors about these symptoms?"

Dr. Sharrad paused, and Titus realized he was waiting for confirmation. Titus wondered why, since it was all in there. "Yeah, so?"

Ugh, he hated how bratty he sounded.

"So," Dr. Sharrad continued, "those doctors recommended more tests, and I think we should proceed with them. More to the point, I'd like to bring in a new specialist."

Titus watched the waves crash against the rocks ten feet below. They were violent today, likely a storm off the coast sending out its rage for miles.

"What kind of specialist?" he heard himself ask.

"A rheumatologist. For musculoskeletal diseases and systemic autoimmune conditions. That's my hunch looking at these notes from . . ."

Dr. Sharrad's voice faded as Titus's concentration fragmented. He drew a hand down his face, scraping his nails along his jaw, maybe drawing blood. *Push it away. Focus.*

"Does anyone else have access to my medical records?"

"What?"

"Does my grandfather? My parents?" For as long as Titus could remember, he'd been subjected to regular health checks that his guardians had sent along to his parents, but at ATA there might be a sliver of a chance at privacy . . .

"Well, you turned eighteen last month, didn't you?" Dr. Sharrad said, clearly startled by the sudden pivot. "Yes, you did. So now, technically you're an adult."

Had he? If it was late September, then yes. But he'd never celebrated a single birthday.

"And according to the laws of your nation," Dr. Sharrad continued, "no one can access your medical records unless you sign a medical information release form. Your parents signed for you upon your admission to this school, but now that you're eighteen, it's up to your discretion moving forward."

Titus sagged against the rock wall. He raised a shaky hand to his head, fisting his hair, pulling at the roots, his mother's words echoing over Dr. Sharrad's.

"Titus, we don't have time for this anymore. There isn't a single doctor who can name anything wrong with you. Besides, kings must show no weakness."

"U-understood. Thank you. I'll stop by the infirmary this week."

"Titus, we really should—"

But Titus had already hung up. Then, with every bit of strength he had left, he chucked his phone out into the waves below.

16

EMMELINE

It felt like a needle was drilling into her skull, right at the base. Emmeline hissed out a breath and pressed the heels of her palms into her eyes.

Soothing classical music played in her ears, but rather than Chopin or Tchaikovsky, it was the 2005 *Pride and Prejudice* soundtrack. That movie might've been the one thing that she and her old governess, Heather, had agreed on. After a rotten day, they'd watch together in quiet solidarity, both mouthing the lines they knew by heart. Now, listening to "Liz On Top of the World" on repeat was keeping a migraine at bay.

She was supposed to be focusing on her Technology Entrepreneurship reading, but the words were bleeding together, sounding an awful lot like *I don't trust you, and you wouldn't trust me.*

The words that Titus used to utterly dismiss her. And then the last thing she overheard before he disappeared from the ramparts—*Hello, Mother.*

That gutted her. It shouldn't have. She knew his parents had already been in touch. But now she had witnessed it. They were calling him. Caring about him.

But not Emmeline's. Not yet. A whole month at Almus Terra, and no contact. Why, why, *why* hadn't they at least sent an email? That wasn't a lot to ask. She'd happily take a text. But...nothing.

FWUMP. Emmeline jerked straight up in her desk chair as a pillow hit the dorm window with surprising precision.

It wasn't hard to guess who'd thrown it, but Emmeline *was* surprised to see Danica and Oliver—of all people—behind an out-of-breath, angry-looking Oakley.

Earbuds in, Emmeline hadn't heard the three of them enter the dorm, but here they were, and Emmeline was quickly trying to assess her appearance. Yoga pants and a cashmere sweater, a fishtail braid, no makeup—not ideal, but her skin was flawless. She considered toeing off her fuzzy socks but decided against it. Oliver wouldn't think any less of her.

"Problem?" she asked. Her eyes lingered on him a beat too long. She hadn't spoken to him since that night in the bailey, only seen him in the Technology Entrepreneurship class they shared.

Oliver, meanwhile, was intent on looking at anything *but* her. Danica had him by the arm, and his panicked expression indicated he was absolutely mortified to be in their room.

"Ollie's hours in the computer lab for his Software Development project got changed from eight to midnight. Freaking Elites got his time slot instead."

He pushed his glasses up his nose and shook his head. "Oakley, it's fi—"

"It's *not* fine," Danica snapped. "It's unfair and elitist. You have as much right to those servers as anyone. Way more, even. You're a million times smarter. Now you have to get special permission to be out of the dorms past curfew, and sacrifice sleep."

Emmeline bit her tongue, annoyed. Oakley was right. It wasn't fair. Emmeline might be as spoiled and bougie as the rest of the student council, but she wasn't an idiot. She understood the importance and power of the middle class, the masses, the popular vote. Lose their support, marginalize others, and you have a huge political problem.

Plus, there was the whole morality question—*what we owe each other* and all that.

Not for the first time, she wondered if there was something to be done about it. Something *she* should do. But then…*heir apparent.* She could not screw that up. The risk was too great. She'd set her sights on greater change once that title was hers and her royal footing was more secure.

"I'm sorry, Oliver," Emmeline said, and she meant it. "That's not okay."

Finally, those deep-brown eyes landed on her, and Emmeline's stomach erupted in butterflies.

"Thanks, Emmeline."

Oh no, she found that she loved her name in his baritone.

"I can't believe you're still considering that awful student council," Oakley snapped bitterly at Emmeline.

Tearing her eyes from Oliver, Emmeline replied calmly, "This is precisely why I *should* consider it. I can stop decisions like that." *Eventually.*

Oakley contemplated this, nodding. "I see. Infiltrate from within and whatnot. But seriously, good luck making a difference. That Calixa is a thirteen-itch."

Danica snorted. "That joke is like a decade old, babe."

"Still works."

As Danica and Oakley bickered in their flirty way, Oliver tried to slip out. But Emmeline was watching his every move.

"Oliver," she called, "have you finished the section on Silicon Valley cluster dynamics and context?"

He froze, his gaze sliding over to her.

She smiled and tapped the edge of her laptop. "You know, from our homework?"

He cleared his throat. "Uh, yeah. I'm on the conceptual frameworks for analyzing tech ventures."

"Then... would you mind helping me study?"

Emmeline couldn't remember ever trying so hard to get a boy's attention. Going to an all-girls' school may have only allowed for limited interactions, but they'd been easy.

"Er... yeah, sure." After a brief moment of hesitation, he delicately moved the chair from Oakley's desk next to Emmeline and sat down awkwardly. Suddenly the space felt a lot smaller with him by her side. So close she could smell a warm combination of herbs and soil. Like he'd spent more time in the greenhouses earlier that day.

"So... how can I help?"

Emmeline liked that he asked. "Start from the beginning," she prompted.

He shot her a look as if he didn't quite believe she needed *that*, but at her smile, a corner of his lips tugged up in return. "All right, well, most people think Silicon Valley began primarily from skilled science research within university departments, but there was a lot of government intervention that contributed to its success, like permissive regulation and steady spending from the US Department of Defense."

Emmeline scooted closer, listening to his voice and smelling his fresh herbal scent, her migraine dissolving almost entirely, even with Danica and Oakley giggling in the background.

True to her word, Emmeline continued meeting with the student council, but she bided her time. Besides focusing on the competition for heir apparent, she needed to understand how much power Calixa and Kavi possessed. There was no point in acting too soon, or arguing on the Scholars' behalf, before she even knew if she could win. That would be foolish and surely not gain her any points with the king.

Attending the council meetings also served another purpose: using Sebastian Bane. Seb was her best chance at surpassing Titus. And after her cousin had dismissed her so easily, she was eager to take him down a peg. He would rue the day he didn't see her worth.

Since her last "date" with Sebastian, they'd met up a few times, mostly around student council meetings. She'd let him talk about himself, laugh when he wasn't funny, flip her hair, and casually press up against him when they walked arm in arm. But none of it seemed to charm him enough to betray his roommate.

He knew they were playing a game. And Sebastian had the better hand.

"I can't wait to see how the Norms react tomorrow morning," Sebastian chuckled as they descended the stairs of the council's tower.

Emmeline said nothing, thinking about the new amendment to the student bylaws that had passed not even fifteen minutes ago. Apparently it had been in the works for a while, and the final vote tonight had merely been a formality.

Oakley would have a fit. Danica would be quietly angry. Oliver, in his very Oliver way, would say nothing.

"Honestly, I can't believe it's taken so long to pass it. Seeing as how they attend this school for free, they should at least work for their supper, so to speak," he continued.

A queasiness brewed in Emmeline's belly and Seb's comments made her want to claw the sneer right off his face.

"Titus was almost late today," Emmeline said. "And he didn't check his phone once. Doesn't he seem a bit...frazzled?"

In truth, the difference in her cousin hadn't been *that* remarkable, but she remarked on it anyway. She needed to get *something* out of this walk, other than wasted time.

Seb let out a booming laugh that echoed through the dark corridor. Emmeline almost hushed him since it was well past the eleven o'clock curfew, but council members could technically be out whenever they wanted.

"That's because the bloody idiot accidentally dropped his phone off the side of the ramparts. He's waiting to get a new one. Can you believe someone can be that careless? Definitely monarch material."

No, Emmeline couldn't believe Titus had been careless. The boy—she was loath to admit—was a paradigm of poise and grace. Her gut clenched as alarm bells went off in her head. Titus had destroyed his phone on purpose. *Why*, she had no idea. But he must be hiding something from his parents and the king.

Illicit content? Or perhaps evidence that he and his parents had broken the Ashland king's rules a second time? Surely that would eliminate him from the running once and for all.

"C'mon, Emmeline..." Titus's tone, so annoyed, so tired, so utterly dismissive of her, cut through her mind. She hated him. Hated how he'd talked to his parents all along and she had yet to hear a single word from hers. Hated how he'd had never felt lost or alone or...

"Emmeline?" Sebastian nudged her and she looked up, pulled out of her thoughts. He was clearly annoyed.

Shit. Had he been talking? "I'm sorry, what did you say?"

Seb sighed. "Never mind. Let's just get you back to your dorm."

The way he said it, so exasperated, made her think she wasn't getting escorted anywhere again. She was wasting his time. Other girls would pay him more attention.

Maybe Emmeline had worried none of his information would be useful—until this. Now, for better or worse, he'd confirmed that these dates were time well spent. She wasn't yet sure what she'd do with this piece of information about Titus's missing phone, but that hardly mattered.

What mattered was that she was right from the start: Sebastian was a strategic ally. And she wanted to ensure he would not get bored of her like his other dates.

Passion in the pursuit of perfection. Her mother's words echoed through her ears as Emmeline yanked on Sebastian's necktie and pulled him into the first dark classroom she saw.

He stumbled in after her but quickly caught up to what was happening. Emmeline knew, with certainty, that he'd done this many times. The door clicked behind them, and Sebastian's hands were on her waist, his fingers digging into her hips to press her closer. Emmeline let him, her hands sliding up his chest to skate across his shoulders and up into his thick dark hair.

"Yes, Your Highness?" Seb murmured, his hand dragging up her side to pull her flush against him. His chest was solid, and his arms were enveloping. His cologne was cloying, but being held...ugh, it felt *good*.

Heather had never hugged her. Neither had the nanny before her. Nor had any of her "friends" back in Manhattan. She was ashamed to admit, but Oakley might've been her first legitimate embrace. It left her starved for human touch.

So she took what she could get. Her body pressed into his, feeling the warmth of his skin through his shirt. While her fingernails scraped against his scalp, he nipped her bottom lip as if testing her. To see if she really wanted this.

And yes, she *did*. She didn't want this embrace—even if it was with Sebastian—to end too soon.

With another hard yank, Emmeline tugged him down, his hands tightened, and their lips met in what could only be described as battle.

Sebastian's lips were cold, pressing against hers in a play for possession. Everything about his kiss felt victorious. Domineering, overpowering. She disliked it, and yet...she didn't. How he held onto her—strong and a little desperate—it felt good. Because for all his faults, at least Sebastian wanted her.

Emmeline had grown up believing she was unwanted, and she couldn't so easily shake a lifetime of emotional starvation. The need to be touched. To be loved.

This was not love. But it was want. And that was close enough. She *craved* it.

Suddenly, Sebastian pulled away. The illumination from blinking tech in the room and the moonlight coming through the window cast his face in harsh shadows.

"I think it's time I get you back to your dorm, princess." He placed a kiss at the corner of her lips. As if to take away the sting of his words. Of stopping.

Emmeline blinked, absolutely floored. What...was happening?

She grabbed his arm as he started to release her, and she hissed her frustration. The feeling of being in his arms, the intensity of being desired, she wanted more. "We're not done."

Sebastian lifted a brow. "Is that a royal decree?"

"Cut the crap, Sebastian," Emmeline growled, annoyed. "No more kid gloves. Kiss me for real."

Sebastian seized her, his grin wicked, but it thrilled her nonetheless. "As you wish, princess." Then his mouth devoured hers.

First it was a caress of his tongue against the seam of her lips, then he did as she commanded. He kissed her *for real*. Deep and slow, then fast and desperate, and Emmeline, for all her limited experience, could barely keep up. He was talented. She hated to admit it. This was technically accomplished *and* passionate. A dangerous combination.

Fortunately she didn't have feelings for Sebastian—otherwise she'd be in trouble. It was a good thing this wasn't...

Of course now that she'd thought of him she couldn't stop. Imaginings coursing through her like side effects. She smelled fresh herbs and sunshine soil instead of smothering sandalwood and spice. Warm brown skin and a soft T-shirt under her fingers instead of a stiff cotton button-down.

"Yes, Emmeline," he whispered against her lips.

Emmeline's nails dug into the base of his neck; she fantasized about smooth shaved sides rather than thick curls. Her tongue stroked against his, soliciting heat all through her body and sending frissons of electricity down her skin. Firm hands grasped the back of her thighs and lifted her onto a nearby desk.

The movements never slowed their kiss or doused her fire. Oliver's fingers dove into her long waves as he shifted the angle of his mouth to slant hotly over hers. The desk rattled under them, loud over the gentle whirring of the blinking computer servers.

Then there was another sound slicing through Emmeline's fantasy. The door opening, the flick of a light switch—

"*Oh.* Crap, s-sorry—"

The deep baritone voice was like an ice pick gutting Emmeline's core and sending blizzards of cold realization through her. Oliver was standing in the doorway, *not* propping her up on a desk. Oliver had his hand on the light switch to the computer lab, *not* tangled in her hair.

"Occupied, idiot," growled Sebastian with his British accent and tenor tone and stuffy cologne.

"R-right," Oliver choked out. He stumbled out the door and slammed it. Emmeline could hear his rapid footsteps flying down the hall. Her chest hurt, her lips stung, her gut roiled with disgust—at herself.

Sebastian kissed the corner of her lips, gripping her lower back. "Where were we?"

17

SADIE

THE ROPE TWISTED BACK AND FORTH, SLOWLY ROTATING THE body silhouetted against the setting bloodred sun. Sadie stood, frozen in time, disbelief and denial coursing through her like shots of a poisonous drug—destroying her molecule by molecule. Her blood pumped in time with a chant in her head. *Not. Real. Not. Real. Not. Real.*

I just want to give up.

Sadie jerked awake with a gasp. A loud tearing sound echoed through the silent, dark library. The book page she'd fallen asleep on, which had been stuck to her face, ripped down the middle.

With a groan, Sadie gingerly peeled the page from her wet cheek and pushed the nightmare away into the recesses of her memory.

Great, she'd destroyed library property. Mrs. Harakka would kill her when she found out. Especially after she was nice enough to let her stay late today. . . .

But Sadie didn't mean to stay *this* late. Her phone said it was almost midnight. When had she even fallen asleep? The last thing she could remember was reading an Anthropology book, and Herodotus had been discussing ethnographies of Egypt and Syria.

Sadie was packing up her things when she heard the library door open, quick, harried footsteps, and short breaths. Curious, she moved around the stacks on the second floor to see the library doors in the dim lighting of the few lamps scattered on the heavy mahogany tables.

"Oliver?" she guessed, peering into the shadows.

Oliver looked up, his glasses catching the lamp light. "S-Sadie?"

Sadie quickly made her way down to meet him. "What's wrong?"

She didn't know Oliver well, only by association, really, thanks to Danica. He was usually pretty shy or reserved, but now he looked distressed. Or at the very least, uncomfortable.

"Nothing," Oliver said quickly, rubbing his chest in a circular motion, his expression clearly saying *Not nothing*.

"Oh, well." Sadie glanced around at the empty library. "Why are you here so late?" she asked after a beat of awkward silence.

Oliver moved his long fingers to rub the deep shadows under his eyes, pushing his lenses up near his brows. "I was *supposed* to be in the computer lab using the servers for my project."

Sadie started to pick up on his frustration. "But you're not allowed in? I thought the computer lab had assigned time slots."

"It does," he said roughly, pulling out a chair and plopping down, his big shoulders slumping in defeat.

Another obnoxious Elite took his slot, if Sadie were to hazard a guess. "I'm sorry. Can you talk to your professor?"

Oliver sighed heavily and checked his watch. "Nah, probably just a...misunderstanding. But that's a night's work out the window," he grumbled.

He looked so dejected that Sadie couldn't leave him like this. She wanted to help if she could.

"Anything you can do without the server?" she asked, sliding into the chair next to him.

Oliver shrugged. "Well, I map out my phases of work expecting to use the ATA server. It has access to almost half the world's national banks' databases. It allows me to test my code."

"You're writing code for a bank? Is it financial software?" she asked, impressed.

"Er, not exactly. It's like...imagine if you could invest in humanity, you know? The more a charity flourishes, the more it can help others. Well, I'm working on an app that charts the progress of philanthropy. It utilizes company shares and national banks and projects' investment growth for charities. You can donate money into the charity of your choice, buy and sell shares in the name of that charity, and invest your wealth into the well-being of others."

As he talked, he pulled out his iPad with designs and prototype wireframes of this app. It looked incredibly complicated but so well planned. Not to mention totally inspiring.

"Oliver...that's...that's amazing," Sadie said, admiring the software in beta mode. There were data feeds she didn't understand, and dashboards charting financial numbers that flew over her head, but it sounded and looked ingenious.

"Thanks." Oliver smiled. "I think it'll be great once I finish it. *If* I finish it."

"I'm sure you will," Sadie said, patting him on the shoulder. "You need to. The world needs people with big brains, big ideas, and even bigger hearts."

He chuckled. "Wow, that's cheesy."

She elbowed him in the ribs. "Rude." She was glad she'd made him smile, but hers was fading. Ever since she'd heard Almus Terra existed, she'd wanted to come here because it was supposed to help the world—promote peace and foster advocacy. Yet all she'd done so far was worry about a rivalry she had no business being in. Her Philanthropy project with Titus was *something*, but it paled in comparison to Oliver's ambitions. His work made her want to do more.

And who's to say she couldn't try? Yes, her studies took up a lot of her weeks, but she didn't have any friends. Titus was a study partner and Trang mostly still kept to herself. In short: Sadie had time to spare.

"Are you allowed to be out this late?" Oliver said, checking the time again and pulling her out of an idea germinating in her head.

Sadie sighed. "No, I fell asleep. But my room isn't far."

"I'll walk you back," he offered. "I have an official pass thanks to that late computer lab time slot."

"That you didn't even get to use," Sadie pointed out.

"That I didn't get to use," he agreed with a flash of white teeth.

Ten minutes later, they were already at Sadie's door. "Thanks again, and good luck on your project, Oliver. It sounds incredible."

"It's not really that..." His words trailed off as his gaze homed in on a spot above Sadie's left shoulder.

Sadie turned to find Emmeline coming to a halt at the other end of the hallway. For the first time ever, Emmeline looked...unkempt—waves frizzy, clothes slightly wrinkled, and her lips and eyes all red and puffy. Like a deer in headlights, Emmeline stared at Sadie, then slowly moved her gaze to Oliver.

Sadie could feel Oliver stiffen at once. He mumbled something that sounded like *Thanks, good*, then quickly took off, hiking his bag up his shoulder.

Before Sadie could say a word or try to understand what had just happened, Emmeline approached with fury in her eyes, her hair flying behind her. "What were you doing?" she spat, squeezing Sadie's arm.

Cold indignation spiraled through Sadie. What the *hell*?

Rather than knuckling under, like she always did, she shot back, "Can you answer the same question?"

Emmeline reacted as though she'd been slapped.

Tearing her arm away from Emmeline's viselike grip, Sadie slipped into their room and slammed the door in her face.

"Good thing I wasn't sleeping," a voice muttered behind Sadie.

Sadie whipped around to find Trang in her bottom bunk, illuminated by the light of her laptop. The blue glow of the screen made her jet-black hair look almost blue. In a rare moment, her headphones were off, charging on her bedside table.

Shoot. She was right. Luckily Oakley seemed to be out, but Trang was clearly still awake. Sadie waited to see if Emmeline would come in, but she remained on the other side. Maybe she went off to collect herself, potentially even to Danica's dorm if that's where Oakley was.

Whatever. Sadie didn't care. She walked over to the other bunk bed and sat down heavily, dropping her bag. "I'm really sorry. That was... Emmeline. She just... anyway. I was careless."

Gaze on her laptop screen, Trang continued in a sardonic tone, "Wow, Emmeline pissed someone off. Unheard of."

Sadie snorted. They were quiet for a moment as Trang clacked away on her keyboard. Then Sadie suddenly remembered. "Oh! I kept meaning to thank you."

Trang gave a confused frown. "For what?"

"That day in the dining hall. You really saved me there. I'd been... totally zoning out and I would've been *so* late if you hadn't shaken me out of it. So, yeah, thank you. I really appreciate it."

For maybe the first time, Trang really seemed to focus on Sadie. Honestly, Sadie had never gotten the vibe that Trang was rude or antisocial, just extremely cautious. Like everyone around her had the potential to be disappointing or ask for something she couldn't give.

"You're welcome," Trang finally said.

A seed of hope sprouted in Sadie's chest. "Are you working on Anthropology? I just fell asleep in the library reading Herodotus."

It was Trang's turn to snort. "That old fart would put anyone to sleep."

"I know, right?" Sadie laughed. "Well, except for the Battle of Thermopylae."

"Yeah, we can't all be Spartans, though." Trang shifted on her bed and shot Sadie a side-eye. "I'm working on my Cradle of Civilization essay."

"Oh! I finished mine yesterday. Do you..." Sadie stopped herself, then pushed forward nervously. "Need help? Maybe we could swap when you're done."

Trang regarded her for a moment before giving her a slow nod. "That'd be helpful."

"Great!" There was another beat of awkwardness before Sadie cleared her throat. She didn't want this interaction to end so soon. "So...um...has Emmeline pissed you off?"

Sadie instantly regretted her words. Trang's brows furrowed and she glared at her computer.

"I just thought...based on what you said..."

"She thinks she knows everything," Trang said. "Like what she said about Ramon's family and whether he could afford Almus Terra next year. I mean, she shouldn't assume one way or the other."

"Agreed," Sadie said softly. Sadie sensed it was far more personal than Ramon's family, but this relationship was new, and she didn't want to ask any more than Trang wanted to share.

They fell into a lapse of silence and Sadie searched for something else to say, anything....Suddenly a sports announcer's blaring voice cut through the silence and Trang lunged for her computer, desperate to silence a video that clearly started playing accidentally.

"And Reigns finishes with the Diamond Cutter! The headlock nearly—"

Trang stabbed her finger on the volume key, forgetting the mute button altogether in her haste, and gradually the announcer's voice faded to nothing. But it was too late.

Sadie sat there, momentarily lost for words. "Was that...pro-wrestling?" she asked after a minute.

Trang covered her face with her hands, clearly mortified. "Maybe."

In that moment Sadie realized she didn't just want to get to know Trang for the sake of filling a friend slot. She wanted to get to know Trang as a person.

Because a girl who happened to like both cozy task-management games *and* pro-wrestling was someone Sadie would surely regret not befriending.

With a grin, she leaned over and turned Trang's volume back up.

The next morning's breakfast was tense. And not just because Sadie and Emmeline kept shooting eye daggers at each other. Beyond that, the entire school seemed to be holding its breath. They'd all just received a memo outlining a massive change to the students' bylaws, voted on and approved by the student council.

Amendment Twenty-Three: Students accepted into Almus Terra on a scholarship, by the grace of the Academy's charity, are expected to take on custodial duties for any student-run club or organization, including but not limited to Mu Alpha Theta Club, Junior Classical League, ATA Astronomers, Thespians United, the robotics club...

And the list went on. It also included several new parts of castle upkeep that were usually done by staff. Apparently this amendment resulted in the dismissal of three full-time employees, saving Almus Terra thousands of dollars in salaries and benefits. But that work didn't just disappear. It was inherited by the Scholars.

"Oh, I bet the school board is just singing that bitch's praises right now," Oakley seethed, not so quietly, at the table over their breakfast. She speared a veggie sausage and started cutting at it viciously, the squeak of the metal knife on glass piercing.

"Babe, chill," Danica whispered, noticing everyone else glancing at their table.

"I will *not*. This is abhorrent." Oakley stabbed her fork in Emmeline's direction. "I thought you were supposed to prevent this kind of thing. Being on the council and all."

Emmeline was back to looking perfect. Maybe even more gorgeous than usual, if possible. "This has been in motion since last year. No way could I stop an amendment three weeks in," she said calmly.

"You should've at least tried," Oakley replied.

Emmeline inspected a nail. "Are you blaming me for something you could've prevented yourself? Let me guess, you had a chance to be on the council last year, but you turned it down. And now you're feeling guilty? Don't put that on me."

Danica sucked in a breath. Oakley stood, slamming her hands down on the table and making dishware rattle. "Screw you, Emmeline."

With that, Oakley grabbed her breakfast tray, turned, and left, Danica following behind. All around, murmurings erupted, but not just from Oakley's outburst. Arguments and complaints in hushed voices. To Sadie, it felt like a tectonic range getting ready to split. Dissent as thick and poisonous as magma destined to explode.

Though Sadie wanted to support her peers, she knew she was already on thin ice. Taking a stand against the student council when she had detention? Maybe not her best move.

A red sunset and a slowly rotating silhouette flashed through her mind, and Sadie bowed her head and picked at her breakfast. She had to stay at Almus Terra, no matter what. There was no going back. No one to go back to.

18

ALARIC

It took two weeks for the rage to recede to a place inside where Alaric could release it, controlled, on the track. Where he could run until his lungs nearly burst. Like if he only ran just a *bit* faster, he might turn back time.

But he wasn't some superhero. Even though Jacob's cheers made him feel like one.

"Eleven point eight seconds—Alaric, that's amazing!" Jacob jumped and punched the air, letting out a whoop.

It wasn't anywhere near Olympic levels, but Alaric was satisfied just hitting the asphalt hard enough to neither hear nor feel anything else.

He caught the towel Jacob threw at him and wiped down his neck, breathing through the burning in his lungs.

"Go again?" Jacob asked, holding up the stopwatch.

"Jaysus, are yeh tryin' to kill me? Nah, I'm done. Let's go." He slung the towel over his shoulder and grabbed his water bottle, Jacob following him like a pup.

In truth, he didn't mind. Ever since they'd bonded over their favorite band, Jacob sought him out—in the dining hall, in corridors between classes, in the bailey or ramparts, where Alaric would stretch out and listen to music. At first he worried the fourteen-year-old would be annoying, but Jacob was anything but. He was a sharp kid—studying robotics—and seemed to like a lot of the things Alaric did, like electronica, anime, graphic novels.

Slowly, Jacob introduced Alaric to other Scholars he knew, and it began to feel a bit like being back in Dublin. Having friends, talking about shows and music, complaining about teachers and homework. It felt *normal*, not like the royal hell that had brought him here. On good days, Ashland and his sorry excuse for a family only crossed his mind a few times. On the best days, he forgot about them entirely.

"Jacob." Alaric shut his gym locker and shouldered his bag, frowning at the younger boy. "Oy, what are yeh doing?"

Jacob was nearly ready to fall into the laundry bin, his torso tipping over its edge as he dug for nasty, rank towels, then tossed them into a cart. "Taking these down to wash."

Alaric cocked an eyebrow. "Isn't that someone's job?" He'd been using the gym facilities almost every other day and not once did he clock students doing the laundry themselves.

Unearthing the last towel, Jacob gave him a funny look. "Didn't you read the schoolwide email from this morning?"

No. Alaric didn't care what those council tools had to say. Alaric pulled out his phone and with every word he read, a familiar rage crept up inside him. He let out a string of expletives so foul that Jacob dropped his armload of towels.

Amendment twenty-three might have been the thing that tipped Alaric over the edge. Ever since he was young, he'd found outlets for his anger. A drunk foster dad hits you? Find a bully targeting a weaker kid and hit him instead. A neighbor blames you for cigarettes on her lawn when you don't even smoke? Spray-paint the side of her garage. A social worker yells when you're kicked out of another home? Escape into a make-believe world in your mind.

He'd coped. He'd survived. But meeting his father, hearing those words that made everything inside him crack, feeling Sadie's trembling arms trying to hold him together...it all just kept building and building. And now his only friend was made to dig through dirty laundry.

It was too much. He went back and ran some more, until he thought he was going to pass out. He showered a second time. He pushed the foul-smelling laundry cart downstairs and started the machines. He went to the dining hall. He stood, not getting a dinner tray, not sitting down, just staring and leaning against the wall, watching everyone eat, rage expanding in his stomach.

Until a girl he recognized passed by—Lotta, of all people. The one who harassed him for photos. Without a second thought, he grabbed her tray and slammed it against the wall. The contents underneath exploded in shattering glass, splattering food, and splashing liquid. Lotta stepped back, eyes wide, but not a single speck landed on her. Instead, the mess dripped down the stone wall and onto the floor.

Alaric let the tray fall, plate pieces and silverware clattering to the ground. The entire dining hall went completely silent. Every pair of shocked eyes on him.

"Damn," he said with a dramatic sigh, arms folded, looking down at the broken dishware and smashed food near his trainers. "What a mess."

No one said a word, uncertain of what he'd do next, but eager to find out.

Rolling his shoulders, Alaric stepped toward one of the middle tables. He found a C-Suite, the daughter of a rich Singapore landowner, took her half-eaten lunch of cooked vegetables and dumped it on the ground. She gasped as he grabbed the sandwich of a German functionary's son and smushed it into the table. The boy had simply frozen mid-chew while his fries tumbled to the floor.

When he turned to an Elite from America—the vice president's son—the kid sprang from his seat and said, "What the *hell*, man?"

"Oh, sorry." Alaric stepped back, looking around in mock surprise. "Aye, made a right mess there, haven't I? S'pose yeh want me to clean it up?"

"Of course—*you* freaking did it," the guy—Alaric finally remembered his name, Roderick—snarled.

"An excellent point." At that, Alaric clapped him on the shoulder and used the position to hoist himself onto the nearest table. Sidestepping someone's glass of water, Alaric casually walked down the long dining table. Kids slid away from the benches, away from his imposing presence, some even standing back from their tables to stare up at him.

"And that's pretty logical, right? If yeh made a mess, yeh should clean it up yerself?" he asked the dining hall, not even needing to raise his voice. The hall was deadly quiet as he scanned the sea of his peers.

Alaric's gaze landed briefly on Sadie, who sat two tables down. She stared back at him with wide eyes and parted lips, but he quickly looked away. Other familiar faces jumped out as well—Jacob's friends, Bea and Assane, Emmeline . . .

Her eyes narrowed, but she gave nothing away. What any of them thought, Alaric didn't care. He was done comparing himself—to her, to them.

"But why is this school so special?" he asked. "Why is it that after a club meeting, or the end of a filthy day in the locker room"—he found Jacob's stunned face—"we get others to clean up our messes? Because, Roderick, IF yeh recall," Alaric spun, pointing to the American Elite, who stared back with an open mouth like a fish, "a new amendment says *I* don't have to clean this up. All because I was born with a golden spoon lodged down my throat."

Murmurs resumed throughout the dining hall. Soft, but Alaric could feel the energy begin to sizzle among the crowd, reminding him of before a concert when the headliner took the stage.

"Alaric!"

Slowly, Alaric rotated toward the sound of the voice—behind him, near the doors to the dining hall. His golden counterpart, Titus, stood there flanked by a South Asian boy and a pale blond girl with pink-tinged curls. They looked at Alaric with murder in their eyes.

Alaric just grinned. "Cousin, thanks for joining us."

"You're making a fool of yourself. Get down."

"Right. I should probably pose for photos, yeh? Lord knows they'll be taken without my permission anyway." At that, Alaric crouched down and held out both hands with his middle fingers extended. As expected, several students raised their phones.

"*Alaric!*"

"Oh, fine," he said, rolling his eyes, and he jumped off the table, his swagger cool and measured until he reached Titus. "I'm glad yer here, actually. Maybe the lot of yeh can tell us: Why do Elites and C-Suites not want to clean up after themselves?"

Utter silence followed. Titus's jaw tightened, but he didn't step back. The two leaders of the student council said nothing, but Alaric could see the gears turning behind the blond girl's gaze. Looking for weakness. She'd find none.

"Is it because we think we're better?" With every word, Alaric began to raise his voice. "Better because our parents have enough money to pay? Better than the kids who studied till their eyes bled and labored to make ends meet?" More buzzing energy from the surrounding crowd. Students parted for Alaric to turn away from his cousin and step back onto the table. "ATA is MESSED. UP."

He was shouting now, blood boiling under the surface.

"AND WE NEED TO CLEAN IT UP."

Then someone gave a whoop. More cheers followed, then words started to form. Alaric couldn't tell who started the chant, but it quickly gained momentum.

"ATA is messed up! Student council, clean it up!"

Now half the dining hall was standing, loud, angry, and gaining courage. Alaric was yelling the chant too, punctuating each word with a punch in the air.

"ATA IS MESSED UP. STUDENT COUNCIL, CLEAN IT UP."

Screams hit the twenty-foot-ceiling. Nearly a hundred students had swarmed the table where Alaric stood chanting. It lasted for a long time, long enough for the students to start getting hoarse, until a piercing whistle cut through the clamor and silence followed.

The headmistress had arrived.

Alaric stared at the same Japanese tea set from the last time he was in the headmistress's office. It was quite beautiful, though Alaric knew next to nothing about ceramics. Veins of shimmery gold spiderwebbed through the cups, creating the most elegant, hypnotic patterns.

It was easier to lose himself in art than to think about what might happen next. He wouldn't be surprised if expulsion was on the table.

"It's called kintsugi."

"What?" Alaric asked, looking up at Headmistress Aquila, who sat at her desk, her pen flying across papers.

"Mending broken pottery—my tea set—with gold-infused lacquer. It's the Japanese practice of honoring the flaws and imperfections of the object, rather than trying to hide it. The cracks are part of its history. Quite lovely, isn't it?"

Alaric sat back, staring at the tea set with renewed interest. "Uh... yeah."

"So, Alaric, that performance was quite impressive."

His head snapped over to her. "Uh... thanks?"

Headmistress Aquila did not even look up from her papers. "I believe most of the students have cleared out by now. You're dismissed."

Alaric stared at her, confused. "Yeh mean dismissed from the Academy, right?"

More pen strokes, scratching across paper. "No. Dismissed from my office."

"Yer not...expelling me?"

Finally, she met his gaze. "Is that what you'd like?"

"I...no. But...I don't get it."

With a sigh, Almus Terra's headmistress set down her pen and looked over at him, a hint of annoyance evident on her features. "Listen, Alaric, what did I say at the start of the term? We're in the business of creating world leaders here. The student council exists to allow students to learn how to govern in as realistic a setting as possible. Some leaders invoke change by starting revolutions—case in point. How would this simulation be realistic if I'd interfered with either side—no matter my personal beliefs?"

Alaric stared at the woman with her sharp eyes and her black and purple and gray braids, and for the first time he was beginning to understand her. Understand this academy.

For good measure, he stated the obvious, just to see what she'd say. "But it's unfair to the Scholars."

A smile curved at her lips. "Then they bloody well ought to *do* something about it."

19

SADIE

"Here you go, Sadie," Jacob said, handing her a new sponge.

"Thanks, Jacob." After removing the drying pasta and specks of vodka sauce with chopped parsley with her previous sponge, Sadie took the new one and glided it across the wall, creating a streak of warm soapy water.

Sadie had a mountain of homework to do, but when she noticed a few students' not leaving the dining hall after the "Scholar Rally," as many had started to call it, she'd lingered. Sure enough, those who had stayed knew Alaric—one in particular, Jacob, seemed to know him fairly well—and were so moved by his actions they wanted to help absorb the damage.

Every so often, someone, usually Assane, a boy with dark brown skin and a thick Senegalese accent, would pull up the Academy forums on his phone and start reading out comments. "Oooh, listen to this one. 'Alaric Eldana's rhetoric was extremely effective in showing the injustice that's been happening at ATA for years. The *Norms* have no business serving their peers. All students should be responsible for making the school a better place. Just as we aspire for the world. Let's start here.'"

Bea tossed back her head of green curls and laughed. "Yeah, but did you see the memes with Alaric flipping the birds? 'Not Today, Oligarchy'?"

Jacob held up his phone. "Those are gold. My favorite is 'Who's got two fingers and wants to start a revolution?'"

"No, the best is 'That moment when you're flipping off Calixa and everyone cheers'!"

The small group of friends paused their work, all joining in on the laughter. After the misery of the morning, it was nice to witness such solidarity. This surge of optimism and hope was important. Sadie only wished she'd had the courage to join their chants.

As she scrubbed harder, trying to get particularly stubborn vegetable puree off the wall, a large hand plucked the sponge from her fingers.

"Oy, what're yeh doin'?"

Sadie glanced up to find Alaric standing over her, a deep scowl on his face.

"What's it *look* like I'm doing?" she huffed, bouncing on her toes to grab back her sponge.

But he pulled it higher out of reach. With a squeeze, the soapy water trickled down his fingers and wrist.

"And the rest of yeh—what the hell?" he barked at Jacob, Bea, and Assane.

They stopped and glanced at one another. Then Jacob brightened and waved his phone in the air with a huge grin. "Alaric! You're a meme!"

Like he did on the dining tables an hour before, Alaric stalked toward them with all the brute power and natural authority he inherently possessed and yanked away Assane's mop.

"Did yeh miss my whole *feckin point*? I'll clean up my *own* mess," he growled.

Sadie frowned as the three friends exchanged uncomfortable glances. "Don't be a jerk. They wanted to help."

Alaric rounded back on her, his eyes flashing. "I didn't ask for help."

"Friends don't have to ask," Sadie said, folding her arms.

"Yeah, man, we just thought—" Jacob started.

"Well, yeh thought wrong," he said with a snarl. "Yer not meant to clean up mine or anyone's mess. Yeh don't work for me."

"Don't insult them, Alaric!" Sadie snapped back, striding toward him. It was unbelievable how he could do the right thing one minute, and then the next his spikes would flare up like a porcupine. "They know they don't work for you. It's a gesture of *kindness*. Ever heard of it?"

He cocked one scornful eyebrow at her. "And is that why *yer* here? Out of the goodness of yer heart?"

Sadie reeled back like she'd been slapped. He was mocking her. Rubbing it in her face that he'd been strong enough to do what she hadn't: Stand up and speak up.

Rage and shame sizzled across her skin, forcing a hot red flush across her cheeks and down her neck. This boy had a talent for eliciting physical reactions she couldn't contain. She reached into the nearest trash bin, seized a handful of mushy food, and chucked it with surprising precision.

Disgusting slop splattered Alaric square in the neck. Specks of veggie puree hit his jaw and juices of eggplant and pasta sauce dribbled over his shirt's neckline.

Jacob whispered, "Whoa," and Bea stifled a laugh, turning it into a cough.

Alaric stared at her, not moving. Without a word, Sadie stormed out of the dining hall. It was only when she stepped into the shower to wash off the smell of five global cuisines that she realized, *Oh butter biscuits. Sunday detention will be a reckoning.*

"You're shaking the table."

"Hmm?" Sadie looked up. Trang pointed to Sadie's knee with her pen, showing how it kept hitting the table and making it vibrate. "Oh, sorry!"

They were in a small self-study room reviewing each other's edits on their Cradle of Civilization essays. Sadie was distracted by her detention later that afternoon, and she hoped Trang wouldn't get annoyed by all her nervous ticks. It was their first official study session, and she didn't want it to be their last.

"Worried about your detention?" Trang asked, hitting the nail right on the head.

"Ugh. Maybe," Sadie groaned, dropping her head on the table.

"Why?" Trang glanced at their Anthropology book then back to her laptop screen. "You were in a decent mood after the last one."

"It's just... after the whole rally, Alaric said something insensitive, so I chucked food at his face," she mumbled.

Trang burst out laughing. "You didn't."

"I did," Sadie said miserably.

"Then you better watch your back. What's the assignment today?"

"Prying barnacles off an old boat down by one of the piers in the village."

"I'll keep an eye out for corpses along the coast."

"Trang!"

"I'm kidding!" Trang exclaimed, giggling, which made Sadie smile in turn. "Okay, but in all seriousness, Alaric seems like a decent guy. I mean, all the stuff he said back there was right. Do you stand behind what you said?"

Sadie nodded, tapping her pencil on her notebook. "Yes, he was being mean to his friends. That's inexcusable."

"Well, there you go. If he's really a decent guy, he'll own his mistake."

It was good advice. And a good segue. "Speaking of the rally... what'd you think?" Sadie truly didn't care about Trang's social stratum, but she could still be curious.

Trang frowned slightly and tilted her head, hair falling down her shoulder. "You want to know if I'm a C-Suite or a Scholar, don't you?"

"No!" Sadie denied quickly, then sighed at Trang's pointed look. "Not really, I mean. I just want to get to know you."

And know if you want to be friends as much as I do.

"My background matters that much?" she shot back, her tone sharp. Then she stood and started to gather her things. "Maybe we should just—"

"Wait!" Sadie jumped up, almost knocking over her chair. "This whole heir thing makes it hard to know if anyone really...I didn't mean to insinuate. What I mean is...I'm sorry."

After a moment of hesitation, Trang sat back down, and Sadie followed suit. The two girls regarded each other before Trang finally sighed, glancing away. "The truth is I'm kind of both."

"Both what?" Sadie asked.

"Scholar and C-Suite." Trang stared at the table, curling a long strand of hair around her finger. "My family has a long history of attending Almus Terra. But recently...our company's been struggling. My father is a proud man, though, and he loves me so much. He wants me to go to ATA, but the money just isn't there. Luckily, he was able to negotiate a sort of payment plan with the headmistress. In a way, I'm halfway on a scholarship and the other half..."

Sadie quickly shook her head. "No, I get it. I wouldn't even be here myself if not for the king. Thanks for telling me. I didn't mean to force it out of you."

It made sense now why Trang closed herself off from others. In a school like Almus Terra (or any prep school, she supposed) if you didn't fit neatly into one category, you felt like an outsider.

Trang rested her chin on her palm and smiled. "S'okay. I kinda wanted it off my chest anyway. And for the record, I don't have ulterior motives in this friendship. You can be straight with me. I might not be forthcoming about my life, but I'd never lie about it either."

One thousand percent, Sadie believed her. Maybe it helped that she wanted to, but mostly it was because Trang seemed genuine in every way. When she was upset, she *acted* upset. And once she opened up about the things she liked, she didn't shut up about them. That one night, Sadie had to finally cut Trang off at one AM when she was still explaining the differences between the Dallas Diamond Cutter versus the RKO created by infamous pro-wrestler Randy Orton.

"So, uh," Trang started, pointing at Sadie's laptop, "you done reviewing my final edits? I want to turn this thing in and get it over with."

"Oh yeah! Let me just—" Sadie's ringing phone interrupted her. She glanced at the number, readying to silence a spam call, but when she saw the ID she jumped out of her chair. "Sorry, I have to take this."

Sadie stepped outside of their little classroom and answered. "Hello? This is Sadie."

"Sadie Aurelia?" The tone was sharp. "As in one of the heirs all over the news?"

She winced. Tucked away at Almus Terra, she forgot about all the publicity. Most of her social media feeds were curated to content she wanted to see—and she hadn't wanted to see herself at all.

"Y-yes."

There was a crackle of static over the phone like someone was blowing out a harsh, annoyed breath. "Is this some kind of joke?"

"I'm sorry?"

"The new heir of Ashland wants to help my little charity free of charge?" The woman—she assumed Mrs. Colliander, president of the Ashland Sea Mammal Conservation—snorted. "If this is a prank, thank you for wasting my time."

"N-no, it's not!" Sadie cried, desperate to keep her on the phone. "Mrs. Colliander, hang on. Please. I've long admired the ASMC, and I really do want to help. I've gotten pretty good at web content management, and I can help run your social media accounts. I'm not asking for money—er, clearly I don't need it." It wasn't like Sadie was personally rich, but she had no needs at Almus Terra.

"It would be hard to have long admired the ASMC since it was only founded—"

"Two years and eleven months ago," Sadie finished for her. "Your work to save the North Atlantic right whales is really inspiring."

Sadie took the silence on the other end of the line as surprise, and quickly pushed forward. "I realize this is a little unconventional, Mrs. Colliander, and honestly I didn't think of the whole royal heir thing until this moment. But I...I miss home." *And I was really lonely when I came up with this idea.* "And I love sea animals. My grannah used to take me to watch the sea lions in the harbor at Farach. If you're willing to trust me with your accounts, I can help."

The idea to volunteer for a charity she loved came from her talk with Oliver in the library, and her philanthropic project with Titus had only reinforced her desire to do more. Plus, she'd spent so much of her time studying alone, she wanted to feel connected to something. Even to Ashland, though it was still painful. But because it was a cause she loved, that made it easier.

"Very well." The woman's tone was still stern. "But I want approval from the king's office for this. I won't have my charity take the fall because your involvement isn't—I don't know—sanctioned or something. If I get written approval, I'll give you access."

"Let me put you in touch with Ms. Halvorsen—she'll get you whatever you need. Thank you *so* much, ma'am."

"Mm-hmm." Mrs. Colliander hung up, clearly not the warmest of people. But she had to be tough. Her charity was something she did in her own time. The Ashland economy had improved but was still so fractured. Charities were rare and certainly couldn't offer people full-time work.

Sadie didn't care, though. She was excited to help. Plus, posting content about adorable baby seals and otters and majestic whales was hardly work. Slipping her phone into her pocket, Sadie headed back into the classroom to work with Trang. *Eat your heart out, Aquaman.*

Because Sadie didn't want to chance meeting Alaric on the way, she headed to detention earlier than she had to. In a cruel twist of irony, he must have had a similar notion, because he was already there, wearing gloves and sitting cross-legged next to the boat. A scraper was already in his hand, and he dug its metal edge into the hardened calcium plates. With care, Sadie stepped around the bow and sat on the other side, toward the stern and as far from him as possible.

He glanced up but said nothing as she sat and picked up her tools. The sound of scraping and the lapping of gentle waves against the docks filled the tense silence between them.

Sadie would *not* be the first to talk. He'd pushed her buttons one too many times and he deserved gross food all over his stupid muscular chest.

Except with each passing minute, Sadie grew angrier. Was this *it* for the rest of the semester? Sundays spent in annoyed silence while doing semi-manual labor? She wanted to scream.

Instead, she hacked at the barnacles with vigor. Bits of calcium flew every whichway as she attacked the hardened crust with all the frustration she couldn't verbalize.

"Oy, oy, oy!" Alaric finally shouted, leaning across the boat and snatching away her scraper, just like he did the sponge. Which only infuriated her more. "Yer going to damage the hull."

"No I'm not," Sadie snapped. "Give it *back*."

"Yeah, nah," he drawled, spinning the scraper in his large palm. "I think I'll hang onto my future murder weapon."

Sadie leapt to her feet. "You are the WORST. You better have apologized to Jacob and his friends. They did a nice thing because they actually *like* you. God knows why, but they do."

"Oy, hang on—" he started, getting to his feet, but she wasn't done.

"They look up to you for taking a stand on behalf of all the other Scholars, and I—I did too. Maybe I was too much of a coward to do anything like that myself, but I thought you were amazing. And I was inspired. I thought if I hung around to clean up, I'd find the courage to tell you as much. But noooo, you had to go and pooh-pooh all over—"

She was cut off by Alaric's bare hand scooping behind her neck and jerking her face up to his. He'd been moving closer to her as she ranted, peeling off his gloves, but she'd ignored his advances, never dreaming he'd do something like *this.*

Sadie closed her eyes, bracing herself, but at the very last second, he stopped just shy of kissing her. Instead, his forehead pressed upon hers. His nose brushed against hers as warm breath clouded her face in faint steam, a result of the chilly seaside air.

His other hand gripped her upper arm, while her gloved palms pressed against his chest, her heart racing. "Wh-what are you doing?"

Had he been about to kiss her? Had he thought better of it? Or maybe he was still debating? Sadie felt her stomach swoop at the idea. Like the possibility of being a royal heir: It was incomprehensible. Kissing Alaric Eldana did not compute.

Alaric's fingers dug gently into the base of her skull—it felt like he was playing with the hair that had escaped from her ponytail. His mouth tilted up into a crooked grin, and against her wishes, her heartbeat skipped.

"Seeing what it takes to shut yeh up."

UGH!

Sadie slapped his chest and tried to push him away. But they were on a dock surrounded by a barnacle-covered boat and ice-cold water, and there wasn't that much space, so Alaric held onto her even tighter.

"Easy there," he murmured, sliding the hand that held her arm over to her waist and expertly moving her away from the edge. "No need to get all riled up again. Can't have yeh taking us both into the sea every week."

"You're. An. Ass," she seethed, but stopped struggling. He was too darn strong.

"What, yeh can hold on to me, but I can't hold on to yeh?"

Sadie went quiet, her anger doused the way sand smothers a fire. That was the first time he'd referenced their moment in the office. When she'd thrown her arms around Alaric to stop him from doing something he'd regret forever. How he'd trembled under her hold. Her heart broke for him a little.

At her silence, Alaric gave her another squeeze. "Nah, Sadie, don't be gettin' all pitiful on me."

With a jolt of surprise, Sadie looked up, their faces too close for comfort. But she stayed put. Her eyes moved between his dark ones, searching for something.

"Is that what you think? That I pity you?"

His brows furrowed, something flashing across his features that Sadie couldn't identify. Then he shook his head. "Not...anymore. I mean, yeh just called me amazing."

"Yeah, well, now you're back to being a jerk."

With a chuckle so light Sadie almost didn't catch it, he released her and handed back her scraper.

"Yes I did," he said, crouching down and picking up his gloves.

"Did what?" she asked.

He sighed. "I did apologize to Jacob."

Pleased, Sadie knelt back down. It seemed that perhaps Trang had been right. He was a decent guy. "And Bea and Assane?"

He rolled his eyes but nodded.

A needle of jealousy poked Sadie's heart. Alaric had already found friends who seemed to like him for who he was. Maybe even in spite of *who* he was. Sadie barely had one. She wasn't best friends with Trang, but she hoped to get there.

"I deserve an apology too," she said, turning her scraper back to the barnacles.

He snorted. "I'm sure yeh will live."

"Fine. I take back what I said entirely." She snapped a barnacle off and flung it into the water behind her. "You *weren't* amazing. You sounded arrogant and condescending."

Alaric clicked his tongue. "Can't have that. Too much like your boyfriend."

With a forced swallow, she said, "Titus is not my boyfriend. Those are rumors."

"The pictures from the library look pretty real."

Sadie's stomach roiled and she leaned against the hull, feeling sick. *Pictures?* She hadn't seen those. But she knew gossip traveled like wildfire. Case in point, Lotta went through the trouble of ruining her (only) nice outfit.

Still, the idea of dating Titus Eldana made her brain short-circuit. Like kissing Alaric Eldana. *Incomprehensible.* They were her princes. Ashland's princes. Despite what the king decreed, she was not on their level. Nor even their same stratosphere.

"He was getting an eyelash."

Ha. That didn't sound convincing even to her own ears.

"Aye, cailín," Alaric said, flinging a barnacle over his shoulder. "Whatever yeh say."

20

EMMELINE

"Just go, babe. You can do it. Apologize. Be strong."

Emmeline looked up from her laptop. She was in between Bach pieces filtering through her earbuds, and the voices on the other side of the door were loud and clear.

"It's so much easier when you're dating someone. Because then you get to do fun stuff afterward," another voice grumbled—Oakley.

Eager to get this over with, Emmeline put her tech away and wrenched the door open to find Oakley and Danica standing there.

Enough was enough. "Oakley, I'm sorry I was so harsh. I hated you thinking I didn't care about the amendment," Emmeline said quickly and with practice. It had been in her head awhile.

As much as she hated to admit vulnerability, she missed Oakley. And it had been an awkward and lonely couple of days since their waspish argument a few mornings ago. She'd already spent far too many hours out in the archery fields, letting her arrows fly with her anger. Time to move on.

Oakley blinked, shocked. Then, recovering quickly, she launched herself at Emmeline and squeezed her tight around the neck. "I'm sorry too, Emmie. I totally overreacted. It was unreasonable of me to put all that on your shoulders. I mean"—Oakley drew back and smirked—"not even hot royal revolutionaries can take down the oligarchy in a day, right?"

Irritation flooded Emmeline's veins like a hit of morphine, but she forced a smirk right back. "Right."

All weekend she'd had to pretend to be as impressed with Alaric as everyone else. It was a delicate dance. She wasn't about to have Oakley find out that she disagreed with Alaric's actions, and she couldn't let the student council hear her support Alaric's rally.

In truth, she was infuriated. Alaric had managed to do the one thing that governments feared most: Incite a revolution.

He'd started with some clever rhetoric and low-grade destruction, but his movement was growing. On the forums, in classes, in clubs, the Scholars were no longer putting their heads down. They fulfilled their responsibilities, but always with sass and sarcasm. They had taken Alaric's words to heart. The school was messed up, and they weren't going to be subjugated by C-Suites or Elites. Which, in turn, was making the other two factions absolutely incensed.

So much so that an emergency council meeting was called for this coming Thursday. Emmeline dreaded it. As much as she agreed with Oakley and Alaric in the general sense, she was still too wary to pledge her support. Their trip to Ashland was approaching and she didn't want to do *anything* to upset her grandfather. The king could either dismiss Alaric for throwing food like a child or admire him for provoking change like a revolutionary. Impossible to predict.

"Okay, so now that the awkward make-up convo is out of the way," Oakley said giddily, grabbing Emmeline's jacket on the chair and tossing it to her, "come pick some produce from Danica's garden so we can sell it at the village farmers market."

Of course Oakley was in a great mood. She'd loved Alaric's speech. Despite being a C-Suite, she was the Scholars' biggest supporter and one of the amendment's biggest opponents.

Needing a break from her studies, Emmeline shrugged on her jacket and followed her friends down to the greenhouses.

As soon as she entered the glass dome with its towering plants, humid air, and neat rows of crops, she wanted to turn right back around. The soil and herbs and fall sunshine, all of it made her think of Oliver. Every time Emmeline thought of him lately, her stomach gave a painful clench. They had not spoken since that night. And she imagined they might never speak again. Remembering the look on his face when he came through the door, Sebastian's hands on her— it all played in a recurring nightmarish loop when she let her guard down.

It was probably for the best, though. It's not as if Oliver, with his lack of pedigree and connections, was a viable partner for the Ashland princess—no matter how often she thought of his warm brown eyes and callused hands. She couldn't get attached to someone who wouldn't impress her grandfather.

So she brushed the longing aside and helped Oakley and Danica pack up carrots, potatoes, squash, and cucumbers into several large sustainable cloth bags and heave them onto a cart. Because the greenhouses were located at the bottom of the hill on the edge of the castle grounds, they only had to take a short gravel road to reach the outskirts of the village.

The shops were cute and quaint, made of old stone and brick that looked hundreds of years old. But the sky-blue paint and coral terracotta shingles were new. Or as new as the turn of the century. Wood signs hung out front—boutiques that claimed to sell fashion from Milan and Paris, handmade artisanal furniture, and Venetian glass. Stalls for the farmers market were set out in the tiny square. Cheese from Italy, wine from Paris, fresh-caught fish, local herbs, handmade jewelry, pottery, candles, bath salts—it was quite an operation.

Oakley caught the look on Emmeline's face and smiled proudly.

"A lot of these are student-run. Like the art club has an entire booth where they sell their work."

"Sell to whom?" Emmeline wondered out loud. The village was tiny. She doubted locals had disposable income to splurge on art students' paintings.

Danica stopped pushing her cart of vegetables and pointed toward the docks, where a ferry was coming in. "Every Sunday, the island is open to tourists. Except during the off-season, which starts in November. Tourists aren't allowed anywhere near ATA, but they can go to spots around the coast to take pictures of the castle. Mostly, though, they shop at the market."

Emmeline didn't have a clue, but then her focus was always elsewhere. Either on her studies, the student council, her rivals, or her still-silent parents.

Danica made a beeline to a booth with an elderly French woman who wore a brightly colored handwoven shawl. As Danica greeted the woman in French and began to set up their vegetables with price tags, Emmeline inspected the delicious-smelling sourdough bread, rosemary rolls, and chocolate croissants in tidy baskets across the table. In front of the woman was a sleek white tablet set up to process credit cards. Based on their rapid conversation in French, Emmeline picked up that the students had supplied Madame Rosseau with the tech to sell her goods so long as she sold the horticulture club's vegetables and donated the club's profits and leftover produce to a local food bank in Marseille.

Sure enough, throughout the market, Emmeline saw students working and interacting with vendors. It had been a long time since she'd done any leisurely shopping, and Emmeline was itching to explore, but then she spotted something five stalls over that made her heart stop.

It was the same shattering crash that had occurred a week ago. In the hallway, in front of her dorm room. Sadie and Oliver.

There they were again. Oliver was bent over an old man's laptop, his dark brows furrowed in that sinfully attractive mix of concentration and dedication. Sadie leaned over the table, the end of her braid touching Oliver's shoulder as she watched him work. She said something and Oliver glanced up at her, cracking an easy, handsome smile.

Emmeline's chest tightened, as did her throat, resulting in a harsh stinging sensation in her eyes. Blinking rapidly, she turned her back on them.

"Emmie, you've got to try this sourdough. An ATA student from San Francisco taught Madame how to make it like twenty years ago. Tastes just like the States. Give it a burl," Oakley shoved a piece of fluffy white bread and rock-solid crust near her face.

Emmeline jerked back, feeling nauseated. "Uh, next time. I'm not feeling well suddenly."

"Cramps?" Oakley started digging in her fanny pack. "Hang on—I think I have Midol."

"I just need to lie down, thanks." Before anyone had a chance to respond, Emmeline started across the square, maneuvering around students, booths, and incoming tourists.

She really *wasn't* feeling well, but lying down or Midol was not going to help her. A feeling of loss spread from the center of her chest. Silent, yawning, and devastatingly infinite—a chasm growing inside her, consuming everything precious.

Halfway up to the castle, Emmeline stopped and pressed her hand against a tree, steadying herself. She tried to push the feeling out, out with the pain and the bitterness of seeing that girl with yet another person who should be Emmeline's.

First her cousins, and now Oliver. Sadie seemed to be close with every person who should belong to Emmeline.

Just stop, she urged herself.

It wasn't logical for her to feel so possessive. It's not as if Emmeline wanted Alaric and Titus romantically (ew)—the way she wanted

Oliver—but they were her family. Rivals or not, they shared blood. Perhaps they couldn't be best friends or have a normal family life, but they were still *hers*. Not Sadie's.

Though Emmeline couldn't remember how she'd gotten there, somehow she ended up back in her dorm room and was dialing.

Dialing. Yes. *No*. She shouldn't. But she had the phone number memorized and her fingers were already flying across the glass screen.

Emmeline's breath came out in rapid bursts as the phone rang thousands of miles away and right next to her ear.

The ringing stopped. "Hello?"

It was a woman's voice. Elegant, slightly accented, clipped, *regal*. Emmeline's stomach seized and she almost hung up. Her heart was careening off a cliff, brakes screeching and horn blaring. *Don't say it. Don't say it.*

"Mother?" she said, breathless.

There was a slight pause. "Is this Princess Emmeline?"

Emmeline's eyes slipped shut, her heart meeting the rocks at the bottom of the cliff, exploding in fire and smoke and ash. Her mother would never refer to her like that.

"Yes," Emmeline said, trying to steel her shaky voice.

"Ah, I see. How wonderful to meet you. I'm Georgiana, your mother's private secretary."

Emmeline dragged her rose-pink nails across her forehead. "This isn't my mother's private number? Ms. Halvorsen gave it to me weeks ago."

There was a tapping sound, as if Georgiana was typing, distracted. "No, Your Highness. Your mother gives out her private number herself. I'm not allowed to distribute it."

Emmeline squeezed her phone so hard she imagined it cracking. "Not even to her daughter?"

There was silence over the phone. Emmeline sank into her desk chair, staring into nothingness. "I see," she muttered.

It had been a month since her parents received Emmeline's contact information. Weeks since she sent that email. *Years* since she first dreamed of meeting them. Of knowing them.

Georgiana said something, but Emmeline ended the call. She was angry at her parents and hurt and *hateful,* and she wasn't sure where to direct it.

Then her eyes landed on the desk across the room—Sadie's. All neat and tidy with a few cute notebooks and a pencil stand decorated with images of a cartoon sea lion. Her laptop sat in its charging station unguarded.

Emotions so sharp they tasted like metal had Emmeline unplugging Sadie's laptop, tucking it under her arm, and ducking out of the dorm. Had her speed-walking across the western ramparts, down the old stone steps to the craggy rock shore. Had her reeling back and throwing the laptop as hard and as far as she could.

Had her not thinking about the consequences. Had her not *caring.*

The computer cracked and bounced on the sharp rocks, its sleek metal parts disappearing into the frothy white waves. Like she suspected Titus had done with his phone, Emmeline sought to destroy. Not incriminating evidence, but her competition's work and success, and maybe her happiness. Because Sadie didn't deserve any of it.

Emmeline might deserve it even less, but no one could accuse her of not trying. Trying to be what she thought her parents wanted her to be. Not that they cared enough to tell her one way or another.

21

SADIE

"You didn't have to help, you know," Oliver said, carefully setting the old laptop into one of the tech room's many drawers.

"Sorry, did I slow you down?" Sadie stood back as Oliver dug around for a bulky battery pack.

"That's not what I meant. I just figured you had homework to get to rather than helping the software club. Midterms are next week."

Sadie shrugged. Yes, she *did* have loads of studying, but she was doing well in her classes, and she'd managed to finish her next big section for the Philanthropy project with Titus.

After detention with Alaric, she figured she had time to check out the farmers market. In her wanderings, she had run into Oliver, and he'd explained that the software club, of which he was a member, helped maintain the vendors' tech. It was one of the many symbiotic relationships that ATA students had with the outside community. Curious, she'd asked to tag along as he made several visits to old fishermen and artisans selling their wares, none of whom had any clue how to log in to their payment processing platforms.

But alas, at the mention of midterms, Sadie was forced to confront reality. With a sigh, she checked her watch. "This was fun. But I probably should get back. See you later, Oliver."

They parted with a friendly wave and Sadie headed to her dorm, devising a study plan for the evening as she walked. First, she'd take a hot shower and wash away the chilly salt air; next, she'd curl up with a mug of tea and study inflation graphs on her laptop for International Econ; then she'd read about the origin of *Sí, se puede!* (Yes, we can!), Dolores Huerta's slogan for the National Farmworker's Association in the United States, for her Advocacy Studies homework.

But those plans flew out the window the moment she tossed her jacket on the back of her chair and paused at the strangely vacant desk. Where was her laptop? She could've sworn she'd left it charging. With a frown, she crossed to her bag and dug around. Empty. *What the hell?*

Taking deep breaths, Sadie began to thoroughly tear through the room. She unmade her bed, thinking it might be in the inner depths of her sheets and covers. She looked under beds and rugs, rifled through drawers, and dug into closets.

With each place she looked, her anxiety grew. She thought of upcoming midterms and the email she'd just sent to Ms. Halvorsen and Mrs. Colliander about working for the Ashland Sea Mammal Conservation. She'd gone ahead and started designing a new website in the hopes that her help would be welcome. That was gone, too, if she didn't find her laptop.

After digging through her desk for the third time, she sat back on her heels and tried to fight off waves of panic. Could it be in the library? Another classroom? *No,* she very specifically remembered working at her desk this morning during a rare moment that she'd had the dorm room completely to herself and could play lo-fi music as loudly as she wanted. Had someone . . . taken it?

Sadie quickly dismissed the thought. There were no thieves at Almus Terra. Although . . . she did have a few enemies. Lotta, Remy, the girls from Titus's fan club, to name a few. Plus, Emmeline hated her to be sure, though stealing didn't really seem like her style. Not to mention, if the king found out, that surely wouldn't elevate her in his esteem.

But once the thought took root, another wave of alarm spread. Sadie lunged for her bedside table. Her hands clumsily pried open the bottom drawer, and she shoved aside some of her favorite graphic novels, a deck of Dutch playing cards, and her passport, then gripped the edges of a small, worn journal.

Sadie sagged with relief. Feeling the familiar leather binding and embossed letters slowed her heart rate. *This* was safe. She held her father's journal to her chest and let the scent of old paper fill her nose. It was safe.

"Sadie?"

With a gasp, Sadie fumbled the journal back into her drawer under the few other personal effects she'd brought from home.

"What's going on?"

Oakley stood in the doorway rightfully confused. The room was a mess. Sadie had torn it apart. Clothes, textbooks, shoes all sprawled across the floor in a way that looked a little manic.

Sadie swallowed, her gaze darting to Emmeline, who had appeared behind Oakley. The princess's expression was just as concerned as Oakley's, which set off a warning bell. Her acting was almost *too* good. Normally she'd look bored.

"My laptop is missing," Sadie said.

Oakley's brows knit together. "Ah, she'll be right. Let's look for it. You'll help too, yeah, Emmie?"

"Of course," Emmeline said.

For the next hour, the girls went through their room, top to bottom. All the while, Oakley hedged her with questions. "Are you sure you left it here?" "Maybe we should ask the admin staff to put out a note." "When was the last time you backed up your data to the cloud?"

At that terrifying thought, Sadie logged in to her student account in the cloud via Oakley's laptop. With a drop in her stomach, she realized the last time she backed up her data had been a week ago. She'd lost seven days' worth of work. Not to mention the website she'd started for the ASMC, and a few poems she'd written in her spare time.

Sadie sat there, somewhat numb, mentally calculating how far this would set her back, when Oakley squeezed her shoulder. "Sorry, Sadie. We're headed to dinner. No drama about the mess. We'll clean later. But might be best to give up now and report it stolen, yeah?"

Sadie didn't hear anything after *give up*. Those words were like triggers firing off in her brain, unlocking memories that she had to keep in a cage in order to function.

The door closed behind her roommates with a soft snap, but Sadie didn't hear it. She sat there trying to push back floods of panic. She couldn't remember how to breathe. Her lungs wouldn't cooperate.

A week's worth of work. Gone. Her breaths came out in short, stilted bursts. How could she possibly catch up? What if she flunked her midterms? What if that was enough to send her back to Ashland?

The room spun, dizziness making her crouch down to feel solid ground under her hands and knees as she fought for breath. *Back to Ashland.* Where would she live?

Flashes of those same merciless images whirled around in her head like a tornado. The bloodred sunset, the silhouette against the horizon, hands grabbing her shoulders as she tried in vain to pull at the rope, her fingers grappling for life, wanting to save, to do what she could, there had to be something, *anything*, please don't be . . .

Suddenly a sharp slap whipped her head to the side. Pain exploded on her cheek so hard and fast that it forced her to draw in a deep breath as a shocked gasp. Oxygen made its way into her lungs. Her vision began to clear, her muscles slowly unlocking.

Trang crouched in front of her. "Breathe, Sadie. Listen to me right now and breathe," her roommate instructed harshly.

Sadie blinked and nodded, coughing and sucking in deep lungfuls of air. "Th-thanks."

Only then could Sadie see the worry and mild fear on her roommate's face as Trang pulled on her arm. "Can you stand? We're going to the infirmary."

The big bruise forming on Sadie's cheek was the ailment that got the most attention—not the panic attack. She sat on a semiprivate infirmary bed with an ice pack cradled against her cheek.

Trang leaned against the wall, arms folded, as Ms. Martinez pumped at the blood pressure cuff on Sadie's arm and watched the dial. "Eighty-three over sixty-three. Blood pressure is fine. Sip your juice and eat your crackers, and I'll get you some ibuprofen for your cheek."

While Dr. Sharrad hadn't been available to see Sadie, Ms. Martinez, his no-nonsense Argentinian nurse practitioner, had diagnosed Sadie with a single look. A panic attack? Commonplace at Almus Terra. Students were under such extreme pressure to perform that there was at least one a week.

That wasn't exactly healthy, but who was Sadie to judge? She wanted to excel just as much as anyone. And the thought of what she faced—midterms and a week behind on work—made her short of breath all over again.

"Thanks," Sadie said again softly to Trang, shifting the ice bag on her aching cheek.

Trang blinked at her. "I'm surprised you're not mad. I hit you pretty hard."

"Nah, you reset my breathing. I don't know if it was the best way to do it, but I get it."

For a heavy minute, Trang just stared. Then she pushed off the wall and sat on the bed next to Sadie. She laid a tentative hand on Sadie's shoulder. "Don't worry about Anthropology. I'll give you all my notes and help you study. Plus, you emailed me your essay, remember? You don't have to start from scratch."

Sadie blinked to stave off a sudden urge to cry. Naturally, she'd had to explain to Ms. Martinez how the missing laptop triggered her panic attack, but she hadn't realized she needed comfort so badly until that moment.

"That would be amazing," Sadie replied thickly.

Trang just nodded. Then she tapped her cheek. "I'm really sorry about the bruising."

"Seriously, I'm fine."

It looked as if Trang were about to say something else when the door across from the beds opened and the last person on earth Sadie expected to see locked eyes with her.

"Sadie?" Titus looked just as surprised but recovered faster, closing the distance between them with brisk steps and stopping just shy of her knees. He wore a simple crew neck sweater and dark-wash jeans, and his gold hair was handsomely disheveled. Frowning, he reached for the ice pack on her face. "What happened?"

Sadie dodged his hand. "It's nothing," she said just as Trang said, "I slapped her."

Titus glanced from Trang to Sadie, then back to Trang. "What?"

For the second time, Sadie explained her missing laptop, her panic attack, and the ingenious slap that reset her breathing. As Titus listened, his expression one of deep concern, Sadie noticed Dr. Sharrad and another man leave the same exam room that Titus had emerged from, but she pushed that curious fact aside.

"Don't worry about the project. I have it all backed up," Titus assured her as soon as she finished.

Sadie exhaled. "I was desperately hoping you'd say that."

Trang squeezed Sadie's shoulder in support then stood. "I'm off. I'll send you those notes. Feel better, 'kay?"

Warmth blossomed in Sadie's chest. "Thanks, Trang."

When her roommate was gone, Titus took her spot and timidly patted Sadie's knee. "And I'll get you my notes too. I'm so sorry this happened, Sadie. If there's anything else I can do, please let me know."

She looked down at his innocent hand on her knee. It was a kind gesture. And so was the squeeze on her shoulder from Trang. But Sadie could really use something less subtle at the moment. She was a firm believer in hugs. Coming from the right person, a hug could give people energy and strength to withstand any hardship or stress.

And she'd missed them. With the exception of Oakley's welcome embrace (and holding onto Alaric, though she wasn't sure that counted), Sadie hadn't felt the healing powers of a giant, enveloping hug in over a year.

Choosing to be vulnerable, she let herself lean into him. Her voice was small as she mumbled, "Would you think me weak if I asked for a hug right now?"

Titus didn't hesitate. His arms came around her warm and strong, squeezing her gently into his massive chest and pushing her face into his shoulder.

Holy moly. She couldn't stop her heart ricocheting in her rib cage as she inadvertently took a deep pull of his clean evergreen scent. And she swore that he was breathing her in too.

Then he pulled back, and Sadie felt somehow relieved *and* resentful he'd let her go. He kept an arm around her back, though, and his face was awfully close. She didn't move away, still basking in the warmth of that blissful hug. Besides, there would be no one in the infirmary to spy on them. No #TeamTitus fan club to drench her with tea or steal her computer.

"When are you going to forget about that stupid email?" he groaned.

"When you're properly remorseful. I mean, look how *incapable* I am," she teased back.

"You know full well that's rubbish," he argued. "Think about all the rich people with amazing security who are victims of theft. I mean, look at the *Ocean's Eleven* franchise."

Despite everything, Sadie was smiling. Titus also happened to be smiling... at her.

After a few moments, she felt his hand rub down her arm, his fingers sliding under her palm resting on the bed. Her pulse picked up as he carefully maneuvered her hand into the cradle of his much larger one. His fingertips tickled her skin, drawing patterns over her palm, and Sadie's heart catapulted into her throat.

Suddenly everything felt too warm. And too good.

"Doing better, Ms. Aurelia?"

Titus dropped her hand and Sadie leaned away the instant Ms. Martinez pulled the curtain all the way back.

"Much!" She quickly jumped to her feet, the ice pack slipping from her fingers and almost falling to the floor. Titus managed to catch it just in time, however, and stood smoothly. Like he comforted girls and drew featherlight caresses across their skin all the freaking time. It was only then that Sadie suspected Alaric's accusations had any merit.

That hug had been from a friend. But that look, then his soft caresses, held something more.

"I'll head back to my dorm now," she told the nurse practitioner.

Titus placed a gentle hand on her lower back. "I'll walk you back."

Sadie bit her bottom lip. His offer was sweet but also confusing, especially after that moment. For right now, though, she wouldn't read into it. Not when she had so many other worries plaguing her.

When Titus dropped her off, Sadie had been prepared to clean up the whole room by herself. Instead, she found it immaculate.

Another surprise was Trang on the bottom bunk below Sadie's bed, folding her sweaters to place them neatly back in the chest of drawers where they belonged.

"You...you didn't have to do all this," Sadie said meekly, a stinging sensation starting in her eyes. How pathetic was she for such simple acts of kindness to make her cry?

Trang just folded another T-shirt—an old one that had a cartoon puffin on it that read *Cap'n*—and said with a smirk, "You have weird tastes in clothes."

With a laugh, Sadie dropped herself onto the bed next to her. "I'll have you know, that's peak Ashlandic fashion."

"I doubt that. It does scream *you*, though."

Sadie was weirdly elated to be close enough with someone for them to "get" her fashion sense, or lack thereof.

But the feeling quickly faded as she realized something important. Trang had cleaned her mess—a perfectly wonderful thing to do—but that *also* meant she'd just gone through her stuff. Yet another stab of terror suddenly had Sadie dropping from the bed and to her knees, diving into the bottom bedside table drawer. And when she couldn't find it there, she swiped her hand frantically under her bed—

"If you're looking for your journal, here."

Sadie froze as Trang stood and reached into Sadie's top bunk, sliding her father's journal out from under the pillow.

"I just thought it would be easier up here since sometimes you read it at night, but you have to get down from the top bunk to fetch it."

It took a lot of restraint not to snatch it from Trang's outstretched hand. Careful not to look upset when Trang had been nothing but courteous and kind, Sadie accepted her father's journal and breathed a sigh of relief when it was back in her arms.

"I didn't mean to scare you. It was under the bed when I was cleaning, and—"

"No, no, thank you," Sadie said quickly. "You were right. It's a good idea. I just...It's important to me. It was my father's, and I don't have many things from him."

This being the *only* thing.

There was an awkward beat of silence before Trang said softly, "That's rough."

It was such a simple commiserating sentiment that Sadie couldn't help appreciating it. "Actually, the more accurate statement is that it's really my mother's. She told me it was my father's, but I never knew him. He died before I was born, and Mah didn't like to talk about him. He was just a civil servant, but...he liked to write poems." Sadie waved the little book in the air; it was full of musings that objectively weren't very good. But they were hers and her mother's all the same.

Smoothing her hand over the old leather was the assurance she needed that it was right here. That she hadn't just lost it a second time. At least it helped her put things into perspective, though. A laptop and all its hardware and data could be replaced.

22

TITUS

"Titus!"

Titus locked his phone screen and laid it on his thigh under the table, though it was obvious to everyone he'd been staring at it, *not* paying the least bit of attention.

"Pardon?"

"I said," Calixa seethed, giving him a look that could turn any creature to stone, "do you have any ideas on how to combat this rebellion?"

Titus looked at the tablet in front of him, its browser opened to the student forums, where another new TikTok trend had started to circulate—Scholars doing their chores over a sound clip of Calixa's speech from last year sped up and mixed with the "Imperial March" from *Star Wars*. It was brilliantly clever, not that Titus could ever say that.

"I already gave my suggestion. You didn't like it," he said evenly. He was tired of this conversation. Over and over, he'd heard Calixa and Kavi and the rest of the Elites and C-Suites complain about the Scholars' resistance incited by Alaric's dining hall rally. Predictably, Calixa was incensed, and every ounce of her energy was now focused on how to punish them.

It was all so juvenile, and truthfully, Titus deeply regretted his own involvement. He should've kept his mouth shut. Let Alaric have his moment. But he had been *fetched* by Calixa and her minions to "control his kin," and Titus was in no position yet to disobey.

"Doing nothing is not a suggestion," Cal snapped back. "These ungrateful nobodies have no idea what they're dealing with. Real power is control. It's leverage."

"Cal," Kavi said gently, laying a hand on her shoulder, which she brushed off.

Titus resisted the urge to pick up his phone again. It wasn't his official new phone, but a spare he'd paid a Scholar for so his parents wouldn't have access to any of its data. It was the best way to keep his secret safe.

"If I may..."

He glanced over to where Emmeline sat, looking self-assured as usual. Cal nodded for her to continue, though her gaze blazed with intensity that would make most people shrivel.

"I propose we give them a voice. Give them a chair at the student council."

Everyone was silent. Titus swore Calixa's irises flashed a demonic red. "You can't be serious."

Emmeline rolled her eyes, never one to be intimidated. "Come on, Calixa, a chair doesn't equate to any real power. Not yet. But it will *feel* like they're part of the decision-making. We can say they have a voice, even if it's not a loud one. It will also calm the backlash and make their anger look petulant. And then in practice, we pile them with work. Show them what it really means to be in charge and all the effort it entails. We intimidate them into submission."

Calixa was silent, the rage subsiding. She drummed her long nails on the wood surface, her favorite way to think. "I'll... consider it."

Titus bit the inside of his cheek to keep his expression neutral even as irritation arced through him, Emmeline's smug gaze meeting his own.

*　　*　　*

The wind whistled through Titus's hair, whipping his tie over his shoulder and chilling his clammy skin. The western ramparts faced the sea, but for all he could tell, the landscape might as well be a desert. It was well past sundown on a new moon, and the only light came from the walkways' lanterns and the glow of his burner phone's screen.

His thumb hovered over the link within the SMS message from Dr. Sharrad. His test results. Logically, he knew that reading them wouldn't give him any real answers because he didn't know what they would mean, but it was the *implications* of them. The fact that Dr. Sharrad had asked to see him so they could talk through the tests together with the specialist. Titus refused. He didn't need anyone witnessing a meltdown if the news was . . .

Honestly, he hadn't expected it to all happen so quickly. He understood that it often took months to meet with the right expert, especially leading physicians from different countries. But that was the power of ATA. For all he knew, the specialist who'd examined him had either attended ATA or was a good friend of an alum.

A part of him deep inside wanted a real medical explanation for all this—to know it wasn't just stress or in his head—but the larger part of him feared the truth.

With a sigh, he locked the screen and headed back to his dorm. He'd procrastinated returning because he didn't want more of Seb (or Emmeline if she was with him) right after that frustrating council meeting. But the moment he walked into the dorm, he wished he'd come earlier.

Sadie was on the floor, Oliver next to her, and Alaric lounged on his bed, looking over her shoulder, their attention focused on the new computer in her lap.

Sadie glanced up for only a moment, shooting him a quick smile, then went right back to typing. "Hey, Titus."

It took him a solid twenty seconds to register why Sadie was here. Of course, she desperately needed help since her laptop had disappeared, but it took him far too long to realize that Sadie wasn't just relying on *him*.

Naturally. Titus wasn't in all her classes. Alaric and Oliver had to be sharing notes for the ones they had together.

But it really annoyed him that she'd come here without him. He'd invited her twice to work on their project in his room, but she'd found some excuse to politely relocate. Yet here she was with Oliver. And Alaric.

Fighting the impulse to form a fist, Titus stuffed his hands into his pockets. "Getting some help?" he asked with an easy smile, one he hoped didn't look forced.

"Yes," she said with a sigh, blowing a stray piece of ginger hair away from her face. Dark circles had formed under her eyes and her cheeks seemed hollower than last week. Was she fitting in meals between classes and cram sessions?

"My first midterm is tomorrow. International Econ. Alaric is quizzing me. Oliver is helping with Advocacy Studies. He's converting videos I had to watch to audio files so I can listen on the go. Neat, huh?"

Alaric didn't look up from Sadie's laptop, but Oliver gave Titus a sheepish smile. Titus didn't have the energy, or defensible cause, to be mad, but frustration coursed through him all the same. It was draining to have a living situation where hardly any of them were on friendly terms.

His only relaxed interactions on campus seemed to be with Sadie once a week when they worked on their project. Though lately he'd had the good fortune of seeing her every day to help with all her lost midterm work.

"You're all set, Sadie," Oliver said, tapping a few keys on his computer.

She squeezed his arm as he got to his feet. "Thank you so much, Oliver."

"You're missing the entire recap section on Economies of Scale," Alaric said, falling back on his pillows. "It's the second half of the notes I sent you."

Sadie's shoulders fell. "I haven't gotten there yet."

"Then you better cram tonight. It's definitely on the test."

"Right," she grumbled, shoving her new laptop into her bag, and stood.

She was leaving already? Titus moved to open the door for her. "We're all set for our cram session tomorrow night, yeah?"

Sadie nodded. "Yep. Eight o'clock. I'll see you then."

"Let me walk you back," he offered, even though he was tired and his feet hurt.

But Sadie shook her head and pulled out her headphones. "Thanks, but I really need to listen to these audio files." She gave them all a little wave. "Bye, guys."

Oliver waved back. "Good luck, Sadie."

The door shut behind her and Titus was left aggravated and rejected. The first sting was par for the course, the latter was new.

Alaric snorted, lifting a graphic novel up to read. "Girls don't like try-hards."

Titus wanted to punch him. Instead, he turned to his desk. He had his own midterms to ace. His parents would expect nothing less.

It took everything Titus had to remain standing on the tarmac and not pass out (in other words, to avoid a face full of asphalt and a busted lip). Unlike the other students at Almus Terra, Alaric, Emmeline, Titus, and Sadie weren't allowed to enjoy the first day of their fall break by sleeping in. After three days of exams and nearly two straight weeks of cramming and writing reports, the four Ashland heirs were required to meet Ilsa Halvorsen at three AM for an early boat ride back to the coast of continental France and another car ride to the Toulon airport.

Thankfully, it wasn't just Titus who was dead on his feet. Alaric crouched on the ground with his gaze half-lidded and his cheek resting on his fist. Sadie sat on top of her luggage, burrowed in her hoodie with her eyes closed. Only Emmeline and Titus remained standing while they waited for boarding, both unwilling to appear weak to any of the king's associates.

Titus took solace in the fact that, while Emmeline's posture was flawless, her sunglasses were on before the crack of dawn. He was quite certain her eyes were closed, just as exhausted as the rest of them.

Every so often, he would discreetly massage his knuckles and wrists. They ached much more frequently with all the nonstop typing and note-taking. Still, he had not opened those results or, more importantly, set another appointment with Dr. Sharrad.

Finally, the flight crew opened the door to the jet and the guards went to grab their suitcases so they could be stored in the underbelly. Titus gently shook Sadie awake and helped her to her feet. Emmeline was first up the steps and picked a massive fancy leather chair next to one of the windows. Alaric was second and, with little care, dumped himself into another seat. He tugged his ratty beanie over his eyes and stuffed his hands into his jacket pockets.

Sadie took a seat opposite Alaric, and Titus sat behind her, next to Emmeline. No one spoke. Just like no one had spoken during any other leg of the trip. Since the first day in Headmistress Aquila's office, the four of them hadn't had a real conversation. But Titus wasn't about to attempt it. What was the point? On some level, they all disliked and distrusted one another. Well, except for Sadie. He wasn't entirely sure how she felt about her new life. That's the one topic they had wisely avoided during all their project meetups.

As the door to the jet closed and the guards took their seats at the back of the plane, everyone settled into sleep they so desperately craved.

But they were roused minutes later by Alaric's grunt of protest as Ilsa ripped the beanie off his head, revealing disheveled dark hair.

"Listen up," she barked. "We land in Ashland in five hours and fifteen minutes, at which point the four of you will be greeted by the press. It's your first appearance, so we need to spend most of the flight preparing."

If they had been normal teenagers, there would've been a collective groan. Instead, no one said a word. Though Alaric's scowl deepened, and Sadie hugged her stomach. Emmeline only glanced out the window as the jet began to roll forward for taxying.

"There's a bathroom in the back where you can change into suitable attire, and I have a stylist on board for hair and makeup when we get closer. Now, let's review your notes. I just emailed your vetted talking points."

On cue, their phones pinged. Titus had to pause and remember in which pocket he'd stored which phone. He didn't need Ilsa or anyone else seeing his burner phone.

"Sorry—are yeh codding me? Yeh really expect me to say this?" Alaric growled, his thumb scrolling through the email. "'I am honored to return to my homeland after these last sixteen years abroad. In many ways, my own horizon has broadened.' I sound like a tool."

"Not those exact words, but yes. That is what I expect you—all of you—to say."

"Will I, yeah?" he snarled.

Ilsa scrolled through her tablet. "If you want to return to Almus Terra, yes. One of the many reasons King Leander sent the three of you away is that he wanted you to get a wider worldview than any childhood in the Heres Castle would've provided. But most importantly, and what can never be discussed beyond the Ashland royal family, is that the three of you were in danger. With no named heir and a history defined by war and unrest, any one of you was a target. Either for murder or manipulation. Publicly disclosing such vulnerability would compromise everything that your grandfather has built. We must prove to the world that King Leander's decision to remove you three from the public eye was made for your own developmental benefit, and nothing more. Growing up away from the media's attention, you're instantly more relatable. Now, Sadie, your talking points are quite different...."

Ilsa then turned her attention wholly to Sadie, and Titus was left to stare at his phone with his stomach churning.

Every line of this script felt like a lie. And he wondered if the press would be able to sniff out the actual truth. They were sent away because King Leander didn't want his grandchildren to end up like their parents. Simple as that. Everything else was just a smoke screen.

Titus imagined that stepping onto Ashlandic soil would feel like a missing puzzle piece sliding into place. Or something more profound. He didn't expect it to be like a homecoming, because he hadn't been here since he was a baby, and he wasn't the sentimental type. But he expected...something. Unfortunately, as his shiny shoes hit the tarmac of the Durah airport, it felt no different from the tarmac back in France. Except it was colder here. Even his charcoal-gray wool coat wore thin against the incoming fall wind.

Ashland sat east of Nova Scotia and just south of Greenland, and the chill in the air was an easy reminder of it. The sky was yellow, pink, and orange and full of puffy stratocumulus clouds rolling over the Labrador Sea.

The cliffs were impressive already, visible in the distance over rolling green slopes, carving their way out into the icy waters like stone giants of the old Ashlandic pagan stories. Raised to one day be king, Titus had studied his heritage well. He knew Ashland's history and geography better than the other heirs by far. Except Sadie, as this had always been her home.

Though she did *not* look happy to be back. Her shoulders were tightly bunched, like every muscle was prepared to take several blows in a fight. It drew her ginger-red waves around her cheeks and neck, and her navy-blue coat hid the tailored dress that Ilsa had forced her into. She was rereading the talking points for the reporters. The journey from the small jet into the airport was short, but they'd been instructed to wait outside while Ilsa prepped the press.

"You'll do fine," Titus told Sadie quietly.

Sadie glanced up at him, then over at Alaric, who was standing like a statue and looking out at the cliffs, and then at Emmeline, who was glaring at the airport doors, as if willing them to open.

Then she blew out a harsh breath full of steam. "I didn't think we'd have to talk to the press so soon. How does she expect me to memorize all this?"

"She doesn't. It's just an idea. Knowing what not to say is more important."

Sadie pursed her lips, rolling them through her teeth. The lipstick the stylist applied was a caramel nude color and made the freckles on her nose and cheeks attractively stand out. He was having a harder time remembering how he'd ever thought she was plain.

"Are you nervous?" she asked him suddenly.

Titus rolled his shoulders back and took a deep breath. "For the media? Not at all. What happens after..."

Sadie's brows furrowed as she looked up at him. Without overthinking it, he poked her right between them. "Careful. V brow."

Her brilliant smile was worth the scathing looks from both Emmeline and Alaric. He ignored them, like he ignored the small voice inside that told him what he was feeling was not the triumph of victory, but something far more genuine. And dangerous.

Just then the doors opened, and the royal guards surged forward, herding the heirs inside, where flashes were already going off like fireworks.

Showtime.

23

ALARIC

WITH A LEVEL OF CONTROL ALARIC DIDN'T KNOW HE POSSESSED, he resisted the urge to take the microphone shoved into his face and hit the reporter with his own gear—in a classic "why are you hitting yourself" move.

"Sure, I miss Ireland as much as the next lad," he said, trying his best not to sound as gruff as Ilsa claimed he usually did. *Speak like a Homo sapiens instead of a Homo habilis.* Ha-ha, she was calling him a caveman. Hilarious. "But there's always something missing. Home. Ashland."

The words felt like a lie because they were. What a load of crap. He'd been just shy of two years old when they shipped him off to Dublin. There hadn't been anything *to* miss.

But he delivered his lines as dictated. Despite this heir nonsense, he did want to go back to Almus Terra. The school was challenging and had everything he was interested in. So he used the preapproved responses.

"Having grown up abroad, do you believe the public will have trouble accepting you as their potential king?" the reporter asked, moving the mic back to Alaric.

Alaric bit his tongue to stop himself from saying, *I don't think that's how monarchy has ever worked.* The people of Ashland will get whomever

Leander chooses. Though, to be fair, this country was known for its coups and civil wars. Maybe public acceptance was critical.

This time, he pulled the response word for word from memory. "I believe the king has done what's best, and if the Ashlandic people have trusted him for the last fifty years, then they should continue to do so." That answer in particular was one that Ilsa had drilled into them.

With a glance over, he noticed Sadie also speaking to a reporter. A royal guard stood menacingly next to her, ensuring no one got too close. Apparently the press had been all but strip-searched before they were allowed anywhere near the heirs. Not to mention, judging from the glass-domed airport lobby, Alaric could tell the place was crawling with security. The king had spared no expense in protecting his heirs. No surprise there, really.

At last, Ilsa's voice rang through the lobby. "All right, we'll stand for pictures and then the heirs will be on their way. The airport must open back up to the public."

With Sadie and Emmeline in the middle and Titus and Alaric on the ends, picture after picture was taken. Ilsa mouthed *smile* at him with a murderous look on her face.

More photos were snapped as the four of them were ushered through the vacant airport out to a line of shiny black cars with little Ashlandic flags fluttering in the breeze. He and Emmeline climbed into one, and Titus and Sadie climbed into another. He tried not to notice how easily Titus seemed to adopt the spot beside her.

"You did well," Emmeline said after a few minutes of driving through a city that looked a heck of a lot like Dublin. But then, he supposed a lot of old cities looked the same. Historic stone buildings mixed with new monstrosities of metal and glass.

He cocked an eyebrow at his cousin. It was the first real overture she'd made that didn't drip with condescension. She faced the window, but her back was rigid, her whole body tense.

"Your approval means so much to me," he said dryly.

As expected, she shot him an annoyed look, then muttered something under her breath that sounded like *dick*.

Perhaps that had been a real compliment, but he didn't need one. Not from her. Or Titus. Now more than ever, he felt the massive divergence between him and his cousins. And it went deeper than money and class. It boiled down to blood. Family. His mother was dead, his "father" hated him, his genes were Eldana and the only reason for his being here.

The procession of royal cars drove into the older, historic district of Durah, the capital of Ashland. Alaric could see old Gothic churches next to pubs and renovated clubs for the younger generation. There were gift shops of old pagan lore, new fashion boutiques, art galleries of seascapes, and even... an Apple Store.

Alaric didn't know much about his country of origin, but he'd read everything Wikipedia had to say. While most countries launched into industrialism following the world wars, Ashland had been embroiled in its own internal struggles. Since the fifteenth century, five families (two in particular) had wrestled for power, causing rebellions and coups and endless fighting. Meanwhile Ashland suffered, its economy surviving entirely off its sea trade and ports.

The current regime didn't begin until Leander Eldana, heir to one of the five families, had returned to Ashland after studying abroad during America's Cold War and brought home weapons and strategy that enabled him to quash the Sixth Civil War. Taking over Durah and its harbors, King Leander opened trade beyond fishing and mercantilism. He brought in factories and foreign corporations—in short, he created jobs. The economy grew exponentially, and Ashland had been steadily catching up to the outside world ever since.

But perhaps not fast enough. Poverty was evident along the drive. As they looped through forests on twisting roads that slanted upward on the way into Durah, Alaric noticed meager stone cottages on the fringes of run-down towns that had been left behind in the way of city progress.

As the cars raced by thick evergreen trees, he caught his own reflection in the window. He took in his slicked-back dark hair, high starched collar, and deep blue tie, and poisonous words echoed in his head. *You're not my son. You're a bastard.*

With a low breath, he closed his eyes and leaned his head back into the seat. *What am I even doing here?*

Heres Castle was different from Almus Terra in many ways, having been updated and expanded throughout the years, depending perhaps on which family controlled it.

Alaric didn't know the architectural terms, but he was able to pick out certain styles like layers of history. The eleventh-century Windsor and Edinburgh Castles had been its base, using that classic old stone medieval foundation, then topped with the towering spires of Neuschwanstein Castle in Germany. In later decades, it had been clear that stained glass, silver-and-pearl trim, and painted blue-and-green walls were adopted from the palaces in Russia, like the Winter Palace in St. Petersburg.

The result was a fortress of chronicled time, a patchwork of the country's royalty, and a personification of its turbulent history, unable to determine its own identity amidst years of bloodshed and unrest.

Emmeline had gotten out of the car and started up the steps, following Ilsa. But Alaric hadn't been able to move. He was seriously considering an escape. If they refused to drive him back to the airport, was he strong enough to take out one of the guards and hijack the car? Was Almus Terra really worth what he was about to go through?

"Alaric, look!" Sadie called from the stairs. They were lined with tall flowering trees that had decorated the stone steps with little white blossoms. She swept her arm over the castle's entrance with double doors, stone bordering, and silver iron designs. "It's an ogival arch!"

Her smile was huge, her knees curled inward like she was ready to jump up and down right there. *And slip and fall.*

That thought had him climbing up the steps after her. "I see, I see. Don't slip, yeah?"

Her smile turned into a scowl. "Will you let that go? I'm not as clumsy as you think."

Alaric joined her on the step, ignoring Titus next to her, who stood staring up at the door with a clenched jaw.

"Hurry up, you three. We're due to meet the king *now*," Ilsa snapped from the doors, held open by two towering guards in full military uniform with real swords at their sides.

Great, Alaric thought. Hopefully that didn't include the rest of the royal family. He needed more time for mental preparation to face Lord Erickson and not punch the living daylights out of him.

They were led through a massive entrance hall with tapestries that hung from the twenty-foot arched stone ceiling, which depicted great ships with dragonheads, cliffs, and thunder clouds. Ilsa's heels clicked over the marble as she marched them up a grand staircase and down a long corridor that opened to an antechamber of old stone statues and interior landscaping with living walls and modern water features.

Through yet another ogival arch, the heirs were led into a large sitting room with a gold-plated map on a wall, windows that overlooked the cliffs and the sea, and a long couch with armchairs and chaise lounges.

Beyond the furniture, Alaric's gaze was drawn to a rug at their feet. It was not just a richly colorful scene of the island's natural landscape—of its jagged cliffs, rocky beaches, rolling hills, deep forests, and serpentine rivers—it held crests. Crests he recognized from his brief Google search into Ashland's chaotic history. They were as old as the fifteenth century, dating back to when the country first began carving itself up.

The Eldana crest was threaded into the left middle of the tapestry, while Thorane and Reynar were in the bottom corners, and Bredahl was woven into the right. The crest at the very top looked fiercer than the rest, a sea dragon curled around a trident with the name Scealan.

A heel nudged his shoe, and his gaze jumped up to Ilsa, whose chin jerked toward the center of the room. *Pay attention,* her irritated glare said.

King Leander stood next to a desk, greeting them: "Ah, you're here. Very well done."

He gestured to the massive flat screen on the opposite wall of the gold-plated map, and Ilsa unmuted a news story of Emmeline speaking clearly into a reporter's mic. Her youthful face was everything the press wanted. The news clips jumped to Sadie, Titus, and Alaric in various sound bites, highlighting the stories they had been fed on the plane.

"I would say your first media hit was a smashing success. While you're here, we've stacked up a few more appearances. All strategic. Ilsa?"

"Yes, Your Majesty. We have the Durah City Memorial Hospital visit, a Harbor excursion to launch the maiden voyage of *Riretha*, a football match with our premier league team—"

"Yes," he said with a sharp nod, cutting her off. "Have Richard confirm those details." Clasping his hands behind his back, he strode over and regarded each with a fierce gaze, though Alaric had a hunch that this was Leander's look of approval.

"Ilsa will show you all to your rooms. We can discuss your progress so far at school during the family dinner tonight. I've already received a full report of your midterm results. The rest of your time here will include lessons in our country's etiquette and history, along with Ilsa's approved events. You'll fly back Saturday to catch up on work before classes resume."

"Your Majesty, the cabinet meeting—" a bald man by the entrance started.

King Leander checked his watch. "Ilsa, I leave them in your capable hands."

Ilsa straightened and Alaric could almost feel her pride radiating from ten feet away. "This way, Your Highnesses," she said, leading them out of the room and down the hall.

Alaric was keenly aware that none of them had said a word to the king. It hadn't felt the least bit necessary, even. As they were heading back the way they'd come and the king turned in the other direction, Alaric caught sight of a tall figure with a face painfully familiar.

As the king strode into the room, Alaric's father turned his back and the doors shut.

24

EMMELINE

WITH HARDLY A GLANCE AT THE DECADENT FURNISHINGS OF HER room, Emmeline crossed into the bathroom for a mirror. Already, her makeup from the plane was slowly fading into heinous dark circles. She'd seen a hint of them during her TV close-up and her chest had almost seized in panic.

Her first appearance on the news and she looked tired? She could've strangled Ilsa for her poor planning. What was that woman thinking, putting them in front of a camera after a week of all-night cramming sessions?

Emmeline dropped her head and heaved a sigh, massaging her temples. What she really needed was to eat, but she was ready to pass out where she stood. They'd had little time for sleep or food since they left Almus Terra, and she was feeling it.

A knock sounded, and a maid entered with a tray of food and hot tea. Emmeline quickly washed her hands and toed off her heels. She checked the time and surmised that if she ate quickly and asked the maid to unpack for her, she could fit in a power nap. Plus, sleep might placate the nervous hornets buzzing in her stomach ever since the king had said *family dinner.*

But the prospect of a nap evaporated when her phone went off—

Oakley's cheery smile lit up her screen. She snatched it from her bed and answered immediately. As soon as FaceTime connected, Oakley was yelling, "Lemme see! Lemme see!"

Emmeline smothered a smile and pretended to be exasperated by rolling her eyes. "It's just another castle, Oak. We already live in one."

"Says the princess who has her own suite. Quit yapping and show me the goods, yeah?" Oakley had elected to stay at Almus Terra during fall break to spend time with her girlfriend *sans* roommates, and Emmeline could see Danica's *League of Legends* poster in the background.

With a grin, Emmeline switched the phone's camera to show off her room, and Oakley gasped. "Blimey! An honest-to-god canopy bed. Does your closet speak to you? Like some *Clueless* AI that tells you what to wear?"

"As if I'd ever let a computer dress me." Emmeline tapped the camera back so Oakley could see her face and plopped down on the bed. "Did you see the news?"

"When you landed at the airport? Of course," Oakley scoffed, tugging on a curl. "What kind of friend would I be if I didn't watch your big debut?" Then she grinned and winked. "You were perf, by the way."

Emmeline laughed. Oakley gave her five times the energy that a nap or a cup of coffee ever could. "Thanks. Ilsa informed us about the press conference on the way."

"That checks out. I was wondering why you didn't tell me. But no worries, I have a Google alert on your name."

"My, my, my, should Danica be worried?" Emmeline teased back.

"Emmie dearest, straight girls are not my type." They laughed and there was a shuffling of the phone as Danica's forehead came into view, then the sight of her gold-brown eyes and tan, freckled cheeks.

"Emmie! How's the home country? Everything you dreamed?"

A gnawing ache bloomed in Emmeline's chest, but she forced a smile. "You bet."

"That's great. Oh! Do you wanna say hey to Oliver? He's here too, vibin'—Ollie! Come say hey to Emmeline."

That ache quickly became a sharp pain as Emmeline's heart thudded. "Sorry, Dani. I've got to get ready for the next thing the king wants us to do." *Lie.* "Talk later!"

Then she hung up and tossed the phone away, groaning at her own cowardice. She'd better get it together before dinner. She had a feeling she'd need all the courage she could get.

Emmeline studied her reflection one more time in the ornate full-length mirror. She wore a deep purple dress with a cowl neck and thin straps, mid-length, that bunched the silky material together in a patchwork of amethysts. More of the same gems hung around her neck and on her ears. Her golden light brown hair was swept back in a jeweled barrette that pinned her waves to cascade down her bare back, while her makeup was done in tones of lavender and silver.

Ilsa's stylists took the lead, but Emmeline had chosen her own jewelry and dress, and she was pleased with the result. What parent wouldn't want her as a daughter?

Uncurling her fingers so her nails didn't dig into her palms, she slipped on heels and headed for the door, where an attendant waited to escort her to dinner. It was seven minutes until six, and as she walked she focused on her breathing. On placing one foot in front of the other.

This was it. She was about to meet her parents. The thought made her dizzy, but she had to be composed. Perfect. Always.

She was taken to another sitting room that was much larger than the first. The space contained one wall made entirely of bookshelves, several couches, and chairs with small tables and tea sets centered around a large stone fireplace.

The last of the heirs to arrive, she quickly noted everyone's locations like placements on a chess board. Alaric leaned against the bookshelves, holding a crystal lowball glass of what Emmeline guessed was whiskey. Titus sat, predictably, next to Sadie. Not, she observed, next to the adults she recognized as his parents. Crown Prince Magnus and Lady Calliope, both blond, elegant, and looking exactly like the photos that Emmeline had scoured online.

Neither her parents nor Alaric's father were anywhere to be seen. And Sadie was an orphan. Articles had confirmed as much, but her parents' causes of death could not be made public due to minor protection laws. Emmeline would've mustered a little sympathy for the girl had she not felt like Sadie was stealing Emmeline's family for herself.

Remembering her Ashlandic royal etiquette, she approached Prince Magnus, who stood behind his wife, perched at the end of a wingback armchair, and curtsied, her left hand touching her right shoulder in the traditional military salute. "Your Highness."

"Charmed, Emmeline," Lady Calliope replied with a clipped, high-class accent. "Look at you, all grown up." Then her smile turned smug, bordering on cruel, paired with: "Your parents must be so excited to see you."

Emmeline's jaw clenched hard. The sting of her aunt's words was cushioned only by the hatred in her own heart. *Vindictive old witch.*

But she smiled back and straightened. "As excited as Titus was to see you."

Lady Calliope's gaze turned icy.

Emmeline stepped over to an empty chair and took her seat, subtly apprising her cousins and Sadie to see if they were as visibly on edge as she.

Titus and Alaric wore suits tailored to their frames, complete with cuff links of the Eldana family crest and open soft collars. Sadie was prettier than Emmeline had ever thought she had the potential to be. Her dress was a deep maroon, the color pairing well with her fair, freckled skin, and ginger-red waves, and its slim cut and square neck accentuated her curves. Rubies adorned her ears, and her hazel eyes were made larger with simple black liner.

Conversations down the hall caused a subtle ripple of tension throughout the room. Five seconds later, King Leander entered, followed by two attendants, his voice thundering, "Tell the king of Norway I don't care what he thinks of our docking taxes. They're my ports. If he wants to anchor his supply ships on the way to Canada, he'll pay whatever I decide. Now, do not disturb me until after dinner."

The men bowed and murmured, "Your Majesty," before turning on their heels and going back the way they came.

King Leander headed straight for the decanter of alcohol, pouring amber liquid into a crystal glass. After taking a deep swig, he turned to give Emmeline, Alaric, Titus, and Sadie a brittle smile. "Ah, the joys of ruling. Something one of *you* will learn firsthand."

The dig at Prince Magnus and Lady Calliope pulled the tension in the room that much tighter. And Emmeline relished the strain. But she didn't get to enjoy it for long, because the next moment a peel of laughter echoed down the hall, and the doors were thrown open.

A woman in an off-shoulder dress with beadwork so fine it looked as expensive as a Lamborghini sauntered in holding a champagne flute. "Freddy, we're not going to Santorini again," she called over her shoulder, flipping a piece of long honey-gold hair away from her face.

Emmeline recognized her mother at once. Lady Chloe, a young Ashlandic actress who was so gorgeous she'd managed to snag herself a prince at the tender age of sixteen. Though she'd been a young bride, she didn't have Emmeline until she turned twenty.

Looking at Chloe in the flesh, Emmeline could see that pictures online did not do her justice. It felt like all the energy and life in the room had suddenly been drawn to her like a spotlight. She was vibrant and beautiful and magnetic.

A tall man as attractive as his wife sauntered in behind her. Prince Frederick, Emmeline's father, and King Leander's youngest son. "We need not stay. Damien's—"

"Ohhh, Emmeline!" Chloe gasped, jeweled nails fluttering across her chest in surprise. "Of course! That's why Georgiana was so insistent about family dinner tonight. How exciting. Look how beautiful you are."

It took every muscle, every ounce of self-control for Emmeline's face not to drop like her stomach. Her parents had forgotten they were seeing her tonight. Her parents had forgotten *her*.

Emmeline stood robotically and accepted the awkward embrace that her mother gave her.

Lady Chloe smelled like roses and red wine. She caressed her daughter's face with the soft pads of her fingers.

"Simply stunning. Absolute perfection. She looks just like me, doesn't she, Freddy?" But there was nothing loving in her mother's touch, merely vain admiration.

The dining room was as extravagant as the rest of the castle thus far. It was easily the size of a small church, with high ceilings and long windows that opened to a balcony overlooking the Labrador Sea. Decorated with silver and crystal, one long dark wood table with high-backed chairs took up the center of the white rug.

King Leander resided at the head of the table, while Emmeline, Alaric, Sadie, and Titus were instructed to sit on his right side; the chair to his immediate left remained empty. The other side of the table was filled with Titus's and Emmeline's parents, and it took Emmeline far too long to realize the empty chair was intended for Alaric's father.

Except when Lord Erickson entered—obnoxiously late—he did not approach his king. Instead, he took the seat next to Emmeline's father.

Ah, the spot was left in memory for Alaric's mother, the late Princess Rhea.

As the first course—something pale and mushy swimming in garlic and butter—was brought out, King Leander cleared his throat and raised his glass of wine.

Everyone joined him except Alaric's father, but King Leander simply chose to ignore it.

"A toast to our prodigal young heirs, finally back home. Grandchildren, we are so happy to celebrate your return, and your continued success at Almus Terra. And Sadie, we could not be more pleased for you to join our table as an honorary member of the Eldana line."

Emmeline had to school her features at that, but they all drank—some more aggressively than others. She noticed Alaric's father and her own parents take big gulps.

"I want to congratulate each of you individually on your excellent midterm results and progress in your studies," the king continued, his gaze roaming over their faces like he was scanning a piece of legislation.

"Titus," he began, swirling his wineglass casually. Titus straightened, and his parents stopped eating. The king pretended not to notice any of this and continued, "I've been informed you're top of class in both Intro to Foreign Policy and Global Economic Statistics. Well done."

"Thank you, sir," Titus said after a beat. Prince Magnus and Lady Calliope went back to chewing.

"Emmeline," King Leander said, setting down his glass and fixing her with his full attention. Emmeline stared back at her grandfather and avoided her parents' eyes. From her peripheral vision, she saw her mother checking her phone. Her father was spearing a piece of lettuce with his fork. Neither of them seemed remotely interested. The wine in her stomach soured.

"Your Ancient Political Rhetoric speech captured the attention of Dr. Limbaugh, and your midterm for Energy Conservation 101 also received the highest grade. Additionally, you showed amazing marksmanship in your Archery class. One of the most promising young archers in the last decade, according to Ms. Rylander. Impressive."

Emmeline's nails dug into her palm as she nodded politely and said, "Thank you, Your Majesty." Her mother was still on her phone.

King Leander moved on. "I am most intrigued by your progress so far, Alaric. You may not have top marks in any class—but your professors have all told me you spark the most rigorous debates, turning the Socratic method back on them in International Economics and Democratic Republic Studies. I've also heard your projects in Cyber Security and Data Analysis have both of your instructors eager to see the final products."

Alaric said nothing, nor did he even nod. He just glared at his drink, his dark brows furrowed. Lord Erickson kept eating as if he hadn't heard a word.

Unfazed, King Leander turned finally to Sadie, who looked like she might pass out at any minute. She'd barely touched her food, probably not knowing which utensil to use.

"Professor Chamapiwa is most impressed with you, Sadie. Your passion in Advocacy Studies rivals that of her own colleagues, she tells me. I've also been informed that you received the best grade on your Anthropology midterm."

"Th-thank you, Your Majesty," Sadie practically squeaked.

As the next course was served, a Chilean sea bass with butternut squash risotto, King Leander took the opportunity to have his wineglass refilled. He was drawing out his remarks on purpose, making everyone sweat to know who, exactly, was pulling ahead in the race for heir apparent.

He swirled the dark cherry-red liquid in his glass, brought it to his nose to take a deep whiff, then tasted it with the flourish of a top-tier sommelier.

"You are all doing very well. That much is indisputable. But your studies are not the only thing I am evaluating. As the year goes on, I urge you to consider every moment to be pivotal in your path to my throne. Like Titus's alignment with Calixa Chevalier and Kavi Sandhu on the student council. Or Alaric's rousing speech to the Scholars, even Sadie's extracurricular work for a small Ashlandic charity. I am watching"—his gaze slowly moved to Emmeline, as she was the obvious exclusion—"all of you. Very carefully."

Dinner was painful. Hardly anyone spoke. It wasn't that Emmeline wanted to engage in conversation when her skin was sizzling with shame—it's that the ordeal went on far too long. She wanted to go to bed so she could stop reliving the moment where her grandfather left her out in his final speech, as if all her academic work meant nothing. Most of all, she wanted to get away from her parents so they could continue ignoring her from all the way across the castle, instead of across the table.

Perhaps the cruelest part of this was that damn letter. It had given her hope for something more. But sitting here, a mere two and a half feet away, her mother commented only on Emmeline's appearance.

Watching her mother and father now, Emmeline wondered if it was even Lady Chloe who had written to her, and not Georgiana. Judging from her mother's vapid remarks and constant selfies during dinner, Emmeline doubted Lady Chloe even knew the word *entelechy*.

She downed her second glass of wine. With that last gulp, she started to feel a little woozy, but then . . . she was beginning to care less and less. Hard to tell if that was the effect of the alcohol or the fact that her father was leering at one of the maids.

Yes, Emmeline was starting to feel quite sick.

"Dessert will be served in the study, along with some of our finest Ashlandic tea," King Leander said, rising from the table. "Emmeline . . . I'd like to see you in my office."

Emmeline's head snapped up and her temples pounded painfully. She tried not to wince. Gingerly, she got to her feet, her stomach and head swimming. "O-of course, Your Majesty."

Her blood ran cold, but her skin felt feverish as she followed the king out of the dining hall and down the corridor. They climbed marble stairs in silence, and though she'd never concentrated so hard just to walk in heels before, she now felt like it was deeply necessary. Nausea rolled through her. She had to breathe carefully so as not to lose her dinner at the feet of a marble statue or an ancient glass vase.

This was it. She wasn't good enough. This was where her grandfather eliminated her from the running for heir apparent. She would just be a grandchild. And that—as she was discovering—didn't count for much in this family.

Bypassing a guard, her grandfather opened the door to his office and stepped aside to allow her to pass. With squared shoulders, and hoping to exemplify more dignity than she felt, Emmeline strode through and took a seat in one of his massive chairs.

Leander circled his desk and pulled open a drawer. Silently, he retrieved printed photographs and slid them across the polished wood to Emmeline. The images were stills of video feeds from ATA halls in which Emmeline carried Sadie's laptop.

"Let me guess, you threw it into the sea?"

Years of Heather's lessons in manipulation had prepared Emmeline to keep her expression completely neutral.

Of all things to disqualify her from the throne, she couldn't believe it was *this*. The one time she lost control. The one time her emotions got the better of her. It was achingly pathetic.

"I've told Zuri they need cameras out on the ramparts. But she refuses to put them out there. Says she doesn't want footage of teenagers making out," Leander continued, his tone light.

It took all her power not to crumble on the spot. Not to show any shame or remorse, even though she was in danger of passing out. With a face of calm indifference she did not feel, Emmeline met the king's appraising look. He said nothing, waiting her out.

"Was I expected to play nice, Your Majesty?" she asked coolly.

The corner of King Leander's mouth twitched into a wicked smile, then a slow, deep chuckle started in the back of his throat. Emmeline's nails dug into the armchair, but she let him laugh, not knowing what to expect next. She was bleeding out, and she'd rather that he just put an end to her misery.

King Leander leaned back, regarding her with those sharp gray eyes, still smirking. "I hope your tactics proved fruitful."

Emmeline stared back at him, completely confused. Was she... not out of the running?

Leander hummed in the back of his throat, hands folded across his abs. "Your cousins are full of surprises. I've known for years Titus's parents disobeyed my orders, but I was intrigued at the notion of one of you knowing while the others did not. Even Alaric's upbringing might serve him better than he can see at the moment. But you, Emmeline," he continued, his gaze locked with hers, "are everything I'd expected you'd be."

Emmeline's heart skipped, and her nails dug deeper into the leather of the chair.

"Elegant, strategic...ruthless." His eyes narrowed. "Every mark of a royal. No, a solider."

Emmeline lifted her chin, the wooziness and warmth from the wine evaporating like steam on her overheated skin.

This. This was what she wanted. What she craved. Acknowledgment. To be seen.

"Do what must be done to win, Emmeline. Let no one get in your way." Then he scooped up the photographs and tapped the edge of them on the wood. "But next time, don't get caught."

25

TITUS

THOUGH TOTTENHAM WAS HIS FAVORITE FOOTBALL CLUB OF ALL time, Titus was expected to root for Ashland's team. Not that he'd want to be rowdy in the royal box either way.

No one had spoken in the last fifteen minutes, much less cheered. Even the few reporters covering the heirs' PR appearance looked bored. Ilsa was typing on her laptop and the guards stood around behind them, not touching the buffet of Michelin-quality food.

He, Sadie, Alaric, and Emmeline all sat in the box seats over the field, either watching the match or sleeping with their eyes open, one of the two. It was their third day in Ashland, and they'd been up at five every morning, to bed after eleven, with classes and meetings stacked back-to-back, learning every possible aspect of life in Ashlandic Court.

The game was their second PR event, and though it was significantly more fun than watching a massive tanker pull away from the harbor, it was still draining. The stylists dressed them not in suits, but in deep-blue sweaters with the Ashlandic Sea Dragons logo and jeans. The girls wore the kits of Ashland's star players, and Sadie looked incredibly cute in hers.

She also might have been the only one *really* watching the game.

She was vibrating in the seat next to him, wanting desperately to jump and scream as Malaevik raced across the field with the ball, heading straight for the goal with no defense blocking his path.

"Why're you holding back?" Titus asked quietly.

Sadie shot him a look, then one to the stoic guards behind them. "It's a little tense in here."

"So? Ignore them."

"Yeah, right."

"If Malaevik scores, I'll cheer with you."

Sadie spared him a quick glance before focusing her attention back on the field as the ace striker danced around Tottenham's tardy defense. "Really?"

"Definitely."

As if on cue, the Ashlandic player made his shot. The ball sailed through the air, hitting the net right between the hands of Tottenham's goalie.

Sadie burst from her seat, shrieking with excitement. "YAH, MALAEVIK! GO DRAGONS!"

Though the rest of the stadium exploded in cheers and screams, Sadie was alone in the royal box. She was screaming for less than ten seconds before she realized the silence around her and dropped back into her seat face flaming, clearly mortified.

Laughing, Titus tried to shield himself as Sadie punched his arm. "Oh my god, you vicious liar."

"Easy there, Sadie. No one likes a violent fan."

Their antics were cut off as someone loudly cleared their throat. Emmeline was glaring at them with daggers in her silver eyes. Alaric, on the other hand, ignored them entirely.

When Titus saw the reporters watching, he settled back, and Sadie did the same. Their short-lived fun died a quick, judgmental death. This week could not end soon enough.

*　　*　　*

After the first night, they mercifully hadn't had any more "family din-ners." Food was brought to them between court lessons with Ilsa, and apart from her and a few random castle attendants, the heirs saw no one else. Not even their parents. *Thank God.*

Seeing his parents in person hadn't been much different from expe-riencing them over the phone. Cold, strict, and scathingly unpleasant. Their hugs were pathetic. He'd had warmer embraces from his Elton John–impersonating piano teacher back at Eton.

But a part of himself—which he hated—still craved their attention. Still wanted their approval and...love. So when they summoned him that evening, Titus felt mostly trepidation, as well as a smidgen of hope.

Each of the heirs had their own living quarters, which took up most of the second floor of the north wing. And while he rarely saw Alaric or Emmeline out of their rooms, Sadie was surprisingly com-fortable roaming the halls.

As he straightened the collar of his dinner jacket, he noticed her in a small alcove sitting on the thick window ledge and watching the sea rage below the cliffs. Looking lost in her own world, he didn't inter-rupt. Besides, his mother would not tolerate even a second of tardiness.

Right before he entered the room where his parents waited, his burner phone buzzed in his jacket pocket. Cursing, he reached to turn it off. He didn't need his parents discovering that he had a second phone. That's when he saw a missed call, voicemail, and another text notification. All from Dr. Sharrad.

His stomach plummeted. The one good thing about being so busy was that he hadn't been able to worry *too* much about the appointment waiting for him when he returned to ATA. But how could he forget entirely when every day the dull aches and incessant throbs seemed to grow incrementally worse?

Soon. He would have to deal with this soon. Today he chose to be ignorant. He confronted one nightmare at a time.

Offhandedly he considered why he even bothered carrying around the burner phone if he wasn't going to answer it right away. He couldn't risk accidentally revealing the secret phone. With that in mind, he turned it off, tucked it back into his dinner jacket, and knocked on the door.

"Come in," his mother said from the other side.

The room he'd been summoned to was another study—smaller, private, and not far from the gardens. His mother sat at the desk, laptop open, reading glasses on, the light of the screen reflected in her lenses. His father was on the couch reading on his tablet.

Neither of them looked up when Titus walked in. Before he even had a chance to say good evening, Lady Calliope was turning around her laptop, showing a news article with Titus and Sadie smiling and laughing together at the football game.

"What's this?" Her voice was eerily calm.

Titus felt every muscle in his body tighten. "It's good press," he replied quietly.

His mother seized her teacup and chucked it just over his shoulder, the porcelain shattering against the wall. Titus didn't flinch when it came hurtling toward him, more from shock than lack of reflexes. Tea drenched the wallpaper and his left shoulder, splashing some of the leather-bound books.

"Don't be cute," she said quietly, even as the sound of breaking porcelain echoed in the study. "Do you think your grandfather sees a future king in this silly little teenager?"

Titus resisted the urge to heave a sigh. That would only make her angrier. "I don't pretend to know what the king sees or thinks."

Lady Calliope stood, eyes flashing dangerously. Thick rivulets of steamy liquid rolled down the wall as his mother took a steadying breath. "Emmeline is on track for heir apparent."

Every instinct told Titus to panic. But not in front of his parents. He kept his voice even. "Emmeline and I had matching success in our midterms. We are both chairs on the student council. There is nothing she has done that I—"

"Don't be *foolish*, Titus," his mother seethed through clenched teeth. "Why else would your grandfather receive her *alone* in his office? Certainly not to dismiss her. Haven't you noticed her renewed confidence, despite knowing what a joke her parents are?"

It felt like someone was tightening their hand around his throat. It was getting harder and harder to breathe. "He has not named her yet," he managed to croak.

"That's the only reason you're still standing here now," his mother hissed. "Otherwise, we'd do well to disown you."

Pain wove its way through his body, but not the pain that he'd steadily grown accustomed to. This pain originated from his heart.

For a brief moment, Titus imagined telling his parents about Dr. Sharrad. About the specialist waiting to see him again. About the fact that he might need more time to cope and understand whatever was going on...but then he heard the drip of the tea down the wall, reaching the ground. The shattered cup lay at his feet.

"Now," his mother began, "what more can you do?"

Always more. Never enough.

He'd known for years he was nothing but a biological asset to be used at his parents' discretion. But experiencing deep-rooted trauma in person was something new. Something he wasn't sure he could tolerate, or overcome.

26

SADIE

Sadie felt something tapping her head.

It jolted her from old memories. From piercing tea kettles, old jigsaw puzzles, knitting needles, and warm embraces that smelled like peppermint oil and turmeric.

She tipped her neck back, finding the person she least expected standing behind her. "Hey, Alaric."

He stood there in jeans and his well-worn olive-green Henley, Ilsa's approved outfit already abandoned. "Fancy a walk?" he grumbled, jerking his thumb over his shoulder.

Sadie blinked in surprise, but she wasn't going to say no. The sting of grief had been nearly debilitating the last few days, ever since returning to her homeland. At one point during a lesson, Ilsa had mentioned something inane about the king's favorite place to visit in southern Ashland and Sadie bolted up from her chair. She barely made it out of the room before bursting into sobs. The casual mention of a beach she'd once visited with her mah and grannah riled up so much heartache.

She found that roaming the breathtaking palace grounds helped ward off some of those moments. So she bounced to her feet. "I'd love to. Have you been to the gardens yet?"

Alaric shook his head and Sadie pointed down the hall. "This way. They're really special. There's a full grove of wisteria."

He let Sadie lead the way. She had no idea what had possessed Alaric to seek her out, but she was glad for the company.

One silver lining is that she'd managed to snap some beautiful landscapes for Ashland Sea Mammal Conservation's socials. Due to midterms and losing her laptop, she'd barely been able to work with them so far, but Mrs. Colliander had given her account access as soon as Ilsa Halvorsen signed off on Sadie's participation. She had already connected accounts to a social media scheduler app and begun preparing posts. So far, her video of the massive tanker, *Riretha*, pulling away from the docks with her caption of an old Ashlandic sea prayer had gotten almost a thousand views. Followers loved celebrating the seafaring economy in tandem with protecting marine life.

Working on the accounts had filled most of her spare time (not that she had much), but tonight, for whatever reason, she hadn't been able to shake off the past. She was grateful for Alaric's invitation. Exceedingly so.

They walked in silence for a bit before Sadie choked out a laugh. "So that was embarrassing, huh?"

He cocked an eyebrow. "Yeh'll need to be more specific."

Sadie stuck her tongue out at him. "You know, when I jumped up and screamed at Malaevik's goal."

Alaric snorted. "Nothing wrong with cheering for football."

"How come you didn't cheer, then?"

He shrugged. "I happen to like Tottenham. Wouldn't feel right to cheer against one of my favorite teams."

"I guess that makes sense. They've got a crappy defense, though."

"Careful now, or I'll toss yeh off this balcony," Alaric warned. Sadie giggled and the two fell into a more comfortable silence as they made their way to the garden. If possible, the landscaping was even more beautiful than Almus Terra's. It had ivy-clad stone statues of sea dragons, blossoms that thrived in the cold, dank air, and ponds with the beginnings of ice at their shores.

Sadie loved it. She had discovered it on her first night here when she couldn't sleep.

"What were yeh thinking about?" Alaric asked suddenly as they passed a row of evening primroses. "Back at the window?"

Her heart cracked a little in her chest, and she moved her fingers just below her left collarbone, feeling the sting radiate through her blood, carrying grief to every cell of her body. "Old stories my grannah used to tell me," she answered softly.

"Stories," he repeated.

"Mm-hmm." They passed a part of the garden that revealed the sea between the towers of Heres Castle, and she continued. "Ashland lore. From before this country tore itself apart."

Alaric tucked his hands in his jacket pockets. "Yeh know them pretty well, aye?"

"By heart," Sadie answered. When she felt Alaric's skeptical look, she took a deep breath and recited a story her mother used to tell her. Her favorite.

"The giants had only ever known the rocks and the hills and the evergreen, but when they saw the sea in all its majesty, they knelt before its might and offered their queen. The sea gods, fearing the power of the giants, washed them with salt and met them as tyrants. Durah, the giant queen, found her beloved kin covered with brine and crust, so she allied with the wind to smite the sea with every gust. Thus, the cliffs stand still as Durah's giant kin, battling water with stone and wind."

Why her mother loved the story so much was a mystery. But it had been musically recited every bedtime until each word lived in her soul.

"Durah chose vengeance, huh?" Alaric muttered, his gaze on one of the tallest spires.

"It's not like it really solved anything," Sadie said, running her fingers across a hanging freesia blossom.

"Might've made Durah feel better."

"No one heals from vengeance."

"How do yeh know that?"

Sadie peered into Alaric's shadowed face. Light was low in the garden; even so, she could see the hurt etched into a boy far too young to show so many lines. Alaric was here, denied by a father who believed he was a bastard, and probably struggling just as much as she was. But for all of Sadie's loss, at least she'd been loved. Deeply.

Sadie opened her mouth, not yet sure what cold comfort she could offer, but wanting to reassure him all the same, when raised voices pierced through the garden.

Words were hard to make out, but Sadie recognized a voice. It was a deeper register, but it sounded like Titus. Was it his father? That would explain the Ashlandic accent.

"Is that Prince Magnus?" Sadie whispered.

"Drop it, Sadie," Alaric said brusquely. "Don't interfere."

Sadie frowned as the voices grew louder, angrier. Meaner. She only caught every other word, but each one was crueler than the last.

Worthless. Pathetic. Inept. *Disappointment.* What parent spoke of their child like that?

It might not be her place to interfere, but if it was Titus...

Despite their rocky start, he'd become perhaps the closest person to her at Almus Terra, tied with Trang. Their project had brought them together, and against all odds, she enjoyed time with him. He listened to her points, valued her work, and made her smile. And the last few days, he'd checked on her when he could—even making her laugh at the game today...

Sadie started toward the voices. She felt Alaric's fingers brush her arm, as if wanting to stop her, but she easily slipped away from his loose grip. Moving quickly through the garden, nearing the primroses, she got closer to the castle's walls. The voices had stopped. A door slammed. Footsteps crunched across the pebbles. A heavy thud and a rattling breath.

It took Sadie only a few seconds to find him. Titus sat on a stone bench, head in his hands, his shoulders rising and falling with labored breaths. Like he was on the verge of a panic attack. She identified with what she saw more than she cared to admit. That gave her the courage she needed to reach out to him.

"Titus?" she whispered.

He lifted his head, face startlingly pale in the gold glow of the castle windows. Seeing her under the branches of a crepe myrtle, he stood swiftly. But then stumbled. He managed to catch himself by grabbing the edge of the stone bench, but his left knee drove into the cold grass.

With a gasp, she darted forward, looping her hand under his arm to help him. His sleeves were pushed up and his forearms felt awfully cold. But his elbow was almost fiery to the touch. "Are you okay?" she breathed.

"I'm fine." He pushed himself to his feet. Betraying his words, a tremor that did not seem fine struck visibly through his body.

"You should sit." She pulled him toward the stone bench, but he resisted.

"What are you doing here, Sadie?" he said. His voice sounded tired and strained, like everything hurt. Of course, if she had just been verbally abused like that, she'd hurt too.

Sadie sat on the bench, tugging him down with her. "Sit, Titus, please."

He didn't sit, but the muscles in his arm trembled under her touch.

"Or I'll sit on you."

A laugh of disbelief escaped him. "Promise?"

"Sit," she pled impatiently, and his rigid form gave way, allowing him to fall back onto the bench. He let out a breath and another shudder, but then his spine straightened, and a brief grimace crossed his features as he moved his arm away from her touch.

Sadie was left feeling oddly cold. And not because of the weather.

Titus didn't want to show any vulnerability. Not even in front of her, and she felt they'd grown... well, maybe not close, but friendly. At least enough for him not to put up a front.

Maybe it would be better to leave him alone so he could relax, but she found that she couldn't. "So...," she started, picking at the edge of her sweater. "Was that your—"

She didn't even get to finish her sentence, because he was already pushing himself up. "For God's sake, Titus," Sadie hissed through her teeth as she grabbed his arm and urged him back down. She wasn't sure how or why, except that it was clear he was in serious pain. It might be emotional or mental, but in her experience, sometimes that could be even worse than the physical. It also seemed like the topic of his parents was off limits. He'd try to flee again if she brought it up.

With a huff, she threw her calves over his thighs. "There. Now you can't leave."

Even in the dim light, Sadie could read the surprise across his features. But he didn't shove away her legs. If anything, his posture relaxed. A tired smile flitted across his lips as his chest moved closer to her arm.

"I'm pretty sure I could still manage an escape."

Dang, he was right. She scooched closer. Soon she was nearly sitting on his lap, her knee pressed against his abs as she wrapped her arms around her folded legs.

"All right, it would be a little more difficult now," he admitted, laughter in his voice.

If she could make him laugh, this was worth it. And, geez, just like his hugs, it felt good sitting in his lap with all his warmth around her, so close to a real embrace.

After a few moments of silence, their breaths the only sound, Sadie asked, "Are you going to tell me what's wrong?"

His forehead nudged against her temple, hot breath tickling her ear.

Heat bloomed up her neck and into her cheeks. She remembered that moment in the library. She remembered Alaric's teasing words. But she didn't move away. She liked it too much, and she wanted to hear what he had to say. More than anything.

"Nothing's wrong," he murmured softly.

Vicious liar.

"Titus," she probed softly.

"How do you smell so sweet? Like you just finished baking sugar cookies?" He purred against her neck, arm tightening around her, and fingers gently digging into her hip. He was inhaling her. Deep lungfuls against her hair and collarbone.

Butterflies swooped in her stomach, her heart dive-bombing with them. "I stole some of the soap from ATA," she whispered. "It's vanilla."

He chuckled into her skin, and shivers danced down her arms and legs. "Makes sense."

Sadie planted a hand against his chest. This wasn't why she'd been trying to find him, but she also couldn't bring herself to leave. "Titus, listen."

His cheekbone nudged her neck, but the rest of his body seemed to tense. "I'm listening."

Sadie could go about this one of two ways: She could confront him about what she'd overheard and make him feel even worse, or she could distract him with something that might make him feel better, even marginally.

"I had fun today," she said finally. It was the truth—in that brief moment when she let loose and screamed to her heart's content. It had been exhilarating. "I cheered and laughed. Thanks to you."

Against her arm, Titus's chest expanded with a deep breath. Strong but gentle fingers gripped her chin and lifted her face. There were a few seconds where she could've moved her head away, but she didn't. And the next pivotal moment, his lips were on hers.

Tender and warm. Full, but firm.

The butterflies in her stomach were Freaking. Out.

Sadie didn't know much about kissing. She'd only had a few awkward pecks at her old school's dance—but she knew this was good. Titus didn't just kiss with his mouth—his whole body was involved. His arm around her back curled her against him, hugging her body closer, and his fingers dug harder into her hip. His other hand smoothed against her jaw, tilting her face for a deeper kiss. The bottom of Sadie's shoes skimmed across the stone as Titus shifted his legs—his shoulders and large frame surged over her like he was ready to devour.

Sadie's fingers squeezed his shirt as he cradled her cheek and drew another kiss from her lips—then another, then a fourth. Or maybe it was a fifth. How could she keep count when her skin felt so warm, and her head felt so foggy, and her stomach felt so . . . swoopy? *Is that even a word?*

She was being lowered down, her back on the bench and her hair falling over the edge. The nape of her neck felt the chill of stone. He'd kissed her at least six times, but this was the moment that seemed to jolt an eruption of electricity down her spine.

They were not done. In fact, it seemed only the beginning.

"Soft . . ." He sounded entranced as his thumb skated down her cheek and glided across her bottom lip. Her breath stalled in her chest, her pulse stuttering. That felt *too* good.

"Titus."

The warning in her tone, the hesitation and worry—he heard it. Titus pulled away immediately, and Sadie stared at him with wide eyes. His handsome face was flushed, his blond hair slightly mussed, his lips—red. Heat poured through her blood, and she knew she couldn't stay a second longer. Not even to figure out what just happened.

Heartbeat thundering in her ears, Sadie bolted to her feet. Titus didn't stop her until the last moment and his hand captured hers. Not hard, but firm.

"Sadie. Talk to me. Don't freak out."

"I'm not freaking out," she said. Ha, now *she* was the liar.

"You are. Listen. That wasn't—" He sighed, dropping her hand and dragging fingers through his hair. "That wasn't because I had a bad day, all right? I've been *wanting* to kiss you."

Sure, Sadie had read some of the signs. Had them pointed out to her, even. But hearing him say it? Even after living through the kiss? It sounded ridiculous.

"Oh" was all she could say. *Incomprehensible.*

Titus got to his feet, took both of her hands, and tugged her close. With a small yelp, she stumbled into him, her chest bumping his and her heart jumping into her throat. Despite the little voice in her head that said this was a *bad idea*, it felt good—necessary even—for him to pull her close. To remind her that it wasn't something he regretted.

Brushing his cheek ever so softly against her forehead, he whispered, "So think about us. Think about me wanting to kiss you."

"Titus, this isn't—"

"In fact . . ." His head dipped farther, down toward her lips, and she couldn't stop the gasp exploding from her chest. "I dare you not to."

27

ALARIC

Alaric was under no illusions he'd made it into the lower dregs of Durah undetected. But no one had stopped him, so he wasn't sure if they cared. Maybe this whole visit was a test anyway. Let him dig his own grave. Anyone who escaped in the middle of the night only to wander into a pub and drink themselves into a stupor surely wasn't fit for the crown.

Course, he wasn't all the way gone yet. He could still remember the last few hours with painful clarity. Clarity that he was *trying* to muck up. Trying, and failing.

"Oy, another," he grumbled at the barkeep, a slimy old-timer who had no qualms about serving a teenager so long as Alaric's notes rang up the same in his register.

The man poured a shot of whiskey while a rock band from the seventies played in the speakers overhead. A neon sign flashed to his left, casting his hands and forearm in hot pink.

Alaric couldn't remember where, exactly, he was, and he didn't care, but he *could* still remember Sadie on Titus's lap. The picture of her legs across his thighs, of his hand on her jaw, of his lips, slowly but surely, stealing kisses that must be velvet soft—

Wincing, Alaric tossed the shot back, but the burn down his throat didn't dull the images. They enhanced into IMAX quality instead. Blowing up with Dolby surround sound—low breaths, sighs, the rustling of clothes as Titus moved over her...

Alaric muttered a curse under his breath and dug his palms into his eyes. *He didn't care.* Sadie could kiss whomever she wanted. Even a stuck-up arsehole like his rotten cousin.

But of course he cared. Otherwise he wouldn't have settled at the most miserable pub in town. What made this royally pathetic (ha, pun) was that he *never* dulled his mind with alcohol. He'd seen what it did to men twice his age and twice his size. Turned them into blundering fools or senseless monsters. He'd never wanted to be one of them.

Yet here he was. On a bender. Real prince *he* turned out to be.

As he gestured to the bartender for a pint, he swallowed back the ache of missing his life before this nonsense. Sure, it hadn't been stellar, but he had great friends. Kyle. The twins, Pike and Lee. Rodney. Even old Mrs. Tuttle—well, he missed her stew more than her.

His fingers fumbled for the glass, splashing amber liquid on the bar top. Was anyone looking for him?

Surely he'd been seen stomping through the landscaping to get to the road that led out through the evergreen trees. He'd passed several guard houses before he made it to the highway and called a taxi.

The taxi dumped him off at the end of a street in Durah, and he'd stormed into the first pub he'd seen. Now inebriated, he could still remember everything so very well, but his thought processing was much slower. He didn't question *why* he cared what Sadie and Titus did. He didn't think too hard about his father ignoring his existence. And he didn't wonder *why* he was still here.

Sure, he liked Almus Terra. He wanted to stay. But were interesting classes really worth untangling all the messed-up family drama in this asinine competition?

More importantly, were Sadie, Titus, and his father worth Alaric's self-destruction?

When he slung back the next drink, easily his fourth, the answer could only be . . . yes. His foggy brain wondered how many times Sadie had kissed Titus. He wondered if he'd matched it yet in drinks, or if he still had a long way to go.

With a groan, Alaric pulled his hands down his face, then dragged his fingers through his hair. This was miserable. Next to him, a man yelled at reruns of the Tottenham-Ashland football match.

The man roared, splashing his beer everywhere. "Maddison's offside, his whole arm!"

With nothing left to lose, Alaric released his anger and growled back, "VAR shows otherwise, yeh muppet."

And that was all it took to nudge the stranger to the edge. "All right, maggot, *up*. Let's take this outside." The man stood so abruptly his stool fell back, hitting the passing waitress.

She fell to the side, nearly crashing into a table, before Alaric caught her arm and hauled her up. It was like she could see the absolute murder in Alaric's eyes, because the waitress grabbed his arm. "Love, wait there—"

But Alaric wasn't hearing her. This was the outlet he needed: a fight. Something to knock him into oblivion. And while football was a stupid excuse, hitting a woman, even accidentally, was something that he could get behind for a brawl.

Alaric seized the man by the collar and shoved him toward the entrance of the pub. The man stumbled drunkenly against the door.

"Yeh want outside, arsehole? Yeh *first*." On his last word, Alaric reared back and swung. Cartilage crunched, the man's nose folding like a piece of paper under Alaric's knuckles.

He fell through the door from the force of the blow and landed face up on the sidewalk. Alaric's blood roared in his ears as he reached down for the man's collar. Someone tried to grab his shirt, and that's when his fighting instincts really kicked in. He skipped back, his fists raised, but already seeing double. Shadowy figures advanced and he fell against the grimy brick wall.

Flashing lights appeared in his peripheral vision, and rough, strong hands jerked his wrists behind his back and shoved him over the hood of a car. Alaric struggled to see straight. The world was moving. Spinning. Too fast.

For a moment, he felt the cool metal of handcuffs, then he was forced downward, almost rolling his ankle as he slipped off the curb and was pushed into a car that smelled strongly like leather and... flowers?

His messed-up brain had been certain this was a cop car. But he knew from experience those smelled like greasy cheeseburgers and vomit. Not florals or new-car smell.

"Unbelievable," a feminine voice said. "He's completely sloshed. Make him drink."

A strong hand seized Alaric's jaw and opened his mouth, tipping in warm water. Or what Alaric thought was *only* warm water.

Salt flooded into his taste buds and nausea rose like a tidal wave. The car abruptly stopped, the door opened, and his head was thrust outside just as he vomited on the side of the road. It didn't take him long to empty his stomach, all liquid poison.

Done, he collapsed back into the leather seat feeling more like a human. His head pounded, his throat burned, and his right hand hurt from punching someone dead in the face, but the world was no longer spinning.

"Take us back," a sharp voice commanded next to him. The car rolled forward.

Sobering up, Alaric couldn't believe he hadn't placed the voice sooner. Using a smidgen of the strength he had left, he looked beside him.

His cousin sat there in leggings, a winter coat, and boots, holding up her phone. The light from the camera shone right on him, making him squint and blink.

"Are yeh filming this, Emmeline?" he groaned.

She lowered the screen, looking at him like, *duh*. "For blackmail. In case I need it later."

Alaric couldn't even be mad. He closed his eyes, leaning his neck back on the seat rest and relishing the cool leather on his clammy skin.

"Got it."

"You're an idiot, by the way."

A pathetic smile tugged at the corner of his lips. "I know."

If there's one thing he'd always known, it was that. But now he was starting to understand something new. With Emmeline next to him, he realized *why* he'd chosen to drink the night away.

He'd wanted Sadie to be there. When he reached out earlier in the garden, she'd slipped through his fingers and had chosen instead to comfort Titus. Maybe it wasn't fair to put that responsibility on her, especially when he'd been surly most of the time. But hell, he'd wanted someone to choose him. After he'd been sitting in his room thinking about his dead mother and a father who hated him, with no one left on his side. No one *ever* on his side.

When he'd tried to hold onto Sadie, he'd wanted her to stay. Because no one ever did.

"Thanks for the save, cousin," he said as the car zoomed down the highway. She may not have been the person he reached for, nor could she fill any gaping hole inside him, but there was a big piece of Emmeline Eldana he'd misjudged. For better or worse, she might be the only family he had that gave a damn.

"Don't do it again," she muttered. "Otherwise I'll put your drunk ass on the news."

28

SADIE

"W**E'RE SO HONORED TO MAKE YOUR ACQUAINTANCE, Y**OUR H**IGH-**nesses.*" The portly chief of medicine bowed, the edge of his doctor's coat sweeping the floor.

"We are all the more honored, sir," Emmeline said, returning the bow. "Thank you for your service to our people, and for protecting Ashland's health and longevity."

Not for the first time, Sadie was deeply glad for the face mask hiding most of her features. They'd been at Durah Memorial Hospital for almost twenty minutes, which was nineteen minutes too long. The place was full of haunting memories. Of Grannah's final days. Of the hours after her mother . . .

The chief of medicine spoke about their new state-of-the-art MRI machine that the Royal Treasury had approved. Apparently, they could detect 15 percent more early-stage diseases with this one than they had with their old one. *But what about depression? What about bipolar disorder? When will you ever cure those life-threatening diseases?*

Immediately Sadie felt guilty about her resentment. This MRI machine was of course a very good thing.

"You okay?" Titus whispered, his nudging elbow gently returning her to the present. The chief of medicine was walking and talking again, leading them through the new wing built for cancer patients.

Sadie took a deep breath, but it didn't feel deep enough through the mask. "Bathroom," she muttered.

Titus gave a subtle nod. "I'll cover for you."

Ignoring the guilty pang in her chest, Sadie took advantage of Titus's kindness and slipped away from the group. Despite the fact that she'd asked for time to consider his feelings, and hers, Titus was still looking out. And if they weren't in this hospital, she'd probably still be reliving that kiss—*kisses*—like she had for almost two full days.

Sadie passed the bathroom. She knew the clean white floors and the light blue walls all too well, and it was easy to reach the stairwell that connected to the floor above. Her heels echoed down the hall, but other than a medical assistant carrying fresh sheets, there was no one around.

Her phone chimed in her pocket, so she quickly put it on silent. But managed a small smile and quick text back when she saw who it was.

> TRANG: **How's the hospital visit going? Know you were dreading it...**
>
> SADIE: **Yeah, I needed a second...but Titus is covering for me!** ☺
>
> TRANG: **Well, well, chivalry is not dead apparently.**

Sadie ached to tell Trang more about the previous night with Titus and, more than once, had considered asking for a call. But every time she'd gotten close, she'd chickened out.

Maybe she'd known she needed all her courage for this. Room 345 was empty. Part of her hoped it wouldn't be so she could avoid facing her demons altogether. Still, if she couldn't see her grannah's stone memorial while she was briefly home, this was the next-closest thing.

Sadie stood at the foot of the hospital bed, staring at it with surprisingly dry eyes.

Behind her, the door opened. Probably a guard summoning her back. "I'm com—Your Majesty!"

Sadie nearly jumped out of her skin at the sight of King Leander standing in the doorway. She wasn't even aware he'd been at the hospital with them. "I'm so sorry, sir. I just wanted to..." Her throat closed, stopping any more words.

"Visit your grandmother's old room? Yes, I imagined you would. That's why I'm here. To check on you."

Sadie straightened, her eyes widening with shock. But then, as the king, he'd likely known everything about her before allowing her to be part of this competition.

"Thank you, sir. But... I'm all right."

"No need to lie to your king, Sadie," he said, though his tone was gentle. With a few strides, he reached the window and looked out. "I am no stranger to grief. Losing Rhea... it weighed on me for a very long time. Never goes away, actually. Your grandmother died in this bed, didn't she? Four days after she was hit?"

Sadie swallowed hard, then slowly slid her hospital mask down to her neck, so her next words wouldn't be muffled. "Yes, sir. But it wasn't the car that killed her."

The king nodded. "Hmm, that's one way to view it, I suppose."

In Sadie's opinion, it was the only way. Her grandmother had been diagnosed with dementia, but with little money and expensive health care, her mother had no way to care for Grannah. While Mah was at work, and Sadie at school, Grannah had wandered out to the street. She'd been confused and agitated, and was hit by a car.

The driver had the right of way in broad daylight and was totally sober. Grannah had just stepped off the curb when no one was around to stop her. To this day, Sadie still received a card with penance from the driver on the anniversary of her death, though she'd told him to stop.

"But your mother never made it to the hospital," King Leander said, his words so soft Sadie thought she imagined them.

At his expectant look, Sadie realized he was waiting for her reply.

"No sir," she said finally, though her mouth tasted like ash. Her grandmother, she could handle. Her mother...if he talked about her mother, she'd...

"I imagine that must've been quite a shock. Finding her like that. I'm deeply sorry you had to witness such a thing," he said quietly. And he did sound remorseful.

"To lose a parent in such a way," he continued, sighing deeply. "It must leave a deep scar."

Sadie couldn't respond. She just wished he'd stop talking.

"When I sent my grandchildren away, I selfishly thought little about how they might feel in the end. My only goal was to protect them. And I still stand by my choice. Even if they hate me for it."

It took her a moment to believe it, because the king she'd encountered so far seemed incapable of remorse—but she heard it there, in his words.

Some discomfort she'd been feeling seeped away. He was doing a sloppy job of it, but she respected his efforts to console her.

"I don't believe they hate you, Your Majesty." Though she didn't know if that was exactly true or not, it felt like the right thing to say. And she wanted to believe it too.

King Leander regarded her for a moment, then gave her a sad smile. "May I offer you some advice, Sadie? As one who's also lost someone incredibly dear to them?"

"Please, sir."

"Have you heard of stoicism?"

Sadie had, but only in passing in her high school Classical Studies courses.

"It's a philosophy made popular by the Roman emperor Marcus Aurelius. Rather befitting of Sadie Aurelia, wouldn't you say? " He smiled. "Anyway, he dealt with a lot, you see—wars, a plague—his rule was not easy. And yet, he celebrated the hardships. He believed that while you could not change your fate, or the events happening around you, you could change how you faced it."

Sadie's gut churned. On some level, she knew what he was trying to say. And in a way, she agreed. But it felt too raw. Too soon. Perhaps Marcus Aurelius's trials had made him stronger, but Sadie had been decimated.

The king seemed to sense that his words brought internal conflict, so he laid a gentle hand on her shoulder. "Sadie. Look to the path ahead, not behind you. You've been given a chance at something great. A stoic would focus on the opportunities, not the losses. To right wrongs. Not give up."

I just want to give up. For the first time, those wrenching words not only wounded but also steadied her. Grief poured out of her like blood onto the hospital floor. But the king's firm grip on her shoulder spun her point of view with dizzying clarity.

The path ahead. Righting wrongs. She had been given an opportunity as an heir . . . and what had she done with it so far? Nothing.

"What is it, Sadie?" King Leander's gaze ignited like the fire he'd just stoked inside her.

The mask crinkled around her neck as she lifted her chin. It took every ounce of courage she had to answer his prompt. "Why did you pass the Entrepreneurial Exemption Law, sir?"

King Leander's mouth twitched. If he was surprised by the sudden change in subject, he didn't mention it. "It pours money into our economy. Business owners have more to spend, to pay their people more to—"

"They won't pay unless you raise the minimum wage, which you haven't done in ten years." This was true, at least for the eleven large corporations that had ruled Ashland's economy. Small businesses could barely survive among their monopolies. And corporate greed prevented many from getting higher wages. *Alaric hadn't exactly been wrong.*

King Leander's eyes narrowed at her.

Oops. Her pulse spiked, fearing she'd gone too far despite the fact that he'd encouraged her challenge. She had just cut off the king. Was this the moment where she was discarded? Not for getting detention, or kissing his grandson in the garden, but for disagreeing with him? Wouldn't that be hilarious.

And yet…she didn't think he would. He'd seemed to welcome that defiance.

His smile stayed in place. "Our economy has flourished under this law. It's allowed foreign companies to start businesses here because they don't shoulder the burden of taxes."

"But your subjects *do*," Sadie argued. So many of them wanting, trying for a better life. But feeling stuck. Why couldn't he see it?

"Such is the evil of all governments, Sadie. Now," he turned for the door, "let us return to the others. You have a full day ahead."

He dismissed her, but he'd done so much more than that.

Before this moment, Sadie was only interested in the free ride to Almus Terra. Before, she had no desire to rule and couldn't even imagine it. Before, she'd been too scared to refuse the king's trial because she had nowhere else to go.

Now, though, she wanted to compete in earnest. Because she was realizing, for the first time, that she was no longer powerless. The monarch held the fates of everyday people like Grannah and Mah, regulating working conditions, pushing health care reform, establishing economic policies, reshaping their country.

Sadie could not change the past. But if she were queen, she could create the future her family had deserved. The future they all deserved.

The earbud Ilsa yanked from her ear made Sadie's glasses slide down her nose. Her cordless headphones had run out of battery and after wearing contacts for almost a week straight, Sadie craved simple. She wanted sweatpants and sweatshirts, and glasses. No more pantyhose or foundation. That was the rallying cry in her head as they flew back over the Atlantic.

"I know you're tired of me," Ilsa said, waving around her tablet. "But I have one more announcement before I leave you at the Toulon airport. Your grandfather has expressed his desire for all four of you to be on the Hibernia planning committee."

"The *what?*" Alaric continued staring at the book he was reading, its cover folded behind the spine.

"Come on, Alaric," Ilsa growled. She seemed quite ready to strangle them all. "The Almus Terra winter ball, where one of you will be announced heir apparent."

"Oh, *that* Hibernia," Alaric muttered, his eyebrows popping up sarcastically.

"You've been ordered to submit applications to the student council, who will then choose eight students to lead the event planning."

"Ilsa," Emmeline drawled. "It's just a party. Shouldn't our time be devoted to more serious pursuits?"

Sadie agreed wholeheartedly, though she wasn't brave enough to say it.

"It's *not* just a party," Ilsa snapped. "It's Almus Terra's Open House event, which all the parents of the C-Suites and Elites will be attending."

"Of course it's only *their* parents," Alaric said under his breath, but loud enough for everyone to hear over the jet engines.

"Yes, it's only their parents," Ilsa continued, "because they are the only ones with enough power to shape your futures."

Sadie clenched her jaw, feeling those words like a knife to her ribs. Alaric snorted.

"It's a front," Titus said after a beat. "It's not an open house, or a ball, it's a global economic summit masquerading as a family weekend." Everyone looked at him, but he kept staring out the window. "Calixa's been boasting about it all semester."

"I haven't heard anything at the council meetings," Emmeline said, crossing her arms. "Must be when you and Cal are alone?"

Sadie's heart skittered as Titus's gaze jumped to her, and then quickly away. He then glared at Emmeline. "Perhaps you've been too busy with Sebastian to stay informed."

"Children," Ilsa interrupted, sounding exhausted. "Yes, Titus is correct. It's a global economic summit that isn't *technically* authorized by the UN."

"Is this even...legal?" Sadie asked. A secret global economic summit held at the world's most prestigious boarding school hardly sounded ethical.

"What, you think Interpol is concerned about a dance party for rich people and their kids?" Emmeline sneered.

Ilsa sighed as her phone rang. "I have to take this. Try to behave." She stood and headed to the back of the plane.

"So what really happens at this thing?" Alaric asked, his glower pointed at Titus. It was, Sadie noted, perhaps the first time Alaric had addressed his cousin all week.

"I only know what Cal brags about. And it could be just that— bragging. But she's said that agreements are discussed, alliances are forged, and sometimes billions of dollars trade hands from company to country."

Alaric let out a hiss of disbelief. Sadie gaped at Titus, thinking of all the C-Suite kids and their parents. "So you're saying corporations might be bribing governments at this thing."

"That's not much different from lobbying in the States," Emmeline said, flicking her wrist like non-sanctioned global trade agreements were no big deal.

"We're on a global scale here, Emmeline," Alaric said, fuming.

"Oh? And what are you going to do about it?" Her silver eyes flashed with challenge. "The king wants us sitting in front-row seats to watch how the world works. That's all. Grow up and smell the bribery."

29

EMMELINE

THE ARROW BURIED ITSELF IN THE TARGET, JUST A LITTLE OFF-center, but nevertheless where Emmeline intended. Calixa hated to lose.

"Hmm." The student council president tilted her head to the side as she studied the target. "Your form is excellent, Emmeline. But your aim needs work."

Emmeline gave a fake smile and took a step back, gesturing for Cal to take her spot. "Show me?"

"Of course," Calixa replied haughtily. She raised her own bow, giving the string a testing tug before she drew an arrow for herself. "You were saying?"

"Right," Emmeline said as she tucked a spare piece of hair away from her cheek. It was typically windy at Almus Terra, but it wasn't so bad this afternoon as to interfere with their archery practice. "I know you're reviewing the applications for the Hibernia planning committee...."

"Don't worry," Cal said, letting her arrow fly. It found the perfect center with a light *thunk*. Satisfied, Calixa turned back and gave Emmeline a bored look. "The Ashland heirs have four of the eight spots. Your grandfather made sure of it."

Emmeline ignored the dig. They'd be on it regardless of her grandfather. The four Ashland heirs weren't just the most highly regarded students at ATA, they were also the highest ranked. With the midterm results out, Sadie, Alaric, Emmeline, and Titus had all made the top ten list of first-year students.

"I wanted to discuss a scholarship student we should add to the committee," Emmeline began carefully.

Calixa's gaze was so sharp it rivaled an arrow driving right into Emmeline. With a click of her tongue, Madame President busied herself with another one from her quiver. "I'm already giving you a Norm for the council," she said.

"Yes, and I stand behind that idea. But I've been reading up on Hibernia and—"

"You mean Sebastian has been telling you," Cal cut in, sending another arrow flying at the target. This one hit just below her first and she let out a swear.

As if Calixa didn't use relationships for her benefit as well. Kavi may be her official boyfriend, but he was *not* the only person she'd manipulated. Yet she had the gall to judge Emmeline for it.

"You'll be shocked to hear Seb isn't as useful as I'd like," Emmeline said with a smirk, leaning into Calixa's baiting with good humor. "But I've gathered there is some kind of fee for parents to attend Hibernia."

After learning more about ATA's infamous winter ball, Emmeline had discovered that all students could attend free of charge—just like any other high school dance. However, their parents were required to pay, and the fee happened to be exorbitant. Not to mention the cost of travel itself. Only the insanely rich would be able to attend, eliminating the parents of Scholars. Which, she assumed, was by design. Especially due to the secret global summit for which Titus had claimed Hibernia was a cover.

Calixa huffed. "It's an event. We're selling tickets, Emmeline."

"Sure, tickets," Emmeline said, waving her hand. "Whatever you want to call it. Almus Terra is collecting money from interested parties who'd like to attend. And it's not like . . . a hundred bucks."

Calixa dropped her bow, tossed her head back, and laughed. "No, five hundred grand is hardly pocket change."

Don't stab her with an arrow. Must. Not. Stab. Emmeline tightened her hand on her bow. "So how does the committee go about collecting all that money for the school? Hundreds of millions flow into one bank?"

Calixa dumped her bow and quiver on the bench where a Scholar would later have to pick it up. "It's not difficult. An attendant is sent with every check."

Regrettably, Emmeline left her equipment the same way. If Oakley saw her, she'd rip Emmeline to pieces. But the princess had to hurry to catch up to Cal, who was already halfway across the archery field. "That's my *point.* Paper checks are ancient. What is this, 1990? We should use a payment portal so they can purchase a ticket online."

At that, Cal stopped at the entrance to the covered parapet that led back toward the dorm wings. "We cannot use someone else's portal to accept money. A check can be written off as a donation to the Academy, but—"

"I know a third-party banking application defeats the purpose," Emmeline interrupted. "As students, we are supposed to control every aspect of this event. I understand it's a learning experience. And I get it, a check donation is clean and straightforward, and easy for us. But it's also outdated. We have students here building financial software. I mean, think of the kind of credit we'd get if we could pull that off."

Calixa cocked an eyebrow, finally picking up what Emmeline was putting down. Creating their own online portal would be completely student-run and extremely impressive. They'd be the first Almus Terra council to move Hibernia into the future. Anyone using the portal—a CEO or prime minister, for example—would find it quite notable. What kind of teenagers built a custom payment platform? Almus Terra students, of course.

"I'm assuming you have someone specific in mind?" Calixa finally said. "Otherwise this entire conversation is pointless."

"I do. But...he happens to be a Norm," Emmeline added, circling back to her initial proposition.

"Speed is critical. It's the end of October and he'd have less than a month to get it ready."

"He can handle it."

An exasperated sigh blew from Cal's lips as they hovered at the threshold of the parapet walkway. "What's his name?"

"Oliver Jackson."

Cal's eyebrows lifted slightly with recognition. "He's top of the class in your year, isn't he? He beat you."

Yes, she came in second, Oliver first. (Titus third.) Though Emmeline should have felt a surge of envy, she felt only pride. "Sounds about right," she said with a shrug. "I just know he's very good with computers. My roommate's girlfriend is his ambassador. They talk about his projects a lot. He could build our portal, no problem."

Calixa hummed as they strolled across the parapet, their high-heeled boots clicking across the stone. "All right," she said at last, "but he must apply. Applications are due at midnight."

Emmeline could count on both hands the number of times her nerves had nearly shown through—her fourteenth birthday, when her friends had decided to throw an impromptu party with boys from their neighboring school; the first day of Almus Terra; meeting her parents; her grandfather calling her to his office; and now. Approaching Oliver.

They'd seen each other in passing over the last few weeks—in classes and down the halls. Apart from when she'd almost said hi to him over FaceTime in Ashland, they hadn't talked since *the incident*. Every time she thought of it, her brain did a hard reboot, pretending it never happened. But the feelings were there. The gnawing, souring guilt and shame.

In a rare sighting, Oliver had no computer. He was sitting at a table in a student lounge reading a book. Emmeline recognized the title *Groundwork of the Metaphysics of Morals*, by Immanuel Kant. She was embarrassed to know Oliver's schedule by heart, and he wasn't taking Moral Philosophy. Meaning *this* was the kind of stuff he read in his downtime. Why did that make him hotter?

Without a word, she dropped a dark blue folder with the embossed gold word *Hibernia* on the cover right under his nose.

Oliver jolted backward, his gaze shooting up to find her there on the other side of the table, her arms folded.

"Emme—"

"You should apply for the Hibernia planning committee. We need your software skills." It was her nerves making her sound snippy. Before, she would've done her best to flirt. Like when they studied for their Technology Entrepreneurship class, she'd sounded much sweeter.

But what if Oliver thought she was with Sebastian? Or maybe he wasn't thinking of that night at all. Maybe he didn't care who she made out with. Somehow that thought was worse.

Oliver's brow furrowed as he flipped through the velvety-soft application papers. "Half of this is already filled out."

At that, Emmeline blushed. "The application is due tonight at midnight. I didn't want the time crunch to stop you from going for it."

His dark eyes pinned her while his lenses sat low on his nose. Finally, he closed the folder. "I really appreciate this, but the student council isn't looking for a Scholar on—"

"I already talked to Calixa," she said quickly, ignoring the way her cheeks burned with the admission. When had she ever worked so hard for someone else? She didn't want to confront that question. "You're in, if you apply."

His brows shot up, disappearing into the twists that grazed his forehead.

She could feel her skin going red, from her hairline down to her neck. She started to turn away from his table. "Apply or don't, I just thought—"

His warm hand caught hers. Long smooth fingers, curled around her own.

She glanced down at their joined hands, and her gaze painstakingly traveled upward. He'd gotten to his feet, was leaning across the table, staring at her with something close to wonder.

"Sorry," he said quickly, letting go. For a moment, Emmeline thought he was apologizing for holding her hand, but then he scratched the back of his head. "I didn't mean to sound ungrateful. I just didn't think there would be any point. What I mean is . . . thank you, Emmeline."

After a nervous glance away, his eyes found hers, and Emmeline felt like a riptide just sent her out to sea. He was so generous, and so honest, that she felt herself wholly unprepared.

She was starting to regret this master plan of hers. Wishing she hadn't ventured to get credit for making Hibernia look more professional *and* get closer to Oliver in one fell swoop.

Their rift may have been a blessing in disguise. She didn't have time for distractions.

But . . ., she bartered with herself as Oliver excitedly started going through the answers she'd filled in for him ("Wow, you already listed out all my coding languages!"), . . . *too late now.*

30

TITUS

"I SAY WE MAKE IT A RAGER. OR WHAT ABOUT ONE OF THOSE silent discos? Everybody gets their own pair of wireless headphones and we just—"

Nearly every committee member at the eight-person table began chuckling before Sebastian slammed his ice coffee down. "Bloody hell, Oakley, Hibernia is not a joke. It's an Almus Terra institution. If it's poorly planned, everyone will remember *who* screwed it up."

"Chill," Oakley deadpanned, all amusement gone. Sebastian, as usual, had a way of dramatically punishing anyone who stole his spotlight, and the rest of the room settled back in mild disappointment.

Titus slowly clenched and unclenched his hands under the table, relieving some stiffness. The tightness across his joints reminded him of the upcoming appointment he could not miss.

"I'm taking this seriously, but we've spent the last two hours on spreadsheets," Oakley said, gesturing to the laptops that everyone had out. "It's time to get creative. You know, come up with something that people would actually *enjoy.*"

"Aye, it's true. Folks love silent discos."

"Thank you." Oakley nodded to Alaric, who sat with his feet up on an empty chair.

"If everyone is familiar with the budget," Emmeline said in a placating tone, "let's move on to branding. We can't get started with decorations until we have a theme for Hibernia."

Titus had to hand it to her—Emmeline was skilled in balancing the two very different personalities of Sebastian and Oakley. This was only the first meeting of the Hibernia planning committee, and they'd already gotten into it four times.

"What's there to brand? Don't we already have a name?" Sadie asked. Her phrasing implied sarcasm, but her tone was genuine. After all, Hibernia's name was a constant.

"It's tradition," Emmeline said curtly. "Every year, Hibernia gets a new theme, a new tagline, a new aesthetic. It's an exercise in marketing and event planning, and why would anyone want to attend the same exact event year after year?"

The only thing she held back was a *duh* at the end. Sadie pressed her lips together and Titus resisted the urge to stick up for her—he didn't need Emmeline becoming more vicious.

"I want to know what Alaric thinks," Lotta said, obnoxiously batting her eyelashes in his direction. It had been apparent from the beginning of the meeting that Lotta, a rich corporate heiress who grew up in the Netherlands and the States, had joined the committee for one reason alone: to hit on Alaric and Titus.

"Me? Why?" Alaric's annoyance was not subtle. He seemed to detest the girl, and for once, Titus saw eye-to-eye with his cousin.

"Hibernia is the classical Latin name for Ireland," Lotta continued sweetly. "Since that's where you're from, I just thought you'd have some cool ideas."

"He's also from Ashland," Emmeline quipped, "and the reason the ball is named Hibernia is not for Ireland, but for its derivation, *eternal winter*. But since you're so invested, Lotta, why don't you and Sadie be in charge of the theme and branding? Anyone up for decorations?" She typed away on her laptop, quashing all discussion.

"Alaric and I can do it," Oakley said, batting Alaric's arm with enough force to bruise. "Need a big guy to hang all those twinkling lights."

"Yeh, all right," Alaric said, probably just relieved not to be paired with his biggest fan.

"Stick to your budget, Oak," Emmeline said, jabbing her index finger at the screen.

Titus's vision swam and the letters on his laptop screen blurred—a consequence of not enough sleep last night. A low-grade fever kept him up, which was new. *Definitely need to make that appointment.*

So when Emmeline suggested he and Sebastian take the "private event" for the adults, which was code for the unofficial global trade summit, his head wasn't clear enough to argue. He just needed this meeting to be over. He hated how he'd inadvertently let Emmeline take the wheel, but his foggy brain left him no other choice.

"So, all that's left is the online ticketing and managing the guest list. I suppose Oliver and I can take care of that," Emmeline said with a few more taps of her keyboard.

"Wait. Hold up. I don't like my partner," Lotta said point-blank.

Everyone stilled. No one said a word as all eyes shot to Sadie, her cheeks blooming cherry red. Titus's hands clenched under the table, but this time from sheer rage. *What the hell?* He should be destroying this petulant girl, but it was a struggle to even keep up with the conversation.

"Pardon?" Emmeline asked, as if even she couldn't compute Lotta's tactless affront.

"Why do you get to be in charge of who partners with whom?" Lotta snapped. "Just because you're a princess? My father has more money in his savings account than your country's entire treasury."

Oakley let out a low whistle. Her eyebrows popped in disbelief as she mouthed, *Wow.*

"Listen, I'll—" Titus started, but he was too slow on the uptake.

It was Oliver who said loudly and quickly, "Then I'd like to partner with Sadie."

Damn it. As regret mixed with weariness pulsed through him, Titus resisted placing his head on the table and closing his eyes.

"If that's okay," Oliver added, asking Emmeline for approval.

Though Titus couldn't be sure, he thought for a second he saw Emmeline's eyes blaze with fire.

"Of course," Emmeline said. "We're all members of the same committee—no one needs my permission for anything. Though *some* of us need to be checked." She looked pointedly at Lotta. "So, Sadie and Oliver for online ticketing and guests, Alaric and Oakley for decorations, Sebastian and Titus for the adults' private event, and Lotta and I will run theme and branding. I can make sure she doesn't ruin it," she added, typing away.

With an offended noise in the back of her throat, Lotta sprang from her chair and left.

"Let's meet again same time on Saturday with a first draft of our plans. It's November second, which means we have just over six weeks to make this all happen," Emmeline said, closing her laptop with a snap.

He hadn't been fast enough to offer his own partnership, but Titus wasn't going to be second in line to check on her. Immediately he stood and rounded the table to meet Sadie as she started packing up.

"Are you okay?" he asked quietly.

Sadie's cheeks darkened, and she shoved her new laptop into her bag. "Absolutely. I mean, it's no secret Lotta and her"—she cleared her throat—"friends don't like me. It all worked out."

But Titus didn't think so. It had been humiliating and he couldn't help but remember their Philanthropy project. She hadn't wanted to be paired with someone who detested her. Nobody would.

"Let's grab some hot tea," he said. "We can—"

His burner phone buzzed loudly in his pocket, the vibration so intense the phone nearly hopped out of his jacket. Ah hell, he really needed to start leaving it in his room.

Sadie glanced at where the buzzing persisted. "Sounds like you're busy. Really, Titus," she said, smiling. "I'm fine. But thank you. Oliver and I have planning to do. Catch you tomorrow."

She patted his arm, then hurried for the door, where Oliver waited on her. She greeted him with a nervous laugh, and Titus's gut twisted. He also didn't miss Emmeline's glare as Sadie and Oliver left the class-room together.

Dr. Sharrad had positioned himself next to the exam room door in case Titus tried to make a break for it. It was a sensible tactic, really.

"So nice you could finally join us, Titus," Dr. Konkin said. His face over the Zoom call was slightly grainy, but Titus perceived his annoyed expression regardless.

It had been nearly two and a half weeks since the rheumatologist asked for a follow-up appointment to go over Titus's bloodwork and X-rays. The specialist had done a full work-up—he'd watched Titus walk from point A to point B; examined his joints; ordered blood tests for RF, anti-CCP, and blood count; and ordered several X-rays of his hands, feet, knees, hips, and spine.

"My schedule made it difficult," Titus said, mirroring Dr. Konkin's expression. It wasn't a complete lie.

"Titus, I believe you have rheumatoid arthritis," Dr. Konkin said matter-of-factly.

Titus blinked. He hadn't even had time to brace himself. The blow came in like a right hook to the solar plexus, knocking the wind out of him.

If Dr. Konkin hadn't already explained to him possible diseases (on top of his own anxiety-induced research), this would've come in a lot harder. Weirdly though, his first reaction now was to chuckle. Before he knew it, he was laughing and laughing, deeply, from his gut.

"Titus?" Dr. Sharrad said, reaching for his shoulder.

But Titus threw up his hand as if to warn him—*don't touch me.* When he'd finally withdrawn a deep breath to calm himself, he straightened. "Titus has arthritis. It bloody *rhymes*, isn't that hysterical, doctor?"

Dr. Konkin glanced at Dr. Sharrad and then sighed. "I know this is a lot, but the disease is more manageable these days. Rheumatoid arthritis—RA—is an autoimmune disease that essentially means you have overactive white blood cells. Your cells attack your joints when there is nothing else to fend off, treating your own body as the enemy. But over the years, we've made some great strides in its treatment. The medications out there now—"

"How do you know for sure?" he interrupted, knowing this wasn't an easy disease to pinpoint. And maybe the doctor was wrong, maybe it was still just stress. . . .

But that didn't give him any relief either. Deep down, Titus wanted some explanation for all this. And if he was being *really* honest, he was glad to finally have an answer. At least there was a reason.

"Well, if your symptoms were more recent, I wouldn't be as confident. But you first reported symptoms almost nine months ago. That is a significant time period. The disease's progression and your . . . reluctance . . . to seek help sooner—"

"Who said it was *my* reluctance?" Titus snapped, his tone leaking aggression. If his parents hadn't dismissed his complaints . . .

"Sorry," Titus muttered after a stint of awkward silence, realizing that, yes, he had avoided this appointment.

Dr. Konkin cleared his throat. "To your point, Titus, it might be connective tissue disorder, but medications will help us narrow this down. Which is why I'd like to start you right away on . . ."

Titus sucked in a breath, squeezing his eyes shut as the rheumatologist's voice faded into the background. He could not hear about next steps, nor about how this was all going to be okay. Because if this diagnosis got out—to his parents, or his grandfather—that would be the end. They'd see it as a weakness and never let him be king, discarding him once and for all. That final blow would obliterate him.

God, he wished he could say they would stand behind him. That they believed he'd succeed and navigate chronic pain for the rest of his life. But he knew better than to expect any goodness from them.

"Titus . . . are you listening?"

Titus just shrugged, having trouble getting out any words.

Dr. Konkin's sigh sounded like a blast of wind through the computer's speakers. "Titus, I know this is difficult—"

"No. You don't." And in a gesture so rude that it surprised even himself, Titus reached forward and slammed the laptop shut, cutting off Dr. Konkin's virtual session.

"Titus!" Dr. Sharrad admonished.

If he'd been Alaric, Titus might've stood up, knocked over his chair, and stormed out. But he was ashamed of what he'd just done.

Dr. Sharrad likely sensed this turmoil because he waited a long time before quietly saying, "This doesn't change what you can do with your life."

At that, Titus let out a cold laugh of disbelief. "You don't know my family."

"They will support you, Titus. Regardless of this disease, there is nothing you can't do."

Titus wanted to scream at the condescension. Of course he was capable. Of course he'd be a brilliant king no matter what. Of course he could carry on through whatever shit life threw at him. *Of course.* He'd come this far. But what he believed—what he knew in his bones—didn't matter.

Not in the eyes of his parents. Nor his grandfather's. Ashland had always valued the strong. And damn it, he was strong. They were just too prejudiced to see it.

"We need to get Dr. Konkin back on to discuss a medication

regimen. There are certain drugs that will take time to see what will work."

Titus scoffed. He had classes, Hibernia, the race to his crown. He did *not* have time to figure out what drugs he should be taking, and then deal with adjusting to their side effects.

"I need to get back to my studies."

Titus started to get up, but Dr. Sharrad caught him by the elbow.

"Let me rephrase. If we do not address the disease now, your white blood cells could cause joint damage within a year, and once that damage occurs, it is generally irreversible. At least until it warrants surgery."

Slowly, Titus lowered himself back down and waited as Dr. Sharrad fiddled with the laptop. He didn't know what was going to come next, but he knew for sure he'd have to hide this. As long as possible. Because Dr. Sharrad was wrong. His family would not support him.

For a meetup space, Titus and Sadie booked a small self-study room at the top of one of the flanking towers on the east side. It was neutral territory. Nobody's dorm, but pretty romantic, all things considered. The sunset coming off the sea was utterly brilliant from this vantage point and it was cozy, with cushioned chairs.

"If you add any more to this action plan, it won't be three years' worth of work, Sadie," Titus said, dropping his stylus on his tablet. It clattered on the glass surface as he flexed his stiff and aching fingers. "It will be a decade's."

Though they were plenty ahead on their Philanthropy project, Sadie insisted they keep working relentlessly. To the point where Titus knew this was more than just a grade for her.

Sadie nibbled on her bottom lip and his glance, like a magnet, was drawn to it. With her entirely focused on their Google doc, Part D of their One-Year Strategic Plan (which had evolved into a Three-Year Plan), he could take his time counting the freckles on her nose. Not that he'd mind her noticing him noticing her. After that night in the garden... why hide his attraction?

"But if we just add one more objective into year two, we can—"

Titus was tired of school and everything else that occupied his mind, including the impending timeline of trying out medication for his new diagnosis. Tired of everything but Sadie.

With a sigh, he dropped his head onto her shoulder and felt her freeze under him. She didn't move away, though, so he let himself breathe her in. That warm vanilla scent, like sugar cookies, filled his senses. Just like in the garden.

He'd told himself it was all part of the plan. Kissing her that night. But the truth was, he kissed her because he couldn't help it. She'd caught him at perhaps his most vulnerable. And with one weakness come others.

"Go ahead, I'm listening," he muttered, head still resting on her shoulder.

"N-never mind."

With a grin, he looked up and found her already staring at him, her gaze unfocused. Carefully, he let his fingertips drift across her flushed cheek before sliding a piece of hair behind her ear. When she sucked in a breath and her own hand went up to his jaw, he took that as invitation and leaned in to kiss her.

She responded immediately. Like she'd been waiting for it. And he was elated—for reasons that had absolutely nothing to do with becoming king.

He kissed her a bit harder than before, his hand wrapping around the back of her neck as hers slipped to the collar of his shirt.

Mindful not to get too carried away, he pulled back, his fingers threading through her ponytail.

She looked utterly lost, her lips bee-stung, and it all made him want to kiss her again. How lucky he was to be attracted to the very girl he needed to seduce.

"You did it again," she said finally, pulling those lips into a small frown.

"Did what? Kiss you?"

"Not that—well, yes, that—but you distracted me from asking what was wrong."

He tried not to draw back, though it was instinctual. "You can ask me anything," he replied.

"Okay . . . why do you like kissing me?"

He blinked at the straightforward question and choked back a laugh, a smile breaking through his features. "I just do."

Sadie raised a brow. "Romantic."

"Fine, okay. Since the day you called me out on all my crap, I've been interested. I was a bloody git, and you gave me another chance. You're passionate about things you believe in with your whole heart, and I think you're beautiful. . . . Does that help in your decision to give us a go?"

Clearly ruffled at his unexpected speech, she shook her head and mumbled, "I—I haven't decided yet."

"Ah." He shut her laptop slowly. "Anything I can do to help?"

"Titus, we've been busy. Remember, Hibernia?"

"I haven't forgotten Lotta's tantrum." His blood still boiled at that. "I should've been faster to say I wanted to be your partner. Because I do."

Sadie let out a nervous laugh. He knew it was nervous because she tucked strands of her hair behind her ears and shifted in her chair. "C'mon, Titus. With the heirs' obligations, our project, then planning Hibernia? All that time together, you'd get sick of me."

"You know that's not true," he practically growled, the words coming from deep in his chest. "I want more time with you, Sadie Aurelia. I want to date you."

He saw her shiver. "Titus, it's not a good idea."

"It's the best one I've ever had," he murmured. And it was true. Every moment he spent with Sadie confirmed that. She was a force to

273

be reckoned with: passionate and brilliant, sharp and strategic when it came to things she really cared about. Not just that—the people of Ashland had come to adore her. Case in point: Her outburst at the football match had gone viral. A royal heir who was one of *them*. He did not want to go against her. He wanted to be on her side.

As he leaned in to kiss her again and she met his lips with a small whimper, Titus hoped he had her. But then she pulled back—just a bit, her hand between his collarbones, her fingers across his throat.

"A little more time, Titus. Please."

With nothing else left to do, Titus kissed her forehead and said, "Of course, Sadie. Anything you need."

Time. The one thing it felt like he didn't have.

31

SADIE

"I'LL GIVE YOU . . . SEVEN MINUTES." KAVI TAPPED HIS SMARTWATCH, starting their countdown.

Oliver and Sadie exchanged glances, a silent conversation happening between the two of them. *There's really no one else we can ask about this?*

Hibernia has been student-run since the dawn of time. No one on staff can, or will, answer our questions.

Okay, Sadie wasn't positive that was what Oliver was asking, since she wasn't telepathic—but as Oliver began to build out the portal for donations, they needed to have a better understanding of the users' expectations. Calixa had given them explicit orders to make the portal sophisticated, whatever that meant. Which is why they were currently trying to get more concrete information about the planning of past events from the president's boyfriend.

"Six minutes and forty-two seconds," Kavi said.

Sadie took the vacant seat across from Kavi in the dining hall and Oliver followed suit. "R-right. So, Calixa told you Oliver is building out a portal for the guests attending Hibernia. And we were wondering what sort of features they would—"

"Where's the guest list coming from?" Kavi opened the note app on his tablet with a flick of his stylus.

"Oh, um." Sadie opened the file that the school's head secretary,

Mr. Hassani, had sent her on her tablet. "It's the list of C-Suites' and Elites' parents. Their private email addresses."

Kavi snapped his fingers and gestured for the tablet.

With another glance at Oliver, who looked just as uncomfortable, Sadie handed it over.

"No, this isn't all of them. You're missing parents of prospective students, and past alumni."

Meaning, other world leaders and corporate tycoons that should be a part of their unsanctioned global summit. Sadie bit her tongue, literally.

"Don't worry, I'll get them to you." Kavi made another note on his tablet. "How are you going to secure their access to the portal? Nothing will hit their inboxes without authentication."

Oliver cleared his throat. "The invitations to the portal can include a link that will allow them to register as a user via an almusterra.edu email. I've already checked with the IT staff."

"Not secure enough," Kavi said sharply.

Oliver blinked, taken aback.

"We're dealing with presidents, Norm. Billionaires. Not someone who worries about 401(k)s or phishing scams. Got it?"

There was a moment where Sadie felt, for the first time, that Oliver was actually going to get mad. He had such an even temper that she'd never once seen him angry. Even when his computer lab slot was taken, he'd seemed more worried than infuriated.

"We can mail them a code," Oliver said finally, his expression blank. "Their code can verify their registration. Then use 2FA and double encryption prior to log-in. Is that sufficient?"

Either Kavi didn't register the sarcasm or he chose to ignore it, because he then proceeded to list twenty other features he wanted the portal to be capable of. It wasn't until Kavi mentioned that there should be two places to pay that Sadie froze and stopped taking notes. "Wait, what? Why two?" she asked.

"The direct deposit into the school's fundraising account for whatever donation they'd like to give to ATA," Kavi continued, "and five hundred thousand pounds into this account." He typed rapidly on his tablet and an email went to both Sadie's and Oliver's accounts with a swoosh.

"Where does this account go to?" Sadie asked with a frown. Was it a fancy Swiss account, or was that just the way it worked in the movies?

"Your seven minutes are up," Kavi said right as his watch chirped, and he dismissed them.

It was freezing out on the docks Sunday afternoon. As Sadie and Alaric cleaned buckets of freshly harvested mussels, she couldn't help thinking two things: one, that she was immensely glad this would be their last detention, and two, where on earth was all that money going?

"I bet that second account is for a global country club or something," Sadie grumbled partially to herself as she tore a bit of the mussel thread away from its navy-blue shell.

"Where might that be? On the International Space Station?" Alaric mused.

"You're mocking me." Sadie narrowed her eyes as Alaric chuckled. "But the ISS would make the world's *coolest* country club."

"Who said I was joking?"

"Okay, forget about the country club, that was a dumb idea. But it's for *something*. Seriously, what could they possibly be using all that money for? Maybe it's their own secret poker game."

At that, Alaric barked out a laugh. "What?"

"Haven't you ever seen *Casino Royale*? What if they're putting all that money in one pot to see who will take home the winning hand?"

"I think yeh've seen too many movies."

"I'm just *saying*," Sadie growled, "it's really shady that people who control so much of the world's wealth are using it to play around. If that is in fact what they are doing. What's with all the secrecy? Why use our school as a front?"

"Dunno." Alaric shrugged. "Yer guess on the psychology of rich arseholes is as good as mine. Maybe ask yer boyfriend?"

Sadie flinched so hard the mussel she'd been cleaning popped right out of her hand, bounced twice, and fell off the docks into the water with a plop.

"He's not my boyfriend," she said, though this time it was with much less certainty. And Alaric, like a shark smelling blood in the water, homed in.

"Aye, but he could be," Alaric guessed, flicking another mussel into the cleaned pile.

Sadie's cheeks burned. It felt odd talking to Alaric about this, though she wasn't sure why. Alaric teased her, never showing any *actual* interest. Even if he had, Sadie didn't like him like that. And honestly, the same could be said for Titus.

Yes, she'd been kissed a little senseless once—twice—and succumbed to how good it felt to be cradled and caressed, especially by the golden prince of Ashland. But that didn't mean she wanted to date him. Truth be told, she wasn't sure if she had any real feelings beyond the butterflies in her stomach whenever they kissed. And she was smart enough to be able to separate the swoony feelings from real ones. Wasn't she?

Titus had been an impossibility. Even as he began showing interest, it had been easy not to dwell on his advances because every other aspect of her life was so overwhelming.

Being a student at Almus Terra had changed her life. Becoming an heir had changed her world. Deciding to actively pursue the crown to her best ability had changed her future. During the days, she was consumed with her classes, helping the charity she loved in her spare time while also studying court etiquette or royal responsibilities. At nights, when she was trying to fall asleep and there wasn't anything to study or read, she still ached with grief.

There was no room left in her life for romance.

Additionally, if she wanted to become heir apparent, how could dating Titus, who *also* wanted to be heir apparent, bode well for either of them? Rivals dating? Probably not the best idea.

Though his words the day before made his interest much harder to ignore. He'd called her passionate and beautiful. . . .

"Yeh haven't said anything in three minutes. I'm taking that as a yes."

Sadie blinked down at the mussel in her gloved hand. "Take it however you want," she grumbled, yanking out the threads and tossing the mussel into the bucket.

"Easy there, yeh seem stressed."

"Oh, and you're not? Our schedules are practically the same. Classes, Hibernia, whatever Ilsa has us doing for Ashland."

"Unlike you, I know how to unwind when the pressure gets . . . too much."

Jealousy sizzled through her like a burn from a curling iron, the sting lasting well after the initial touch. Alaric did have friends—Jacob and his group. In fact, after his stunt in the dining hall, she was sure loads more Scholars had gravitated toward Alaric.

At least now Sadie had Trang. They were now texting throughout the day and hanging out and studying most evenings. Though it felt presumptuous to say they were *best* friends, Sadie didn't feel nearly as lonely and adrift as she had a month ago.

"All right, enough." Suddenly Alaric stood. He reached down and yanked her hand, pulling her to her feet as well.

Startled, she gaped up at him. "Enough what?"

"Enough with the mussels. Enough with the moping. I'm taking yeh to unwind too."

"I . . . where . . . what do you mean?"

"Just go wash off the fishy smell," he said, patting her on the head, "wear warm clothes, and meet me at the east ramparts at eight. Got it?"

Later, Sadie would hate how she didn't even try to challenge his orders. But she was anxious to get her mind off Titus and the heir apparent, now that she'd decided it was something she truly wanted. So if Alaric was promising her a night as a normal teenager, she wanted to do it.

"Do you even know where you're going?" Trang asked with a frown in their dorm bathroom as Sadie attempted, and failed, to add waves to her hair.

"Nope," Sadie said, trying to rotate her wrist to produce the perfect casual wave. Disheartened, she dropped the wand on the porcelain counter.

"Here, let me." Trang took the wand and ran the plates through Sadie's hair, flipping the ends naturally. "I don't know, Sadie. Sounds sketch to me."

Truthfully, Sadie was really touched Trang cared enough to worry like this.

But maybe that was to be expected. Their friendship seemed to be growing every day, and there was hardly an hour that passed by without the two chatting in some format. It had now gotten to the point where Sadie knew about Trang's not-so-secret love affair with American medical dramas, and one particular telenovela that she'd fallen so in love as to learn Spanish in addition to already speaking Vietnamese, English, and Mandarin.

"Alaric won't let anything happen to me." That much Sadie knew. He'd saved her from the ocean and fretted about her clumsiness more than once. Despite his gruff exterior he was a protective person.

Trang moved on to the next section of Sadie's hair. "What about Titus?"

"This isn't a date," Sadie said quickly, her skin prickling with a mix of excitement, nerves, and guilt. *Not a date.* She had absolutely no reason to feel guilty for hanging out with Alaric when she hadn't even told Titus she'd be his girlfriend. It had been inevitable and a relief when she'd confided to Trang about it all. She'd needed to talk to someone or she'd explode.

"Ooookay, if you say so." Trang's tone was a little snappy. Not at all like her usual self since they'd become close. Trang was sardonic at times, but never waspish.

Sadie caught her friend's gaze in the mirror. "Hey . . . is everything all right?"

Trang stopped, dropping the next piece of Sadie's hair and snapping the heating tool in a nervous gesture. "Yeah. Well, not really." Her brow furrowed, and she went back to her task, still talking. "I talked to my bố yesterday. The company was in the red again this past quarter."

Sadie kept quiet. Unlike her shows and pro-wrestling, Trang didn't often open up about her father and their family's company, but it seemed like one day she'd be expected to take over. Apparently, he was trying to impart the realities of leadership and running a multimillion-dollar business.

"So I'm just . . . worried," Trang said finally, flipping the last piece of Sadie's hair over her shoulder.

Sadie turned and gave Trang a fierce hug. At first, Trang was stiff, then she melted into the embrace too.

Sadie pulled back and grinned. "Well, don't worry about me. Are you sure you don't want to come? Alaric won't mind." He would, but Sadie didn't care.

Trang shook her head. "Nah, not for me. Besides, I'm close to finishing this quest in *Stardew Valley.* But—" She gripped Sadie by the shoulders and looked sternly into her eyes. "If he does *anything* to you, I'm gonna kick his ass."

*　　*　　*

Fifteen minutes before eight, Sadie stood smack-dab in the middle of the eastern ramparts, rocking back and forth on her heels. She wore a pair of thick leggings and boots, with an old Ashland Sea Dragons sweatshirt, a sturdy denim jacket over it, and a scarf knitted by her grannah wrapped around her neck. She was cozy for now, but no matter how warmly she bundled she knew the wintery sea wind would be merciless.

Alaric turned out to be early too. She spotted him coming up the steps from the side of the boys' dorms holding a paper bag in his loose grip. He wore jeans, a black shirt, a zip-up hoodie, and another thick jacket on top, with a beanie covering his dark hair.

Reaching her, he gave her a once-over, then pulled the beanie from his head, ruffling his short waves. He tossed it to her, and she took the hint. She lamented messing up Trang's waves, but then the scent of mint and fresh rain tickled her nose, and she quickly shoved the beanie over her hair and ears.

It's warm. Unwanted goosebumps traveled down the base of her neck and spine.

They crossed into one of the covered parapets of the castle's outer walls, then slipped through an iron gate that led to a staircase of stone carved right into the island's rock. It went all the way to a tiny beach that was mostly covered by a dense patch of woods along the northern part of the island. The bright half-moon and smattering of starlight illuminated a clear path along the rocky coast.

They were quiet as they moved across the pebbles, broken branches, and hard sand, so Sadie heard voices before she saw them all. Her jaw dropped at the scene—fifteen or twenty shadowy figures all lounging on blankets across rocks and sea-breeze damp grass.

"Hey, Al," one of them called as Alaric joined the group. "Warm us up, yeah?"

Alaric dumped his paper bag into the center of a ring of stones and logs of dry driftwood. "Told yeh not to call me that, Kenny." He knelt and retrieved a lighter from his pocket. He flicked it once, twice, then a spark ignited under the paper bag. There must have been kindling in the bag because the fire blazed up immediately, catching the driftwood.

The dark enclosure was suddenly illuminated, revealing Jacob, Bea, Assane, Danica's roommate Ross, and a few others she knew from classes, all from different countries and class years. The one thing they all had in common: They were Scholars.

"Another Elite? For Christ's sake, Alaric. What if she tattles on us to their overlords?"

Sadie's gaze jerked to the person who'd spoken. He was someone Oakley talked to. Artem...or something like that.

It took Sadie far too long to realize he had a bottle of vodka in his hand. They were drinking. *Was this what Alaric meant about unwinding?*

"Sadie's one of us," Jacob said, throwing an arm around her shoulders.

"She didn't grow up rich like the rest of the nobs." Alaric held out his hand and someone tossed him a dark bottle. With little effort, he popped off the cap and handed it to Sadie. "Time to unwind."

Artem lifted his arm, still holding the bottle of clear liquor. "I want to hear her swear she won't say a word. Better yet—" He nodded, and a phone camera flashed in the darkness, burning her retinas.

Perfect. They took her picture holding a beer. That could ruin her in about a thousand different ways. She could be expelled for this; the press would destroy her potential as an heir for underage drinking; King Leander—she didn't even want to think about what he'd do. But this was their insurance. Everyone's insurance. If she told, they told.

"I won't say a word," she said, taking a swig from the bottle. Instantly, she gagged and spit it out. That was foul.

A roar of laughter erupted around the campfire.

"Give her a cider!"

"Or a seltzer!"

Sadie ended up nursing a canned cocktail that had flavors of peach and lemonade with a tart aftertaste. She didn't know what was in it, but it sure was tasty. Music played in the background while students enjoyed the fire, talked, laid back and watched the stars, made out, played card games, and generally relaxed.

The alcohol seemed to be present not to numb their senses or their minds—they had scholarships to maintain, after all—but to make ceremony of solidarity.

Even Sadie understood the appeal. The drink in her hand was delicious and it seemed to quiet the too-loud thoughts in her head. Thoughts about being the better heir, dating Titus, whether Emmeline had stolen her laptop, how much she hated Lotta, how much she missed Mah. All the thoughts were still there, but they felt softer.

After playing a fun new card game and chatting with Jacob and Bea about Professor Reyes and his annoying habits, she noticed that Alaric hadn't even taken a sip of his own drink. The gross beer that had once been in Sadie's hand.

"You don't like it either?" she asked him. Her beverage was half-way gone.

Alaric startled, then glanced down, as if he forgot he'd even been holding it. "Oh. Nah. No drinking for me. Had a bad go of it not long ago."

His explanation left no room for questioning, though Sadie was curious. She took another sip and hummed with the strange, fizzy feeling spreading through her bloodstream. "I've never had alcohol before tonight."

"Shocking," Alaric muttered under his breath.

She hit his arm. "Stop doing that."

"Ow—doing what?"

"Being so reductive. You don't know me." Sadie lifted her chin to meet his gaze. They sat on a flannel blanket on a flat rock in front of the fire. For a while, Jacob and his friends had been around, but they'd moved away to watch a game of Dutch Blitz, an insanely addictive card game. Now they were alone.

Alaric was all hard lines and shadows. His gray eyes just like a stormy sea. Sadie imagined those were the eyes of an old Ashlandic sea god. Like one from the stories that Mah and Grannah used to tell her.

"I don't?"

As she tilted her face up, he tilted his down, their noses so close they almost touched.

A smirk curved his lips. "Then tell me I'm wrong. Tell me yeh don't wanna date Prince Golden Retriever because he's everythin' yeh stand against."

Sadie jerked back, shock rippling through her enough for that hazy feeling to recede.

"I don't know what you're talking about," she whispered.

Oh, but she did. And she hated that he was right. She hadn't allowed herself to think of it, but yes. A piece of her *would* be ashamed to date him. Titus was rich, powerful, comfortable with his place in the world because he'd always been at the top. It wasn't like he was a bad person. He was kind to her, gentle, smart, and dedicated—she'd witnessed all that herself. But he'd also never questioned authority or fought for what *should* be instead of what was.

But Sadie was compelled to challenge the injustices. Ever since that moment in Grannah's hospital room, talking to her king, she knew she wanted to make changes for the better. Had to. Her cowardice held her back, but it was something she was working on.

Cold fingertips grabbed Sadie's chin and gently turned her head back to his. Alaric's stormy gaze held hers. "I know yeh well enough, Sadie."

His whisper was low, and his words held a weight as heavy as gravity.

"You don't." Her breath fogged in steam over his face. "You don't know that I want to be queen. You don't know what I carry inside. And you don't know your eyes look like the sea back home and that they're the most beautiful things I've ever seen. But sometimes they make me so sad I want to cry whenever you look at me."

Her head was buzzing now. She wasn't sure of all the words she'd just said because her ears were slow to catch up to her tongue. But it must've been something strange, because Alaric stared at her for a long time, his brows furrowed.

He took the can from her grasp and dumped the rest on the rocks, then tossed it into a nearby trash bag. Alaric said something to the group while Sadie's attention went back to the flames twirling and twisting like magic.

Gentle hands helped her to her feet. Then Alaric wrapped an arm around her waist and, as he guided her over the rocks and up the stone steps, she leaned into his solid strength.

"Am I drunk?" she asked while walking across the ramparts. Her brain was catching up now, away from the campfire smoke and into the brisk night chill that helped clear her head.

"Yer tipsy," Alaric said, though he didn't sound amused like she thought he'd be. "I'm taking yeh back to yer dorm."

"Wait—" Sadie gasped, grabbing the edge of the stone ramparts. "Not yet."

"Sadie...," Alaric said with a sigh.

"No, no, listen, this was great. Thank you. I had fun, I..." Sadie leaned her body away from Alaric's to rest her cheek on the cold wall. "I stopped. Just for a bit."

"Stopped what?"

"Stopped missing her." Sadie sucked in a breath, and suddenly she could feel the tears threatening to fall. "It was just for a minute. Maybe three or four. But down there with Jacob, when we were playing Phase 10 and I was thinking, *Heck yes, I really need two more sevens....* I wasn't thinking of Mah and how much I miss her. Or how I could've—should've—done something to help her. And—"

Sadie pressed a hand over her mouth, feeling woozy, but not entirely nauseated. She felt like she needed water, probably because of the alcohol.

With a sigh, Alaric reached down and picked her up like she weighed nothing—just like the time before—but now his hold was like that of a prince holding a princess.

She blabbed on. "I want to change Ashland, Alaric. I know you haven't lived there so you don't know, but there's so much wrong. The poor are too poor. No one cares about the mentally ill or senior citizens—which is over half the population. Veterans from the last war can hardly hold down jobs. The economy grows, but only a small portion of the country benefits." On some level, Sadie knew she should stop talking, but she couldn't.

"Grannah's gone because we had no way to take care of her. We're her family, we were supposed to, and Mah did everything she could, but it wasn't enough. And when we lost her, it became so hard. Just too hard for Mah to keep working. To keep living. She just..."

At some point, she was set down outside her dorm. Tears were rolling steadily down her cheeks, but there was a water bottle in her hand. She didn't know how it got there, though it must have been from Alaric. He took care of her, weirdly. Sweetly.

Warm thumbs brushed her cheeks, smearing salty tears across her cold freckled skin. She caught his hands and met those gray eyes that were lovely and devastating all at once.

"I lost them, Alaric. I lost them because my government failed. Our country deserves better. I don't know if I'm the one to fix it, but I want to try, you know? At first I didn't want any part of this, but I can't stop thinking that now...I actually want to win."

It was a waterfall of words. She wasn't drunk, but Sadie was uninhibited enough to let it all flow out like a faucet. Stuff she'd been itching to say for weeks—for a year, in some sense.

"Do you...do you think I can?" she asked softly. She wasn't sure why she was asking him. Well, no, that wasn't true. When he'd rallied the students, she'd admired him. His strength and courage and sense of morality. He was rough around the edges, but he cared.

Alaric studied her for a moment, his hard expression unreadable. With his hands still holding her cheeks, he pulled her face closer to his. So close her breath caught. Like he was going to kiss her. And in her warm, tipsy, vulnerable state, she almost wished he would.

But then he said one word that sobered her up faster than any hangover cure ever could.

"No."

32

ALARIC

ALARIC WATCHED HIS RESPONSE LAND LIKE A PHYSICAL BLOW. Her half-lidded gaze blinked rapidly as she took a step back from him and stumbled into her dorm. With a sniff, she ripped his beanie from her head and shoved it into his chest. Even with her ginger waves flat and full of static, her cheeks flushed, and her red-rimmed eyes, she still looked cute. Adorable.

Out of nowhere, he had the urge to nestle her back into him, maybe find out what Titus already knew—how she tasted. But that would border on cruel after what he'd just said. So he took his beanie back and shoved his hands into his jacket pockets.

"Drink all that water before yeh go to bed." He nodded to the bottle he'd given her.

She nodded dully. "Right." Her voice was small. "Thanks for inviting me out. That was fun."

For feck's sake. He'd just decimated her confidence and here she was, still *thanking* him. He glowered down at her, hating how she made him feel. When she'd been crying, he'd wanted to kiss away her tears. When she'd been snogging Titus in the garden, he'd wanted to shatter her heart into shards. She swayed him to extremes far too easily, and he had to shut that shit down.

So when she asked him whether he thought she could become heir apparent, and some day queen, he'd given an answer he knew would hurt her.

He needed to put distance between them, despite himself. But there was another reason too. A more important reason.

Sadie was too *good*. Too gentle. Too kind. Too obliging. To win against the Elites, who were raised to believe they deserved the world on a silver platter, she would need to be ruthless. Cutthroat. Strategic. Cunning. Ready to sacrifice her values to win.

Sadie was not that person. She couldn't compete in that world. Not really. Better to face it now, in the shadows of a vacant corridor, than under the bright lights of news crews.

With a sharp breath, Sadie lifted her gaze to meet his. The dewy-eyed look was gone, and she stared at him with something like determination.

"Good night, Alaric." She opened her door, stepped inside, and shut it right in his face.

He'd expected nothing less. Still stung, though.

Mid-November was rather cold to be on the track field—for most students. But this was southern France. It was practically balmy for Alaric's Irish blood, and besides, he needed to run. He felt the tension in his muscles urging him to move until the memories from last night faded into the background and the ache in his legs and burn in his lungs took over all else.

You don't know your eyes look like the sea back home and that they're the most beautiful things I've ever seen. But sometimes they make me so sad I want to cry whenever you look at me.

He winced, flinching like the words had struck him across the face. Much like his *No* had struck her last night. Perhaps that was another reason he'd said it. To drive her so far away she'd never know how much her tipsy admission had affected him.

He was about to place his foot against the starting block when a voice echoed.

"Don't you dare, Durham!"

His old surname made him freeze. Not many people here used it, so his curiosity made him straighten and turn toward the entrance.

Oakley stormed across the turf wearing a long coat with a hood, a cutoff top, and overalls. "Seriously? You bail on our last two meetups and ignore my texts? I'm gonna murder you!"

Alaric tipped his head back and groaned. That stupid planning committee. He had half a mind to quit. He was seriously considering just asking about scholarship opportunities and figuring out how to stay at Almus Terra without being an Ashland heir. He'd ranked sixth out of the first-years in midterm results—surely he'd proven he was smart enough to be here, royal lineage or not.

"What's there to talk about?" he snapped as she grew closer. "Yeh said we couldn't start decorating until we had the new theme."

Oakley didn't stop until she was right under his nose. "We still need to contact vendors. Landscapers, ice sculptors, interior designers. Do you have *any* idea what it takes to decorate a castle? Blimey, last year I counted the Christmas trees and there were eight *just* in the ballroom."

Alaric dug his trainers into the track's polyurethane. "How'd yeh even find me?"

Oakley snorted. "Please, I knew Jacob and his crew long before you two became best buds."

"Is there anyone yer *not* friends with?"

"Seb, Calixa, and most of the student council. Stop changing the subject. Look, either *you* help or *I* grill Sadie on why she came back last night smelling like hard seltzer and cursing your name under her breath."

Another full body wince. So she'd been angrier than she'd let on. He wasn't sure if it felt better or worse to know.

"Fine, fine," he growled. "I'll call a bloody Christmas tree farmer, that what yeh want?"

"Of course not. This isn't some Christmas jamboree. We're an international school with about a hundred different cultures and religions represented."

"But yeh just—"

Oakley shoved her phone into his face the next moment, with an email he couldn't read two centimeters from his nose. "If you ever checked your email you'd see that Emmeline sent our theme this morning. It's 'legions.' I think she wants to go with a military aesthetic."

Coming from Emmeline? *Sounds about right.* She declared war against anyone who stood in her way. She may have saved him that night in the pub, but he had no doubt that she'd use that blackmail video if cornered. Without hesitation.

Oakley held out her hands like she was imagining the set of a movie. "Frosted suits of armor. White walkers. Ice dragons. Fake snow sprinkling down in the ballroom. It'll be like Elsa of Arendelle threw up everywhere. Whadya think, mate?"

"Fine. Brilliant. Can I run now?"

Saying yes to decorating sounded easy enough at the initial meeting, but faced with Oakley's enthusiasm, he now wondered if Sadie would switch with him so he could work on Oliver's software instead.

Who was he kidding.

Oakley stabbed Alaric in the chest with her sharp nails. "Listen here, Durham. I was bluffing when I said I'd grill Sadie. That girl is one crack away from breaking, and I'm not going to push her off the edge. But I'm serious about getting help. This is too big for me alone.

You either commit to this or I'll get someone who will. Keep in mind, it won't look good if you drop out now. In or out—tell me by the end of the day."

With that, Oakley left, her long jacket fluttering as her purposeful strides carried her back across the track field.

Now too drained to run, Alaric changed out of his track clothes and packed up. His phone dinged with an incoming email. He almost ignored it, but he remembered Oakley's accusation.

> **To:** aeldana@almusterra.edu
> **From:** head-secretary@almusterra.edu
>
> Mr. Eldana,
>
> Please come to the front office at your earliest convenience. We've received a letter addressed to you.
>
> Regards,
> Omar Hassani
> *Head School Secretary*
> *Almus Terra Administrative Offices*

A letter from who? He and the lads in Dublin chatted on a Discord server. They never sent emails to each other, much less actual mail. And any contact from the Ashland crowd came via email through Ilsa Halvorsen.

In any case, he went to retrieve it. The last time he ignored a letter, two men in suits showed up at his flat and shipped him off to a school where he learned he was a prince. Maybe this letter would reveal he was a wizard. Fingers crossed.

Mr. Hassani was a no-nonsense kind of man who wore small circular glasses and, Alaric was fairly certain, used scented oil on his bald head. With a sip of tea, he passed Alaric the letter.

Weirdly, there was no return address, no fancy seal, and the handwriting was unrecognizable.

Alaric was barely out of the school's front office and into the cold air before he ripped open the envelope. The letter was handwritten, on something close to a notepad-type paper, without even an introduction. No "Dear," not even "Alaric," just—

> Renounce your claim to the Ashland throne and you'll be taken care of. I can provide the balance of your tuition at Almus Terra, any postgraduate studies, and twelve million pounds a year for the rest of your life. You'll be rich with the freedom to do whatever you like.
>
> You can't lose.
>
> I await your reply.
>
> Mikael Erickson

For a long moment, Alaric stood there, the paper trembling in his hand. He'd been in the doorway of the bailey, so several students had to skirt around him, shooting him confused looks. But he didn't budge, even when another boy brushed his shoulder aggressively. He just kept staring at the letter from his father, staring and staring.

This...this changed *everything.* Just like the acceptance letter from Almus Terra, it jerked the trajectory of Alaric's life the way a change in gravity altered a spaceship's orbit.

On its surface, the offer was an out. A chance to do whatever he wished without catering to the demands of some old geezer in a castle. He could walk away.

But looking deeper, this was meant to erase Alaric once and for all. Renouncing his royal blood would cut Alaric off from any future in the Eldana family. His father was doing everything in his power to make sure a bastard didn't end up on the throne.

Still frozen in that same spot, Alaric pulled out his lighter from his back pocket and touched the flame to the piece of paper. It lit up easily, like the kindling in last night's campfire, and the offer vanished into smoke.

Ashes fluttered to the ground. He stepped on them as he pulled out his phone and dialed Oakley. "Hey. I'm in."

33

TITUS

Not for the first time, Titus regretted not speaking up in his Hibernia planning meeting.

Sebastian had been grating his last nerve. Changing his mind every other day about the location for the unsanctioned summit or which cocktails and hors d'oeuvres to serve. The final head count was just over fifty-five adults, and there were only three lecture halls with that capacity, but Seb *still* couldn't make up his bloody mind.

"It's a school. Alcohol can't even *be* on the premises," Titus argued as Seb tossed Titus's favorite paper weight—a football globe with the World Cup's winning teams' flags—up and down in the air.

"Get real, mate, it's a meeting for companies to bribe governments, and you're worried about a little booze?"

Titus hated whenever Sebastian made a good point. "Then just give them a full bar."

Seb shrugged and tossed up the ball again. "Where's the sophistication in that?"

For the love of . . . Titus did not have time for this. He still needed to finish his Ancient Political Rhetoric speech, study for the Global Economics Statistics test, and wrap up his Cyber Security project.

One of the reasons he hadn't argued too hard about his role in planning Hibernia was because it was the easiest part, and he needed all the extra time he could get, especially as he started the medication for his RA. But thanks to Seb, it was taking far longer than it should.

Titus was about to make his own executive decisions when a timid knock sounded at the door. Sebastian and Titus glanced at each other. Oliver and Alaric never knocked, and Sebastian's hookups texted him for a meetup rather than coming to their dorm. But Seb checked his phone anyway while Titus rolled his eyes and stood to answer.

"Sadie?" She was a bit farther from the door than was normal. Almost like she was still deciding whether to run away. Though classes had ended two hours ago, she was still in her uniform and her hair was adorably unkempt.

"Hey, Titus...I..." Cheeks stained strawberry, she stared at her hands twisted in front of her. "Sorry, you busy?"

"He's not." Sebastian clapped Titus on the shoulder, coming to stand behind him in the doorway. A smirk pulled at his lips as he regarded Sadie. "Come in, Sadie."

"Oh no, that's—"

In a gesture that was far too practiced, Sebastian guided Sadie into their dorm room. "No, really, I insist. I've got to get going anyway. You two can have the room."

As Sadie took a tentative seat on Titus's bed, clearly uncomfortable, Sebastian hooked his arm around Titus's shoulder and leaned in close to whisper, "You can't say I never did anything for you. Now, enjoy, mate. You need to relax."

If not for Sadie's presence, Titus would've actually punched him.

The door snapped shut and Titus took a seat at his desk, giving her space on the bed.

"Is everything okay?" he asked after a few moments of silence and her avoiding his gaze.

Finally, she looked at him. Her hazel eyes were a little bloodshot, as if she'd been crying or sleep-deprived. Lashes fluttered against her freckled cheeks as she took a deep breath. "*If* we dated, what would that be like?"

Titus straightened in his chair as he reacted to her words. He had *not* been expecting that. "What do you mean?" he asked, not quite sure how to answer.

Her pink cheeks turned pinker. "I've never dated anyone. I don't know what—I don't know the rules."

Titus tried not to smile. Or laugh. Not because he thought it was funny, but because he was so happy. And she was so cute. Hell, he'd never really dated before either, though he'd done stuff.

"No rules. We'd just do what feels right. For us. Whatever makes us happy. And comfortable," he added hastily.

Sadie nodded slowly, her gaze far off, like she was actually considering this. *Please let her want this too.*

"Look, Sadie," he said, resisting the urge to move closer to her, "the only reason I asked you out is because I like you. And I want to spend time with you."

Liar, an evil voice in his head whispered. *Vicious liar.*

She looked up at him through her lashes, her shoulders hunched like she was shielding herself from an incoming blow. "What if..." She pulled her bottom lip between her teeth. "What if I wanted to date in secret?"

Titus didn't need to think about it. If that's what a yes looked like, that was fine for him. Besides, dating in secret never worked. It would get out eventually and by then, hopefully, she'd be too in love with him to care. "That's fine, but can I ask why?"

Though he had a very good idea of why. Apparently there was an unofficial Ashlandic Prince fan club, and he couldn't imagine the kind of grief these obsessive fans would cause his girlfriend. Jealousy knew no bounds.

"Take a guess," she huffed. "But it's not just jealous girls, Titus. What would your grandfather say? We're both Ashlandic heirs."

Titus scoffed. "We're not related, Sadie."

She flushed. "I'm talking about the rules for this...succession. Obviously."

This time he did laugh. "Again with the rules. What rules? My grandfather never said we couldn't date each other. Why would that even matter?"

"That's my point—we don't know *what* matters."

"Sadie." Unable to stay away any longer, he moved next to her on the bed, their thighs touching. "Believe it or not, but you're the only person in this school I've felt close to all year. Sebastian's a git. Emmeline and Alaric want nothing to do with me. And anyone else who tries to be my friend is motivated by the wrong reasons. Tell me you don't understand."

Her gaze searched his. "I do."

"Then give us a try. Sure, we could be just friends, and if that's what you want, I'll leave it at that. I swear. But I really like kissing you. Do you like kissing me?"

At that, Sadie cracked a smile. It was so bright something in Titus's chest clenched painfully. He ignored it.

"It's all right."

He matched her smile, reaching up to cup her cheeks. "Just all right, eh?" he murmured, brushing his thumbs over her freckles. She giggled, but he quickly interrupted her laughter by pressing his lips against hers. Over and over, until she was breathless.

It had been three days since Titus last felt an arthritis flare-up. Three days, incidentally, since Sadie had agreed to date him. Correlation? Perhaps. Dr. Konkin had said the disease was stress-related and ever since that day in his dorm, the first seventy-two hours of their relationship had been rather blissful.

They'd met for studying every night, and the last fifteen minutes of their sessions ended with his hands woven into her hair and her vanilla scent all around him.

He moved slowly, though. The last thing he wanted was to scare her, so while he was *dying* to make out with more tongue, he kept it chaste (for the most part).

For the first time in weeks, his hands and feet didn't ache, and his joints weren't as stiff. Then again, it might have nothing to do with Sadie, and everything to do with the new medication he was on. According to Dr. Konkin, the steroids were meant to reduce his inflammation. With the drug, he was supposed to look out for mood swings and high blood pressure, among other concerning side effects. But, so far, so good. And today he was truly looking forward to his fencing class.

Among other things, Almus Terra didn't really have a normal physical education program. Students signed up for a "gym" period, where they could choose any sport that encouraged discipline, dedication, and focus.

He'd learned fencing at Eton when he was a boy and enjoyed the rigidity of the sport. The intricate footwork and wicked fast movements kept his mind sharp and his attacks sharper.

Most people had their gym period at either the end or the beginning of the day, so the locker room was usually full while Titus changed into his gear. Today was no different, and Sebastian hovered, waiting for Titus so they could get on with their practice.

"So you're not going to give me a single dirty detail," Seb complained loudly, sliding on his gloves.

Titus jerked on his fencing jacket with a little too much force. "There's nothing to tell," he said. Sebastian had kept hinting at wanting to hear what happened with Sadie. It appeared he was no longer hinting.

"C'mon, you prat. She came to our dorm. I gave you the room—"

"Sebastian," Titus hissed, "shut the hell up."

"Someone's touchy. Okay, fine. But you'd be an idiot not to go for it. She's pretty fit, all things considered. Fiery little gingers, amiright?"

Before Titus could grab for his roommate's throat, a locker slammed with such force it made everyone in the vicinity jump. Titus turned and his blood ran cold at the look of murder on his cousin's face. Without a word, Alaric stalked out of the locker room, his killer gaze still locked on Titus.

"What happened to him?" Seb muttered.

I'll bet I know.

Titus didn't have to wait long to verify his assumption. After his second round with Sebastian, a hush fell over the gymnasium. Students released their yoga poses, paused their grappling, stopped doing burpees—everything ground to a halt as Alaric stepped onto the fencing mat brandishing a saber.

The whole school knew Alaric was a runner. He dominated the track and was rarely in the gym except for calisthenics. Never on fencing mats.

The way he stalked toward Titus screamed aggression, his eyes as cold as the low-carbon steel of his sword. "Fancy a match, cousin?"

Titus had removed his protective mask, so his view was clear as he glanced around the gym. The ceilings were high and arched, gothic patterns etched into the stone walls—walls that were wide enough to accommodate three different classes at once. At least a fifth of the school was watching. Over fifty kids ... waiting to see what the princes would do.

Titus tightened his grip on his sword, then let his wrist hang loose, as if this were nothing. "I wasn't aware you knew how to fence."

He looked casual, but in truth was fighting back a queasiness that had started halfway through his last round with Seb. It was one of the reasons he'd removed his mask—so he could breathe through the creeping nausea.

What had he had for lunch earlier? *Oh no*...had he skipped it because he'd needed to finish his Ancient Political Rhetoric paper?

Alaric shrugged, moving his saber from one hand to the other. "I think I can manage." Then his voice lowered dangerously, his eyes narrowing. "Unless you're scared."

Students were edging away from them now, clearing the area for the looming battle. And unfortunately, Titus didn't see a way out of it. Problem was...the nausea was getting worse. He could feel it. And with a surge of panic, he realized this could be a side effect of the steroids.

But if he refused the challenge he'd look weak, and not just in front of the whole school. His grandfather and parents would be mortified to know Titus backed down from a match where he had the upper hand.

Alaric couldn't know how to properly fence, but Titus understood this wouldn't end in victorious strike points on either fencing jacket.

Not with the look in his cousin's eyes. Not after what was said in the locker room.

Well, shit. Titus promptly saluted Alaric and took his stance in accordance to fencing rules.

Alaric didn't salute, and he had no stance. Without warning, his saber cut through the air with neither poise nor form—but brutal and accurate, nonetheless.

A collective gasp echoed as Titus leapt back, narrowly dodging the sharp steel. He was ready for Alaric's next swing and met it with his own épée. The handles clashed, the vicious sound echoing into the arched rafters.

They were close, nearly nose-to-nose, and pressing their swords against each other in a battle of sheer will. This was no longer fencing, not that it ever pretended to be.

"She said yes to you, didn't she?" Alaric hissed low through gritted teeth, his eyes flashing.

The question shocked Titus into letting his guard down. Alaric took the opportunity to drive forward with his shoulders, his elbow smashing hard enough into Titus's forearm to shoot a tremor up his spine.

With a grunt, Titus pushed back, moving his épée up Alaric's saber in a clash of scraping steel. Their swords freed from their lock, Titus slowly stepped to the side and Alaric mirrored his movement—the two circling each other.

"Don't know what you're talking about," Titus finally muttered.

He'd always wondered whether Alaric had feelings for Sadie. Sometimes the way he looked at her, or *didn't* look at her, had made Titus think that maybe . . .

Well, he had his answer now. Regardless, he wasn't shocked by Alaric's feelings.

What had really caught Titus off guard was the fact that Alaric knew Titus had asked her out. Had Sadie told him about it? Were they closer than Titus realized?

"The hell you don't," Alaric rasped, then lunged.

Shouts came from the students as their swords met again in another lock. The handles clanged together, and their shoulders trembled with force as they pushed against each other.

"You're a lowly maggot for talking about her with that arsehole," Alaric seethed, rotating his sword with a twist of his wrists.

"And what does that make you?" Titus panted. Though he deeply wished he wouldn't need to talk. The nausea was overwhelming now, and he didn't want to throw up all over the mat. "Using her as an excuse to challenge me in front of an audience? Could've done this anywhere. But you manufactured a spectacle. Just like the dining hall. You're a lot more like *us* than you know."

Titus had only a few seconds to revel in both the fury and horror on Alaric's face as the truth hit his cousin in the gut.

Then he recovered, too quickly and too violently. Alaric reared back and headbutted Titus in the forehead.

Thanks to the weapons, the move was not as effective, but it did its job well enough. A new kind of pain detonated in Titus's skull, forcing him to drop his sword. Alaric did the same, grabbing Titus's shirt collar and thrusting him backward into the piste. Every instinct of self-preservation kicked in and Titus remembered how to fall—a tactic most athletes in competitive fighting sports were taught.

As his back hit the mat—his shoulders, not his spine, carrying most of the impact—he thrust out his foot, digging his heel into Alaric's hip bone and using the fall to propel Alaric over his head. His cousin landed with a thud, and a roar came from the students.

Cheers. Egging them on. Maybe it had started as a fencing challenge, but now this was royal infighting, and Norms wanted this. Elites and C-Suites wanted this.

Alaric's pull on his fencing jacket had loosened the ties, so Titus shred it from his torso, tossing it to the ground as he stood. The material had barely touched the mat before Alaric went for him again, but Titus raised his forearm to block just in time.

No longer content to stay on the defensive, Titus dropped and swiped a kick at Alaric's shins. But either through training or experience, Alaric was skilled in combat as well and dove forward. He rolled across the mat, popping back up for another strike.

Ignoring the roiling in his gut, Titus dodged and wove as Alaric advanced. They traveled across the gym, out through the open doors, and into the courtyard's November sunlight. Students swarmed out after them, but their shouts were incomprehensible. Titus heard only the roar of his blood.

I can't keep this up. I'm going to fall. I cannot fall.

Rattled thoughts flashed through his head like bolts of lightning. The panic felt worse than the dizzying cramps in his stomach. As he ducked and shot forward with an uppercut—water, ice-cold, hit him square in the chest and face. He sucked it up through his mouth and nostrils, doubling over and choking as Alaric did the same.

Blinking through freezing droplets falling from his hair and lashes, Titus glimpsed a familiar figure holding a garden hose.

Emmeline, dressed in yoga attire, had her hand on the nozzle, ready to spray a second time. "Are you gentlemen *quite* done?"

34

EMMELINE

For good measure—and because she really enjoyed it the first time—Emmeline blasted her cousins with another face full of icy water.

"Feckin hell! All right, Emmeline!" Alaric barked, shaking the water from his hair.

Titus hadn't moved, soaked down to the bone, his shirt clinging to his chest and arms. Alaric was just as wet, and even more muscly than Titus, so Emmeline had no doubt the prince fan clubs were going wild. Videos and pictures were being taken by students who'd had enough foresight to grab their phones when the fight started.

"Anybody else who doesn't want to get sprayed better clear out!" Emmeline shouted at the gathered students. She swung the hose toward the crowd, and they immediately scattered like hungry rats. Most of them escaped back into the gym, closing its doors on the feuding royals.

She'd been in yoga class when she saw Alaric approach the fencing piste and knew something bad was bound to happen. As they'd fought their way into the courtyard, she'd followed them out and grabbed the hose from the landscaping team.

If only their barbaric fighting was enough to get them expelled, or better yet, removed from the line of succession. Naturally, there was not a single instructor in sight to distribute punishment, and even if there had been, Emmeline had no doubt they'd have gotten away with it. The professors at ATA regarded their pupils as adults, expecting them to solve their own problems. As for her grandfather, he'd probably be thrilled to see his grandsons brawling. *Ugh. Men.*

Once most of the students had trickled back inside, their thumbs flying across their phone screens, social media activity exploding, Emmeline dropped the hose down by her side. She glowered at her cousins. "Go warm up before you get pneumonia. You morons."

Alaric grunted and turned on his heel, heading for the lockers, wringing out his sopping shirt. But Titus didn't move, he looked dazed.

"Titus," Emmeline snapped. "Is there water in your ears? Did you hear me?"

The moment Alaric was gone, Titus dropped to his knees and promptly vomited.

Emmeline jumped back, shocked more than revulsed. "Oh my God—Titus! What's wrong?" As Titus continued to cough through the burn of bile in his throat, Emmeline went to help him up. But he knocked away her hands.

"D-don't touch me. I'm *fine.*"

Clearly he wasn't, but Emmeline was not about to double down when she wasn't wanted. "Yeah, this *screams* fine."

Titus shot her a piercing look, his iron-gray eyes fierce with annoyance and pain. Then he stood, snatched the hose from her grip and washed away his sick.

"Just leave me alone, Emmeline." His words were as cold as the frigid water.

There it was again. That sharp stab into her heart whenever Titus pushed her away. Whenever Alaric snapped back.

Why did it have to be this way? She wanted to be Ashland's queen. More than anything, she wanted her place in the Eldana family. The two boys who were her *blood*, they could be like the brothers she'd always wanted...

But they didn't trust her. They maybe hated her. And there was nothing she could do about it.

"Relax, you're not on camera." Mainly because she didn't have her phone. "Just get to the infirmary. If you can."

Titus tightened his jaw, still staring at her, hunched over on his knees.

She clicked her tongue. "Didn't think so. Why are you in such bad shape?"

Finally Titus got to his feet, and though Emmeline herself was tall, he still towered over her. "It...he got me in the stomach, that's all."

With that, he turned and started walking toward the castle, not the locker room.

"He's going to drip all over the castle floor," Emmeline muttered to herself before she went back into the gym.

She found Sebastian fencing with Roderick, son of the US vice president. Too annoyed to wait for them to be done with their three-minute round, she slammed her hands on the mat and yelled, "Sebastian!"

Roderick got his hit, thrusting his foil into Sebastian's padded jacket, and the light dinged with a point.

Sebastian held up his hand to his opponent and tore off his mask, then walked over to Emmeline, who stood at the edge of the piste.

"Princess?" Seb cocked an eyebrow, irritation threading through his tone.

Emmeline ignored it. "Go check on Titus."

Seb raised his brows in surprise. "Why? It was just one hit."

"He's in bad shape. Go."

"Again, why should I?"

"Because I asked, and you're his freaking roommate."

308

Sebastian muttered a curse, stabbing his foil into the mat. "Consider it done, princess."

But Emmeline didn't know if it was "done" for several days. Not until after their biweekly Hibernia meeting, which was moving at a snail's pace.

She was going through her agenda as fast as she could, but Lotta had questions about every. Single. Thing. And none of them were the least bit relevant.

"Ice dragons?" Lotta snorted as Oakley pulled up sketches from the ice sculptors. "Really? That's so... dorky."

Before Oakley could lunge across the desk and suffocate her, Alaric cleared his throat. "They were my idea."

"Oh," Lotta turned pink and pressed her lips together. "W-well, they are pretty cool. And match the theme. Very... military chic."

Nearly everyone at the table rolled their eyes. Emmeline pushed forward, tabbing through to the next slide. Lotta had been invited to Emmeline's brainstorming sessions but always had some excuse to skip. If Alaric and Titus were out of sight, so was Lotta. Emmeline had therefore done all the work herself and even got an art student to come up with the "Hibernia Legions" logo.

"We're sticking to the decorations budget?" Emmeline asked, looking pointedly at Oakley, but it was Alaric who spoke up.

"The ice sculptors were the most expensive, but I managed to cut some costs for the landscaping and lighting."

Emmeline stared at him, her gaze bouncing to Oakley for confirmation, who nodded enthusiastically with her thumbs up.

"Cut costs... how?" she asked skeptically.

"We're going with blue spruce for most of the interior plants, so I contacted some foresters within the Ore Mountains on the German-Czech border, a blue spruce forest. We'll pay for the shipping and handling of ten crates, but they'll give us the boughs for free. As for lighting, we'll need to rent the lights, but the labor costs will be covered by the students."

Emmeline loathed the fact that she was impressed. What had flipped Alaric's switch? In their three previous meetings, he'd barely said a word. What changed?

"Students have never done exterior or interior lighting for Hibernia. It's too delicate," Sebastian said, folding his arms.

"I've done electrical work." Alaric glared back. "As long as I have the right plans and equipment, I can direct the team."

"Very well, moving on," Emmeline said, cutting off further debate.

She clicked to the slide that Titus and Sebastian had submitted, and her eyes shot over to her cousin. He looked normal—no more pale or tired than he usually was. But he'd been quiet.

"The summit will take place in the Magna Carta Lecture Hall," Titus said, his attention on the screen. "We've decided to go with an electronic pad that scans the guests' wristbands. When they check in, each guest will receive a corresponding band, and depending on their registration status, they will have exclusive admittance to this room. When the meeting is ready to start, the band will vibrate with a notification, prompting them into the hall."

Emmeline turned to Oliver, who sat with his laptop open, his fingers flying. He hadn't stopped typing since they all sat down. "And that's all possible?" she asked, trying not to admire how dexterous his hands were, moving across the keys.

"You bet," he said in his deep timbre. "Sadie ordered the wristbands from the vendor two weeks ago. I just need to program them once they arrive."

The rest of the meeting was devoted to Oliver and Sadie taking the committee through their prototype of the registration dashboard. According to Oliver, it was in beta phase. With another week of tweaking, it would be ready to send out. Which was good because Hibernia was almost exactly three weeks away. Paper save-the-date invitations had been sent out as soon as the theme had been determined, but Calixa and Kavi were laying on the pressure.

It was driving Emmeline up the wall. "See you all this weekend. The electronic invitations *must* be out by Friday, and the vendors booked and paid for. Meeting adjourned."

Sebastian started to get up next to her, but she pulled his arm right back down, nearly popping his shoulder out of the socket.

He waited until the last person—Oakley—was gone before he sucked in a breath with a foul curse. "Christ, Emmeline."

"You're ignoring my texts, Sebastian," she said in a deadly tone. She was actually furious it had taken them this long to connect. Titus was her family, and she'd been *worried* about him. "What happened to Titus?"

Sebastian sighed, lacing his hands behind his head and rocking on the back legs of his chair. "Nothing, all right? By the time I got to our room, he seemed fine. Dunno."

Emmeline pushed. "He didn't go to the infirmary?"

Now Sebastian was pushing back. "Aren't *you* the doting family member. No, princess, Titus didn't go to the infirmary for a *bump*. He used to get hurt all the time at Eton and he never told anyone. Bloke could have internal bleeding and you'd never know it. That happened once actually, playing rugby when we were twelve—"

"It was much worse than a bump," she snapped. "Some friend you are."

At that, Seb's brows furrowed and for the first time, he looked angry. "Hey. Don't put your family shit on me, Emmeline. I'm telling you he had an ice pack on his forehead and was texting on his royal phone. *Normal.*"

Emmeline blinked, confused. An ice pack on his forehead? Didn't Titus get punched in the stomach? Granted, she hadn't actually seen the whole fight because she'd been fetching the hose. But that's what he'd told her.

Just then something else she'd heard made those other questions vanish.

"His royal phone?"

"His other phone. The one for Ashland stuff."

"Right, we all got one." Emmeline lied, wanting to keep this intel to herself so she could process it later. "I'm just surprised he had it out. Well thanks for trying, I guess." Emmeline stood, grabbing her bag.

Then Sebastian caught her wrist. "There might be something else..."

Emmeline was too preoccupied with the second phone that she didn't much care what else he had to say. "Yes?"

"Sadie and Titus are dating." Emmeline froze and Sebastian's smirk widened.

Okay. She cared about *that*.

"How can you be sure?"

"She came to our dorm room last week. Titus is now constantly on his phone. Smiling." Sebastian paused, then put the nail in the coffin. "He's been out every evening, coming in late, smelling like a girl."

"That's not concrete proof," she argued, though she knew deep down it must be true.

"There's no other girl in school he's paid the least bit attention to. Trust me. They're snogging in secret."

"Why secret?" Emmeline wondered out loud.

"Who cares?"

Emmeline did. She cared very much because Titus was succeeding. As she'd predicted, he'd set out to seduce Sadie, effectively eliminating one of his rivals if he managed to get her to fall in love with him. And Sadie was so innocent and vulnerable, there's no way she wouldn't fall for a prince's charms. Even if the prince was boring Titus.

At least she's dating Titus and not Oliver.

Wow. That thought came out of nowhere. That should not be

what's important right now, and yet she hadn't been able to stop the flood of relief that came with it.

"What's with the face?" Sebastian asked, his arm draped behind her chair and his slouch casual and confident. "Upset your cousin started dating someone before you did?"

"Hardly," she scoffed. But her thoughts and emotions wrapped around a certain someone were becoming more and more of a hindrance.

Sebastian's eyes flashed with interest. "That wasn't very convincing, *Emmie.*"

She wanted to snap at him not to call her that. Only certain people were allowed to use that nickname, but he was trying to get a rise out of her. Trying to make her reveal more of herself.

"If I didn't know better, I'd say you're angry that Titus has the better strategy," he continued. "You know how everyone loves a power couple."

Son of a . . .

He was right. King Leander might even be delighted that two of his heirs are dating. If he'd liked Sadie enough to add her to the running for his throne, he may even support a royal engagement, despite the fact that they were barely eighteen. What if Titus was named heir apparent and Sadie his fiancée?

That could *not* happen.

Emmeline turned her gaze sharply to Sebastian. "But that's only if their relationship is strong enough to weather a storm."

35

SADIE

"WHAT WAS I THINKING?" SADIE ANNOUNCED AS THE REST OF the class packed up around her. They'd just had their most jam-packed Anthropology lecture of the year and Sadie was pretty sure the Trobriand Islands ethnographic study results were leaking out of her ears.

"You'll have to be more specific," Trang said, shoving her laptop into her bag.

"Planning Hibernia before the finals. I may never sleep from now until December eighteenth."

Sadie hadn't moved from her desk, still staring blankly at the screen where Bronisław Malinowski's monographs had flashed by in record speed.

"Can I borrow your stuffed sea lion then?"

That finally made Sadie tear her gaze from the screen and look at her friend, confused. "You want to borrow Una?"

Grannah had gotten her Una when she was nine. Sadie had picked it up in one of the tourist shops of their little seaside suburb of Durah, called Farach, and she hadn't been able to put it down.

That reminded her—she needed to finish the content calendar and scheduling for all of December's posts for the Ashland Sea Mammal Conservation's social media. Their follower count had grown since Sadie took over, but her work had suffered recently due to planning for Hibernia and studying for finals. Mrs. Colliander hadn't complained (as she was getting free labor), but still, Sadie didn't want to disappoint her.

"You always look so serene cuddling that thing," Trang teased, nudging her out of the chair and out of her worries. "I don't think I've *ever* been that peaceful, and my uncle's a Buddhist monk. I had to study at his temple for the whole summer when I was thirteen."

Sadie gathered up her laptop and books and shoved them into her bag. "I'll never part with Una. She'll be buried with me out at sea."

"So that's a real thing, huh?" Trang asked as they headed into the corridor and turned down the stone staircase, bypassing one of the castle's old statues of some angelic-looking saint.

"Being buried at sea?" Sadie asked, her stomach sinking, already regretting the topic she'd accidentally brought up.

"Yeah. Every country is obviously different, but Ashland doesn't bury anyone in the ground, right? I heard they carve names of the deceased on rocks by the sea."

An image of her mother's name embossed in gold on the rock wall outside Farach's port flashed through her mind and Sadie stumbled on the steps. She had to grab the statue's edge to keep from falling.

"Sadie!" Trang cried, reaching for her.

"I'm fine, sorry. Just—rolled my ankle," Sadie said with a self-deprecating laugh. Good thing Alaric wasn't around to be further convinced she was just as clumsy as he treated her. But that thought alone was painful. She hadn't spoken to him since the night of the bonfire. Nor had she told Trang about what happened—she didn't want her friend trying to "kick his ass" as she'd threatened to do.

Ultimately, Sadie doubted she could stomach seeing him or talking to him yet. Knowing someone had absolutely no faith in you, that they thought so little of you—it was unbearable.

Maybe that's why she'd gone to Titus two days later. It wasn't the best reason to date someone, but Titus made her feel better about herself. Made her feel beautiful and happy. Shouldn't dating be as simple as that?

It helped that when Sadie had told Trang about her leaning toward saying yes to Titus, her friend had been wholeheartedly supportive. After all, the blond Ashland prince was the only person whom Trang witnessed looking after Sadie as much as she did. First in the infirmary after her panic attack, and then later when Sadie texted that it had been Titus who'd kept her afloat in Ashland. It was clear he cared.

So she gave it a shot. For better or worse, she'd made her decision. She tried not to think about all the complications and instead enjoy their moments together. In the present.

"Hey, Sadie...why's everyone staring?" Trang asked her suddenly, dragging Sadie out of her thoughts about Titus and their "study session" last night.

They had entered one of the school's most trafficked corridors, the western wing, the hall connecting the admin offices and the dining hall. Nearly every student they passed scanned Sadie with eyes wide, then quickly ducked to return to their phones.

"Oh no." Trang stopped in her tracks, her gaze also glued to her phone.

"What?" Sadie asked, though she wasn't sure she wanted to find out. No, she was certain she didn't.

Trang winced, holding up her phone. "You're trending on TikTok."

Blood drained from her face as Sadie watched herself on Titus's lap, his mouth devouring hers in their study room. His hands threaded into her hair and angled her mouth to meet his skilled tongue. Some Doja Cat song played on a loop with fire graphics bordering the screen.

"Oh my god."

It was from last night. The first time Titus had attempted a deeper kiss that made Sadie's toes curl and her mind go wonderfully, deliriously blank.

She grabbed Trang's phone and started scrolling through the comments. Nearly all of them were hateful—except…the ones that weren't from school. These had Ashlandic hashtags, making their national news. Actually, it was world news. And people were *losing it*.

The video had reached hundreds of thousands of views, and it was climbing. People were going wild for the two Ashland heirs hooking up. A Cinderella story as old as time—an impoverished girl with a prince. Everyone loved a rags-to-riches story, and the icing on the cake? They were rivals falling in love.

Falling in love? Absolutely not. It hadn't even been a month. They were simply enjoying quiet moments together, a little bit at a time. But that's not what the rest of the world saw. The comments and the varying opinions were endless.

> **@jinn_k23** EEEEE does this mean a royal wedding soon?? #heirOTP

> **@rayraycake** dannnnng those Ashland princes can XXX #royalmakeout

> **@Pr!nc3ssRee** And this was only what they caught on camera. What a slut.

> **@hans-iver** We're so proud of our girl. Bring our prince home, Sadie! #AshlandHeirs

Sadie's head started spinning, her chest tight. Students in the hallway weren't just staring now, they were whispering. At the end of the corridor, Sadie spotted Lotta and Remy and their friends looking like they were ready to blow something up.

Sadie could only watch in horror as the ticks went up on her video. The question of *who* had filmed and posted it hadn't even crossed her mind, and it didn't matter anyway. What was done was done.

Trang squeezed her shoulder, muttering something in Sadie's ear. But Sadie couldn't hear anything but a high-pitched buzzing.

"Sadie!"

A sharp voice rang through the hall and Sadie looked up from the video. Titus was striding toward her, his golden brows pulled together, looking downright furious.

Furious at *her*? His uniform and hair were immaculate as always. Of course he looked unscathed. It was never the guy who got dragged with caustic remarks. It would never be him being called a slut for the whole world to see. He was the prince and could bestow his affections on whomever he pleased. Titus could do no wrong.

Sadie was prepared to explode in his direction. If he even *suggested* this was her fault in any way, she'd lose it, she'd—

His hands were suddenly cupping her cheeks, smoothing over her freckles as they'd done so many times over the last few weeks. Concerned eyes searched her face, as if looking for any sign of damage, or any hint of tears.

"Are you all right?" he asked, almost out of breath. Had he been running to find her?

Sadie wasn't sure if she could even speak right now. They were in a busy corridor with people staring, probably . . . recording.

With a hard swallow, she gently tried to push his hands down. "I'm okay."

"I'm so sorry. I don't know how this happened. I'll find out—"

"Titus," she said, her eyes widening with alarm. "I think we're being filmed. Let's just . . . talk when we're alone, okay?"

Titus muttered a curse, then touched his forehead to hers. "Yeah, okay." Then, for their audience, he placed a gentle kiss on her lips.

Hoots, whistles, and catcalls echoed through the corridor. Sadie blushed and let Titus take her hand and lead her into the bailey, some place away from the masses.

That place ended up being underneath some desks in one of the art rooms. Titus had pulled her between his legs with her back pressed against his chest and his chin resting on her shoulder. His arms held her waist as if worried she'd bolt.

And, well...she might.

Being at ATA, it was easy to forget about the outside world. She'd only thought about hiding it from other students. She hadn't even considered hiding it from the rest of the world.

"On a scale of one to 'I'm ready to move to Antarctica,' how badly are you freaking out right now?" Titus asked.

With him curled around her like this, in the fortress of desks, she felt...safe.

"Not quite Antarctica level. Maybe...Madagascar?"

"Then let's go. Those lemurs are cute, and I hear they throw really great dance parties."

"Titus," Sadie said, giggling and elbowing him in the stomach.

He chuckled, his chest vibrating behind her. Then he fell quiet. Both lost in the prospect of what they'd soon have to endure.

"Are you going to be okay with this?" he finally asked. "I...I don't want to lose you so soon, Sadie."

She hesitated, and for whatever reason, Alaric's face flashed through her head. The look he'd given her—with the campfire casting shadows across the planes of his face, his sharp jaw, and deep-set eyes.

For the tenth time, she wondered about that gym fight. Naturally, like every other student, she'd heard it was the best fight in ATA history. She'd even watched a few videos. And she'd been more than curious to know what set Alaric off to challenge Titus.

Had it been about the crown? Was it about Alaric's parents—or lack thereof? Had Titus said something cruel, or had it just been Alaric's bad temper?

Didn't matter. It was none of her business.

Dating Titus in the open would involve a world of baggage, but Sadie had a better support system now. Trang felt like more of a sister these last couple weeks. And thanks to the Hibernia committee, she was becoming real friends with Oliver. Titus was caring and protective. She wanted to draw on their strength to do well in finals and pull off the Hibernia planning so she could gain favor with the king.

Sadie blew out a breath and tilted her head to place a soft kiss on her boyfriend's cheek. "You're not losing me. Promise."

36

ALARIC

IF ALARIC SAW THAT VIDEO ONE MORE TIME, HE WAS GOING TO destroy every cell phone in the school. The kicker? It wasn't even on his feed. He followed a total of thirty accounts—his friends back home and some gaming and animation studios and bands he liked. No, it was on everyone *else's* screens. Popping up while they scrolled in class, the student lounges, or dining halls.

With every exposure, he felt sick. That, combined with the fact that he couldn't get away from their relationship. No matter where he was, it always seemed to come up.

Even in a student lounge one evening where he'd decided to take a break from preparing for his Democratic Republic Studies final and read some web comics on his phone.

"One million views," Ross said as they slid into a table across from Jacob, who was testing his new robotic arm on shuffling a deck of cards.

Don't say it, Alaric prayed.

"What's one million views?" Bea asked, not looking up from sketching on her iPad.

In answer, the Doja Cat song played.

"I can't believe her. One minute she was hanging out with us and the next she's sucking face with one of *them*," Bea practically snarled.

"It kind of makes sense, you know?" Assane said calmly. "I've never seen her around with other students. I don't think she has many friends. And I heard Titus is a partner for her school project. Maybe they just grew close."

"It doesn't matter. She switched sides. End of story." Bea tapped her stylus on the table with every word.

"Annnd we've heard from Bea the Betrayed. Jacob?" Ross asked. "Thoughts?"

Jacob put down his tool and the robotic arm dropped the cards. They spilled across the table. Sighing, he said, "I think it sucks for Sadie all around. Most Scholars don't trust her now, and Elites have been saying she's 'dating above her station.' So I hope Titus is worth it."

With that, Alaric stood and grabbed his bag. "Going to bed," he grumbled, though it was still three full hours before curfew.

It wasn't like Alaric hadn't already heard those things in hallway whispers or classroom gossip, but it stung to hear them from his friends.

He'd even caught some Elites claiming she was "gaining favor with her country." Which had become undeniably evident. More and more, public support compounded for Sadie as the heir apparent. After her initial wave of popularity in September, it had only seemed to grow. Her display at the football match. Her sweet, genuine nature made visible through Ilsa's PR events. And now dating Titus, the gilded prodigal son.

On top of the sick feelings brewing in his gut that he refused to acknowledge, Alaric was faced with something entirely new: worry.

He worried about Titus and Sadie gaining favor with King Leander, about the succession that he'd never cared about until a few weeks ago.

For the first time, Alaric confronted the same anxiety and stress that Emmeline and Titus seemed to live with. Who was pulling ahead? Which of their actions gained points, or lost them? It was maddening.

Now that he'd finally decided to really go for the throne, he was lost.

All he could do was throw himself into his finals and planning for Hibernia. Those decorations turned out to be far more than he'd bargained for, yet they were the only thing in his life he had control over.

"You know the Roman standards of legions with the eagles on the top?" Oakley asked, interrupting his review of the type 4060 digital counter with the built-in oscillator.

He ground his teeth. "Yeah?" He sat in the bailey after classes, just a week shy of finals and exactly twelve days away from Hibernia, reviewing the castle's electrical plans on his laptop alongside Oakley, who had taken the theme Legions very seriously.

"What if we made them *dragons* instead of eagles?" Her hands spread out like she was imagining the finale of a Christopher Nolan film.

"Brilliant."

"I hear your sarcasm and I'm choosing to ignore it. By the way, you could've told Lotta the ice dragons were my idea. I would've torn that brat to shreds."

"Exactly why I didn't. Would've taken too long," he muttered, tabbing through to the next electro schematic. "I don't get yer obsession with dragons."

"Okay first of all, anyone who's not obsessed with dragons is clearly a lizard person in disguise. That's why they lie to everyone about how they're not obsessed with dragons."

"I am trying very hard to read this schematic, Oakley."

"Hey, guys."

Alaric suppressed a groan at Emmeline's arrival. She'd changed out of her uniform and wore a fuzzy jacket that sparkled and black leggings. Her long honey waves were tied into a fancy braid, and she cradled her laptop in her arms.

"Emmie! Eagles or dragons for the frosted standards?"

Emmeline cocked an eyebrow. "Dragons. Is this a trick question?"

"Just proving you're not a lizard person, babe," Oakley said cheerfully, jumping to her feet and pecking Emmeline's cheek. "Blimey, I'm late for my date with Danica. Al, you'll fill in our fearless leader, yeah?"

Alaric grunted as Emmeline took a seat at the stone table and Oakley grabbed her stuff and skipped off.

"So . . .," Emmeline started slowly, "how's it going?"

"The blue spruce is arriving on the docks tomorrow. We'll start the setup the day after finals. That gives four days to—"

"Not Hibernia," she interrupted. "I can read an email report."

"Then why are yeh here?" he asked, maybe too harshly, as he typed an email back to the lighting vendor requesting an additional hundred strings.

"Oh, just wanted to chat."

"About?"

"Why you suddenly care about our line of succession."

Alaric stopped typing, his gaze shifting over to Emmeline, who sat across from him with a pleasant smile.

"C'mon, Alaric. You can't expect me to believe you randomly became obsessed with evergreen boughs and exterior illumination."

"And yeh can't expect *me* to believe the night before that video was released yeh showed up at our dorm to see that British prick for no other reason than to drop off tea before bed."

Emmeline was quiet for a moment before she clicked her tongue and muttered, "So you admit you care about the crown now?"

"Do yeh admit yeh used Sebastian to do your dirty work?"

Her eyes sparked with rage. "Is that judgment I hear?"

Alaric smirked and went back to his email. "Pride."

Emmeline folded her arms and drummed her painted nails across her elbow. "Can I ask you something?"

"Depends."

"Was Oliver in the dorm room that night? I didn't see past Sebastian when he opened the door."

Alaric pressed send, heard the *whoosh* of the traveling email, then slowly closed his laptop. He regarded Emmeline, noting her abnormally rosy cheeks, and considered messing with her.

In the end, he figured the truth would pack the biggest punch. And since she'd been the mastermind behind that video, he was all too pleased to dish out a little pain himself.

"He was."

Emmeline mouthed a foul curse word.

"Yeh like him."

She briefly stiffened, then dropped her elbows on the table with a huff. She surprised him by not even trying to deny it.

"So? Doesn't matter."

"Emmeline, he's leagues better than Sebastian."

"You think I don't know that?" Her words hissed like the most venomous serpent. Eyes flashing like a basilisk, instant death in her glare. For a long moment, neither of them said anything. His cousin continued to glare at him as she rested her chin on her palm.

"Oliver is a Scholar from Middle America. His parents are nice, I'm sure, but they don't have access to government regulations, nor do they control millions of dollars. He may be a genius, but smart doesn't always equal powerful. There's no point in getting attached if I can't keep him. Unlike you, I'm willing to admit what I want. And what I want will *not* be sacrificed at the altar of my stupid hormones."

Alaric said nothing. Because as much as he hated to agree with her twisted logic, it made sense. And there was something in her words that resonated a little too well.

"Besides, why would I risk messing with a boy I actually care about?" she mumbled, and Alaric wasn't sure if she realized she'd said it aloud.

A few awkward moments passed before Emmeline glared pointedly at Alaric. "Well, what about you and Sadie?"

A prickle of irritation started in the back of Alaric's neck.

"That fight was about *her*, wasn't it?"

He clenched his teeth and glanced away, a muscle ticking in his jaw.

"You sent Titus to the infirmary. Punched him in the gut."

Alaric's gaze shot over to her. "What? No, I didn't. I landed a headbutt. That's it."

"He says you did."

"Trust me. I don't take credit for hits I don't land."

Emmeline pursed her lips. "Interesting. Hey, did you get a new phone in Ashland?"

Alaric stared at her, totally thrown. "No. Why? Did yeh?"

"No. But Seb says Titus has two phones."

It's possible that Titus did and Alaric didn't know. He tried to stay out of their dorm room as much as possible to avoid both Titus and Sebastian.

"So you swear you didn't get one?" Emmeline prodded when he didn't respond, nudging his knee under the table with her leg.

"Why on *earth* would I need two phones? Ilsa texts me enough on this one as it is," he exploded.

But his frustration barely registered. Instead Emmeline clicked her tongue. "Why, indeed."

"Are we done?"

She let out a light, annoying laugh. "God, that video must be killing you."

He opened his laptop back up. "I've got work to do, yeh can get out of my face now."

"Fine, fine. Just tell me this, Alaric."

She waited until he was staring into her silver eyes. "What do you really think of Sadie?"

Soft, sweet, kind, with a heart to hold the pain of everyone around her, while she buries her own. In a word? Breakable.

"She knows what I think of her."

37

EMMELINE

It didn't take long for Emmeline to figure out that her plan had backfired. Sebastian had more or less warned her of the risk. But she'd honestly thought Sadie and Titus wouldn't survive the turmoil of being discovered. And at first, the fallout was predictable. Scholars didn't like Sadie now that she'd "crossed to the dark side," and Elites and C-Suites thought she was dating Titus to gain favors. The rumors and reactions had turned vicious. Exactly as she'd planned.

What she hadn't predicted? How good of a boyfriend Titus would be.

He walked Sadie to class when he could. Sat next to her in the dining hall, which encouraged a combination of Scholars, C-Suites, and Elites to sit with them—an inclusion coup that had only been pulled off in the past by Oakley and Danica. They studied in public places now, like the student lounges, and everyone saw how sickeningly cute they were together.

Titus seemed to really care about Sadie and went to great lengths to protect her. Even going so far as to pull Lotta aside and warn her about any bullying. Lotta had complained about it to one of Oakley's friends, and Oakley reported it back to Emmeline. Which just galled her even more.

It was *fake*. It was all fake. She knew why Titus was doing this, and it wasn't because he was falling for Sadie. What's worse is that their popularity was soaring not just within the school, but across pop culture worldwide. Strangers on social media were invested in Sadie and Titus's relationship, and the general consensus seemed to be rooting for love. #Ashland5ever

At this rate, the public's approval for Ashland's young lovers would force King Leander to fold in that direction. To make them happy. And she could *not* let it come to that. Not after all the sacrifices she'd made. But what could she do? What leverage did she have?

As finals wrapped up and Hibernia marched closer, Emmeline could only watch on as Sadie and Titus became ATA's de facto power couple, easily dethroning Calixa and Kavi.

The final blow for Emmeline unexpectedly came in the form of an email from Ilsa.

To: eeldana@almusterra.edu, aeldana@almusterra.edu, teldana@almusterra.edu, saurelia@almusterra.edu
From: royalsecretary-office2@ashland.gov

Your Royal Highnesses,

We need to confirm the final fitting for your suits and dresses for Hibernia. The royal seamstress can be on-site December 14 at 4PM. Please clear your schedules so she can make any last-minute adjustments.

Sadie—Your fitting will have to be the following day as she's had to change your gown to match Titus's suit. The king would like the two of you to appear as a couple for the press.

Your Loyal Subject,
Ilsa Halvorsen
Royal Private Secretary
Office of the King, Ashland

Emmeline lay in her bed staring at the email until the words became blurry. *This isn't happening.* She'd been close. So close. A month ago, she was sitting in King Leander's office as the chosen one. Now...

She drew in a breath and pressed her arm over her eyes.

No, she was not going to give up. She just had to get Titus to admit what Emmeline already knew to be true. And she wouldn't sleep until she figured out how.

If Emmeline's nerves had been close to the edge before, they were now hanging by a branch over a rocky abyss thanks to the strange scene in front of her.

She'd come back after an archery session with Calixa, where she'd once again been grilled over the preparations for Hibernia. The student council president was a terrible micromanager.

Upon entering her dorm, she found Sadie, Trang, and Oliver sitting on the floor in a circle, laptops out, appearing to have a group study session before the last few days of finals.

Oliver gave her a smile that melted her insides a bit. "Hey, Emmeline."

Trang didn't acknowledge her, but Sadie chimed in with her usual irritating kindness. "Sorry, are we in your way? Oliver and I were just checking on some things within the Hibernia portal. Trang offered to help us sort through the responses."

"Trang isn't on the committee," Emmeline said before she could stop herself. What did that even matter? But seeing Oliver here had thrown her off-kilter.

"So?" Trang said with a frown. "Alaric has gotten a bunch of people to help with the decorating."

"That's not the same thing. These responses are from—"

"*VIPs*?" Trang interjected. "Very important parents? Only the rich and powerful ones allowed to attend Hibernia?"

Emmeline swallowed her words as Oliver pointedly stared down at his screen. Discomfort roiled through her stomach like old tuna. She suddenly wished to be anywhere else.

She folded her arms, refusing to look at Oliver, whose parents were very obviously *not* going. "That's out of my hands."

"Yeah, so you say," Trang muttered, looking back to her laptop.

Emmeline hated her in that moment. Hated how Trang had made her look, but knowing full well she'd once again follow the traditions of Almus Terra, despite what she believed in. Her grandfather wanted her on this committee, and this unsanctioned global economic summit was too important to attempt change. She needed to become heir apparent first, *then* she could challenge the customs. Play the game first to win, then modify the rules. That had always been her strategy.

Sadie, who had been looking nervously between the three of them, suddenly bolted to her feet with her phone in her hand. "Oh, um, Titus is calling. I'll be right back."

She hurried out the door and in the silence that followed, Oliver started packing up his things. "Well, I think I've got what I needed. Trang, I appreciate the help. Emmeline, I'll... catch you later."

Before Emmeline could ask herself what she'd expected out of her interference, she tried to step in front of Oliver to stop him. She wanted to tell him she didn't agree with leaving out his parents, or any of the Scholars' parents—but the sudden movement startled Oliver and he stepped back quickly, bumping the bunk bed Sadie and Emmeline shared. His shoulder grazed the top bunk's comforter, and the shuffle caused the pillow to slide, and a little leather book tumbled to the floor.

"Oops, I'm so sorry." Oliver bent down to grab what looked like a journal, when Trang dove for it instead, snatching it up before he could get it.

"I got it—thanks, Oliver."

Emmeline raised her eyebrows. She'd seen that book before. Sadie had stuffed it into a drawer after she'd torn the dorm apart looking for her laptop. It was Sadie's—but Trang knew about it. Knew that it was important to her.

"Oh sure, sorry again," he said as he sidestepped Emmeline, giving her a wide berth and heading for the door.

That would have hurt if Emmeline wasn't so absorbed in an idea beginning to coalesce. In her peripheral view, she watched Trang discreetly slide the journal into her bag.

It was time she got to know her fourth roommate a little better.

Sadie stood in front of the mirror wearing a gown of deep crimson red. Mrs. Kendle, the royal seamstress, adjusted the skirts, adding in pins to pick up the train just a bit more—for waltzing, as Titus pointed out. Though he didn't need to be there, Titus had offered to accompany Sadie to her dress fitting and Emmeline had invited herself as well. It was as good an excuse as any.

And he watched her, practically entranced, as Sadie turned from one side to the other in her gown.

Emmeline hated that Sadie did, in fact, look stunning. The red satin highlighted her ginger hair and pale complexion. The off-the-shoulder sleeves revealed alluring freckles across her creamy skin.

"There should be something on her neck," Emmeline spoke up from her chair in the corner, tapping her collarbone. "A diamond collar or a festoon."

Mrs. Kendle stepped back, looking over her work. The gown was tight in the bodice with pink silk sleeves that draped across Sadie's arms, then it cinched at the waist in a bow and expanded out in a gorgeous cascade of satin fabric and tulle petticoats.

"Yes, I believe you're right."

"Um, no collar, please," Sadie piped up, her fingers nervously scratching her throat.

"Don't worry, Sadie," Titus said, getting up from his chair and kissing her on her bare shoulder. "You don't have to wear a necklace if you don't want to."

Sadie blushed and Emmeline couldn't stand another minute of this. Time to act.

"Titus?" Emmeline said sweetly. "Could I have a word? About Hibernia." She gestured out to the hall.

Titus's eyes narrowed, but in front of Mrs. Kendle he predictably didn't refuse.

He followed her into the hall and into another vacant admin office, the same one where Sadie had been primped before their initial family portrait.

"What's this about, Emmeline?" he asked, wasting no time, his expression annoyed.

"Just wondering if you needed this."

The moment Titus saw his second phone in her hand, Emmeline knew she'd guessed correctly. His jaw went slack, his face paler than a ghost's, and he stared from the phone back to Emmeline, like she'd just stopped time.

This is yours, right?"

"Emmeline . . ." Titus's gray eyes moved back to hers as he pressed his lips into a thin line.

It hadn't been easy finding the secret phone, but accessing Titus's dorm room was child's play thanks to her relationship with Sebastian, who conveniently left her alone in their room whenever she sent him to fetch her a drink, or to collect her laptop when she "forgot it" at the library.

"Now, if I were to *guess*, there's something on this phone you don't want Mummy or Daddy seeing. Rest assured, I haven't bothered to hack into it, and actually I don't even care. All I needed to know is that you're hiding something. I'm sure our family would be much more motivated to find out what—"

"STOP."

Emmeline looked up, her gut twisting at how distraught her cousin looked. His face was exhausted, haggard. One hand was on the nearby desk, supporting his weight, while the other dragged through his tousled blond hair. She took no pleasure in this cruelty, but Titus was winning. Sadie was winning. And that was unacceptable.

"Just…stop," he said. His gaze shot to her, wary and full of hate. "What do you want?"

With a hand she commanded to *stop shaking*, she held out her phone. "Record a message telling Sadie why you're really with her."

Titus stared at the phone, then blew out a breath, pain flashing across his features. "Emmeline, that would crush her."

"Should've thought about that before you executed your strategy to seduce her."

What hypocrisy. As if she herself hadn't done whatever she could to get ahead. From filming Alaric while he vomited his guts out, to destroying Sadie's laptop, and using Sebastian to learn how to blackmail Titus. Emmeline hated herself for this. And she hated herself even more for what she was about to do.

But there was no going back. It was either this or give up her dreams of ever being loved and respected by her family. *Never.* She'd come too far.

Neither of them moved, but then he finally reached for the phone and took it with trembling fingers. Like Emmeline, he was shaken, forced to confront what he'd done.

They knew their sins.

"How can I be sure you won't tell anyone, even if I do this? How can I trust you?"

Emmeline crossed her arms, her sharp nails digging painfully into her skin. "You can't. You never have. But I swear on my blood I won't tell a soul if you do this for me. And your blood is the same as mine. That must count for something."

After a long tense minute, Titus opened the voice memo app, and before pressing record, he told her with sad, reddened eyes, "Trust me, our blood is not the same."

38

SADIE

"Just a few final touches, dear, and you'll be done," Mrs. Kendle promised, adding another pin to the train.

"I don't mind, take your time," Sadie said with a smile. The dress was magnificent, and she looked *hot*. Standing in front of the mirror like this, she admired the way it accented her slim waist and lifted her breasts—she also loved the way Titus couldn't keep his eyes off her in it.

Just then, Mrs. Kendle's phone rang. "Oh, if you'll excuse me. I'm so sorry." The royal seamstress bowed her way out the door.

Sadie turned back to the mirrors, a grin on her face. The fire in the hearth crackled and popped, filling the room with warmth.

For the first time in weeks, the stress of the semester felt far away. Hibernia was almost ready, and she'd aced her finals. Not to mention, she had people to enjoy winter break with.

Ten seconds later, the door opened again.

"That was fast—oh, Emmeline."

The princess entered and closed the door behind her with a snap. Sadie frowned, her brows pulling together, along with the strings of her heart. Like a premonition, something felt wrong.

"Where's Titus?"

"Oh, Seb needed him for their part of Hibernia," Emmeline said, flicking her wrist dismissively.

"Mrs. Kendle is on a call. I think she's almost done—you don't have to stay," Sadie said, knowing Emmeline didn't care for her. Didn't even pretend.

"Oh, it's fine. I don't mind." Emmeline smiled, taking a seat in one of the plush armchairs. Probably the exact one she'd sat in for the family portrait. "So . . . you and Titus are going pretty strong, huh?"

Sadie fiddled with the material of her skirts and the rustle echoed in the room, second only to the sound of crackling flames in the fireplace. "I . . . I guess."

"Don't be shy, Sadie. He seems to adore you. And everyone is really shipping you two. I actually had to look up what OTP means." Her laugh was sunny but hollow.

Sadie swallowed hard, discomfort climbing into her chest. "That's just the internet."

"Uh-huh," Emmeline said, her gaze locked with Sadie's through the glass of the three-paneled mirror. "Can I just ask . . . are you falling in love with him?"

Sadie's heart jumped into her throat. She turned quickly on the spot to face Emmeline, hopefully not losing any pins in the satin gown's train in the process.

"No, no, I like him a lot, but we just started dating. And really . . . it's none of your business."

Emmeline blew out a breath. "That's a relief. Because this would've been freaking *tragic*." Then she pulled out her phone and tapped the screen, her nails clicking.

Suddenly Titus's regal voice filled the room, piercing her heart like one of Emmeline's stupid arrows.

"I'm dating Sadie Aurelia with the intention of seducing her to form an alliance. If she loves me, I expect she'd renounce her position as a potential heir to support my rightful claim to the throne of Ashland. Our relationship has also won the support of the Ashlandic citizens and boosted my own popularity. Any intimacy between us is a matter of strategy. Nothing more."

Silence, apart from the crackling flames, resonated in the small room after the end of Titus's message.

Time seemed to slow. Creeping forward at a glacier's pace, spreading its icy, killer devastation through Sadie. A thousand emotions hit her at once. Hurt, humiliation, anger...She licked her lips and asked in a quivering voice, "What do you have on him?"

Emmeline's expression didn't change. "Does it matter? Every word is true."

The fragmented shards of Sadie's heart beat pathetically in her chest. As much as she wanted to give Titus the excuse that he was being forced, or blackmailed, whatever—she couldn't deny this.

Yes, it had to be true. Because the alternative would be absurd. *Her? With a prince?* It was laughable. And yet...the entire world had believed in their fairy tale. Maybe because people loved love stories, whether they were true or not.

Hot shame washed over the cold realization, and Sadie couldn't stay upright. She found herself sinking in her gown, trying hard not to cry. Not to break down in sobs in front of Emmeline.

Even though she wasn't in love with Titus, he'd been her friend first. A friend who was using her. It was all fake. The way he'd lured her in using her own fears. He'd never actually cared for her, in any way. She was a pawn in their royal game of chess. His captured queen.

Her eyes burned, but she clenched her fists so hard that her nails pricked her palms and a new pain exploded in her hands. She took a shuddering breath and gritted out, "Go away, Emmeline."

Emmeline stood, tucking her phone into her purse. "Renounce your claim to Ashland's throne."

Sadie's jaw dropped. "You're joking."

The Ashlandic princess tapped her nails on her hips, her eyes flashing like moonlight on snow. "Does it look like I'm joking?"

A bolt of anger seared through Sadie's blood. "Go to hell."

Instead of fighting back, Emmeline just sighed, her shoulders falling and her eyes rolling. "Sadie, please don't make me do this."

"Do what?" Sadie rasped, getting to her feet on shaky legs. "What else could you possibly—"

But her voice cut off in a strangled gasp as Emmeline pulled out a little leather journal from her purse. An old, beaten, *loved* journal.

"Where—where did you get that?" Sadie asked, her voice feeling disconnected from her body. She felt herself slipping. Everything falling around her.

Emmeline glanced at the journal with a frown. Then opened it, the worn pages flipping with the movement of her thumb across the edges.

"Trang gave it to me."

Another stab. Another blow.

"You...you're lying. She wouldn't," Sadie said, nearly choking. But even as she was saying it...doubt clouded her heart. After all, if Titus had betrayed her, why not Trang as well?

"The name in the back is *J. Aurelia*. Your dad's...I assume?"

Sadie couldn't speak. She tried to open her mouth and willed words to come out, but there was only a pathetic squeak.

"You better start figuring out who your real friends are, Sadie. And start taking stock of who's watching you. News flash: You're a royal. It's everyone."

Now it was impossible to breathe. She tried. But her lungs refused to work.

"Didn't take much to get this either. Just a substantial loan—no interest rates—for her family's business in Vietnam. And that was the cost of betrayal."

As the words sank into her skin like scorch marks, Sadie struggled to pull in oxygen. No, *no*. They—they were best friends. Sadie knew Trang's favorite wrestler; she knew how many times she'd watched *Grey's Anatomy* season four (fourteen); how much Trang loves her father, how much she worries about him. But…maybe that's exactly why she'd do this. For her family. Part of Sadie couldn't help but sympathize.

She didn't want to believe it, but it made sense. Trang knew the journal's hiding spot: It had been her idea to place it under Sadie's pillow ever since that day her laptop went missing.

After all, Titus, who worked so hard to win Sadie's heart, had been using her all along. A friend with so much more on the line—her family's future—could just as easily betray her, too.

"Emmeline, please—" Sadie said, stumbling forward, reaching…

But the princess was graceful and easily sidestepped Sadie, moving right next to the fire.

"Renounce your claim." She raised the journal. The only thing left of Sadie's father. The only thing her mother had kept.

"Please, we can—"

"Wrong answer." Emmeline threw the book into the flames.

"NO!" Sadie shrieked, diving for the journal, but Emmeline caught her and shoved her back. Sadie tripped over the long train, felt a pin stick the bottom of her foot, and landed in a pile of tulle and satin.

She watched as the flames consumed the little book. Twirling, twisting, an illusion of chemical combustion. She'd thought it so beautiful once upon a time.

Her vision tunneled as air couldn't reach her lungs, as the fire ate up her oxygen, ate up the last remnants of her heart. Everything went black.

Dr. Sharrad and Ms. Martinez allowed Sadie to stay in the infirmary for a whole day and a half, and she couldn't express her gratitude enough.

After waking up in the infirmary, still in that stupid gown, she'd collapsed into body-shaking sobs. Ms. Martinez had been so patient and gentle helping Sadie out of the gown, even through streaming tears.

She barely thought about the gown, or Hibernia, or even Titus and Trang. Instead she thought of her mother. Of what she'd lost when Emmeline tossed that journal into the flames. It had been her mah's most prized possession, probably the last thing she looked at and cried over before her life ended that day. What had meant so much to her parents, Sadie let slip through her fingers so easily.

She hated herself for that. Hated her weakness as she'd simply stood there, watching Emmeline destroy the remnants of her family. Too shocked from the betrayals of Trang and Titus, the two people closest to her... in her life.

Shadows moved across the infirmary wall, marking the passage of time as the day wore on. Sadie didn't move from her bed. Didn't eat or wash her face. Tears crusted on her lashes, her hair felt greasy, but she didn't care.

For the first time, she began to understand wanting to give up. And that just made her cry harder. She cried until it hurt. Until her head pounded and her lips were chapped with dehydration. It felt like losing her mother all over again. And she was starting to wonder how she could get through this a second time.

It was evening when Ms. Martinez pulled back the curtain around her infirmary bed with another glass of water. The nurse looked down kindly at Sadie. "You have a visitor."

Sadie didn't move. "I don't want to see anyone." If Titus showed his face she'd probably slap him.

"You will see your king," a harsh voice said from behind the nurse.

The command of King Leander had Sadie sitting up so quickly pillows flew off her bed.

"Your Majesty," she croaked. The room spun, but she forced herself to focus on the most powerful man her country had seen in over three hundred years.

"Please give us a moment," King Leander said to the nurse.

Ms. Martinez looked uncomfortable, but she gave a short bow and left, her footsteps and the click of the door echoing behind her.

Ignoring the dehydration headache was a struggle, but Sadie didn't dare reach for the glass of water at her bedside. King Leander had pinned her with his cold iron gaze, and she found she couldn't move. Especially under eyes that looked so much like his grandson's. That signature Eldana gray, each with their own unique shades, his—Sadie noticed for the first time—most closely resembled Titus's.

"You were found fainted on the floor," he said, his tone neutral, almost casual.

That was an extreme oversimplification. She fainted because of the emotional distress his granddaughter had inflicted on her. The cruelty of something so selfish. She wet her lips and started to croak, "Emmeline—"

"Don't speak," King Leander said. It wasn't harsh or loud, just authoritative. "It doesn't matter *why* you fainted. Or what she did to put you in such a state. The fact is, you couldn't handle it."

Sadie's eyes widened, her body locking.

"I thought we'd come to an understanding, Sadie," King Leander said with a withering sigh. "I'd hoped you'd follow the path of Marcus Aurelius. I'd hoped you'd be able to forge ahead with grace and fortitude. Instead, you've disappointed me."

His words shouldn't hurt as much as they did. He was an imperfect monarch—like everyone who'd come before him—but he'd led Ashland through fifty years of peace, which was unprecedented. And he was still her king.

Just like with Alaric, she'd admired Leander, and now he'd been disillusioned. By her.

"Yes, your past is tragic, but if you cannot overcome it, I'm afraid I can let you go no further. Weakness is the root cause of Ashland's eternal suffering. Rulers who crumble in the face of adversity might easily be overthrown by a little coup here, a small uprising there, a stab in the back—it is the downfall of this country. For the sake of our land, my heirs must be strong. Based on the last couple days I know that you, sadly, are not."

For the first time since she saw her father's journal curling into black flecks of ash, Sadie felt something other than grief stirring in her chest. If his idea of strength meant stepping all over others, maybe she *was* weak.

Suddenly everything became painfully clear.

"I gave you a chance, Sadie. I had hopes you'd overcome the tides that set you out at sea. That your triumph, your resilience, could set the stage for Ashland's next chapter. For the rebirth of our great nation. But now I can see . . . it was all for naught."

He leaned down and took her chin in his weathered, callused hand. "Such a pity, darling girl." His gray eyes bored into hers, resolute. A hint of a tattoo peaked out under his shirt sleeve on his wrist. "You're dismissed, Sadie Aurelia. You're going back home."

Sadie's fingers curled into her bed sheets, that stirring feeling growing and growing. Oh yes, it was all *so* clear. Like in the hospital, her king had a way of making her see things in a new light.

King Leander dropped her chin and started to leave, his steps echoing across the stone castle floor.

"Your Majesty," Sadie called.

He turned, raising an eyebrow.

"Can I stay until after Hibernia?"

"Naturally. You'll be expected for photos. And all four of you should be present when I appoint my champion."

Sadie waited until the door was closed and his footsteps were long gone from the hallway before she threw off her bedsheets. Her knees stung as she dropped to the floor and floundered for her bag that Trang had left when attempting to visit her.

Bless the old sea gods. Her phone was in the bag. She dialed Oliver with shaking hands—hands coursing with something much stronger than sheer will alone. Sadie had never felt so charged, so driven, so powerful in her entire life.

"Oliver? I need a favor."

39

TITUS

Titus lay in his bed, eyes wide open, looking up at the underside of his top bunk. But he didn't see the outlines of the wood, or the textured material of the mattress cover. Instead, he kept seeing Sadie's face. In different, lovely expressions but always revolving back to one in particular: betrayal.

He was a coward and hadn't seen her yet, but he imagined her reaction all the same. Quite vividly.

When Emmeline had held up that second phone, all he could picture were the lengths his parents would go to discover what he'd been hiding. And when they did, the mental and emotional abuse they would inflict on him for having a disease. For something he had, not something he chose or did.

But Titus's behavior was hardly admirable. Whatever his reasoning, he'd chosen to hurt Sadie. All because he was scared of his family's punishing biases—of what they might deny him, when the crown was *all* he'd ever worked for.

Above him, Oliver clacked away on his laptop. Working through the night, just as he had yesterday. On what, Titus didn't know or care, really. Finals were over, the registration portal for Hibernia was closed. The ball was *tomorrow.*

And he still didn't know how Sadie was. Hadn't seen her. Hadn't texted her. He knew she wouldn't answer, so what was the bloody point?

He'd hate himself—maybe forever for this—but he'd be king. Because he could live with hating himself, but he couldn't live with his entire eighteen years being a waste.

Almus Terra Academy had been transformed. Titus hated to admit it, but Alaric had done a brilliant job. Cold blue and warm gold lights wound around every pillar and lined every rampart within the castle. Each door was laden with blue spruce and red winterberry wreaths, frosted with ATA crests in the center. Ice sculptures of faceless roman soldiers with standards of dragons lined the road. Suits of armor within the castle had been artificially frosted as well, and fake ice carved pathways through the corridors and across the courtyard guiding guests to the grand ballroom.

Most of the Norms had gone home for the holidays, with the exception of third-years and a few who'd helped Alaric and Oakley with the decorating. Of course, all were welcome to attend Hibernia, but because *their* parents couldn't afford to attend, many elected to go home in silent protest and solidarity. The C-Suites and Elites who remained greeted their parents as they arrived, all dressed in extravagant gowns and custom-tailored suits.

Titus watched from the steps leading off to the headmistress's office, his arms folded across his chest. Oliver and Oakley worked together to check in the guests using a laptop to confirm their attendance and give them the correct electronic wristband.

Titus knew which guests were to attend the unsanctioned meeting because Oakley reached for *those* wristbands under the table.

He watched Kavi's parents, owners of one of the world's largest media groups; Calixa's mother, the president of France; and Seb's father, prime minister of England. Oakley's dad, the wind farm tycoon of Australia and New Zealand. The sultan of Oman, the king of Morocco, the largest landowners in Singapore and China, the vice president of the United States, an oil tycoon from Saudi Arabia, a Brazilian CEO controlling the country's exports in sugar and corn, the queen of Denmark . . .

"Waiting to greet your parents, Titus?" a voice said, startling him from behind.

He turned to find Headmistress Aquila coming down the stairs. She wore a pantsuit of sparkling silver, a train of silk falling behind her by way of a skirt. Her braids had snowflakes spun in, making her grays look like glittering frost instead of the sign of age.

"Ah, no, ma'am," Titus said, coughing into his fist. "I believe they're already inside with my grandfather." Which is why he was out *here*.

He didn't mean to be caught standing around, but his job was done. He'd checked and rechecked the meeting room. Drinks were ready, hors d'oeuvres were waiting in the kitchen, the student orchestra was playing in the ballroom. Emmeline had the event running tighter than the freaking Olympics. Everything was accounted for. Everything was perfect.

And he *still* had not seen Sadie. That was either a good or bad thing and he honestly couldn't figure out which.

"What a ridiculous soiree," Headmistress Aquila said, sighing.

Titus glanced over at her with surprise. "Ma'am?"

"You heard me. But the donations pay for seventy-five percent of our scholarship students. So . . . I can't get rid of it," she huffed.

"And the *other* donations?" Titus asked in a low voice.

His headmistress didn't look at him, but her gaze narrowed at the moving crowd below, in jewels and glittering gowns and pin-striped suits.

"I'm sure I don't know what you mean. Enjoy your evening, Titus." Then she continued down the steps, waving hello to a man with dark brown skin in an expensive-looking dashiki.

Yeah, he should've expected that. The headmistress couldn't know about any unsanctioned meeting to discuss global trade affairs. He knew she did, of course, but she could never admit to it.

With a sigh, he headed down the steps and followed the frosted pathways through the bailey—illuminated brilliantly in lights all woven through hundreds of plants and shrubs. His breath fogged in front of him as he walked. The cold made his joint pain worse, but he bit back the grimace and strode confidently through the courtyard.

Dr. Konkin had said it would take a few months to see if the steroids were truly helping with the inflammation, so he'd need to exercise patience. The problem, as evidenced by the "fencing incident," was the side effects. The trial and error of how, when, or how much to eat in order to minimize his nausea was not exactly glamorous.

Ignoring the pinch in his toes, he headed up the steps, through the antechamber, and into the ballroom. If possible, it looked even more stunning than the rest of the castle. The high ceilings had hidden snow machines in the rafters so artificial snow (a soap mixture of bubbles that emulated snowflakes) floated down and disappeared before hitting the floor. The ballroom chandeliers had been decorated with hanging icicles, while sconces of blue flames threaded with more blue spruce and red winterberry hung in the halls. Gold-frosted armor and weapons accented tables of Almus Terra's diverse cuisines, savory dishes, and desserts from hundreds of cultures.

Couples waltzed across the dance floor in strict Viennese style, their arms held aloft in perfect formation, and their heads turned away from each other like they were all competitive dancers. Titus almost laughed at the absurdity of it all. Technically, this was a *school dance.*

"Hey." A hand suddenly grabbed his arm, surprisingly hard. He glanced down at the pale, slender wrist, then faced Sadie's dormmate staring him down.

The rare times he'd seen her up close, Trang had always worn tiny amethyst gemstones in her ears. She'd forgone the small studs and instead wore dangling multicolored sea pearls. Her black hair was wound into a fancy updo. The bodice of her ombré gown was a deep teal that blended into a light aqua at the hem.

"What the hell did you do to Sadie?" Trang demanded, her short aquamarine nails digging hard into his arm through his suit jacket.

Titus struggled to muster through the pressure bursting at his temples. Why had he not anticipated *this*?

"Trang, our relationship is—"

"Don't you dare say 'none of my business,' Eldana. I trusted you to make her happy. I—" Trang said, her voice rising slightly, enough to make one couple turn around and give them looks. "I encouraged her to go out with you."

And now she was feeling guilty. Titus had half a mind to ask Trang how Sadie was doing. In fact, in a moment of weakness, he was about to do just that, when Trang dropped his arm in disgust, her eyes glassy with frustration.

"I've barely even seen her the last four days. I tried to see her in the infirmary, but I was turned away, and then she's suddenly out and nowhere to be found. She comes in the middle of the night and leaves before dawn—I've tried to catch her, but she just ignores me. You did something and I want to know what."

Confusion, along with a fresh wave of guilt, surged inside him. He knew that he'd hurt her, but he'd hoped she'd been able to lean on Trang. Sadie had been so excited and happy to have her as a friend. Had he upset her so deeply that she didn't want to trust or rely on anyone?

Titus swallowed and shook his head. "We ended it, Trang. But tonight is not the time to talk about this."

Trang's lip curled in disgust as she regarded him like she would a cockroach—a justified look. He was every bit as detestable as she thought. "Forgive me for the inconvenience, Your Highness." Then she turned on her heel and disappeared into the crowd.

Everything in him screamed to go back through the antechamber, through the bailey, and into the cold night air to find Sadie. Find her and somehow make this right. But the same reasons he broke her heart in the first place kept him rooted to this spot while the rest of the ball moved on around him.

Eventually, more self-preservation got him moving. He noticed Lotta making eyes at him from across the dance floor with a neckline so low he could almost see her belly button. So he changed direction toward the front of the ballroom, focusing his attention on the Eldana family near the edge of the stage, where the orchestra played. Alaric, Emmeline, her parents, King Leander, all looking beautiful—quite the royal family, weren't they?

Emmeline was chatting with their grandfather, looking pristine in a gown of icy blue. Unlike Sadie's dress, it was slim and fell down her legs using comparatively little material. See-through glittering fabric coated her arms and back like a second skin dusted in frost. She looked the part. Like a princess ready to take on the world.

He despised her. He'd thought he hated her before, but that was nothing compared to this. Now he hated her almost as much as he hated himself.

But he could admit she'd won. This round at least. She'd destroyed his relationship with Sadie and destroyed *her*.

"Titus." It took every ounce of control he had not to run away from the familiar voice. Slowly, he turned around and plastered on a handsome smile.

"Mother, welcome to Almus Terra."

His mother was dressed in a gown of deep chrome, like the material was made of a thousand blades. Her eyes narrowed at him in quiet rage. "Are you making light of the fact that I was never sent here?"

Honestly, no. But now he kind of wished he'd milked it a little. He dipped his head. "Of course not, Mother."

She stepped closer, grinding her back heel into the top of his foot. He clenched his teeth in response. "Your grandfather will announce his heir apparent tonight. We'll see if you were worth the eight hours of labor you put me through. I'm not holding my breath."

She leaned away just after he caught a whiff of her perfume. His mother always smelled like the finest fragrance money could buy. But it was a vile scent. He wanted sweet, warm vanilla. He wanted Sadie.

Lady Calliope lifted her champagne flute to her lips and muttered before taking a swig, "The good news is that little peasant is out of the way."

Wait . . . what?

"Out of the way?" he asked before he could stop himself.

She shot him a pitiful look. "Did you really not know your grandfather dismissed Sadie Aurelia? Something about her being too weak. Good thing, anyhow. Or I would have made you break up with her. Honestly, dating someone so below your station. Disgusting, Titus. Even for you."

That little peasant. Too weak. Not long ago, Titus had perceived Sadie in a similar light. Now he saw that judgement for what it was: his mother's poison. His rotten parents didn't excuse the person he'd become, but perhaps they were the root cause of his self-loathing. And finally, he'd had enough.

Though he was about to do the very thing that he'd sacrificed Sadie's heart to prevent, at least here, he could speak for himself.

"Mother, I have rheumatoid arthritis."

She choked on her champagne. The bubbly liquid dripped down her chin as her face jerked toward her son with wild eyes.

For the first time in his life, Titus addressed his mother from a position of strength. "Do with that what you will."

He turned and left her frozen, speechless.

The truth was, this disease was consequential in his fight for succession. Because *nothing* would stop Titus from becoming who he was born to be.

40

ALARIC

Being around so many fancy people gave Alaric hives. Either that, or he was allergic to the material of this suffocating suit. In a pathetic attempt not to scratch, he kept his hands in his pockets while Emmeline chatted with King Leander, occasionally giving Alaric credit on the decorations. On how *enchanting* the castle looked.

Hell, it did look enchanting. Oakley had nearly wept when it was all up. "This might be the best thing I've ever done," she'd said, overcome.

Alaric would never, ever admit it, but in that moment, he'd agreed with her. For the first time in his life, he'd created something beautiful instead of tearing things down to rubble.

"Yes, yes, the castle looks sublime, my dear," King Leander chuckled, patting Emmeline on the back. "But we're most impressed with the registration portal and electronic wristbands. You and your team have advanced this tradition into the present. I truly commend your efforts."

Emmeline practically beamed, radiating winter sunshine. "Thank you, Your Majesty. The programmer did an excellent job."

"Hmm, and what's his name?"

"Oliver Jackson," Emmeline said.

"Ah-ha, the top seed in your class," King Leander said with a nod. "Yes, I look forward to meeting him."

At that moment, King Leander's wristband vibrated. As did the wristbands of other registered attendees. In the crowd of students and their parents, drinking, talking, and waltzing to the music, it was hard to detect, but select adults slowly started moving toward the exit of the ballroom. It was time for their summit.

Before King Leander could get very far, Alaric fell into stride next to him. "May I escort yeh to yer destination, sir?"

Leander's eyebrows raised in mild surprise. "I've been here many times, Alaric."

"I understand, sir. To be frank, I need an excuse."

Out in the corridor, behind a few other attendees, King Leander chortled. "I do love your honesty."

Of course he did. Because all arrogant men love when their egos meet a match.

"An excuse for?"

"Seeing my father. I assume he'll be in attendance, as yer treasury secretary."

King Leander looked quite amused. "Indeed. You have some business with him, I assume?"

"He sent me a letter with a proposition. I was just planning to answer in person, for good measure."

The king of Ashland nodded sagely, and Alaric wondered if Leander knew of the bribe that was sent to him. About the ultimatum. If he did know, he certainly didn't seem to care. They turned the corridor at that point and Alaric's gaze shot to the end of the hall like a magnet.

There he was: Mikael Erickson, standing by the door to Magna Carta Lecture Hall. The man his mother claimed to be his father, and the man who denied him with every ventricle of his cold, shriveled heart. He'd avoided the ball entirely and had gone straight to the meeting but refused to enter without his king.

"Then be my guest, Alaric." King Leander gestured to his son-in-law, and with a brush of his wristband, the keypad beeped. "I'll see you inside, Mikael."

The door clicked shut behind the king, leaving Alaric alone with the treasury secretary.

"Evenin', Da," Alaric said, just to piss him off. It worked.

Lord Erickson didn't greet him, hardly even looked him in the eye. He just said stiffly, "Have you considered my offer?"

Alaric pretended to think. He nodded thoughtfully. "Aye. I have."

"And?" Lord Erickson growled.

"I just wanted to tell yeh, face-to-face, that once upon a time, I didn't give two shites about the crown." Alaric stepped so close to his father they were almost nose-to-nose. "But now, after that letter . . . I promise yeh this: There *will* be a bastard on the throne. And I'll make sure yeh live to see it, Da. Mark my words."

Lord Erickson jerked back. His eyes blazed red with fury, but he didn't take a swing. This was not the place. Now was not the time.

But he *did* spit on Alaric's shoe. Then turned and knocked his wristband against the pad. He pulled the door open and slipped inside.

The moment he was gone, Alaric let out a long breath. *Damn, that felt good.*

Alaric turned down the hall, back toward the ballroom, but stopped when he saw a small red-headed figure thundering toward him. "Sadie?"

She wore her Almus Terra uniform, her slate-gray jacket and skirt pressed and neat, and the first-year emerald-green tie knotted perfectly around her slim neck. Her hair was done in soft waves, flying behind her as she walked. She looked . . . well, it didn't look like she was heading for the dance floor.

"Hello, Alaric," she said, striding right past him toward Magna Carta Lecture Hall. In her hand was a wristband.

His eyes widened. He caught her by the elbow. "Oy, what are yeh doing?"

When she met his gaze, Alaric almost retreated.

This was not the Sadie he knew. Her hazel eyes glinted, her lips were set in a firm line, and if he looked past all that, past her hard expression...he feared what he saw.

In light of her relationship with Titus, he'd stayed as far away from her as possible, and though he hadn't seen the power couple around lately, he hadn't thought much of it. He'd been worked to the bone mounting this whole production.

She tried to jerk away and keep walking, but he held on, not knowing what to say or how to make it better. Because something inside her—he was pretty sure—had been broken.

Before he could do anything else, Sadie clawed at his hand on her elbow, her nails scratching his skin, but not hard enough to draw blood. He jerked away with a hiss, shaking his wrist. "*Ow*, Sadie."

"Stay out of my way, Alaric," she warned, then bumped the wristband against the pad.

He watched in continued shock as she charged straight into the clandestine assembly of world leaders.

"What the hell did they do to yeh, cailín?" he muttered as the door shut behind her.

41

SADIE

WHAT SADIE HAD ALWAYS THOUGHT SHE NEEDED WAS COURAGE. If she'd been brave, she could've stood up to Lotta and her friends. But if she was going to inventory her faults—or more precisely, what led her to this moment—she might as well be thorough.

If she'd been less trusting, she would've confronted Emmeline back when her laptop was stolen. If she'd been more wary, Titus and Trang would never have been able to betray her so utterly. If she'd been less sensitive, she would've listened to Alaric when he told her he didn't think she could do this. And if she'd been stronger, she could've done more for her mother in those final days.

But now Sadie knew better. She knew that she hadn't needed courage. She hadn't needed strength or wariness or anything else. She needed to have nothing left to lose. She needed to be broken.

The moment Sadie entered the Magna Carta Lecture Hall, she felt every pair of eyes zero in on her small form—on her uniform and the wristband in her hand, on her pale red hair and freckles—and then dismiss her immediately.

She was just a student. Likely here by mistake. Maybe to check the technology in the room for their meeting.

The lecture hall for Political Science was similar to their Economics classroom. Rows of seats on levels leading down into its center. The hall's projector tarp was already lowered with the Almus Terra crest as a default image, waiting for someone to cast their screen.

After a few moments, a woman with raven-black hair and light brown skin eyed Sadie with annoyance. She wore a golden sari and gold jewelry down her arms.

"We're about to start," she said. "Are you here for something?"

Sadie just smiled and made her way down the steps to the center of the room. Then she finally heard the voice she'd been waiting to bait.

"Sadie." She didn't have to turn to find him. King Leander was on his feet in the second row, his chair almost perfectly in the center.

"Hello, Your Majesty," she said with a wave. "Enjoying your evening so far?"

The old Sadie would've shriveled under the look of pure rage from her king. And to be honest, her knees and fingers did tremble. But that fear was nothing compared to the conviction that had burned through her insides until all that was left was smoldering ash.

"I thought I'd made myself clear," he said, his voice low enough that only a few people in the first two rows would be able to hear.

Good. She was embarrassing him. Everyone in the room had recognized who she was by now. Her public disobedience might just be unprecedented.

"You did, sir," Sadie said, maintaining her pleasant smile. "But before all of you got started on bribing each other to defraud your citizens and reap the benefits of your own greed, I need to share some vital information about your registration fee."

Everyone stopped moving. A few of the guests had been chatting with one another, waiting for Leander to deal with this little girl. But now—*now* they were listening. Staring at her with bated breath. Finally, she had the most power in the room.

At that moment, in perfect synchronicity, the doors opened once more and Oliver slipped inside. He wore a suit, but it wasn't custom, and it wasn't expensive. He held his laptop to his chest and met Sadie's gaze with pride.

Every guest watched in shocked disbelief as Oliver descended the steps, opening his laptop and tapping out a few keys. He stood next to Sadie just as the image of the ATA crest disappeared and a dark dashboard took its place. Set against an indigo background, in bold white typeface, was one very large sum of money.

"Twenty-seven million, five hundred thousand pounds. Or thirty-two million, two hundred ten thousand euros. Or four hundred thirty million, four hundred fifty thousand in Ghanaian Cedi—"

"*Sadie*," King Leander growled.

"Yes, Your Majesty, this is the sum of money sitting in the bank account that was given to us by our esteemed vice president of the student council." Sadie nodded to Oliver. Balancing his laptop on his arm, he typed in a few more keys.

At his final keystroke, the amount began to decrease, the big numbers counting down like the timer on a bomb about to detonate.

"And *this* is the money being siphoned out and donated to charities across the world at a rate of fifty thousand pounds every five seconds."

Slowly, King Leander sank into his chair, his eyes wide.

Sadie stood tall. "Math isn't my best subject, but I'm pretty sure that means all of your money will change hands to people in need in . . . about forty-six minutes."

No one spoke. Probably because no one could believe it.

This wasn't possible.

A student would never dare.

But that's the thing rich people don't understand. When you take everything away from someone, they have nothing to lose.

"You're bluffing," King Leander said finally. His posture was rigid, his gaze stone.

Sadie shrugged as the number on the screen dropped down to twenty million. "I bet someone here has access to the bank account. Check to see if there are funds being withdrawn."

A man next to King Leander, whom Sadie only now recognized as Alaric's father, pulled out his phone and started to tap across his screen. Color drained from his face, and he angled the phone back to the king, who looked at Sadie with a deadly glare.

"Leander!" A sharp voice with a British accent boomed across the room. "*Control* the girl."

Anger seared across her skin at the idea of someone saying she could be controlled, but she didn't let it show. For once, her emotions were not at the helm.

Leander held up his hand to silence Sebastian's father, who sounded just like his son both in arrogance and misogyny.

Other guests shifted in their seats as the number started to trickle down.

Sadie kept her gaze locked with the king of Ashland's, who valued strength above all else.

She didn't blame him for that. In fact, it made sense given his position. But he'd underestimated compassion, all that Sadie would do to make a real change for her country. Because Leander Eldana? He wasn't cutting it. She'd finally seen what needed to be done. What her end game was. What it should've been from the very beginning.

Long moments passed as King Leander searched her expression, probably looking for the dent in her armor.

"Leander," a woman hissed from the third row.

"Can someone lock this account?" another whispered.

Sadie didn't break her staring contest with the king. "You've got twenty-seven minutes. Good luck."

Lord Erickson swore under his breath. "You can't freeze an account while funds are being withdrawn."

Finally, King Leander settled back in his seat and folded his arms.

His chin tilted up as he regarded the girl he'd dismissed and underestimated a mere forty-eight hours ago.

The hint of a smirk pulled at his thin lips. "Your demands?"

Sadie waited thirty more seconds before answering, withdrawing another hundred thousand pounds for people who really needed it.

And then, just because she could, Sadie rolled her eyes. "I'll give you one guess."

42

EMMELINE

Hibernia Legions was turning into Emmeline's crowning achievement. Literally. When her grandfather stood beside her, praising *her*—not Alaric or Titus—on the success of the event, she knew that he'd seen and understood her contributions. Her careful orchestration of every facet of the event.

"That dress is divine," her mother said for the second time, sipping on her fourth glass of champagne. "Isn't it divine, Freddy? Like looking in a mirror. My beautiful girl."

Emmeline forced a smile. "Thank you, Mother." Lady Chloe only ever complimented her dress and her looks. Not her hard work or her outstanding grades. But at least her mother was speaking to her. Her father hadn't said a word, poking around his phone like a teenager at... well, a dance. It was embarrassing.

With disgust that she hid well, Emmeline turned and grabbed Alaric by the elbow. "We're dancing, come on."

"Oh no yeh don't," he grumbled, bracing. But Emmeline was stronger than she looked and succeeded in pulling his arm until he relented. They took up a spot on the floor as the next waltz started.

Luckily it wasn't Viennese, and Alaric was able to lead her well enough through the steps. She was impressed he'd gotten this good after just a few hours of lessons during their fall break in Ashland.

"I'm only doing this so yeh don't have to dance with butt face."

Emmeline smiled. "Yeah, Sebastian's been circling. So thanks, I s'pose."

"Whatever," her cousin said, then eyed her as he stepped out and allowed her to twirl under his arm. "But now that we're here, I have to ask. What on earth did yeh do to Sadie?"

She very nearly tripped. Catching herself and grabbing Alaric's arm as they fell back into step, she cleared her throat. "Nothing."

"Yer usually a better liar than that, Emmie."

Emmeline shot him a glare as he rotated her around the corner, his strides long and sure. "Comparatively, Alaric, I did very little to her. And that's the absolute truth."

Alaric opened his mouth to speak, but he stopped dancing mid-step, his gaze locked on something over her shoulder.

"What're you—" Emmeline's words choked as the crowd began parting on the dance floor and King Leander thundered through the ballroom.

His gaze was focused dead ahead on the stage, and with a single motion of his hand, the orchestra stopped playing.

"Holy—" Alaric said.

Behind King Leander was Sadie. In her Almus Terra uniform. No makeup, no fancy hair style, just the way she always was.

Emmeline couldn't move, as every cell in her body started to vibrate with tension. Something was happening.

Then, to her even greater shock, Oliver followed behind Sadie, holding his laptop to his chest. King Leander rose to the stage and snatched the mic from the lectern that had been positioned off to the side.

"Ladies and gentlemen, I have a quick announcement," he said. His expression was calm, almost neutral, but Emmeline knew something was off. Something was wrong.

"Tonight is the night I name my heir apparent, and rather than keep us all in suspense..." He glanced down at Sadie, who stood at the bottom of the stage. "I would like to do so now."

Emmeline felt her heart slow. "No," she said, her nails sinking into Alaric's arm. "No, no, no, no."

"After years of wishing for a worthy successor to emerge, Sadie Aurelia has proven to be just the young leader I was looking for. I am pleased to announce her as Ashland's heir apparent."

For a beat, no one moved. Then people shifted, looking around, recognizing this moment was odd. No pomp and circumstance. A quick, strangely timed announcement to the world about the most important decision in Ashland's recent history. Emmeline felt like she was going to vomit onto her priceless dress.

At first no one clapped. But then someone started.

Emmeline snapped her head to the left and found Titus clapping, his gaze on Sadie and no one else. Slowly, the rest of the crowd joined in.

The applause soon turned deafening, filling the ballroom like a cacophony of thunderstorms vibrating the castle stones. At least, that's what it sounded like to Emmeline. Something cataclysmic. Something world-ending. After everything she'd done...

She could only watch the next few minutes in stunned denial. Sadie turned and muttered something to Oliver as the crowd clapped. He hastily opened his laptop and typed on a few keys, then gave her a sharp nod.

King Leander marched down the steps of the stage to meet with Sadie and Oliver. Oliver turned his laptop to the king and Leander then patted Sadie on the shoulder. *What is going on?*

Emmeline was walking before she could even think. Walking to Oliver and her grandfather and the bitch who just stole her future.

"Emmeline," Sadie said, smiling brightly. "You look gorgeous."

"Oh, that's right," King Leander said with a nod. "You need proper attire for photos with the press. Is your ball gown available?"

Her grin not faltering for a second, Sadie replied, "I bet it's still in the infirmary."

"Your Majesty . . . ," Emmeline began, her throat dry, her skin tight and prickling. She was seconds away from screaming her head off. "I don't understand what just happened."

"What just happened," her grandfather said, his tone dropping in temperature, "is I discovered you don't have as much control over all this as I thought."

That's when her whole body went from icy cold to burning hot. A full-body flush so fast Emmeline nearly swayed on the spot. Her lashes fluttered with her rapid heartbeat as her gaze drifted over to Oliver.

Oliver. Somehow, and she didn't know *how*, he was the key. His laptop and his genius. She sucked in a breath as their gazes connected. He stared at her with nothing but loathing.

Her heart shriveled, her gut clenched, but by some miracle she remained calm. Years of disappointment and heartbreak had prepared her for this moment.

He *knew*. Sadie had told him. Maybe everything. She saw it written across his face. How he viewed her now as evil, ready to tear down anyone who stood in her way no matter the consequences. Of course he believed Sadie, because who wouldn't? Sadie hadn't flirted with him only to turn around and make out with someone else. Honestly, Emmeline didn't even blame him for hating her.

Just like Emmeline, Sadie had seen Oliver's potential and used it. Slowly, she looked back at Sadie, whose pleasant smile had turned into a triumphant smirk.

"Your Majesty," Sadie said, voice almost melodic. "I could be ready faster if Emmeline helped me with hair and makeup. You don't mind, do you, Emmie?"

Emmeline's skin was scalding to the touch now, burning with hatred and embarrassment. But her features remained cool. Passive. "Of course not," she heard herself say.

"Wonderful," Sadie said and, without hesitation, hooked her arm into Emmeline's.

Students and adults parted to give them looks of curiosity as Emmeline felt her feet move across the dance floor. The two princesses—an heir apparent and a spare—passed through the antechamber and into the cold winter night. As the chilly air doused Emmeline's heated skin, Sadie tightened her grip into something rather painful.

"The next time you threaten me," Sadie whispered, "because you will, I hope you remember this moment."

A shiver passed down Emmeline's spine as she looked at Sadie, a girl she no longer recognized. A girl she knew she'd changed.

"Sadie!" A shout echoed through the bailey, followed by the clacking of heels across stone. Another slap of panic struck Emmeline across the face as she recognized the voice. She wanted to yank Sadie forward instead of turning around, but Sadie stopped and faced their roommate.

"Good evening, Trang."

Trang came to an abrupt stop, as if recovering from a physical blow rather than words alone. "I—I just talked to Titus..." Emmeline watched as Trang's confused gaze bounced from Sadie to Emmeline, Emmeline to Sadie, as if she sensed something wasn't quite right.

"Did you?" Sadie gave her a cold smile. "Well, that makes sense. Snake calls to snake, I suppose. Listen, the next time you make a bad deal, keep me out of it. Cross me again, and I'll take what matters most to *you*."

Trang blinked, her entire body going rigid with shock.

Once again, it took Emmeline's lifelong experience to keep her face neutral during this exchange. While she'd never felt good about what she did to Sadie, it didn't keep her up at night. Sadie had stolen everything from Emmeline and as far as she was concerned, Sadie had reaped what she sowed.

But Trang... Trang was collateral damage. An innocent bystander in a ploy that Emmeline knew would hurt Sadie the most. It hadn't been easy—finding out about Trang's background, potential weaknesses to exploit—but Kavi seemed to have a secret personnel file on nearly everyone at ATA. Given his family's global news conglomerate, it wasn't that surprising.

When she first had the idea to frame Trang, it helped that she'd been furious at her for dragging her in front of Oliver. But she hadn't expected to see the domino effect of her lies unfold firsthand. It didn't feel good, watching Trang's shock crumble into hurt and then morph into anger as Sadie's words landed like bombs in an air raid.

But this was just one of a thousand bad moments in the night from hell. What was one more hit?

"I have no idea what you're talking about," Trang said, her voice clear and sharp through the cold. There was obvious hurt, but indignation as well. Almost disbelief. "And how *dare* you accuse me of something without even talking to me first? We were *friends*, Sadie."

For the tiniest moment, Sadie's hard resolve looked as if it might crack. But then the hint of vulnerability dissolved, and she waved her hand toward the ballroom in dismissal. "I don't have time for this. The press is expecting me. We can talk later."

An uncomfortable silence stretched between the three girls, then Trang looked at Emmeline. Her dark eyes narrowed, as if she somehow knew Emmeline had a hand in this. With a scathing look back at Sadie, she rolled her shoulders and whispered, "So that's how it's going to be."

It wasn't a question. Trang spun and headed back toward the ballroom, skirts swishing, and she nearly ran right into Titus and Alaric as the two princes emerged into the courtyard.

Titus cleared his throat, his eyes meeting Sadie's even as his hands curled into fists at his sides. "Congratulations, Sadie," he said, his voice clear and unwavering. He sounded so professional and composed, Emmeline couldn't tell if he really meant it or not.

And neither, she assumed, could Sadie. But Ashland's new heir apparent didn't seem to care. Her smile back at Titus was vacant. Like nothing he said or did mattered. Not anymore.

Unsurprisingly, Alaric was silent. He just shoved his hands into his pockets and stared at her in quiet resignation.

Finally, Emmeline snapped. She tore her arm from Sadie's grasp and stepped back, the hem of her dress swirling around her heels. "Enough. How did you pull it off?" she said, her voice eerily flat.

Music from the orchestra had resumed, growing louder as a symphony by Tchaikovsky reached a crescendo. Even outside in the castle courtyard, Emmeline could recognize "Waltz of the Flowers" from *The Nutcracker Suite*. It was her favorite. She knew it by heart, loved it with all her soul, and wished *anything* else were playing at this moment.

Sadie tucked her hands behind her back and tilted her head sideways in thought. "Great question. If I owed you anything at all, maybe I'd share."

That response was infuriating, which she was now starting to expect from Sadie. "It was Oliver, wasn't it? What did you make him do?" Emmeline said, mentally preparing for the blow.

"Make him do?" Sadie looked at her with a curious smile, part incredulity, part exasperation. "I'm sorry you think coercion is the only way to collaborate. Maybe I told him the only thing he needed to hear: that I knew a way for millions of bribery dollars to be used for something else—to actually help people."

Then Sadie shrugged, looking thoughtful. "Now, he might have also been moved when I told him you incinerated the last memories I had of my dead father. And that someone as heartless as you should never be responsible for the best interest of others."

This time Emmeline couldn't stop her flinch. There was the blow she'd feel for weeks. Months. Maybe forever.

"Actually," Sadie continued, as if this were all just occurring to her.

It was so fake Emmeline wanted to scream. "Titus, Alaric—I'm glad you're all here."

Sadie's smile dropped and her gaze hardened into crystals, and despite herself, Emmeline shivered.

Titus lifted his chin, bracing himself against his ex. Emmeline had to hand it to him, the prodigal son was nothing if not resilient. Alaric, on the other hand, narrowed his gaze at Sadie. Looking at her, for perhaps the first time, with earned caution.

"Ashland is *my* homeland," Sadie said, steam clouding her face like smoke. "None of you can compete with the sense of purpose that comes from true belonging. If you're arrogant enough to think otherwise, I dare you to challenge me. Now that you finally know what I'm worth."

Silence, except for the final few bars of Tchaikovsky's waltz. Sadie sighed, tipping her neck back as wispy clouds drifted away from the moon, bathing the young royals in its silver glow. "I can't wait for next semester."

Like her governess had taught her through years of practical application, Emmeline knew how to draw strength from a challenge. And how to turn the pain she felt now into a tool to be sharpened and honed. Even after this infernal night, she could feel new strength on the horizon. With a sweet smile, she took back Sadie's arm. After all, they still had to get her into her gown and couldn't keep the king or the press waiting.

"Neither can I."

EPILOGUE

TITUS

Titus watched the girl who despised him smile, trium-phant. It was a brilliant, glowing, dazzling smile as flashes went off around her. The press who'd been allowed to attend Hibernia stole photo after photo of Ashland's new heir apparent.

That beautiful red dress had been salvaged from the infirmary. Her hair and makeup done quickly but no less artfully. Though there was not a sequin, diamond, or jewel adorning Sadie, her silhouette seemed to sparkle with the vivacity of a supernova. Something burn-ing bright, and oh so powerful. She was unrecognizable from the girl he'd started dating even a few weeks ago, much less the wallflower with unkempt hair, messy bangs, and scuffed up Converse from the start of the term.

Sadie Aurelia was no longer an outsider—a peasant—playing at royal.

She had become one of them.

King Leander stood next to her, his hand on her shoulder, a small respectful smile on his lips. Only Titus and maybe a select few oth-ers could discern Leander's true feelings. Titus only could because the king was so like his father. Titus could see, and fear, the quiet rage radiating off his grandfather. If Sadie was a supernova, then their king was a red giant star, blazing fiery hot.

Of course, the same could be said for Emmeline, silently fuming next to the king as they watched the press close in on Sadie. Alaric, as usual, was silent and still—a predator waiting to strike.

"Do you know how she pulled it off?" Emmeline said through her clenched smile.

"I don't," Titus said. *But I'm proud of her* is what he didn't say.

"How about some photos of the happy couple?"

Titus froze. Out of the corner of his eye, he saw Sadie did too.

One of the reporters gestured toward Titus, his camera held up in excitement, clearly proud of himself—that he was the first of the sharks to secure this brilliant photo op. Because Sadie wasn't just heir apparent, she was also dating a prince.

At least, that's what the rest of the world still believed. And adored.

"An excellent idea," King Leander boomed over the voices of the press and the gathering Almus Terra students, their parents, and important alumni. "Come, my boy."

Sadie visibly stiffened as Titus obeyed his grandfather and left Emmeline and Alaric to take up a spotlight of his own making. Leander grabbed his shoulder as soon as he was near and, with surprising force, guided him to her side. Then stepped around them to take both their shoulders in his grip, shielding them momentarily from the press's view.

"I don't care what transpired between the two of you," Leander said under his breath, his gaze locked on Sadie's, who looked as if she was about ready to bite someone. Gone was her starlet disposition. "But you will keep this up until I deem your new status as legitimate."

Oh yes, Sadie was indeed a royal now. She resembled a pit viper ready to strike. "We had a deal," she said viciously.

A deal?

Titus noticed his grandfather's hand squeeze her shoulder. To Sadie's credit, she didn't wince. "But you no longer have leverage now that the money is under our control. I will uphold your title so long as I see fit, mostly because I admire your tactics. But, Sadie, don't be fooled.

You are not my council's favorite. Not even their third choice. I am the king, but I must also answer to advisors. Your relationship with Titus will legitimize your claim. Be smart and get over the heartbreak."

Sadie's hazel eyes flashed in the snaps of more photos. "I am *not* heartbroken."

"Think about it, Sadie," Titus found himself saying, "Do you really want our breakup to upstage your new title? Because it would."

For the first time since she'd been trying on that ridiculous gown in the drawing room, Sadie looked at him. *Really* looked.

He did not like what he saw in her gaze. But it was no surprise.

She was silent for a few brief moments, then the polished smile was back. "Fine."

Leander nodded in agreement, then stepped back to let Titus and Sadie assume the limelight. Titus drew an arm around her as the reporter who'd called for their photo began snapping away. It felt as easy as breathing. Like nothing had ever happened between them. Her familiar vanilla scent, her soft skin, and her small intake of breath as he pulled her close.

That. Thank God. She wasn't completely impervious to him.

"I hope whatever you protected was worth it," Sadie muttered. The first reference she'd made to what Titus had exchanged for that voice memo on Emmeline's phone.

Titus glanced at his mother in the crowd. She stood there next to other Elite parents and alumni. She looked...as unhinged as he'd ever seen her. Which was to say, hardly miffed by a normal person's standards.

Still. It gave him satisfaction to know his reveal, on his own terms, had affected her. That gave him control. Agency. While it was true that Ashland may favor the strong, no one could ever call Titus anything but.

He'd had to withstand the torment he'd suffered as a child under the scrutiny of his parents... and now the torture of publicly pretending Sadie was happy in his arms.

A girl he might—potentially—be in love with, seeing him as evil incarnate.

Titus turned her face toward him as the press started shouting questions and demands. ("Did you know she would be named heir apparent?" "Titus, how do feel about Sadie's victory?" "Any hard feelings?" "Tell us how this might affect your relationship!")

Sweeping his hand across her jaw, Titus pulled her lips to his. It wasn't a brush or even a stunt for the cameras. It was an answer, a challenge, and a promise. A warm, demanding kiss. Sadie had won a battle tonight. But he would win the war. The crown, and her heart.

She pulled back, looking furious that his kiss still managed to leave her breathless.

"I hate you," she whispered.

Titus swiped his thumb over her jaw and gave her a smile for the world to see. "I know."

ACKNOWLEDGMENTS

Fate certainly had a hand in the creation of this book, as it never would've happened without the alignment of some brilliant, shining stars—by which I mean some pretty cool people in the book world.

Jessica Anderson, my wonderful editor whose amazing vision, endless enthusiasm, and kindhearted guidance absolutely made this book what it is. I cannot thank you enough for falling in love with Almus Terra Academy, Ashland, and my broken teenage heirs. Seriously, you rock.

My stellar agent, Masha Gunic, offered me more than just support and advocacy. We brainstormed, we fangirled over the Royal Diaries series, we worked together so beautifully that it felt effortless, and I am so lucky to have her as an agent. She's a colleague and a friend, and I am ever so grateful to her, as well as the rest of the team over at Azantian Literary Agency. Jennifer Azantian, thank you for the loving, inclusive community you have built so naturally.

Watching this book come together through its many stages of publishing has been such a delight. Thank you to the Christy Ottaviano Books/Little, Brown Books for Young Readers team, including Marisa Finkelstein and Caroline Clouse for extremely thoughtful and thorough copy edits, Patrick Hulse and Sasha Illingworth for the stunning cover and lovely interior design, Dassi Zeidel and Bunmi Ishola for proofreading, and Martina Rethman for production manufacturing. Special thanks also to the Little, Brown Books for Young Readers marketing and publicity teams, including Savannah Kennelly, Bill Grace, Andie Divelbiss, Kelly Moran, and Christie Michel—so grateful for your faith in this book!

To my sensitivity readers: Gina Orlando, Trae Hawkins, Johanna Collier, and Tela Vo—thank you so much for your invaluable insight and perspective into the sensitive topics covered in this story. From living with a chronic illness to nuanced race representation, I learned so much, and I appreciate your time and critique more than you know.

I am hugely indebted to Trent Hill, my beta reader and economics instructor. That scene between Sadie and Alaric could not have happened without you. By all means let this go to your head. (I'm just proud I got as far as Ricardo.)

Special shoutout to RuthAnne Oakey-Frost for being an awesome friend and critique partner. Then to Cavalier House Books, Red Stick Reads, and my Swiftie book club—John, James, Tere, Ashley, Madison, Beatriz, Alexandra, and Amanda: heart hands. Lara Ashley for her help with my marketing and publicity efforts, as well as being a great friend and cheerleader.

Thank you to my beautiful family and close friends: Mom, Dad, Jason, Nichole, Christa, Kourtney, and Kelly for all your love and endless patience. Especially when I disappear for deadlines.

Finally, to Meaghan. Thanks for making sure I finished this book on time. You're the best author-assistant-slash-best-friend a girl could ask for. Also, you believed in Not Ivy and kindled my love for YA—so, pretty sure I wouldn't be here in my career without you.

LINDSEY DUGA

is the author of several novels for teens. With a passion for history and mythology, she's always been fascinated with royalty across cultures and fantastical worlds. Lindsey lives in Baton Rouge, Louisiana, with her family and dog, Delphi. She invites you to visit her online at lindseyduga.com and follow her @LinzDuga.